PRAISE FOR BARBARA NICKLESS

Dark of Night

“Nickless’s character-driven mystery

. Engrossing bits of scholarship tuckec le sleuths.”

vs

“Evan and his immediate circle fascinate . . . Fans of religious thrillers will have fun.”

—*Publishers Weekly*

“Captivating, compelling, and completely intriguing! Sherlock Holmes meets *The Da Vinci Code* in this brilliantly written and seamlessly researched adventure, where clues from the ancient past propel contemporary global intrigue. This is an immersive and atmospheric thriller, with an unforgettable main character, and I could not put it down.”

—Hank Phillippi Ryan, *USA Today* bestselling author of *Her Perfect Life*

“Readers rejoice: Dr. Evan Wilding is back, and *Dark of Night* is another great vehicle for his wry brilliance. The novel is fascinating and twisty with unforgettable characters and writing that took my breath away. You’ll want to clear your calendar for this one.”

—Jess Lourey, Amazon Charts bestselling author

“*Dark of Night* had me at Moses papyri. Stolen antiquities, dark forces, cobra bites. What a wonderful read. What an adventure to sink into. What beautiful writing. I loved it.”

—Tracy Clark, author of the Cass Raines series, winner of the 2020 and 2022 Sue Grafton Memorial Award

"Dr. Evan Wilding is absolutely my new favorite fictional human. His witty charm, his intellect—matched only by his wry humor—along with his goshawk sidekick make him exactly the kind of character who captures an audience within a few lines. Add in the talented and tough Detective Addie Bisset, a death by cobra, and a collection of sketchy people all seeking the same priceless artifact, and *Dark of Night* will have you flipping pages well into the night. Barbara Nickless is a phenomenal talent, and she just gets better with every book. *Dark of Night* is her best yet. Bravo!"

—Danielle Girard, *USA Today* bestselling author of *The Ex*

"Missing artifacts? The dark underbelly of the antiquities world? Murder by . . . cobra? Count me in. *Dark of Night* is a top-notch thriller with an unforgettable lead in Dr. Evan Wilding. It's no surprise that Barbara Nickless has fast become one of my favorite authors. I tore through this novel at breakneck speed and can't wait for the next adventure."

—Hannah Mary McKinnon, internationally bestselling author of *Never Coming Home*

"*Dark of Night* is a superb novel . . . After reading the first book in the series, I was hopeful that a second book would be as good or better. I wasn't disappointed. With the new book, Barbara Nickless has solidified a great new mystery series."

—BVS Reviews

At First Light

AN AMAZON BEST BOOK OF THE MONTH: MYSTERY, THRILLER & SUSPENSE

"Well-researched . . ."

—*Kirkus Reviews*

"[In] this intense psychological thriller . . . Evan and Addie race to prevent more bloodshed. Hints of a romantic relationship between the pair enliven the story, and references to *Beowulf* and Viking history add depth. Readers will hope to see more of Addie and Evan."

—*Publishers Weekly*

"Brilliant Evan Wilding, with his goshawk and unusual friendships, will fascinate those who read for character."

—*Library Journal*

"*At First Light* is a winner."

—*Denver Post*

"A high-intensity thriller that will take your breath away . . . Barbara Nickless is an awesome talent."

—*Mysterious Book Report*

"The moment I finished this intelligent and pulse-pounding psychological thriller, I was ready for Book Two . . . Dr. Evan Wilding is one of the most interesting fictional characters I've met in some time . . . Author Nickless's prose is crisp and, at times, poetic. Her descriptions are vivid but balanced. I became immediately attached to her engaging and well-drawn characters. In some respects, *At First Light* is reminiscent of Dan Brown's *The Da Vinci Code*. I highly recommend this book to fans of fast-paced thrillers that include riddles, ancient languages, and literature."

—Claudia N. Oltean, for the *Jacksonville Florida Times-Union*

"*At First Light* is a stunner of a tale. Barbara Nickless has fashioned a deep exploration into moral depravity and the dark depths of the human soul in a fashion not seen since the brilliant David Fincher film *SE7EN*. This wholly realized tale is reminiscent of Lisa Gardner, Karin Slaughter, and Lisa Scottoline at their level best."

—Jon Land, *USA Today* bestselling author

"Barbara Nickless has crafted a dark, twisty thrill ride with a bad guy to give you nightmares, and a pair of protagonists you will want to come back to again and again. Lock your doors and curl up with this book!"

—Tami Hoag, #1 *New York Times* bestselling author of *The Boy*

"*At First Light* by Barbara Nickless is one of the best books I've read in a long, long while. With unique and unforgettable characters who match wits with a devious, sophisticated, and ritualistic serial killer, this complex and compelling story is as powerful as a Norse god and just as terrifying. I can't wait for the next book in the series featuring Detective Addie Bisset and Dr. Evan Wilding! Bravo!"

—Lisa Jackson, #1 *New York Times* bestselling author

Ambush

"A nail-biter with some wicked twists . . . Fast paced and nonstop . . . Sydney is fleshed out, flawed, gritty, and kick-ass, and you can't help but root for her. Nickless leaves you satisfied and smiling—something that doesn't happen too often in this genre!"

—*Bookish Biker*

"*Ambush* has plenty of action and intrigue. There are shoot-outs and kidnappings. There are cover-ups and conspiracies. At the center of it all is a flawed heroine who will do whatever it takes to set things right."

—BVS Reviews

"*Ambush* takes off on page one like a Marine F/A-18 Super Hornet under full military power from the flight deck . . . and never lets the reader down."

—*Mysterious Book Report*

"*Ambush* truly kicks butt and takes names, crackling with tension from page one with a plot as sharp as broken glass. Barbara Nickless is a superb writer."

—Steve Berry, #1 internationally bestselling author

"*Ambush* is modern mystery with its foot on the gas. Barbara Nickless's writing—at turns blazing, aching, stark, and gorgeous—propels this story at a breathless pace until its sublime conclusion. In Sydney Parnell, Nickless has masterfully crafted a heroine who, with all her internal and external scars, compels the reader to simultaneously root for and forgive her. A truly standout novel."

—Carter Wilson, *USA Today* bestselling author of *Mister Tender's Girl*

"Exceptional . . . Nickless raises the stakes and expands the canvas of a blisteringly original series. A wholly satisfying roller coaster of a thriller that features one of the genre's most truly original heroes."

—Jon Land, *USA Today* bestselling author

"*Ambush* . . . makes you laugh and cry as the pages fly by."

—Tim Tigner, internationally bestselling author

Dead Stop

"The twists and turns . . . are first rate. Barbara Nickless has brought forth a worthy heroine in Sydney Parnell."

—BVS Review

"Nothing less than epic . . . A fast-paced, action-packed, thriller-diller of a novel featuring two of the most endearing and toughest ex-jarheads you'll ever meet."

—*Mysterious Book Report*

"A story with the pace of a runaway train."

—Bruce W. Most, award-winning author of *Murder on the Tracks*

"Want a great read, here you go!"

—Books Minority

"Nickless is on my favorite-writers list now."

—Writing.com

"Riveting suspense. Nickless writes with the soul of a poet. *Dead Stop* is a dark and memorable book."

—Gayle Lynds, *New York Times* bestselling author of *The Assassins*

"A deliciously twisted plot that winds through the dark corners of the past into the present, where nothing—and nobody—is as they seem. *Dead Stop* is a first-rate, can't-put-down mystery with a momentum that never slows. I am eager to see what Barbara Nickless comes up with next—she is definitely a mystery writer to watch."

—Margaret Coel, *New York Times* bestselling author of the Wind River Mystery series

Blood on the Tracks

A *SUSPENSE MAGAZINE* BEST BOOKS OF 2016 SELECTION: DEBUT

"A stunner of a thriller. From the first page to the last, *Blood on the Tracks* weaves a spell that only a natural storyteller can master. And a guarantee: you'll fall in love with one of the best characters to come along in modern thriller fiction, Sydney Rose Parnell."

—Jeffery Deaver, internationally bestselling author

"Beautifully written and heartbreakingly intense, this terrific and original debut is unforgettable. Please do not miss *Blood on the Tracks*. It fearlessly explores our darkest and most vulnerable places—and is devastatingly good. Barbara Nickless is a star."

—Hank Phillippi Ryan, Anthony, Agatha, and Mary Higgins Clark Award–winning author of *Say No More*

"Both evocative and self-assured, Barbara Nickless's debut novel is an outstanding, hard-hitting story so gritty and real, you feel it in your teeth. Do yourself a favor and give this bright talent a read."

—John Hart, multiple Edgar Award winner and *New York Times* bestselling author of *Redemption Road*

"Fast paced and intense, *Blood on the Tracks* is an absorbing thriller that is both beautifully written and absolutely unique in character and setting. Barbara Nickless has written a twisting, tortured novel that speaks with brutal honesty of the lingering traumas of war, including and especially those wounds we cannot see. I fell hard for Parnell and her four-legged partner and can't wait to read more."

—Vicki Pettersson, *New York Times* and *USA Today* bestselling author of *Swerve*

"The aptly titled *Blood on the Tracks* offers a fresh and starkly original take on the mystery genre. Barbara Nickless has fashioned a beautifully drawn hero in take-charge, take-no-prisoners Sydney Parnell, former Marine and now a railway cop battling a deadly gang as she investigates their purported connection to a recent murder. Nickless proves a master of both form and function in establishing herself every bit the equal of Nevada Barr and Linda Fairstein. A major debut that is not to be missed."

—Jon Land, *USA Today* bestselling author

"*Blood on the Tracks* is a bullet train of action. It's one part mystery and two parts thriller with a compelling protagonist leading the charge toward a knockout finish. The internal demons of one Sydney Rose Parnell are as gripping as the external monster she's chasing around Colorado. You will long remember this spectacular debut novel."

—Mark Stevens, author of the award-winning Allison Coil Mystery series

"Nickless captures you from the first sentence. Her series features Sydney Rose Parnell, a young woman haunted by the ghosts of her past. In *Blood on the Tracks*, she doggedly pursues a killer, seeking truth even in the face of her own destruction—the true mark of a heroine. Skilled in evoking emotion from the reader, Nickless is a master of the craft, a writer to keep your eyes on."

—Chris Goff, author of *Dark Waters*

"Barbara Nickless's *Blood on the Tracks* is raw and authentic, plunging readers into the fascinating world of tough railroad cop Special Agent Sydney Rose Parnell and her Malinois sidekick, Clyde. Haunted by her military service in Iraq, Sydney Rose is brought in by the Denver Major Crimes unit to help solve a particularly brutal murder, leading her into a snake pit of hate and betrayal. Meticulously plotted and intelligently written, *Blood on the Tracks* is a superb debut novel."

—M. L. Rowland, author of the Search and Rescue Mystery novels

"*Blood on the Tracks* is a must-read debut. A suspenseful crime thriller with propulsive action, masterful writing, and a tough-as-nails cop, Sydney Rose Parnell. Readers will want more."

—Robert K. Tanenbaum, *New York Times* bestselling author of the Butch Karp and Marlene Ciampi legal thrillers

"Nickless's writing admirably captures the fallout from a war where even survivors are trapped, forever reliving their trauma."

—*Kirkus Reviews*

"Part mystery, part antiwar story, Nickless's engrossing first novel, a series launch, introduces Sydney Rose Parnell . . . Nickless skillfully explores the dehumanizing effects resulting from the unspeakable cruelties of wartime as well as the part played by the loyalty soldiers owe to family and each other under stressful circumstances."

—*Publishers Weekly*

"An interesting tale . . . The fast pace will leave you finished in no time. Nickless seamlessly ties everything together with a shocking ending."

—*RT Book Reviews*

"If you enjoy suspense and thrillers, then you will [want] *Blood on the Tracks* for your library. Full of the suspense that holds you on the edge of your seat, it's also replete with acts of bravery, moments of hope, and a host of feelings that keep the story's intensity level high. This would be a great work for a book club or reading group with a great deal of information that would create robust dialogue and debate."

—Blogcritics

"In *Blood on the Tracks*, Barbara Nickless delivers a thriller with the force of a speeding locomotive and the subtlety of a surgeon's knife. Sydney and Clyde are both great characters with flaws and virtues to see them through a plot thick with menace. One for contemporary-thriller lovers everywhere."

—Authorlink

"*Blood on the Tracks* is a superb story that rises above the genre of mystery . . . It is a first-class read."

—*Denver Post*

PLAY OF SHADOWS

ALSO BY
BARBARA NICKLESS

Sydney Rose Parnell Series

Blood on the Tracks

Dead Stop

Ambush

Gone to Darkness

Dr. Evan Wilding Series

At First Light

Dark of Night

PLAY OF SHADOWS

BARBARA NICKLESS

This is a work of fiction. Names, characters, organizations, places, events, and incidents are either products of the author's imagination or are used fictitiously. Otherwise, any resemblance to actual persons, living or dead, is purely coincidental.

Published by Thomas & Mercer, Seattle

www.apub.com

ISBN-13: 9781662509988 (paperback)
ISBN-13: 9781662509995 (digital)

Cover design by Jarrod Taylor

Cover image: © Münzkabinett der Staatlichen Museen zu Berlin / Münzkabinett Online Catalogue; © Napoleonka, © GEORGIOS GKOUMAS, © Pau Buera / Shutterstock

Printed in the United States of America

To my sisters—my found family

All of us contain both god and beast, and the battle between the two, the battle for our humanity, never ends.

—Dr. Morgan Hargrave, PhD,
"Good and Evil in Pre-Adolescent Children"

Know therefore that you are a god.

—Cicero, The Dream of Scipio

"The Use of Classical Myths in the Narratives of Killers"
Excerpt from *Criminal Behavioral Analysis of the "Minotaur Murders" for the Chicago Police Department, August 2018*
Dr. Evan Wilding, Proceedings of the International Conference on Semiotics

The point of myth isn't to prove there are monsters. We don't need proof of what we already know. The point of myth is to reveal where monsters come from. And to show that they can be destroyed.

The Disappearance

July 2008

The storm lay heavy over the fields to the west, the air muggy and oppressive. A quiet rain hissed on the waters of the river near where ten-year-old Colby Kaplan crouched beneath the spreading branches of an ancient cottonwood. The bulk of the storm hadn't reached him.

I'm not afraid, he told himself. *Tav will come, and everything will be okay.*

He pushed to his feet and rested his hand on Rex's head. How could he be afraid when he had the best dog in the world with him? He was just being a baby. Tav had asked him to wait here, and that was what he'd do. Colby didn't have a lot of friends, but he had Tav. Tav was four years older. He was smart and cool and knew all kinds of crazy stuff. Colby wouldn't stand him up because of a stupid thunderstorm. Or because his mom was worried that the Bogeyman might be snatching kids in Illinois. He and Tav were going to study the beyond-weird places where someone had flattened sections of Tom Vandermeer's corn.

Tav said the marks might be caused by the burrowing of something horrible that lived underground, like the giant worms that chased Kevin Bacon in that old movie *Tremors.* Or maybe by extraterrestrials. Colby figured it was probably just local kids having a prank, like his mom said. But it was fun to pretend.

Colby bounced on his toes, watching the clouds for funnels. And spaceships. Out in the cornfields, the wind whooshed like the whisk of a giant's broom, sweeping through the rows of chest-high stalks. Closer by, the trees leaned away from the wind. Some of the elms had dead branches at the top. Colby stared at them, imagining witches rubbing their hands together.

"Just dead limbs is all," he said to Rex. "Just means they're old."

Standing at alert next to Colby, ears flattened against the gale, Rex whined. Rex was the best dog ever. But he sure didn't like storms.

"Easy, boy," Colby said. "We're intrepid explorers, remember? Like they taught us in Scouts. Intrepid explorers are brave."

He turned his back on the cornfields and looked east across the river at the hedge maze in the distance. The kids at school said the maze was haunted. They said a monster lived inside the twining branches of the shrubs, feeding off rabbits and voles and squirrels. Feeding on children when it could find them. They said the flesh of humans was the monster's favorite.

But Colby wasn't afraid of monsters. No matter what Tav said about giant mutant worms or secret government projects that turned people into zombies. He knew serial killers like the Bogeyman *were* real, but he had Rex with him. Rex was a German shepherd, a rescue from the Happy Tails Humane Society in Rock Falls. The happiest day in Colby's life was when he brought Rex home.

He'd like to see a killer get past his dog.

Beyond the maze rose the immense white house his mother called "elegant" on some days, and a "monstrosity" on others, depending on her mood.

Colby had heard the stories. Everyone had. If you lived anywhere near Daysville, Illinois, you knew about the Hargrave family—their money, their fancy cars, their yacht on Lake Michigan. You also knew the story about how Mrs. Hargrave had gotten drunk one afternoon and fallen down the stairs. She'd hit her head and died. Just like that.

Alive for breakfast, dead before lunch, his mom said. She also said alcohol was the devil's drink.

But what you knew more than anything about the Hargraves was Dr. Morgan Hargrave's research. He studied good and evil in children.

As if babies could be evil, his mother always said. *Babies!*

The wind rose. Lightning flared above the fields. Colby counted, just like he'd learned with the other Boy Scouts, tracking the seconds between flash and thunder. He made it to fifteen before thunder rumbled like bricks tumbling.

Three miles away and moving fast.

Maybe Tav wasn't coming. His dad was super strict. He might have told Tav he couldn't leave the house with a storm rolling in. Colby scowled. If his own mom wasn't making him wait until he turned twelve to get a phone, he'd be able to *call* Tav and find out.

Colby's heart gave a sad little flip. Maybe Tav was with his creepy grown-up buddy, Eddie. Eddie was . . . There was something wrong with Eddie. His weird tattoos. The way he rolled his own cigarettes instead of buying them at the market like everyone else. The way he looked at Colby like he was a slice of pizza Eddie couldn't wait to eat.

Colby couldn't understand what Tav saw in a grown-up like Eddie.

He decided he'd take one turn around the area looking for his friend, then go home. He and Rex might be intrepid explorers, but that didn't mean they couldn't get sucked up by a tornado.

He snugged down the hood on his rain jacket, turned his back on the creepy hedge maze and the mansion, and headed toward one of the rocky outcrops where he sometimes met Tav. The ridge looked like a great place for caves, and the grotto guy who came to talk at a Scout meeting told them there were caves around. But Colby had yet to find one.

Colby startled when Rex let loose a sudden volley of barks. The shepherd leapt in front of Colby, hackles raised. Then he took off at a full-out run.

"Rex!" Colby called. The wind tore his voice away.

It must be a rabbit or a racoon. Maybe a fox.

The sky now looked like an old bruise—purple and yellow and green. The wind rose to a roar like that of a freight train, and the rain became a downpour. Colby glanced back toward the Hargrave mansion; a light glowed faintly in an upper-floor window. If things got bad, he could knock on the door, ask to wait out the storm.

When he turned back, Rex was still running toward *something*.

Lightning flashed. Colby counted. Ten seconds. Two miles away.

He ran after his dog.

When he reached the outcropping, he stopped. Someone had placed a row of fist-size white stones along the ground. They were spaced two feet apart, forming a gently curving arc.

Colby found himself smiling. The stones must be a message from Tav, who liked to create what he called mystical mazes.

He followed the stones, which led him around the tumble of rocks, and there was Rex. The dog had scrambled partway up the outcropping and stood with his legs braced, teeth bared, his chest heaving with every bark. The dog had cornered something. When Colby clamored up after his dog, a rush of cool air touched his face—not the storm, he realized with excitement. The breeze came from a gap between the rocks. A cave!

He shrugged off his backpack and pulled out the flashlight, squinting through the rain. The gap swallowed the light.

He and Tav had been through here a hundred times and not seen this opening. The downpour must have dislodged the rocks hiding the entrance.

Firmly, he told Rex to be quiet. The dog's barks changed to a low whine. No doubt some small animal was sheltering inside. All the big predators like coyotes and bears had been run off years ago.

He ordered Rex to sit and stay. Then he edged closer—slipping and sliding on the loose stones—and leaned down to shine the flashlight between slablike rocks.

He smelled mud and decay and the musty scent of limestone. And something else. A whiff of dead things. Maybe a bear *had* denned here once. His light bounced off the back of the cave, which was no more than five or six feet in. Not a real cave, just a little cavity.

"Nothing here, Rex," he said.

Behind him, Rex had fallen silent.

Colby swept the small space with the light and saw what he'd initially missed—a sharp turn where a tunnel branched off to the left. He leaned into the cave's opening. The air current came from the tunnel, which meant that—some distance away—the tunnel led to the surface.

This *was* a real cave!

He turned back to call Rex, but the rocks had become slippery in the rain, and one of the larger stones shifted. He skidded, then slipped partway down the outcropping and screamed as the stone teetered and smashed onto his foot. Biting his lip, he tried to wiggle free. His foot remained wedged.

"Rex!" he shouted.

Rex appeared, balancing on the rocks, his ears and haunches lowered. Lightning flared nearby. The smell of ozone filled the air, mingling with the stink from the cave.

Colby pulled on his calf, trying to free his foot. But neither rock nor foot moved. He pushed against the rock, but he couldn't budge the boulder.

"Get help," he said to Rex, gasping. "Go home and get help. Like Lassie in Mom's old movies. Remember?"

Rex cocked his head. His ears came up. Then abruptly he whined and backed away. He spun on his paws, and five seconds later, he had disappeared around the ridge.

"Good boy, Rex," Colby said, although Rex acted more like a scaredy-cat than like a hero dog on a rescue mission.

Now Colby heard a noise. He turned back to the cave.

Something rushed toward him out of the darkness. Something running low and fast.

Something with teeth.

CHAPTER 1

THE MINOTAUR

July 2018

From my place near the door, the bookstore was an oasis of light and humanity amid the booming snarl of a thunderstorm.

An oasis, at least, for most attendees, present company excepted. I stood at the back, gazing over the heads of forty-six people in folding chairs, their attention riveted to the woman playing a mythical Greek princess on the makeshift stage.

"Take this," Princess Ariadne said to an imaginary Theseus, holding out her hand. Balanced on her palm was a ball of red yarn.

I sneered. Ariadne of Crete: lover of Theseus and traitor to her own brother. She might as well have killed Asterion with her own hands.

"Treacherous witch," I muttered.

A woman in the last row glanced at me and frowned.

I considered smiling to put her at ease. But a smile is submissive, and men like me do not submit. And while my disguise was good, I knew that after the events of tonight, the police would ask questions. I could not afford for this woman to remember me.

So instead, I tipped my head. A reassuring—even gracious—gesture. She took in my neatly creased jeans and the expensive raincoat and—certain now that she had misheard me—smiled before returning her gaze to the stage.

She was here, they were all here, as part of Chicago's citywide reading of Edith Hamilton's *Mythology* and the arrival of the traveling play *The King and the Minotaur*. This woman, like the rest of them, preferred her mythology packaged neatly in the pages of a book or confined, like now, to a stage.

People don't much care to have the myths run free, keeping score and taking retribution.

With effort, I turned my attention away from the stage. I'd come for Ursula and her father. They stood near the front, the father with one elbow propped on a bookshelf filled with history tomes. They'd arrived after all the chairs were taken, and the father looked tired.

They paid no attention to me. They didn't know me in my current guise.

But they would know me soon enough.

They appeared happy. Fat and happy, in the case of the father. Athletic and happy, in the case of Ursula. She had grown up to be quite lovely, which was helpful to the story I was building.

The story of me. The monster.

Asterion.

The Minotaur.

The events of tonight would be a continuation of my katabasis—my journey into the underworld. A journey I wouldn't take alone.

Tonight would be first blood.

Half an hour later, the performance ended. Ursula and her father stood in line to shake Ariadne's hand and then again to purchase Edith Hamilton's book along with a trashy horror novel and a copy of *The Economist*. Throughout, Ursula smiled, laughing up at her father, who laughed along with her. They pulled on their raincoats, and she tucked her arm through his as they headed toward the door. He patted her hand with visible affection.

Yes, definitely happy.

When they left the store, I followed them. I removed my jacket, pulled up my hood, and loped past. I knew where they'd parked. I knew the path they'd take between the garage and the bookstore.

I'd stashed my labrys there, its double blades honed to a glittering edge as sharp and unforgiving as revenge.

CHAPTER 2

EVAN

Not far from the bookstore, as the crow flies, Professor Evan Wilding sat in his office at the Institute of Middle Eastern Antiquities and stared at the computer on his desk while wind howled around the repurposed brick house on Woodlawn Avenue.

He scratched his Vandyke beard and sighed, the sound an echo of the wind through the eaves.

Numbers. Rows and columns of numbers. Terrifyingly large ones, which were the institute's bills. And very small ones, which represented their nearly nonexistent income.

Evan blinked and rubbed his eyes, hoping for a miracle. But the numbers stood their ground.

Outside the single window, lightning bolted across the evening sky. From his second-floor office, Evan could see only the tops of the wind-lashed tupelo trees that grew in a row against the back fence. Beyond the trees, invisible from where he sat, the city's skyline glittered against the stormy heavens, a bastion of civilization etched across nature's fury. Chicago was in the midst of a midwestern monsoon. Overloaded sewers. Flooded basements and roadways. Water poured off overpasses, and there were stories of rats climbing out of manholes and dogs being swept away. *Blame El Niño,* the meteorologists said. This summer was seeing cooler temperatures and more wind and rain. Almost daily rain.

As if reading Evan's thoughts, the skies opened. Drops like silver coins battered the rooftop, drowning out the Beethoven symphonies—currently the *Eroica*—Evan had chosen for the evening's work. Near the door to the hallway, Perro rose and stretched. The Welsh corgi watched Evan for a moment, decided the professor wasn't doing anything of interest, and resettled on his bed. Unlike every other dog Evan had known, Perro was utterly unperturbed by thunder.

In that moment, Evan wanted nothing more than to be Perro. Adored and cared for. Taken for twice-daily walks. Provided with a diet of top-grade food and a steady supply of suitably challenging puzzle toys. Perro had even managed to avoid having his bushy tail docked, thanks to the tender heart of his first human, Evan's research assistant, Diana. It was the perfect life, if you liked dog food. Which, judging by Perro's generous girth, the corgi certainly did.

Evan wondered how his hawk, Ginny, was faring in her mews. No doubt fast asleep, as undisturbed as Perro by the storm.

He sighed again and returned his attention to the spreadsheet.

As an Oxford-educated Englishman, a professor of semiotics, linguistics, and paleography at the University of Chicago, not to mention an interpreter for government agencies on the writings and symbols left by killers and terrorists, Evan loved codes made up of letters and crime scenes strewn with bizarre symbols. *Those*, he could read. Maybe not easily or all at once. But, sooner or later, he would decipher their secrets.

He wasn't much fond of numbers, however. Debits, credits, accounts receivable, asset classes, and other accounting terms—those rattled around in his brain without gaining purchase. Except *insolvency.* That was a word he understood.

And the Institute of Middle Eastern Antiquities was hovering at the brink.

He let his gaze linger on one of the books on the desk. *The Phaistos Disk: An Account of Its Unresolved Mystery.* The undeciphered Phaistos Disc (he preferred to spell *disc* with a *c* instead of a *k*) was where his heart really lay. Almost six thousand miles east on the Greek island of Crete. He'd been beating his head against the brick wall of deciphering the Phaistos since he was in his early twenties. And he had almost nothing to show for it.

Much like the numbers he was moving about on the spreadsheet. He seemed to have a fondness for lost causes.

Speaking of which . . . his eyes caught on another book on his desk: *The Lost Manuscripts of Timbuktu.*

Just outside the window, lightning flared. Brilliant light irradiated the room, and almost immediately, a fury of thunder shook the glass.

The lights flickered out. The computer screen went dark.

Perro barked.

"Looks like that's it for wrestling with the books tonight," Evan said aloud. He tried to suppress his glee. This was serious work requiring serious attention. Could he help it if the phrase *In a thousand years, none of this will matter* kept winding through his brain?

He picked up his cell phone and tapped the flashlight app. The chamber filled with a blue-white glow.

"Let's get candles," he said to Perro.

The dog followed him into the hallway and down the grand central staircase, each of them moving slowly in recognition of the gloom and the fact of their respective short statures. The stairs had not been built with either corgis or dwarfs in mind. As they walked, additional flashes of lightning and the glow from Evan's phone illuminated the painting of a dying Cleopatra and caused the shadows from the institute's urns and the carvings in their niches to leap as he walked by.

At the bottom of the stairs, he made his way through the front room to the windows and peered out to see if the rest of Woodlawn

Avenue was dark. All around, the gloom lay deep. Nary a streetlight nor lamp glowed anywhere up or down along the road.

Perro barked a single sharp warning.

A figure moved in front of the glass, its shape caught in the glow from Evan's phone.

Startled, Evan took a step back. "The hell?"

The figure—a man, judging by his height and girth—bent down. When he straightened, he glanced through the window at Evan. Their eyes met.

The man's face shone pale blue in the light from Evan's phone.

His eyes were wide, his mouth agape, his lips peeled back from his teeth in an expression of alarm.

On his forehead were strange marks: odd signs that appeared to have been scrawled across his forehead in black ink. Rain had caused the marks to blur and run until it was hard to guess what they might have been. A tumble of intersecting lines. Or a child's doodle.

Another blaze of lightning. The man turned and limped hurriedly down the walkway, vanishing into the darkness.

Evan double-checked that the door was locked and that the alarm, which ran on a backup power supply, was still armed. Then he leaned against the door, his heart pounding. He'd had too many run-ins with too many killers to be comfortable with strangers dropping by in the dark.

In the near distance, an engine roared to life. Evan drew a deep breath.

"That was rather odd, wasn't it?" he said to Perro. "A man skulking around near our front door. And those marks on his forehead. What do you suppose he was about?"

In answer, Perro set to barking again. Someone pounded on the front door.

Evan didn't move. Didn't so much as breathe.

The banging stopped. Perro's bark lowered to a rumbling growl.

Then the pounding started up again. Perro howled. Evan closed his eyes.

A voice shouted, "Evan, it's me!"

Evan's eyes popped open. He punched in the code for the alarm and unlocked the door.

A tall man carrying a duffel stood in the doorway.

The man grinned. "Is this how you welcome me to Chicago, brother?"

"Well, I'll be damned," Evan said, his heart pausing its leap toward his throat. "River."

CHAPTER 3

EVAN

Evan glanced up and down the street. "Did you see anyone about?"

River's grin crooked. "On a night like this?"

Evan grabbed River's hand and pulled his brother inside. He slammed the door and locked it.

"Are you okay?" River asked as he handed Evan a padded envelope. "You look like you've seen the proverbial ghost."

Evan accepted the small package. "What's this?"

"It was on your doorstep."

River dropped his battered brown duffel bag and hat on the floor, then bent and hugged Evan. Evan breathed in his brother's scent—rain, hotel shampoo, desert sand, leather. And the familiar River-ness he remembered from their shared childhood.

After a moment, River pulled away. His face looked tired through his smile. It was a long journey from Istanbul to Chicago. "I can't believe I'm here. My visit is way overdue."

While Perro sniffed at River's ankles, Evan placed the envelope on the entryway table.

"I had to inherit an institute to convince you to come to Chicago?" he said. "It would have been easier to have had you kidnapped."

A couple of months earlier, Evan had thrown up his hands at the complexity of wooing donors and applying for grants to support the institute and had asked River to come from Turkey to help him during the dig's off-season. River headed up an archaeological excavation at Göbekli Tepe, Turkey, the site of one of the world's oldest religious structures.

"The institute was just an excuse to come and see you," River said as he studied Evan. "Now, what was all that at the door? The whole I've-seen-a-ghost look you've still got."

"Someone loitering about the building. Gave me a scare. How did you know to find me here?"

"I rang the bell at your home first. When you didn't answer, I came here. You said you've been spending a lot of time at the institute."

"You rang the bell? How'd you get past the gate?"

River laughed and Evan sighed.

"I'd almost forgotten," he said. "You're not much concerned with things like barriers and blockades. Hand me your coat."

River shrugged out of his jacket. Evan took the proffered coat and tossed it toward the wall hooks, where it caught neatly.

River smiled. "Impressive."

"I've been practicing. You want the tour first? Or drinks?"

River gestured toward the padded envelope. "I want to know what's inside. Was it left by your loiterer?"

Evan eyeballed the rain-spattered paper. "Must have been. It wasn't there half an hour ago when I took Perro outside to water the bushes."

"Well?"

But Evan was reluctant. Given his visitor's apparent distress, what if the envelope contained bad news? As far as Evan knew, no bills were overdue and no collectors had been called. But he wasn't much for staying on top of his inbox.

"You first," Evan said. "Tell me why you decided to visit now."

River laughed. "All right, brother. We'll do things your way. The tour first, so long as it's quick. Then a bottle of whatever you have on hand. We can share our stories and open that envelope after we've fortified ourselves with alcohol."

"Now you're being reasonable. Perhaps by then we'll also have a little light."

As if his words were magic, the lamps flared on.

River raised his brows. "Have you been practicing that, too?"

"No practice required. Lights are my superpower."

✣

After a brief tour, Evan directed River to the upstairs bath where his brother could towel off most of the rain while he went into the kitchen to throw together a charcuterie board and fetch a bottle of Hennessy X.O cognac. He retrieved the package from the entryway table and set it next to the cognac. A few minutes later, the brothers sat in the living room in chairs placed before the hearth's cheerful fire while Perro snored at Evan's feet and rain misted the windows.

The institute had all the comforts of home.

"Why didn't you give me a heads-up that you were coming?" Evan said, pouring the Hennessy into snifters.

River stretched out his long legs. He wore travel-stained khaki trousers and boots that had been old before the invention of rope. His blond hair had grown long enough to reach his collar, and his skin had tanned a golden brown. Several days' worth of golden stubble on his chin and cheeks revealed his time on the road. His leather satchel—as beaten up as his boots—sat on the floor next to his hat, an Indiana Jones–style brimmed felt fedora given to him by their father.

Another man might have been uncomfortable wearing a copy of the hat sported by Harrison Ford. But River didn't appear to give a damn, so long as the hat was comfortable and kept off the elements.

And, Evan mused, the fedora was a vast improvement over the tweed sports coat Oliver Wilding had sent Evan, the only acknowledgment of his older son's graduation from Oxford. The coat was a cliché in every way, with its leather elbow patches and leather buttons—Pater Wilding's idea of professorial clothing. Evan couldn't quite bring himself to throw it out; he had hung the coat in the back of his closet, behind his hooded sweatshirts and the formal suit he was sometimes required to wear.

"Instead of phoning, I thought I'd surprise you," River said, shifting his position with lionlike elegance. His long-fingered hands cupped the brandy glass. River Alburn Wilding. *Alburn* was German for "of noble valor," which meant that *courage* was—literally—River's middle name. Everything about him spoke of restless refinement. As if James Bond and Lara Croft had borne a love child. Evan knew that River couldn't care less about his appearance or what people thought about him. His "uncommonly handsome" looks, as their mother put it, just made it look as if he did.

His appearance was a riddle. A paradox. Like the man himself.

Archaeologist. Explorer. Adventurer.

And perhaps an occasional spy.

He was also Evan's baby brother, even if he stood a foot and a half taller than Evan's own four foot five.

"The truth is," River said, "I didn't think I'd be coming for another month. Plenty of time to fill you in on my plans. But we had some issues at the site. A cave-in at one of the trenches. And five of our workers fell ill. We had to end our field season early, so it seemed like the perfect time to come to Chicago. I planned to call you when my plane landed, give you at least an hour's heads-up. But my phone died somewhere over the Atlantic."

"Does this mean you're willing to help me with the institute?" Evan asked. He had popped the question over the phone more than two months ago. "You never answered my question."

"It took some grappling in the desert," River said. "But yes. You're my brother. Ply me with wine, women, and the occasional song, and I'm all yours."

A weight lifted from Evan's chest. River knew all about project management and archaeological ventures, be they digs or organizations. He would know how to fix the numbers on the spreadsheet, how to find grants and attract benefactors. Hell, he probably had a list of artifact-obsessed investors on speed dial.

Evan opened then closed his mouth, momentarily at a loss for words. Finally, he said, "I don't know how to express my appreciation."

River laughed again. "Well, you've already started with a good substitute for the wine. And may the record show that for the first time in our shared lives, I have struck my brother silent."

Evan frowned. "For the record, it was only a moment's failing."

The brothers clinked their glasses. Evan nodded toward the leather duffel. "I hope you packed a few miracles in there. We're going to need them."

"I take it the Watts collection is still tied up in litigation."

Evan nodded glumly. He had inherited the institute from his friend and colleague, historian Elizabeth Lawrence. Along with the institute, Evan should have also inherited an impressive collection of antiquities from the deceased collector Theodore Watts. The collection would have put Elizabeth's institute on the map, ensuring that scholars would visit and patrons would donate.

Unfortunately, Watts's grandson had objected.

"Elizabeth's attorney is certain the judge will rule in our favor," Evan said. "But he's taking his time."

River crossed his legs, resting the ankle of one leg on the thigh of the other. He eyed his brother. "How is it you think I can help?"

"Work some of that magic you're so good at. Find people with deep pockets. And the university has agreed to host any talks you're willing to give. You can share your exploits with starry-eyed would-be adventurers for hundreds of dollars a pop."

"Your exploits are every bit as exciting as mine."

"Ha! What I do involves nothing more than pen and paper. Adventuring is not my skill set, whatever you insist."

River shook his head. "You need more faith in yourself."

"I have plenty of faith in myself when it's warranted. And the good sense to know when I'm out of my element."

River grunted. He gave the envelope another look, eyed his brother, then unlaced and toed off his boots. He flexed his stockinged feet with a sigh.

"What's your interest in Timbuktu?" he asked after a few minutes. "I saw the book on your desk. *The Lost Manuscripts of Timbuktu.*"

"Ah." Evan stared into the flame-lit amber liquid of his drink. "I've received an invitation from the head librarian there. He needs help with some newly discovered fourth-century manuscripts."

"Speaking of adventure," River said dryly. "He's sent you books?"

"He would prefer that Mohammed go to the mountain."

Now both of River's eyebrows went up. "Wait. You've dragged me to Chicago so that you can go off to Mali and get yourself killed?"

"I haven't given him an answer."

River sat up. "The place is overrun with terrorists who love Americans. As in, they love to kidnap them. Torture them. Murder them."

"Terrorist activity makes the work even more important. Before centuries' worth of rare documents are destroyed."

"What's happened to my eminently rational big brother? The one who always looked long and hard before leaping?"

"As opposed to my baby brother, who always leapt first and then winged it. You just told me I need to have more faith in myself."

"Faith, not foolishness."

"Anyway, an idea is *all* it is right now. But it would allow me to truly focus on my work. No teaching duties. No lectures to give. And—for a time—no institute to manage."

"But what about Addie? Aren't the two of you making progress in the romance department?"

Evan looked down. Detective Adrianne Bisset—Addie—had been his best friend ever since she'd tripped and spilled both their drinks several years ago at an art exhibit. For exactly the same length of time, she had also been his secret crush.

"After a whirlwind courtship," Evan said, "her latest guy has proposed marriage. She's giving it serious thought."

"But she hasn't said yes."

"I think she's waiting for the right moment." A sudden melancholia rose like dank air.

River's chair creaked. "Did you say something to her? Tell her how you feel?"

"And ruin a perfectly wonderful friendship?" Evan glanced at his brother, then away. "She's happy, River. And as cliché as it sounds, her happiness is all I ever wanted. Marcus Martin is a surgeon. Brilliant. Well off. A perfectly nice guy."

"I see."

"What do you mean, you see?"

"I see that your heart is broken, so you've decided to take a sabbatical, hand the institute over to me, and run away. I've never known you to be a coward."

"Of the first order. But, I'm not running away. I'm just . . . taking time to reassess my life."

"You aren't fighting for her."

"I want to *win* her heart. Not fight someone for it. Addie and I are friends. It's never been more than that for her. If I go, she'll miss me, just as I'll miss her. But she'll be fine. More than fine." Evan waved a hand in the air. "The topic is closed."

He refilled their glasses, and they both contemplated the flames. At last, Evan picked up the package. No point putting it off any longer.

He used a cheese knife to open one end. Inside was a letter and something small—maybe two inches by two—wrapped in brown paper and sealed shut with clear tape.

"Curious," Evan said.

He unfolded the letter and scanned the first lines.

> Dear Doctors Wilding,
> Will you forgive my forwardness if I call you by your given names?

"It's addressed to both of us," Evan said. "And there are hieroglyphs."

The lights flickered. Through the front windows, lightning raced across the sky.

CHAPTER 4

ADDIE

Detective Adrianne "Addie" Bisset glanced up at the heavens, willing the nighttime rain to hold off long enough for Chicago PD cops to raise a tent and for her to get control of the scene.

She looked back down at the dead man in Couch Place, an alley in Chicago's Loop District. Rigor had yet to set in; she figured the man had been in the alley only an hour or two.

"Cannibals," said Detective Thanh, who stood at her elbow. "See that hole in his throat? If that's not a bite mark, I'll eat the corpse myself."

She'd gotten the call after the detectives on the overnight shift had decided this was a case for Chicago PD's newest division—the Major Crimes Special Investigations Unit, known simply as "the Unit," which operated out of the department's Homan Square facility. Under pressure from the mayor and aldermen, Chicago PD was constantly reshuffling resources and departments in an effort to combat rising crime. The latest shuffle included promoting Addie and Patrick to a squad tasked with handling the most delicate or bizarre cases. What everyone called the "TV cases."

Addie gave it three months before the politicos reshuffled the department again.

She ran the beam of her Maglite over the body.

The victim, a middle-aged white male, lay on his back on the asphalt, naked from the waist up, arms sprawled to either side, legs cast wide. He wore gray slacks, a black leather belt, and dress shoes, no socks. Something—an axe, a machete, a frigging two-handed broadsword for all she knew—had hewn him nearly in half at the waist. His hands were fisted. Maybe they'd get lucky and the medical examiner would find something useful clenched in the victim's hands. If they were really lucky, it would be blood or hair from his attacker.

Of course, she thought as she glanced at the victim, luck seemed to be in short supply.

She focused the beam on the man's hands. Nothing that she could see. But she caught an odd scent above the stench of blood and spilled viscera. A whiff of licorice and . . . honey, she decided.

On the man's chest, above the gaping wound, a series of lines marked his flesh, drawn in what appeared to be the victim's own blood. The blood had run in the earlier rain, leaving little for her to speculate on. Were the lines connected to each other? Had they been letters before the rain smeared them?

Ditto for the marks on his forehead, which looked like they'd been made with a black felt-tip pen. She'd taken pictures shortly after she'd arrived, but according to Thanh and his partner, Garza, the characters or symbols—whatever they were—had been ruined before the first officer appeared on the scene.

The man's mouth and eyes were taped shut.

Then there was the wound Detective Thanh was talking about. A bite-size chunk of flesh torn from the man's neck. Thanh was jumping the gun calling it cannibalism. But it did look like they had a biter. Bite marks had been disproved as a solid method for ID'ing an attacker. But it would mean they'd get DNA.

The rain held off; fog swirled through the alley.

"It's a Jack-the-Ripper night," Thanh said, jingling his car keys. "And now we got this."

There was a lot of blood. It had pooled around the man, with splashes leading from his body to the sidewalk and beyond to the curb. As if he'd been slashed then tossed from a vehicle.

The wound in the neck had also bled, meaning the victim had been alive when something—teeth or a weapon—ripped out a hunk of his flesh.

She aimed the Maglite at the camera placed high on the wall. "Did you ask for footage?"

"You haven't worked this part of town. It's a dummy. A lot of the cameras were moved to higher crime areas." Thanh laughed. "Not sure they get 'higher crime' than what we're looking at right now, though."

"Fork it," she said.

He scratched his nose, then his ear. "Most people don't know they're gone. Even the rumor of cameras makes people feel safer. And maybe scares off a few would-be muggers."

She glanced down the alley at the loading-dock doors, fire exits, and theater posters. The cheerful murals on the doors felt like an affront to the dead man.

"There should be cameras along State and Dearborn," she said.

"We'll scare up what we can."

Couch Place served as a pedestrian thoroughfare between State Street and North Dearborn in Chicago's theater district. It was paved and reasonably well lit, with doors that led to the Neverland Theater and their loading dock plus a handful of other access doors. If the cameras hadn't caught the actual killer, perhaps they could use the footage to identify potential witnesses.

She scanned the area. The unusually intense monsoon rains and the attendant flooding had slowed downtown Chicago almost to a stop. It was a bad night for witnesses.

She checked her phone. Correction. It was a bad Friday morning for witnesses. Only a few pedestrians were gathered at the alley's west end. On the east side, closer to where the body lay, police had closed off the sidewalk and rerouted foot traffic.

"Hurry up with the tent," Addie said to the officers who'd arrived with a three-sided pop-up tent and were now fumbling in their attempts to set it up.

From the other end of the alley, her partner's voice boomed. She excused herself to Thanh and walked down to meet him, playing her light over the ground as she walked, finding nothing more than empty plastic bottles, tossed coffee cups, and cigarette butts. The light hit a vape pen and a beer bottle.

They would collect all of it.

Detective Patrick McBrady's silhouette loomed against the backdrop of a squad car's headlights. A massive Irishman who had firmly embraced his heritage after a trip back to the old country, Patrick was smart, experienced, and occasionally superstitious. He was also as much a father figure to Addie as he was her partner.

Recently, she'd told him of her secret sideline as a watercolorist. She'd expected him to tell her to stay focused on the job. To leave art to the artists, and crime to the cops and criminals.

Instead, he'd given her a gentle ribbing and then applauded. Literally applauded.

"Life's too short to keep dodging your dreams," he'd said. "Go for it."

"You won't tell anyone, right?"

He'd folded his slablike arms. "Nah, lass, I got your six."

Tonight, he was yawning and clutching a thermos of what she was certain was black coffee thick enough to require a knife and fork. Only a few years out from retirement, Patrick carried the weight of the badge with its silver star more with each passing month. These middle-of-the-night calls left him gray skinned and bleary eyed.

He hunched his gigantic shoulders against the night's unusual chill. "How come these special cases never happen during the day?"

"Killers and vampires." She led the way back down the alley toward where the officers had managed to raise the tent.

"Who found him?" Patrick asked as they walked.

She watched Thanh emerge from the tent and step away to take a phone call.

"A couple of out-of-towners heading back to their hotel from a bar," she said. "They're in the back of one of the squad cars being interviewed by Detective Garza."

"You talk to them?"

She nodded. "A pair of college students from Colorado. They drove to Chicago for a concert. Both of them are pretty freaked out."

"Murder's a long way from a rave. Any other wits?" Witnesses.

"Not any that were still around when patrol got here. Thanh's going to check any nearby cameras that are actually working."

"I'll give him my lucky rabbit's foot."

They reached the tent, and Patrick aimed his thermos at the black-and-white artwork on the wall above the body. The tiles—now only partially visible beyond the tent—formed an elegant geometric pattern of textured black lines on white brick.

"Is that supposed to be a maze?" he asked.

Addie nodded. "Nothing to link it to the body so far other than that he was dumped next to it."

"Mazes are supposed to be fun. Puzzles, right?" Patrick shook his head. "Get outta that garden—I never liked them."

Addie took a second to catch up to the Irish idiom—it meant to leave that topic off the table. "That's because you think crossword puzzles are the work of the devil."

"I don't *think*. I know."

"How do you feel about sudoku?"

"Bite your tongue."

He pulled up a surgical mask, and she trailed after him into the tent. A crime-scene tech was running cords to a portable generator to power up a set of lights. They'd have to wait to move the body to look for any ID or other injuries until an investigator arrived from the Cook County medical examiner's office. Cops had the scene; the ME had the body.

Patrick gestured toward the tape over the man's eyes and mouth. "See no evil, speak no evil?"

She pointed out the markings on the forehead and chest. "What do you make of those?"

Patrick borrowed her flashlight and leaned in. He stared in silence for a moment, then grunted. "You're asking the man who would rather play the fiddle with Satan than try a game of tic-tac-toe. It looks like gibberish to me."

She sighed. "The rain has pretty much ruined whatever they were."

"Our killer never heard of permanent ink?" Patrick said.

"Maybe the marks were for him, and he didn't care if we could read them."

"Assuming the killer is the one who put them there." He rubbed the back of his neck. "Are those marks why they called us?"

"That and the guy was practically cut in half."

"There's a point."

"And there's his throat," Addie said.

Patrick leaned in farther. "Looks like our killer shark took a sample bite before proceeding to the entrée."

Patrick kept his voice light, but it was just his form of gallows humor. She knew that every victim cost him something, just as it did her.

"Thanh also thought it was a bite mark," she said.

"You see enough, you get a feel for them," Patrick said. "So to speak."

"Could be that's our killer's mistake."

Most killers made multiple mistakes. But the clever ones—the Zodiac Killers and the Bible Johns—they managed to slide in and out of murder, leaving almost no trace.

"We should be so lucky," Patrick said. The crime-scene tech's lights flared on, causing their shadows to leap onto the canvas. "Let's get to work, then."

CHAPTER 5

EVAN

River moved aside the remnants of the charcuterie board as Evan unfolded the letter, written on thick, creamy paper, and placed it on the table. He read the note aloud.

> Dear Doctors Wilding,
> Will you forgive my forwardness if I call you by your given names?
>
> Evan, we have yet to meet. River, you won't remember me. But although you are unaware of my existence, I feel that I know you both. I have followed and appreciated your work from afar.
>
> And now, it is time for my own humble contribution.
>
> Let the game begin, as they say. I trust you will find it rewarding.
>
> Hygíainete!
>
> TR

Beneath the signature was a line of what, to the casual eye, might resemble pure nonsense, a child's made-up secret code. But Evan recognized the seeming nonsense immediately as signs from three of Crete's scripts: Linear B, the Phaistos Disc, and Cretan Hieroglyphic. Of the three, only Linear B had been mostly deciphered.

There was also a small square maze.

Elegantly penned around the edges of the paper was a narrow border composed of a repeating sequence of seventeen figures from Cretan Hieroglyphic, Crete's third undeciphered script. The glyphs looked hand drawn.

"Undeciphered scripts and the plural form of the word *Hygíaine*," River said, straightening. "An ancient Greek verb used here in the imperative form, instructing us to be of sound mind and good health. Intriguing. Do you know any TRs?"

"There's a Terri Robinson in administration at UChicago. What about you?"

"Tychon Ritsardopoulo. He serves an incredible chilled raki with apricot brandy at a hotel bar in Athens."

"Both unlikely candidates. Keep pondering."

"Someone I bumped into at a conference, maybe? Or grad school?" River pushed back a wayward lock of hair. "That would go back a decade."

Evan turned the piece of paper over, but the back side was blank. He flipped it again to the front, then held it up to the light to check for a watermark—a nearly invisible image that would indicate where the paper had been manufactured. He found nothing, which didn't surprise him. These days, watermarks were used only by high-end paper mills.

The writing was tight and neat, done in black ink, the glyphs skillfully drawn.

"Cretan Hieroglyphic," River said. "Europe's first writing. With Linear B and signs from the Phaistos Disc. And a maze. An intriguing mix."

"But an irrational one. The scripts are three separate entities." Evan raised his chin, scratching beneath it in a contemplative gesture. "The letter itself is rational, if enigmatic. But the glyphs . . . this mix of three different scripts . . . It feels amateurish. Even childish."

"Agreed. Still, when he mentions appreciating your work from afar, he must be talking about your efforts on the Phaistos."

"Not much to admire there," Evan grumbled. "Perhaps he's talking about your time on Crete."

"That was years ago."

"You managed to get a few papers out of it."

River waved a dismissive hand. "Barely worth the trees they took." But then he laughed. "Do you remember that paper we cowrote back when we were in our twenties and still embarrassingly wet behind the ears?"

Evan looked up. "When we thought we'd deciphered the Phaistos Disc."

"And *Archaeological Journal* actually published it."

"What were they thinking?"

"That we'd actually deciphered it, of course. It took us forever to live that one down."

"Those were the days." Evan reread the letter. Pushed a hand through his thick curls. "This note is hardly threatening. The handwriting is controlled, suggesting the same for the mind behind it. TR could be a scholar. Maybe he or she *is* someone you met at a conference."

"Or someone who thinks they've figured out Crete's undeciphered scripts. Like us, all those years ago. That could be his or her 'humble' contribution."

"I have a thick file folder of letters from those dreamers, each sure they've discovered the key. Maybe one of them is TR. But"—he dropped the letter back on the table—"none of this explains why the man who left the letter was so worried."

"Maybe we'll find the answer in that," River said, pointing toward the package. "I'm surprised you haven't already torn it open."

Evan picked up the small bundle and then hesitated. The last time someone had left a package for him—that one at his office at UChicago—it had been the start of a series of gruesome murders that had nearly ended in his own death.

Putting the memory aside, he unwound the tape until the paper opened. Inside lay a silver coin. He moved to pick it up when thoughts of the previous case stopped him.

"Wait a minute," he said, and headed toward the kitchen in the back. In a moment, he returned wearing latex gloves. He handed a second pair to River, then lifted the coin by its edges and held it up to the firelight.

Made of hammered silver, circular in shape but somewhat irregular, the coin showed the image of a bull on one side and that of a maze on the other.

"What is this?" Evan said.

River smiled. "I think we have ourselves a mystery."

His voice held a distinct note of pleasure. Evan felt his own familiar surge of delight, a particular itch that accompanied any enigma laid at his literal or metaphorical doorstep—a puzzle, an unknown sign, a bit of code.

An ancient coin.

Firelight winked on the dull silver of the coin, brightening it.

River pushed up the sleeves of his shirt—revealing an old scar from a battle with bandits in the African Sahel—and pulled on the gloves. Evan, knowing that his brother's expertise in rare coins far exceeded his own, handed over the bit of silver.

"Fascinating," River said. "It's a one-stater coin from Knossos."

"Meaning what?"

"A stater was an ancient coin on the Greek island of Crete. Knossos was the capital city of—"

"Ancient Crete. My admittedly frequent indulgence in alcohol hasn't yet obliterated my brain cells."

"Not yet. But one stater equaled three drachm, the currency of the realm back then. This coin would have been in use around 425 BCE to 360 BCE or so."

Evan studied the image on the coin. "A minotaur," he whispered to himself. The flesh-eating monster kept in the labyrinth below the palace on Crete.

"Very good, brother," River said. He removed a loupe from his leather bag and held the magnifier to his eye and the coin under a lamp. "On the obverse side, we have a naked minotaur shown in a running position. His left hand is fisted, and he holds something in his right hand. On the reverse or 'tails' side," he said as he flipped the coin over, "we have a square maze with five points in the middle. I've seen this type of coin before. Behind glass at a museum, mind you."

"It's rare?" Evan asked.

"Quite rare if it's genuine." River held the rim of the coin between his thumb and forefinger and turned the piece of silver over and over. "The wear and patina, along with the irregular stamping, suggest likely authenticity. Weight and size are good. There's no indication of casting seams or filing."

"You know, in the movies, the expert just bites the coin to judge if it's real."

River lifted the coin toward his mouth, and Evan laughed and raised his palms in a "Please stop" gesture.

"This is why you'll be so good for the institute," Evan said. "Your breadth of knowledge."

"Maybe. But a good fake can fool even the experts." River set the coin back in its paper nesting and returned the loupe to his bag. "There's only perhaps twenty of these coins known to exist. Expensive but not outlandishly so, given its rarity. Worth around fifty-five thousand euros."

"Around sixty thousand US dollars," Evan said. "That's a fair chunk of change to leave on someone's doorstep. No wonder the man looked worried."

"Perhaps he merely wanted to make a gift to the institute."

"Gifts like this come with a request for a receipt so that the donor can benefit from his generosity. Anonymous donors are rare in my field. Especially anonymous donors who look me straight in the eye and then rush off into the darkness."

River picked up his cognac. "A misanthropic donor? A wealthy recluse?"

"The letter is addressed to both of us," Evan said. "Who knew you were coming here?"

"My site manager and the site administrator from Göbekli Tepe. My assistant. A few others."

"Do you trust them?"

"Not to leave a valuable coin on your doorstep? I feel pretty solid on that."

"Then there's the game the writer mentions. What game? And are we to think there's a message hidden in this logo-pictorial-syllabic scrawl?"

"Is there?"

Evan held the letter up to the light again. "If I were to read it straight through—which, for the record, isn't actually possible, it would go something like this: The syllable *de*, followed by the syllable *ko*, and then *de* again. After that is something that might be a maze followed by a figure that I suspect is meant to represent a bee and four little tick marks. We then have a representative of a captive man—a rather unsettling glyph—then the bee, concluding with the syllables *ma* and *de*."

"Hmm," River said.

"Nonsense," Evan said. "Did I tell you or not?"

River finished his drink, then pushed out of his chair with a sudden burst of energy. He paced back and forth in front of the fire. "What are the rules of this game? And how will we know where and when to begin?"

"We wait for the next letter, I suppose." Evan put the current letter and his unease firmly aside. "Perhaps the next missive will be more illuminating."

River stopped in front of the fireplace and propped his elbow on the mantel. "Changing the subject, I heard from Dad."

Evan looked up from his contemplation of a slice of Stilton. "That must have ruined your day."

"He calls every year or so, but each time it's an ugly surprise."

"What did he want?"

"Just to know how we're doing. At least that's what he said."

"To know how *you're* doing, more like," Evan said.

River's eyebrows rose. "If I didn't know you better, I'd say that was self-pitying."

"Maybe." Evan chuckled and was pleased to hear nothing bitter in the sound. "And, also, true."

Now River's expression turned hard. "Look in the Oxford English Dictionary under *poisonous, bunch-backed toad*—to quote the Bard—and the first entry will read Wilding, comma, Oliver J."

Evan laughed. "It does offer me comfort in the middle of the night when I wake up feeling like an orphaned wretch."

"It could have been worse," River said.

"How's that?"

"We could have been poverty stricken as well as neglected."

"Money was a poor substitute for attention."

"True. But it did get us good nannies."

River turned his gaze toward the fire, and Evan watched his brother's face soften again.

River and their father shared some commonalities based on what little their mother had told them. Oliver was an adventurer, a globe-trotting pharmacologist in search of chemical nirvanas, a man who wouldn't allow himself to be pinned down by societal expectations. As in, say, being a doting father to two boys. Evan wasn't surprised that while he heard nothing from his father, River received a call every year or so. What their dad called "checking in" with his boys, although he only ever checked in with one of them.

Evan had made his peace with it long ago. Or so he liked to tell himself.

He jumped when his phone rang out with the opening chords of Helen Reddy's iconic song of feminism, "I Am Woman."

"It's Addie," Evan said, filled with sudden foreboding. There could be only one reason for her to call so late. He eyeballed the coin as he picked up the phone.

"Patrick and I are in the Loop," Addie said. "Couch Place. I need you here. We've caught one of the weird ones."

CHAPTER 6

RIVER

While Evan drove the Jaguar, River rode shotgun, staring out through the rain-spattered windows and trying to piece together his long-ago memories of the city.

He'd been seven when his father had plucked him away from his mother and Evan and his friends in England and deposited him in an apartment on Lake Shore Drive with a nanny and a pet guinea pig—an animal with which he'd felt a certain kinship: both exiles, far from their native land.

The guinea pig had lasted longer than the first three au pairs. River suspected he'd been a handful. *Diabolically defiant,* one of the nannies had said.

But he remembered little of it. Just that he'd been homesick. And alarmed by his father. Oliver Wilding was a big man with a booming voice and a habit of clapping River on the shoulder in a way that felt more like punishment than comradery.

Eventually, when a still very young River persisted in his interest in archaeology, museums, and saber fencing over team sports, Oliver had grown tired of being a dad. After River's mother left Evan with his own nanny in England and returned to the States, Oliver had dropped

River off at her family's Connecticut mansion and disappeared into parts unknown.

River had seen him only four times since.

Which was more than enough. He and Evan had done perfectly damn well without the Right Honourable Oliver J. Wilding, earl of one or another British county, the name of which River continually told himself wasn't important enough to remember.

A silver SUV loomed out of the darkness and sped past them, throwing a wall of water onto the Jaguar. Evan cursed and steered through the sudden deluge, then skirted a small lake in the middle of the street. The puddles were the remnant of the storm that had already passed through; here, the rain had clotted into a mist that obscured everything beyond a few yards.

At least this visit to Chicago was off to a promising start. A mysterious visitor and a maze coin and a murder. Much more interesting than running an antiquities institute, however much he wanted to help Evan.

"Talk to me about mazes," he said.

Evan took another puddle straight on. Water geysered over the passenger windows.

"Unicursal or multicursal?"

River laughed. "Yes. I think."

"If a maze has only one path from entrance to center, then it is unicursal," Evan said. "If there are multiple paths to choose from, then you have a multicursal maze. Or, to use a different terminology that some people prefer, mazes have multiple routes, while *labyrinths* have but a single path. That is, a labyrinth is a unicursal maze. Mazes are considered games now, but they weren't always seen that way. They could be deadly serious. *Penetrans ad interiora mortis.*"

"Penetrating into the interior places of death. That's cheerful."

Evan steered around another puddle. "We *are* heading to Death Alley, after all."

River pulled his gaze from the foggy city. Things kept getting more interesting. "Tell me."

"Today, the walkway is called Couch Place Alley, but in 1903 it was known as the Alley of Death and Mutilation thanks to a fire in a nearby theater. More than six hundred people burned or fell to their deaths or were trampled or asphyxiated. All in a matter of minutes."

"A suitably morbid setting for a murder, then," River said dryly.

"Nothing like death with a spooky side of atmosphere," Evan agreed. "We're almost there."

The flashing blue lights of squad cars appeared, pulsing in the mist. As they drew near, River made out five cars, a crisp line of crime-scene tape, and the white van of the medical examiner's office. Evan pulled to the curb as close to the scene as he could get, then he and River walked the rest of the way along a street rendered almost unrecognizable by the eerily shifting vapors. All around, the megaliths of skyscrapers rose in the darkness, their lights a blurry smear, their vague shapes suggestive of hulking giants.

As they approached the alley, River stared up at the high walls of the buildings on either side. The place looked vaguely familiar. Perhaps he and his father had strolled the length of this alley on their way from the apartment to a restaurant.

"Your Death Alley could be seen as a segment of a maze," he said.

"More like a labyrinth," Evan said, "since it has but a single path through."

They reached the tape stretched across the mouth of the alley. A patrol cop stood guard.

"You'll have to wait here," Evan said to River.

"Take your time. Because you know how much I love creepy fog-enshrouded cities."

Evan stared at him. "You *wanted* to come. And besides, you *do* love creepy cities."

"Only when all the occupants are dead."

"Spoken like a true archaeologist."

Evan signed in with the officer and lowered his head to duck under the tape. River watched as his brother crossed the mystical line between everyday life and a brutal death, heading toward a white tent that had been raised near the east end of the alley. Evan went under a second line of tape—this one red instead of yellow—and a woman came out of the tent and lowered her surgical mask.

She was five foot seven and maybe a hundred and thirty pounds. Her posture carried a barely restrained energy River could sense even from this distance. Her expression was intense, her features fine—delicate nose, a determined jaw, and high cheekbones. Her corkscrew curls were held back in a ponytail.

She had to be Detective Addie Bisset. Evan's friend. And his unrequited love.

She and Evan shook hands. They spoke briefly, then disappeared inside.

River meandered over to where a small crowd had gathered despite the chill and the lateness of the hour. He heard a few startled comments about a dwarf, and then someone said, "That must be the Sparrow. Which means it's definitely a murder. They wouldn't have called him otherwise."

The Sparrow. River smiled at the name, which had been given to Evan by an Oxford don. While most people assumed the nickname had to do with Evan's size, the truth was that—according to the don—seeing a sparrow meant that secrets would soon be brought to light.

Casually, River eased to the side of the crowd to a location where he could study the faces, looking for someone who didn't fit the downtown vibe. He knew that a killer often returned to the scene of his crime, posing as a curious onlooker.

He counted twelve people. There was one older couple in nylon and sensible walking shoes, but the rest were twenty- and thirtysomethings dressed in a mix of dark jeans and camo jackets, animal-print faux fur, or sequined T-shirts that flashed in the police lights. After spending years at dusty archaeological digs in the Middle East, River had forgotten how Westerners dressed—their individuality and their desire to stand out in a crowd.

A whiff of a berry-flavored vape drifted from the group.

River glanced back at the crime scene. Evan emerged from the tent, stared at something on the wall behind the white canvas, then ducked back inside.

River stepped away from the knot of lookie-loos and cops to take in a wider view of the area.

Just outside the reach of the lights from the squad cars stood a tall man in dark jeans and a black hoodie. Although River couldn't make out the man's features, he got the sense that the man was watching the crowd.

River edged closer.

The man pivoted to face him, his features still hidden in darkness. River could almost feel the man taking him in, studying him as if he were a specimen under glass. He radiated a sense of menace, although the threat wasn't anything River could put his finger on. It was nothing more than a gut feeling.

But River trusted his gut.

The man offered a slight nod.

River frowned. What did the nod mean? That they were fellow oglers, morbidly curious comrades? Or was it something more subtle, perhaps more sinister?

Just to see what would happen, he nodded back.

A long moment stretched out. Then Hoodie Man pressed his palm to his chest and tapped his heart three times before he turned on his heel and headed north, moving strikingly fast for a man of his size.

River wasted a few seconds trying to catch the eye of one of the patrol cops before he gave up and hurried after the man, letting the mist serve as cover while his target sped down this block and onto the next, moving in and out of the faint yellow cones cast by fog-veiled lights.

When River neared the next street corner, he spied the man bending down. After a few seconds, the man straightened and glanced back at River before breaking into a sprint. River started his own dash, his boots hitting the concrete with a dull thud.

When he reached the corner moments later, the man had vanished as if he'd never been, leaving only fog-clotted streets. River strained to catch the echo of receding footsteps, but the only sound was the lonely wail of a distant siren.

The street was lined with businesses—Hoodie Man could have vanished into any of them that were still open. Or he could have simply disappeared into the night with its thick vapors.

River pushed back his hat and frowned. He wasn't used to losing his mark.

He glanced down. The man—or someone—had made a series of chalk marks on the sidewalk: six arcs, each no more than two inches long. Next to these was another symbol. Together, the signs formed a bizarre message that most passersby would interpret as nothing more than a meaningless series of lines.

But River had strolled many times through the stiflingly hot Heraklion Archaeological Museum on the island of Crete, where he would stop to admire a display of artifacts with Cretan hieroglyphs: carved gemstones, an altar stone, the Arkalochori Axe. And the famous Phaistos Disc, which shared some of its signs with the axe. Some of these artifacts revealed a numbering system that dated back four thousand years.

The chalk marks on a sidewalk in Chicago could be six curved lines that meant nothing to anyone other than the person who'd made them.

Or—more likely—they could represent the number six written in Cretan Hieroglyphic.

More likely because next to the six arcs was a symbol River recognized immediately as Cretan hieroglyph number 175, per the current standard classification of the glyphs. It consisted of two horizontal triangles bisected by a single vertical line.

It was the symbol for the labrys—a double-headed axe from Crete.

River used his phone to snap a photo, which he texted to Evan. Then he pulled out his leather journal and drew a sketch. It wasn't that he didn't trust technology. It was more that the human eye caught things a camera missed.

)))
)))

He tucked his journal and phone back inside his coat, scanned the streets a final time, then headed back toward the crime scene.

He wondered if this was the game the letter writer had in mind.

And if the opening move was murder.

CHAPTER 7

ADDIE

"It's him," Evan said to Addie and Patrick. "Your murder victim is the man who left the coin and the letter on the doorstep of the institute."

The three of them had emerged from the tent so that the investigator from the ME's office had room to work. The mist was turning to rain, and a few of the onlookers at the west end of the alley began to drift away. Addie knew that Detectives Thanh and Garza would have already talked to them and taken names and phone numbers in case they needed to follow up.

They now had an ID for the victim. Samuel Fishbourne, age fifty-six, corporate attorney and Chicago native. Address in the River North neighborhood. It was a neighborhood Addie frequented—as an artist, she dreamed of someday having a showing in one of the galleries there. Of course, she also dreamed of playing center field for the Cubs, and she imagined the chance of achieving either of these was slim.

Patrol had located Fishbourne's car, a 2015 Lexus ES 350, in a parking garage right next door to Couch Place. They were hauling it to the police garage.

Addie lowered her mask.

A wealthy attorney from an upscale neighborhood dead in an alleyway. A man in dress clothes and with $200 cash in his wallet, along with a platinum AmEx credit card. Plus a photo of him and an attractive younger woman, both smiling as they stood on the stairs in front of the Art Institute of Chicago.

Not the sort of man you'd expect to be delivering packages in a thunderstorm.

"No question on his ID?" she confirmed with Evan.

"Unless he has a twin."

"What time did Fishbourne pay you a visit?" Patrick asked, zipping his rain jacket.

"An hour or so after dark," Evan said. "Nine or nine thirty."

Addie pulled off her latex gloves and dropped them in a bag near the tent. She snugged down the hood on her coat. "Which would mean he died not long after delivering the coin. Did you see or hear anything else? A car? Another person?"

"I heard a car starting up," Evan said. "But River arrived a few minutes after Fishbourne left. It could have been his Uber."

"Uber drivers don't turn off the engine when they drop off a fare," Patrick said. "What kind of vehicle did it sound like? A truck? A sports car?"

Evan shook his head. "Nothing stood out. All I can say is that the man looked worried. Indeed, thinking back, I'd say he was terrified."

"Terrified," Addie echoed. "Of what, I wonder?"

"Not of me, I feel confident. I probably startled him, but I'm hardly frightening. He bent over as if setting something down, then straightened and hurried away. When I opened the front door, I found an envelope on the doorstep, which hadn't been there half an hour before. Inside was a letter and a coin."

Addie tucked her phone inside her jacket as more rain hit the asphalt. "Tell us about the items."

Evan gave her a brief description of the maze-and-minotaur coin, then showed her the photo he'd taken of the letter.

She and Patrick read the note, and she returned Evan's phone. "What is *Hygíainete*?"

"It's an ancient Greek word meaning 'good health.' A typical sign-off."

"If you know Greek," she said, dryly. "And all those other signs?"

"Those around the edge are from a script called Cretan Hieroglyphic, which is undeciphered. The row of figures beneath TR's signature is a mix of two other scripts from Crete—the Phaistos Disc and Linear B."

"Cretin?" Patrick asked. "Isn't that someone with hypothyroidism?"

Addie stared at her partner. "How do you know that?"

"I'm not just the supercop you see before you," Patrick said. "I watch medical TV shows when I take off my Superman cape."

"Patrick's right that the term, spelled with an *i*, originated with people suffering hypothyroidism due to iodine deficiency," Evan said. "These days, though, *cretin* with an *i* means 'stupid' or 'vulgar,' or 'ignorant.' But I'm referring to C-r-e-t-a-n. Cretan with an *a*. Meaning, from the Greek island of Crete."

"But the signs don't mean anything to you?" Addie said.

"Or to any scholar. Not in any traditional sense, anyway. We can't *read* Cretan Hieroglyphic, if that's what you're asking."

She glowered at him and watched him read her subtext.

"Of course, I'll try to extrapolate something," he said. "If there's anything to extrapolate."

"And the game? What kind of game does he mean?"

"No idea. Sorry. But there's a maze on the letter. And a maze on the coin."

In unison, they all turned toward the tiled maze on the alley wall.

She tapped a restless foot. "So, a man drops off a maze coin and a letter that challenges you and your brother to a game, and then he is found dead a few hours later in an alley next to the image of a maze."

"Not only that." Evan turned and pointed toward one of the theater posters. This one lay behind plexiglass and hung near the back door of the Neverland Theater.

Addie read the sign out loud.

The King and the Minotaur

Join us for a reimagining of the famous Greek tragedy!

A vengeful king. A flesh-eating monster. A brave hero.

The king's beautiful, treacherous daughter.

And a dark and deadly labyrinth to lead them all astray.

"The play starts this weekend," Addie said.

Evan nodded. "Probably to go with the citywide read of Edith Hamilton's *Mythology*."

Patrick tugged on his ear. "Meaning maybe our killer is running with the Greek-tragedy theme. He leaves the body near the theater to make sure we get the message."

"For what it's worth," Evan said, "the myth of King Minos and the Minotaur includes not only heroics and romance but cannibalism, bestiality, human sacrifice, and fratricide."

"Let's hope the killer ain't aiming for all those," Patrick said.

Addie spun back to Evan. "Why do you think Fishbourne reached out to you and your brother?"

"The only thing we can come up with is River's archaeological work on the island of Crete and my pointless stabs at deciphering the Phaistos Disc. The disc is a product of the Minoan culture, which thrived on Crete three thousand years before Christ. But I have to point out that the letter writer signed off with the initials TR. Not a match for Samuel Fishbourne. And why would a corporate attorney care about ancient Crete? Presumably, Fishbourne was some sort of go-between."

"Talk about shooting the messenger," Patrick said. "In a manner of speaking."

"Maybe the killer compelled Fishbourne to deliver the package," Addie said.

Patrick brushed rain from his buzz cut. "Using what kind of threat?"

"Whatever it was," Evan said, "it convinced him not to ask for help. I was right there. I could have done something. Called the police. Invited him inside."

Addie heard the anguish in Evan's voice. "And the marks on his forehead? Were they already there when you saw him at the institute?"

"They were smeared by the rain, but yes."

His gaze turned inward, and she could almost see him mentally running down a list of possibilities. Where would the Major Crimes Special Investigations Unit be without this man versed in ancient scripts, strange symbols, and the forensics of murderers with a story to tell?

After a moment, Evan said, "The signs might also be Cretan Hieroglyphic. Like on the letter."

"At least our guy's consistent," Patrick said. "What about the tape over Fishbourne's eyes and mouth?"

"A form of undoing?" Addie suggested. "The killer knew his victim and wanted to keep Fishbourne from seeing him or pleading for his life?"

Evan said, "We should also consider that in light of a possible link to a labyrinth, the killer could have been simulating the Minotaur's maze in which the victim can hear the monster approach, but he cannot see him. And crying for help from the depths of the labyrinth is pointless. In that deep cave, no one can hear you scream. Plus—"

He stopped when his phone buzzed.

"Plus what?" Addie pressed.

"Hold on. It's a text from River. He found something."

Evan held up his phone, and Addie squinted through the light rain. The screen showed a photograph of white chalk marks on a sidewalk. Six small arcs like parentheses along with a pair of triangles bracketing a line.

"The hell is that?" Patrick said.

"River followed a man from the crime scene. He lost his 'target'—that's how River talks—but the man left these markings at the corner of State and Wacker."

"That's a block and a half north," Patrick said. "We'll need a description of the man. If we're lucky, Thanh or Garza will have talked to him."

"Do you think the marks tie into our investigations?" Addie asked.

"The little curved lines could be Cretan hieroglyphs representing the number six. The other image is likely meant to be an axe—another glyph from the letter."

"Six? Why six?" Patrick asked.

Addie recognized the question as rhetorical, but Evan stepped into the void left by Patrick's question.

"Mathematically speaking," he said, "six is the first perfect number because it is both the sum and product of its factors, one, two, and three. As such, it was highly venerated by the Greeks. It was the symbol of Venus, the Greek goddess of love. In the Major Arcana of the Tarot, the sixth card is the Lovers and represents a difficult choice that must be made, often pitting the head against the heart. And, of course, there's the Number of the Beast, which is 666."

Patrick pressed a palm to his forehead. "I should have known even the devil's coffee wasn't going to be enough."

"Starting out, we have to consider everything," Evan said. He typed something back to River, then shoved his phone in his pocket. "But River's discovery provides weight to my guess about the signs on Fishbourne being Cretan hieroglyphs. With your permission, I'd like to try and work backward from the marks, see if I can fill in the gaps caused by the rain."

Addie straightened. "Can these hieroglyphs be used to write words? Is the killer sending a message?"

"I wish the answer to that was yes," Evan said. "But even after thousands of years and thousands of would-be decipherers, Cretan Hieroglyphic has never been decrypted. Which means that any message meant by the killer likely has meaning only for him."

"But you identified the chalk marks that River sent you," she pointed out.

"Numerals are the only glyphs that we *can* read."

"Fork it," Addie said.

"What exactly *is* a hieroglyph? Keep it at the eighth-grade level, please." Patrick nodded toward Addie. "For her sake, you know."

Addie rolled her eyes.

"Keeping it simple," Evan said, "a hieroglyph is a highly stylized picture of something. A bird, a bee, a man, or a woman. The picture can stand for an object, or for a single sound, or a syllable. In Egyptian hieroglyphs, for example, a bird represents the sound made by the letter *a*."

The medical examiner leaned out of the tent.

"Detectives," she said.

Addie turned toward the ME.

Dr. Lisa Sheerin was a chain-smoking, hard-charging curmudgeon with a brilliant mind, a height that didn't much exceed Evan's, and zero tolerance for fools. Addie liked her a great deal.

"You'll want to see this," Sheerin said in her raspy voice. She nodded at Evan. "Him, too."

They pulled up their masks and crowded back into the space. The humid air inside carried the first hint of decay; the scents of honey and licorice still lingered. Addie eased back her hood, then made room for Evan to move to the front so that his short stature wouldn't be a problem.

"I was looking for other injuries," Sheerin said. "We rolled him a bit and found another one of those strange markings. But this one's on his back, technically his trapezius, so it was protected from the rain."

She knelt and lifted Fishbourne's left shoulder. Addie stared at the image drawn in black ink; it seemed to be staring back at her.

"A *cat*?" she asked. More accurately, a cat *head*, with large round eyes and sharply pointed ears.

"Whiskers and all," Sheerin said as she eased the body back down.

"The killer likes cats?" Patrick ventured.

"We probably aren't talking about actual cats," Evan said.

"This is one of those Cretan hieroglyphs?" Patrick asked. "Like on the letter you got?"

"More specifically, it's a syllabogram, meaning it represents a sound. In the case of a Cretan cat, the syllable *ma*. But unless our killer is a scholar, he could be using the sign as a logogram or a pictogram."

Patrick groaned. "Why is it whenever you're around, Professor, I get a headache? What the heck are you talking about?"

"A logogram is simply a picture that represents a word. A picture of a cat stands for the word *cat*. A pictogram is a specific type of hieroglyph in which the picture, rather than representing a sound, the way many Egyptian hieroglyphs do, or standing in for a single word like *cat*, represents a concept suggested by the picture."

"Give us an example," Addie said.

"Consider how a drawing of a foot could represent an actual foot. Or it could denote walking. Maybe a journey. Or an image for a podiatrist."

"Jesus, Mary, Joseph, and the wee donkey," Patrick said. "You mean our cat might be a cat. Or it might be a word for snootiness or walking softly or being a picky eater."

Addie locked her eyes on Evan. "Well?"

Evan ran his fingers uselessly through his damp hair. The curls flopped back into his eyes.

"The cat is definitely Minoan," he said. "The bulging eyes and large ears are typical of Cretan Hieroglyphic cats. But we don't know whether the killer intended this cat as a syllabogram, a pictogram, or a logogram." Patrick glared at him, and Evan rushed on. "That's as much as I can say at this point."

Addie tapped her foot. "We need to know what the cat and these other marks mean to the killer."

"I'll do whatever I can to help," Evan said. "See what I can suss out of the damaged marks and then take a stab at what they might mean. But I'm not sure I'll give you anything helpful."

"We'll be grateful for whatever you can learn." Addie squeezed the bridge of her nose between her thumb and forefinger. She needed coffee. "We'll need the letter Fishbourne left. And the coin. I assume you handled them?"

"The letter. But River and I held the coin by the edge. And we wore gloves."

"You've been watching me work, I see," Patrick said.

"There's one more thing," Evan said. "Do you smell licorice and honey?"

Addie and Patrick both nodded. "His last drink, I assume," Patrick said.

"Could be, but an unusual one. That's the smell of raki, a liquor made of twice-distilled grapes that is popular on Crete. There are theories that in ancient times the liquor was poured over sacrifices."

"Sacrifices," Addie murmured. She puffed out a breath through narrowed lips. A wisp of her hair lifted and resettled. "Get to work, then. I'll send you photos from the scene and whatever else you need."

"Can I talk to River about the case? Use his expertise on Crete?"

Addie glanced down the alley toward the squad cars. A man she assumed to be River—tall and lean, wearing a leather jacket—stood behind the tape. He was sketching something in a notebook, using his body to shield the paper from the rain.

"I'll have Detective Thanh talk to him about the man he followed," she said. "Then, Evan, swear him to secrecy. I'll get a nondisclosure agreement to him first thing tomorrow. Beyond that, use anything that helps. Your brain, your books, your brother. A Magic 8 Ball, if that's of use. We need answers."

Evan nodded. "We're your answer men."

CHAPTER 8

EVAN

After swinging by the institute to pick up a sleepy Perro, River's duffel bag, and the letter and coin, Evan drove south on Woodlawn toward the University of Chicago. He parked his specially modified Jaguar in his designated spot near the Harper Memorial Library.

"Are you sure I can't take you home to catch some sleep?" he asked River.

For himself, he knew sleep would be impossible. He intended to spend what remained of the night in his university office where he kept his literature on Crete's undeciphered scripts.

"Trying to shunt me off so you can keep all the fun to yourself?" River said. He glanced at his watch. "It's lunchtime in Istanbul. And surely you have coffee in that office you tell me you love so much."

"Tea," Evan said.

"I can manage with tea."

"You make a poor Brit, brother."

"Good thing I'm American, then."

Evan killed the engine. Perro pushed his head between the seats and wagged his tail, tongue lolling. Neither man stirred.

"Remember when we were on Crete together?" River said. He sat facing forward; the campus lights illuminated his face.

"Years ago," Evan said, his mind drifting six thousand miles away to Crete. He and River were standing on a windswept knoll staring out at the brilliant blue of the Aegean Sea. He'd been twenty, River seventeen. He on holiday from Oxford, River on a high school field trip to the city of Knossos. They'd taken a hike out of town to get a flavor for Crete the way it must have been millennia earlier when people believed that gods like Zeus visited the earth and heroes like Hercules slew monsters.

"Remember all the cats?" River said. "The glyph cats?"

On Crete, he and River had seen cats like the one drawn on Fishbourne's body. The cats had appeared on storefronts and pub signs. On T-shirts and tea towels. And carved on a segment of bone they'd found in an antiquities shop in one of the alleyways of the island's principal city, Heraklion.

River unfastened his seat belt. "Earlier tonight, while you and I were enjoying our brandies, Samuel Fishbourne was dying in an alley."

"Then let's do what we can for him," Evan said. "Although it's of little solace."

Evan clipped on Perro's leash, and the corgi followed him out of the car. At the door to the library building, Evan used his key to let the three of them inside the soaring building with its elegant Gothic architecture, vaulted ceilings, ornately carved portals, and immense coats of arms. They rode the elevator to the third floor. When they exited, Evan noticed a light shining in the crack at the bottom of the door to his office. It was now well past the witching hour and full into oh-dark-thirty. Who—?

River had noticed both the light and his brother's hesitation and moved ahead of him. Evan realized how comforting it was to have River here. In all their misadventures, River had never allowed so much as a hair on Evan's head to be harmed.

And, if Evan were fair, he'd saved River's bacon a time or two as well.

River's hand reached inside his coat.

"No weapons, River," Evan whispered. "We're at the university, for God's sake."

"Fishbourne is dead," River whispered back. "How do I know you haven't been targeted?"

"You are as much a target as I am. But no guns. Don't you have something else in that bag of yours?"

While they debated, Perro bounded forward, jerking his leash free of Evan's grip. He darted toward the door, tail wagging, butt wiggling, and stuck his nose to the crack. He gave a single happy bark.

There could be only one explanation for Perro's enthusiasm. Evan's guess was confirmed a few seconds later when the door swung open, and the figure of a woman appeared, silhouetted against the light. Tall, athletic, with hair that hung over her shoulders like a shimmering bronze curtain, she resembled nothing so much as a Greek goddess.

Next to him, River drew in a breath.

The woman was Diana Alanis, Evan's friend as well as his research assistant. Diana was brilliant, ambitious, sharp tongued, a frighteningly good axe thrower, and the only American woman with a PhD in Incan quipu.

Diana stooped to scoop up Perro, whose entire body wriggled with excitement. Diana had been his first human before Evan took over dog-watching duties. He licked her face, which, had she been an actual goddess, might have been frowned on. But Diana laughed and pushed back her hair. A white turtleneck sweater set off her burnished skin and hazel eyes. Tight jeans set off the rest of her in a way that was hard to miss but which Evan, as her boss, chose to ignore.

"Diana Alanis," Evan said to River, "my postdoc. Diana, meet my brother, River."

River recovered himself. “A pleasure,” he said, stepping forward to offer a hand. “Evan has mentioned your work.”

“Ah, the Indiana Jones brother. I’ve been wondering when we’d meet.” Diana straightened and shook River’s hand. “Likewise. Still obsessed with Zhou dynasty relics?”

“I’ve moved on to Neo-Hittite sculpture.”

“Less flashy,” Diana said.

“Is that a letdown?”

“It shows maturity.”

“And maturity, I assume, is a good thing?”

“Maturity, especially in the male of the species, is both rare and commendable.” She swung open the door. “Come in, gentlemen. I do believe my night just took a turn for the better.”

✣

Inside the office, Evan watched River take in the space with its large windows overlooking the now-darkened quad, soaring bookshelves complete with a rolling ladder, gleaming wooden floors partially covered by Tuareg, Berber, and Persian rugs, two large desks, and a library table. Through one half-open door was a small sleeping room complete with washroom.

The office smelled of furniture polish, books, tea, and candle wax. Task and floor lamps offered a warm glow.

“Not half bad, big brother,” River said, turning in place. “It suits you.”

“Meaning it’s stuffy, overfilled, and medieval,” Evan said.

“Rather, elegant and filled with wisdom,” River countered.

Evan laughed. “I’ll take it.”

“Tea?” Diana asked.

“If that’s the stiffest thing you have, then yes,” River said, hanging his coat on a peg near the door.

Evan put River in charge of clearing a space on the immense library table that anchored the center of the office. It was an unenviable task—the table was cluttered with student papers, dusty tomes, notepads, several volumes from the Oxford English Dictionary, a scattering of books dealing with ancient Hebrew manuscripts, a new text on semiotics, two laptops, and a miscellany of ceramic sherds from around the world.

But they needed room to work.

Evan joined Diana at the cabinet that served as a refreshment stand where she was rooting around in one of the cupboards. Her hand emerged with a box. "Is Earl Grey all right?" she asked.

"Perfect," he said.

He plugged in the electric kettle. Then, wondering what had caused Diana to be up and about in the middle of the night, he stepped back from the cabinet to observe her. Despite Diana's warmth in greeting them, she looked tired and grumpy, both of which were unusual for his perennially energetic and cheerful friend.

"Why are you here?" he asked.

"I assume it's because my parents loved each other." She pulled out tea bags. "But if you mean why am I working in the middle of the night, why are *you*?"

"Police business."

She turned toward him. "There's been a murder? Why were you brought in? Was it grisly?"

"Should I answer those in order?"

"Come on. Give."

"It's definitely one of the interesting ones. But before we go there, please tell me what's wrong."

She sighed. "I'm buried in the unending to-do lists you give me. There aren't enough hours in the day, so the dark of night seemed like a good time to catch up."

"Diana. The truth, please."

She dropped the tea bags in a ceramic pot. Her shoulders fell. "Diego and I aren't a thing anymore."

Diego. Who'd been constantly at her side for months.

"Oh," Evan said. "Since when?"

"Midnight, give or take a few minutes. He's going home to his mama in Brazil."

"Sounds like a serious lapse in judgment on his part," Evan said.

"Obviously," she said.

"I'm sorry."

"It's just a bump in the road." She sniffed. "*Another* bump in the road."

"Not to be insensitive, but maybe a little rebound work is exactly what you need. Will you help us?"

She turned to him. "On the case?"

Diana had signed a nondisclosure agreement with the Chicago PD, just as he had, which meant he and River could speak freely. It would be good to get Diana's views on the subject.

"Of course," he said.

A faint smile. "Try to stop me."

"With your biceps? I wouldn't dream of it."

She cast a glance over her shoulder toward River, who had finished clearing the table and was now absorbed in studying Evan's bookshelves. He stood with his long legs spread, hands clasped behind his back, his blond hair gleaming in the lamplight. His black shirt did nothing to hide the fact that River was in very good shape.

As if sensing their perusal, River glanced over at them. "Nice collection," he said, gesturing toward the books. "It fits your humble abode."

Diana snorted. "This office is hardly humble. No more than the owner."

Evan sighed. "The place is perfect, except that the staff tends to be rude."

River and Diana both laughed. The kettle whistled. River returned to his scrutiny of the books, and Diana leaned in toward Evan.

"I can't believe you didn't tell me your brother was coming," she whispered, pouring the water.

"He surprised me."

"Me, too." She set down the kettle and pulled a hair tie from her pocket, then twisted her long hair into a bun at the nape of her neck. She brushed away an invisible speck of something from her white sweater. "I look a mess."

Her words startled Evan, who had never known his postdoc to give a fig what she looked like. He'd always assumed that was the provenance of beautiful women—when you were stunning in baggy sweats and stained T-shirts, you clearly didn't have to worry about your looks.

But—watching her watch River—it occurred to him that maybe she just hadn't had a reason to care before. Not around him.

He wanted to warn her that River's interest in human relationships didn't extend beyond brotherly love, a friend here and there, and the occasional one-night stand. Like him and—he assumed—like Diana, River's passion was mainly reserved for his work.

River had gone to stand in front of one of the windows. Now he cast a glance at them over his shoulder. "Is that tea ready?"

"Just about," Evan said, lifting the lid to check.

"Good." River stared out at the darkness. "The night's wasting."

Evan's gaze followed River's out toward the night. "And a monster is afoot."

Chapter 9

Ursula Fishbourne

The first thing that came to Ursula when she awoke was the cold—a bone-biting chill that dug into every part of her with teeth and claws.

The second thing that came back was the memory of being dragged along the ground. She'd gone in and out of consciousness as a dim light in front of her revealed rocky walls and a vaguely human shape. The form hauled her through a tunnel for what seemed like hours before the beast-man left her alone in the darkness.

The third thing that came to her was a memory of her father. He was shouting at someone. Pleading as he was dragged away. And then—

She squeezed her hands into fists.

Was he okay? Had he gotten away from the man who'd tricked them?

Ursula opened her eyes, then realized they were already open. The blackness was entire. She raised her hand and tried to see her own fingers.

Nothing.

She touched her palms to the ground, felt rocks and dirt. The musty air stank of earth and mud and stone. In the distance, water trickled faintly. She strained her ears, listening for anything else. Anything at all.

There came only the water dribbling its faint song.

Maybe she was dead. A ghost. A figment. A soundless dream.

Maybe she was alive and entombed in a crypt.

Or maybe the events of the evening had been a nightmare, and she'd soon wake up in her childhood bed, breathing in the aroma of her father's world-famous cinnamon rolls.

Worst nightmare ever, she'd tell him. *There was this monster . . .*

"Daddy?" she whispered, reaching out.

Nothing—absolutely nothing—reached back.

CHAPTER 10

EVAN

With tea poured and the crime-scene documents from Addie printed, Evan, River, and Diana took their seats around the library table. Diana lifted Perro into her lap, and the corgi sprawled across her thighs with a contented sigh.

"Tell me what happened," Diana said. "Give me all the lurid details."

Evan filled her in on the victim: Fishbourne's background, and that his body had been found in Couch Place, perhaps dumped there.

"How did he die?" she asked.

"You're salivating," Evan responded. "It's a bad look when discussing murder."

"It's the puzzle I'm after. Because if you're involved, I know there's a puzzle. Now please get to it. Cause of death?"

"Still waiting for the ME to determine. But Fishbourne had what could be a bite mark on his throat. And he came very close to being cut in half at the waist."

"Bisected," Diana said softly. Her hazel eyes were bright. "You don't hear that every day."

"It was a common method of execution used by the Mamluks when they ruled Egypt," Evan said. "Which, grisly as it was, I find preferable to their other forms of torture—crucifixion upon the back of a camel or impalement on a greased pole."

Diana stared at him in mock horror. "Sometimes, Professor, you alarm me."

"Not half as much as I alarm myself. I don't know why I remember things like that, yet I forget to buy milk when I go to the market. Anyway, our job is to try and make sense of the markings that someone—we assume the killer—drew on our victim, which were half destroyed by the rain. We have a grouping of signs to analyze for a possible link to Crete."

Diana folded her hands under her chin. "Crete as in the island in the Aegean Sea?"

"It's too early in the morning for you to be difficult. Or, as my students say entirely too often, 'Duh.'"

"I merely ask in the interest of being thorough."

"What other Cretes could there be?"

"There's a city in Illinois, for starters," Diana said. "And Nebraska. There used to be an entire county south of the Mason-Dixon Line."

River's gaze moved between the two of them, his amusement obvious. "Want to take back your 'Duh'?" he asked Evan.

"Also—" Diana began.

"Never mind," Evan said. "*Please*, never mind. We're talking about the island in the Mediterranean. The one mentioned by Homer in his epic poems, *The Iliad* and *The Odyssey*. That's the only Crete I know."

"Book nineteen of *The Odyssey*," River said, and quoted: "'There is a land called Crete, in the midst of the wine-dark sea, a fair, rich land, begirt with water, and therein are many men, past counting, and ninety cities.'"

Diana applauded. "Ah, glorious Crete," she said. "King Minos. The Minotaur. Theseus and Ariadne. The maze and a magical red ball of woolen thread. And a palace at Knossos surely fit for the king of an empire."

"That's the one," Evan said. "If we can focus?"

Diana's eyes lit with curiosity. "A man nearly cut in two. And a bite to his throat. Savagery and cannibalism. Do we have a minotaur walking among us?"

"Now you're catching on."

She raised a brow. "You're talking about a monster with a bull's head and a lust for human flesh."

"Those aspects are yet to be established." Evan turned toward his brother. "River, before we look at the crime-scene photos, did you make sketches?"

River opened his journal and pushed it across the table to Evan. "I sketched the crime scene, the chalk marks on the sidewalk, and Hoodie Man."

"Hoodie Man?" Diana and Evan asked in unison.

River shrugged. "A man wearing a hoodie."

Evan looked at the journal. While crime-scene snapshots were critical to the work he did for the police, photos didn't capture a setting's mood: the ambience that might offer insight into why a killer chose the place he did to commit a murder or dump a body. Although with the Minotaur—as he'd already dubbed the killer—the murderer's choice seemed fairly obvious, and not just because of the alley's more notorious name. Fishbourne's body had lain beneath the image of a maze and across from the playbill for *The King and the Minotaur.*

He's not subtle, our monster, he thought. *But is his message for the police, or is it something more personal?*

Or are the signs merely the scrawls of a maddened brain?

That last option seemed unlikely if the killer was TR, the author of the letter.

A game, TR had written.

Evan pushed aside those thoughts and bent over the sketches. Diana was leaning close to him, her breath in his ear. The sister he never had.

River's first drawing portrayed Couch Place in the darkness and fog. The only bright spot was the white police tent. Evan turned the page and found another view. With amazing accuracy, River had captured the cops and the onlookers. More importantly, from Evan's perspective, he'd caught the alley's feeling of claustrophobia—the closed doors, deep shadows, and creeping mist. The sense that if you were running through the alley, you'd have to run fast to escape out the other end before your pursuer caught you.

Had Fishbourne been running? Or had he been dumped?

River's next drawing showed a man in dark jeans and a hooded sweatshirt. The man's face was in shadow, with just the barest hint of eyes gleaming from the darkness.

"Tell us about him," Evan said to River. "Everything you can think of."

"I couldn't make out anything of his face, but he was tall and graceful. Athletic. Fast. A white man, based on his hands. When he caught me looking at him, he nodded. When I nodded back—"

"You nodded back?" Evan asked.

"We were two voyeurs at a murder scene. It seemed rude not to. Anyway, after our mutual nods, he placed his hand on his heart and tapped his chest three times."

Diana straightened and reached for the teapot. "What does that mean?"

"If we stick with Crete," River said, "then he was expressing gratitude. The chest tap is a common gesture in Greece."

"He was *thanking* you?" Diana asked. "For what?"

River's eyes locked with Evan's. "Maybe for participating in his game."

Evan nodded. "You think Hoodie Man might be TR."

"It's possible, isn't it? The perpetrator returning to the scene of his crime. Leaving more glyphs."

"What game?" Diana asked. "Who is TR?"

Evan refilled his own teacup. "We got a letter earlier tonight. And a Cretan coin of some value."

"Let me guess. The letter was from TR?"

"Those were the initials at the bottom. But the letter was delivered by the victim, Samuel Fishbourne."

Diana glared. "Thanks for sharing that in a timely manner." Her tone was crisp. "A dead man came to see you tonight?"

"He wasn't dead at the time. But I apologize. It's been a crazy night." He filled her in on his late-evening visitor and described the letter and the coin.

She wasn't mollified. "Let's see the letter."

"It's sealed in a bag for Addie."

She held out her hand. "I know you took a picture."

"Oh, right." Evan gave her his phone.

When Diana had finished reading the letter, she glowered at him. "Fishbourne delivers a letter that, presumably, he didn't write and which includes an invitation to a game. He adds drawings of glyphs from what I assume are Cretan scripts." At Evan's nod, she continued. "He also drops off a maze-and-minotaur coin. Then he's killed. I would say this doesn't bode well for the two of you."

"All the more reason for us to figure things out," Evan said.

She sniffed, managing to make it sound righteous. "I haven't accepted your apology. But in the spirit of solving this thing, I'm willing to move on."

"Thank you."

"You're welcome."

Evan turned to River's next drawing, which showed Hoodie Man moving away; River must have sketched it from memory. He'd managed to capture a sense of the man's speed while darkness pressed in from both sides. It was as if the city had vanished, and only the man remained.

"That's seriously creepy," Diana said.

"It was," River said. "*He* was. There was something feral about him. Something . . . hungry."

"You're saying that because of the throat wound," Diana said. "And the whole Minotaur thing."

"Maybe." River didn't look convinced.

The last drawing was of the photo River had sent him—the six curved lines and a symbol that was generally assumed by scholars to represent an axe.

"We don't yet know what the number six signifies," Evan said.

Diana leaned forward. "But I'd recognize a labrys anywhere. In part, because I have one tattooed on my back."

She twisted in her chair and started to lift her sweater.

"No need," Evan said. "We believe you."

Diana lowered her hands. River's face remained carefully blank.

Evan pressed on. "Let's pool what we know so that we're all on the same page. We have the Minotaur."

"The Cretan scripts," River added.

"And a labyrinth," Diana said. "Beyond that, I'm afraid what I know about any of this comes from a high school mythology book."

"Except axes," Evan said. "Clearly, you know a labrys when you see one."

"That I do," Diana said. "*Labrys* is from an ancient word for double-bitted axe. Many scholars assert that the word *labyrinth* is derived from *labrys*, and thus a labyrinth is the 'house of the double axe.'"

"There are hundreds of images of labryses on Crete," River said. "Most of them in the palace of Knossos on northern Crete. In fact, the word *Knossos* means 'palace of the double axe.'"

Evan's eyes rose toward the windows where lightning flickered in the distance. "There are also stories that the axe was used by Zeus to summon thunderstorms."

"Also," Diana added, "the labrys was an important religious symbol in ancient Crete."

"And was potentially a symbolic weapon of sacrifice," River added.

"This is good," Evan said, jotting down notes. "There was also a drawing on Fishbourne's shoulder that is definitely a Cretan symbol."

He searched through the photos and handed the image with the cat to Diana.

He said, "The only semiconclusive thing about any of the glyphs is that the cat head in Cretan Hieroglyphic likely stands for the *ma* sound."

"Like *meow*?" Diana asked.

"Exactly like that. Once you accept that a glyph represents a sound, guessing at that sound isn't too difficult. An initial *m* followed by one or more vowels is used around the world for a cat's meow. *Myau* in Russian. *Miao* in Italian. *Meo* in Vietnamese. And so forth. Whether that is what the killer had in mind is another question."

"Could be he just likes cats," Diana said.

"Even killers have a soft side, is that it?" Evan stood. "Now, before we begin analyzing the signs on the victim's body, let's assemble our tools. We'll need drawings of the Cretan hieroglyphs, the Linear B signs and their phonetic values, and symbols from the Phaistos Disc. Also, charts showing how they're organized."

He had all the glyphs memorized from his work on the Phaistos Disc. He could draw the symbols in his sleep. But sometimes there were small variations in the renderings. Better not to take chances.

His books were arranged chronologically by era. He went to the section on ancient Greece, located the shelf with works on the Minoan culture, then climbed the ladder until he was eight feet up. He grabbed books off the shelf and passed them down to Diana, who stood on the ladder's bottom rung. She turned each tome over to River, who carried it to the newly cleared table.

Seven books in, Evan said, "That should give us a good start."

He climbed down the ladder as Diana moved away, then took a final scan of one of the lower shelves for anything he might have missed. He grabbed a final book.

"One island, four scripts," he said. "The Phaistos Disc, Cretan Hieroglyphic, and Linear A—all undeciphered. And Linear B, which has been mostly deciphered, although it still holds its mysteries. Diana, can you look for Michael Ventris's decipherment of Linear B? It's here somewhere. Ventris's insights might come in handy."

In return, there was only silence. He turned away from the shelves.

Diana and River stood near each other next to the library table and the books they'd gathered. Diana stared down at a volume she'd opened, seemingly lost in thought, her hand resting on one of the pages. With her other hand, she held her heavy bun away from her neck as if the room had suddenly grown warm.

River was looking at Diana with an expression Evan had never seen on his brother's face. The closest he could recall to that look was when he and River had been in the Valley of the Kings, about to enter King Tut's tomb. It was a look of astonishment mixed with a tinge of lust.

Evan cleared his throat, and Diana jumped. She lifted her hand, and the book closed. A flush rose in her cheeks as well as River's.

Something had passed between the two, even if they themselves were only half-aware of it.

"The Ventris book," he said gently. "If you would."

Diana shook herself. "Sorry. Nothing worse than a distracted minion."

CHAPTER 11

ADDIE

Addie stared bleary eyed at the computer screen.

She stood in an office at the Crime Prevention and Information Center at police headquarters. Behind her, Patrick nursed a cup of coffee. At the desk in front of them, with his bulk wedged into a metal-and-vinyl chair, sat Sergeant Devin Delarose.

Delarose laced his hands behind his head. "The PODs were removed from Couch Place and parts of the theater district a few months ago," he said. "The crime rate dropped nearly seventy-six percent in that area after the PODs were first installed. So we moved them to areas with higher crime rates. It's good to keep the criminals wondering when and where Big Brother is watching."

PODs—Police Observation Devices—consisted of remote-controlled video cameras with night-vision capability placed in high-crime areas and moved around as delinquency rates demanded. The videos from the cameras were sent wirelessly to a centralized computer server, where members of the Crime Prevention and Information Center, as well as other officers and departments, could monitor them live or review them later.

"Murphy strikes again," Addie said. "What about along State Street and North Dearborn? Pedestrians would enter the alley from one of those streets."

"We've got a few PODs along there." Delarose lowered his hands and punched buttons on his keyboard, pulling up images. "There were hours of video for the window you requested, obviously. But I have a software program that helps me snip out empty sidewalks and streets. What's left are video clips of pedestrians."

He clicked on an image on the top left of the oversize computer screen. A woman and her dog moved briskly down the sidewalk. The time stamp said 5:30 p.m.

"You can access all of this yourself at your desk," Delarose told her as he clicked on the next image, and two teenagers sprang to life, their gaze riveted by something in a store window. "But I thought it would be helpful if I did a run-through first and gave you anything that looked suspicious. And, of course, I was watching for the victim."

Addie knew Delarose was both thorough and experienced. If nothing panned out on what he captured, they could always go back and review additional footage. But this would give them a good start.

"Did you locate him?" Addie asked.

"Yup. And he wasn't alone."

Delarose's hands flew over the keyboard, selecting an image and enlarging it. He clicked "Play." Addie found herself staring at a very alive Samuel Fishbourne strolling down the sidewalk, unaware that a few hours later, death would be literally just around the corner. He wore the slacks that Addie recognized from the crime scene, along with a white dress shirt and a charcoal-gray suit coat. Standard attorney attire.

And no inked marks on his forehead.

Next to him, her arm tucked through his, walked a woman half his age. She wore black slacks and heels and a white sleeveless blouse.

The woman's face was a match for the woman in the photo from Fishbourne's wallet. Maybe she was a much younger girlfriend. Or perhaps a family member—daughter or niece. The information in Fishbourne's DMV entry listed a daughter, Ursula Fishbourne, as Samuel's NOK—his next of kin. Ursula herself wasn't in the state records. They had to widen the search.

Which meant this woman was either part of the murder, a second victim, or she had left Fishbourne before his encounter with the killer.

Addie leaned in, bracing a palm on the desk, and studied Fishbourne and his companion. No question, they looked content in each other's company. Was this woman now dead? A prisoner? Or safely asleep in her bed?

Addie closed and opened her eyes.

Delarose swiveled his chair back and forth. "This is earlier in the evening, hours before he was killed. Time stamp says six forty. Since the ticket in his car shows he parked near Couch Place at five ten, he and the woman went somewhere before the PODs picked them up heading south on State Street. Then we lost them again."

"There aren't cameras farther along on State?"

"There are. My guess is that they went into one of the businesses before the next camera caught them. Our cameras don't pick up Fishbourne and the woman again for an hour."

Delarose pulled up a satellite view of the area with businesses highlighted.

Patrick crowded in on the other side of the sergeant. "We got stores. Restaurants. Bars. This is going to take a lot of pavement pounding."

"Wherever they were going," Addie murmured, half to herself, "they might have picked up the killer there."

Delarose shrugged. "Wherever it was, the two of them were still together when they reappeared on the cameras an hour later, heading back the way they came. Fishbourne had a bag tucked under his arm. That was new, but we can't see a logo."

Addie pulled out her phone and dialed Sheerin's cell. She knew the pathologist would be overseeing the transfer of Fishbourne's body into the morgue.

"What?" Sheerin answered.

Addie put her phone on speaker. "Is Fishbourne's body at the morgue?"

"He's here. I've got him scheduled for Saturday. A rush job because I owe your partner a favor."

Addie glanced at Patrick, wondering what the favor had been. Patrick shrugged.

She leaned against a wall in Delarose's office as a wave of tiredness hit. "Could you just do a quick external? Check his pockets and take another look at his wallet before you call it a night? Cameras have narrowed down his location, but there are still a lot of options. You'd save Patrick and me and our boys in blue a lot of hours if you find a receipt from tonight."

A long sigh. "You do know what time it is."

"I know," Addie said. "I wouldn't ask if it weren't important."

"Give me fifteen," Sheerin said, and disconnected.

Ten minutes later, she called back. Again, Addie put her on speaker.

"It's your lucky night," the ME said. "Make that your lucky morning. There was a receipt for Petterino's in his back pocket. Two entrées, two glasses of wine. The time stamp is for six thirty p.m."

Addie recognized the name. Petterino's was an Italian restaurant across the street from Couch Place. That explained the missing time between when Fishbourne had parked in the garage and when cameras caught him and the woman on State Street.

"That's hugely helpful," Addie said. "Thank you."

"I got something else."

Addie straightened, almost physically heaving off the exhaustion trying to pull her under. She'd had too many short nights in a row. "What is it?"

"Two tickets for a seven p.m. event at a bookstore on State Street. Looks like he printed them out at work or at home. These older guys don't trust their cell phones to have the information."

"Bingo!" Addie said, pulling up Google Maps. "What's the event?"

"A one-woman performance called *Ariadne*. The ticket came with a copy of a signed program from that play that just came to town."

"*The King and the Minotaur*," Addie said.

"That's it."

"Thanks, Lisa."

"Tell Patrick we're even."

"Not by half," Patrick growled.

Addie disconnected and googled *Ariadne*. According to Wikipedia, she was the sister of the Minotaur as well as the daughter of King Minos and the lover of the hero, Theseus, who slew the Minotaur. She recalled the playbill.

The King and the Minotaur

Join us for a reimagining of the famous Greek tragedy!

A vengeful king. A flesh-eating monster. A brave hero.

The king's beautiful, treacherous daughter.

And a dark and deadly labyrinth to lead them all astray.

Delarose's chair squeaked, calling her back. He said, "I think we just left Chicago and entered the Twilight Zone. Look at this."

While Addie was talking with Sheerin and googling Ariadne, Delarose had continued going through the footage from the previous night.

"We got this old man here."

Delarose showed them a clip of a tall, frail man walking slowly south on State Street. The man moved with a hunched gait, watching the sidewalk as if afraid he'd trip.

"Then," Delarose continued, "with the next camera, the old man has disappeared. Maybe he went inside some place—I don't know what's along State besides that bookstore you just found. But the next camera captures Fishbourne and the woman being passed by *this* guy, who's moving in the opposite direction from the first old man."

Delarose pulled up another video. The footage showed a second older man in black jeans and a hoodie as he appeared on the left, overtook Fishbourne and the woman, then disappeared from view.

Black jeans and a hoodie, Addie thought. *Exactly how River described the man who left the chalk marks.*

"You see what I see?" Delarose asked. "The similarities?"

"Go back to the first man," Addie said.

Delarose rewound the clip. The first man also wore black jeans and a sweatshirt but with a tan trench coat. From what little they could see of his face, he had a sparse gray mustache and spectacles.

"The same clothes," Patrick said. "Minus the jacket. And the glasses."

"If it's the same guy, he picked up his pace," Addie added. "Meaning he's old but not enfeebled."

"He still looks too old by a couple of decades to cut another man in half," Patrick said.

"Here's the footage from the next camera," Delarose said, clicking on a third image.

Patrick leaned forward. "Jesus, Mary, and Joseph. He's—what is that?"

Addie stared at the face on Delarose's computer.

"Enlarge it," she said.

Delarose clicked, and the screen filled with the image of a monster.

"That's the Minotaur," Addie said.

CHAPTER 12

EVAN

"These marks on Fishbourne's skin are what we have to work with," Evan said. "We have the possible glyphs on his forehead plus two on his chest, all partially destroyed by the rain. Let's try and piece them back together."

He printed out close-ups of the rain-ruined symbols from the crime scene and placed them on the table among books propped open to show the signs from all the Cretan scripts. He gave River and Diana each a chart showing the 141 Cretan glyphs classified variously as syllabograms, logograms, klasmatograms (fractions), and arithmograms (numbers). At this point, Evan figured, the classification of the glyphs didn't matter. Not until they had some sense of where the killer was going with his message.

If he was going anywhere at all.

He also printed out the letter from TR.

"Shall we divide and conquer?" River said. "That way, we can sanity-check each other's work."

Diana tapped Evan's wrist. "Shouldn't you give us an overview of the glyphs before we start trying to analyze these signs?"

River made a sound that might have been a groan.

"I'll pretend I didn't hear that," Evan said to him. "And to answer your question, Diana, I think it's better if we start without any preconceived notions."

"But *you* aren't," she pointed out. "And neither is River. I'm at a disadvantage."

"That could be beneficial. Fresh eyes on the problem."

"Humph. Sounds more like a linguistic old boys' club." Her brow wrinkled. "Evan, you gave a lecture on the Phaistos Disc just a few weeks ago. And now we have Cretan hieroglyphs on a murder victim."

River looked up from the chart of glyphs. "Was it a big crowd?"

"There were a few people," Evan said.

Diana rolled her eyes at him. "That's his idea of humility. Evan's lectures are always popular. There were a couple hundred people in the room. You think one of them could be our killer?"

"Surely not." Evan thought back. The attendees had been a mix of students and scholars from the classics department, along with many of his own students. There had also been a generous sprinkling of members of the public. People's fascination with undeciphered scripts never failed to gratify him. "Then again . . ."

"I'll call the registrar and get a list of the attendees," Diana said. "We can look for anyone with the initials TR."

"Excellent thinking," River said.

She gave him her sweetest smile and then selected the photo showing a close-up of the lines inked on Fishbourne's forehead. River took one of the supposed glyphs from Fishbourne's chest and Evan the other—the signs that were drawn in what appeared to be the victim's blood. He also placed TR's letter in front of him.

River pulled a pair of wire-rimmed reading glasses from his pants pocket. Evan looked up in surprise. Since when had River needed readers?

Time seemed to slow as the three bent to their tasks. Rain pattered the windows, but inside was only companionable silence, the occasional rustle of paper, and Perro's soft snore. Evan stopped long enough to make more tea. River paced the room before resuming his seat with a sigh. The clock on Diana's desk ticked softly.

After a while, Diana gave a cry. "I've got it!"

River raised his head. "Impressive."

"Piecing these together is a bit like the petroglyphs I had to reimagine after some jerk took a shotgun to them," Diana said.

"And similar to reimagining the missing sections of some carved basalt that was stolen off a temple in Cambodia," River agreed. He removed his glasses. "I think I'm done as well."

"I've got nothing," Evan said.

"Don't hurt yourself," River said. "We'll wait."

Evan bent again to his paper. "You can't rush greatness."

Diana harrumphed. "Or whatever it is you're doing."

A moment later, he gave his own cry of triumph.

"Figure it out?" River asked.

"Yes. Maybe. I think. A lot of the glyphs are similar. So definitely maybe."

"As long as you're sure," River said. "Let's share. Ladies first."

"That's sexist," Diana said, and looked at Evan. "How about age before beauty?"

"Ageist," he said. He looked at River. "How about if big brother tells little brother to start? And little brother listens."

"Just this once," River said. "If we're dealing with glyphs, then I think I'm looking at syllabogram number twenty per current classification. A honeybee or wasp. Which, for the record, also appears on the letter Fishbourne delivered."

But Evan tapped his chin. "Did you consider sign number fifty-two?"

"Considered and rejected. The lines in fifty-two are in the wrong place."

"You have to think about the medium. Blood is more viscous than ink. It would make a fatter line and could run."

"Blood?" Diana snatched up the photo River was working from.

River said, "Fifty-two doesn't appear on the letter. I'm sticking with the bee. What have you got, Diana?"

She returned River's photo and picked up the drawing she'd made. She held it out. "At the top of the page are the ink marks ruined by rain. At the bottom is my reconstruction. A rather elegantly formed trident. And not just one trident, but three written across Fishbourne's forehead."

"There aren't any known tridents in any of the Cretan scripts," Evan pointed out.

"A couple of the glyphs resemble tridents," Diana said. "And we don't know what *any* of the glyphs are for sure, right? Plus, it's the only thing that fits."

Evan compared the ruined symbols and saw where Diana had filled in the gaps. "It's possible," he agreed. "But why would the killer veer away from known glyphs? And why *three* glyphs? Does he have some thought of a trinity?"

"This much I remember from Greek mythology," Diana continued. "The trident is the symbol of Poseidon."

River snapped his fingers. "The god who started it all."

"Right. By giving King Minos a beautiful white bull, which Minos was supposed to sacrifice to Poseidon. But Minos thought the bull was too beautiful to kill." Diana's voice picked up speed. "So instead, Minos slaughtered a lesser bull."

Evan leapt in. "Which enraged the god."

"Poseidon avenged this slight," River said, "by causing King Minos's wife to lust after the white bull. She mated with the bull—"

"And gave birth to a monster," Diana said. She high-fived River.

"The Minotaur," Evan finished. "Brother to Ariadne. His birth name was Asterion, meaning 'the starry one.' But after he showed a fondness for human flesh, Minos ordered a labyrinth built and locked the boy away before he could eat his way through the locals. This brings things around to my glyph, which I believe is syllabogram number eleven. The head of a bull."

"A bovine," River corrected. "It could be a cow."

"Do you have eyes?" Evan retorted. "The glyph has horns."

Diana glanced at the chart. "It looks more like a geometric figure with two eyes and a weird hat."

"I'm not arguing," Evan said. "It's a heptagon—a seven-sided figure. But with the extension of the line at the top, it has also been conclusively shown by scholars—"

"By *some* scholars," River said.

"By *many* scholars, to represent the male of the species. And it, too, appears on the note."

Diana raised her hands in surrender. "You're the expert. Now we have a bull, a bee or a wasp, and three tridents. Plus, the labrys chalked on the sidewalk—"

"Which also appears on the letter," Evan said. "As does the cat's head."

"*And* the additional glyphs on the letter," she finished.

Evan held up TR's letter. "I may also have deciphered this strange mix of glyphs."

River and Diana stared at him.

"Well?" River said.

"If we use the phonetic values of Linear B and the meanings typically assigned to Cretan Hieroglyphic along with common interpretations of the Phaistos Disc symbols, as well as a simple rebus puzzle—"

"All in a single line of glyphs?" Diana said.

"All in a single line. Then here's what I come up with. The line says, 'Decode or solve the riddle'—or puzzle; I'm referring here to the likely maze image—'before the sacrifice'—and by this, I mean human sacrifice, you note the glyph of a bound man—'is made.'"

River and Diana continued to stare at him.

Diana snatched Evan's copy of the letter. "'Solve the riddle before the sacrifice is made.' If I squint and turn the paper sideways, I can see it."

Evan snatched back the paper.

"I'm kidding," Diana said. "Your interpretation is brilliant."

"Can you state that again for the record?"

River said, "Does that mean we were supposed to solve a riddle in order to save Fishbourne's life?"

"We had no riddle," Evan said.

"Which suggests there will be other riddles? Other victims?"

The two brothers stared gloomily at each other.

Diana slapped her palms on the table. "Come on, gentlemen. Where do we go from here?"

Evan said, "We take a break. We need to let our subconscious minds chew on this."

Perro scratched at the door, and Evan stood.

"Perro's bladder is even worse than mine," he said. "I'd best attend to the wee beast before he embarrasses us both."

"Take a raincoat," Diana said, nodding toward the windows.

"And a stout stick," River said.

"This is Chicago," Evan said. "Not Istanbul."

"My point exactly."

Evan laughed. "I'll be fine. If it's our humble letter writer you're worried about, it's far too soon for him to end the game."

"I'm going with you," River said.

"So am I," Diana chimed in.

"Please. I don't need babysitters. What I need is some air."

He grabbed the keys and his coat, and he and Perro rode the elevator down to the first floor.

Outside, the storm was moving eastward, reducing the rain to a drizzle, and leaving the air thick and muggy. Perro made a beeline for the bushes. Evan tipped back his head and stared at the handful of stars peeking through the remaining tatters of clouds. When Perro returned, business presumably completed, Evan ignored his mental image of the bound man on the letter and took the dog for a short turn around the quad. During the day, the area was always bustling with students and faculty, shouts echoing off the buildings, and visiting parents marching down the walkways with maps firmly in hand.

Tonight, though, the space lay deserted. Evan noticed that the only office light shining in Harper Library was through his own window. The warm yellow light glowed with the promise of comfort and safety.

He headed back down the quad.

He thought of the man who had visited him at the institute the evening before. A man who now lay in the morgue, beyond human reach. It was too soon to know if Samuel Fishbourne had been a victim of opportunity or if the killer had chosen him for a reason.

Had the alarm Evan glimpsed on Fishbourne's face come from knowing someone pursued him? If so, what was this corporate attorney about, dropping a coin on a professor's doorstep?

Or, as he and Addie and Patrick speculated earlier, had he been forced by the killer?

If that were the case, what had the killer held over him?

Patrolling at the end of his leash, Perro suddenly stiffened, his ears straining forward as he came to a halt. Evan stopped, ignored the unease trying to spread through his gut, and wondered what small mammal had caught Perro's attention.

"Let's go, fur ball," he said, jingling the leash.

Perro didn't budge.

Evan caught the steady thump of footsteps on the concrete coming toward them. Tugging Perro's leash, he stepped into the shadows next to the library building.

The footsteps drew nearer, and Perro began to growl. The sound was ferocious for such a small animal, and whoever was behind them stopped. Perro let loose a volley of barks, and Evan thought he heard a low chuckle from only yards away.

But when the footsteps sounded again, they were moving away. Evan let out his breath in a whoosh.

Probably just some poor student with insomnia.

He shook the corgi's leash, and the two hurried back toward the library's front door and the refuge that lay within. Diana met them as they came around the corner.

"I was just coming to find you," she said. "I thought you might want a babysitter after all."

The late-night stroller's low laugh echoed in Evan's mind.

"How about a bodyguard?" he said as they went through the front doors. "That has a better ring to it."

CHAPTER 13

THE MINOTAUR

I found her interesting, this Chicago murder detective. Attractive even as she appeared now: gray with fatigue, her clothes rumpled, her hair falling free from the clips she used to hold it.

I longed to run my fingers through those long curls. Hold her face between my hands. Not for the first time, I wondered if the Minotaur violated his female victims before he tore them limb from limb.

I stood in the morning twilight only a few yards away from the detective, watching as she dug in her purse for her house keys. She held her raincoat folded over one arm and had set a briefcase on the ground near her feet. She hadn't seen me. This was my moment to watch. To evaluate. To see if she, while not my equal, might have the steel to seek me out and the wit to find me.

And a keen wit would be required. For I had created a labyrinthine trail to the monster at the center of the maze. Names—so many names. And my secret language. Identities wrapped within identities, all hidden across time and buried in hieroglyphs.

So, I was curious to know: Was this detective a threat? Or a fly to be swatted away?

Around us, the air hung still and cool, the city quiet, the sun an orange pockmark on the horizon; it would soon scour away the sweetness of the night.

When I heard the jangle of her keys, I stirred from my hiding place and strolled past her. She turned and her eyes followed me, but I could tell that she was reassured by what she saw. I had chosen well for the day.

I nodded. She nodded back.

I pressed my hand to my chest, but I was past her before I tapped my thank-you onto my heart.

CHAPTER 14

EVAN

Evan's phone pinged just as dawn light filtered into his office, easing back the night and illuminating motes of dust in the warming air.

He sat up with a start. The phone pinged again and fell silent.

On the other side of the room, River had fallen asleep on the rug, his hat over his face, his arms and ankles crossed, apparently as comfortable as he would have been in a five-star hotel. Diana had crashed on the cot in the small bedroom off his office, where he occasionally slept.

As for him, he'd spent the remainder of the night studying the seventeen glyphs written in the margins of the note Fishbourne had left on his doorstep. Evan had pondered them, substituted syllables for them, rearranged them. Drawn them over and over until the scribbles made by his tired hand amounted to a child's doodles.

And with all that, he'd come up with nothing. Or, at least, very little.

Still . . . there *was* meaning, however warped. The killer found significance in these seventeen glyphs. He'd chosen them, marked his victim with them. His message—if Evan had interpreted it correctly—made that clear: *Solve the riddle before the sacrifice is made.*

Perhaps the glyphs themselves were the riddle.

We just have to hear his music, Evan reminded himself, *to understand his dance.*

His phone buzzed again. He grabbed it groggily.

Do you have anything? Addie had texted. Followed by, You up?

Wild-ass theories, he typed back. And yes.

Dick's Bar in one hour? They've got green chili.

He sent a thumbs-up emoji, then retreated to the bathroom to wash his face and run a comb through his hair. As soon as they'd shared what they knew with Addie, he'd have to hurry home and feed Ginny. He wondered if there were pet-sitting services for goshawks.

When Evan emerged, River was already up and making tea. He looked as refreshed as if he'd not only slept at a five-star hotel but enjoyed a massage and facial for good measure.

"I'll run Perro outside if you'll finish the tea," River said. "I need a brisk walk to shake off the night."

"Isn't that what the tea is for?"

"I'll have mine when I get back." River gave him the once-over. "You should come with me. Get your blood moving."

Evan mimed looking hurt. "Are you suggesting I need to exercise?"

But River's expression remained serious. "It's just that maybe you can't move as fast as you used to. And if you're thinking of going to Mali . . ." River's voice trailed off, but the idea hung in the air. Evan spent too much time behind a desk. He'd gotten soft. In more ways than one.

Mali Terrorists: 1. Evan: 0.

"In case you've forgotten," Evan said, "I was never much of an athlete."

River's expression softened. "You tell yourself that. But it was never true." He grabbed the keys. "See you in a few."

When the door closed behind his brother, Evan glanced down at his stomach and decided he looked perfectly fine. He searched the cupboards for the stash of protein bars he kept on hand. How could one even think of exercising before breakfast? Even when he took his hawk, Ginny, for her early morning flights, he brought along an egg sandwich to eat while she flew. Otherwise, someone would find him passed out from low blood sugar in the middle of a field.

Still . . . no doubt River was right. He could use more exercise.

On the other hand, what did it matter? He'd never be able to outrun bandits or swing atop a horse the way River could. And it wasn't as if he had a woman to impress. Not since Christina left. Which was all good, he told himself. It gave him more time for his work.

He banged on the door to the bedroom. "Rise and shine!"

He received a muffled curse in response, which cheered him a bit.

✣

An hour after Addie's text, he and River, with Perro in tow, arrived at the pub, their clothes bejeweled with rain. Diana had her regular Friday morning class and promised to meet up with them later.

Dick's Bar was a popular hangout for cops, and the previous times Evan had been here the place had been bursting with light and noise. But this early in the morning the dive was dark and forlorn, quiet except for the low murmur of a television set in the corner above the bar. A few regulars—older men—sat on barstools, working diligently on their breakfasts. Only two booths were occupied. In one, a group of twentysomethings, sullen and silent, hunched over their phones, nursing hangovers.

In the other sat Addie, typing on her phone. She looked up as they approached and smiled tiredly—likely she hadn't slept much, either. She held out her hand to River.

"I'm Addie. Wonderful to meet you."

"And you. Evan speaks highly of you and your work."

"Likewise. And thanks for coming. We're glad for your help."

As River and Evan slid into the booth across from her, she pushed an urn of coffee and two ceramic mugs toward them. While they poured, she removed a document from her briefcase.

"Business first," she said. "River, I ran you last night, and you're clean."

"Crappy firm you hired to do background checks," he said in a dry voice. She gave him a sharp look, to which he responded, "Kidding."

She gave him the document and offered a pen. "I need you to sign a nondisclosure agreement stating that any consulting you do for Chicago PD's Special Investigations Unit will be confidential. I'll leave it to you to read the details. Evan, is Diana going to be part of this?"

"She already is."

"Okay. I need the two of you—and Diana as well—to understand that it's unusual to have an entire team of civilians brought in on an investigation. Please be mindful of the risk I'm running with my department. Your presence on the team was approved by my lieutenant this morning, so we've got that. But it's important that everyone colors inside the lines. Agreed?"

"Agreed," Evan said. River nodded.

"Next, did you bring the letter and the coin?"

Evan slid the two items out of his messenger bag and handed them across the table to Addie. He watched as she read the letter through its plastic sleeve.

She wiped the table with a napkin and set down the plastic-sheathed letter. "The letter is more sinister in the flesh, so to speak, than as a photo on your phone. Do either of you have a theory about who TR is?"

River looked up from perusing the NDA. "No one I can recall."

"Same for me." Evan topped off Addie's coffee, then his own. "But Diana reminded me of a lecture I gave on the Phaistos Disc a few weeks ago. The symbols on the disc share some overlap with other Minoan scripts. Diana thought it might be worth getting a list of attendees, see if anyone with the initials TR was there."

"Good idea," Addie said. "Now what about this game he mentions? Any theories on that?"

"Assuming the writer and the murderer are the same person," Evan said, "we think killing Fishbourne was his first move."

"Pretty dramatic first move. Don't games played between two or more people require both moves and countermoves?"

"That's usually how it works," Evan agreed. "In which case, our countermove is to try and find him." *Or to solve the riddle in the glyphs if there's a riddle to be found.* "A good start would be understanding why he chose Fishbourne as his victim."

River had reached thc last page of the NDA and signed the bottom. He passed the pages back to Addie. "I'm now reliably leakproof."

Addie took a long swallow of coffee and cupped the mug in her hands. "We've got a time line for Fishbourne's activities in the hours before he appeared on Evan's doorstep. He and a companion, a young woman, dined at Petterino's at six thirty, where, according to a receipt found on Fishbourne, they had the Spagehetti E Polpette and two glasses of a high-end cabernet." She set her mug on the table. "Our PODs picked up the pair as they were heading south on State Street in the direction of a bookstore. The bookstore is where, per a pair of tickets also found on Fishbourne, they attended a one-woman show called *Ariadne.* I'll confirm with the employees that Fishbourne and the woman were at the performance. And check in with the waitstaff at Petterino's."

"Ariadne," River echoed.

"King Minos's treacherous daughter," Addie said. "I had to refresh my middle-school mythology last night."

"She was also the Minotaur's treacherous sister," River clarified. "Not that anyone can blame her. Her father and her brother were both monsters, each in their own way."

He fell silent as a tired-looking waitress emerged from the kitchen to take their orders. The bar didn't offer a lot of choices—if you were vegan or vegetarian, you were out of luck. Ham and eggs or thick slices of French toast were de rigueur. There was also the occasional offering of a green chili hot enough to remove your tongue by the roots.

They all ordered eggs with chili.

After the waitress left, Addie pulled out a manila folder, slid out a photo, and passed it to Evan. Evan recognized the man in the picture from the previous night—his mysterious visitor whom he now knew to be Samuel Fishbourne. Hours before his visit to Evan, Fishbourne looked happy and relaxed, a soft smile on his round face.

Next to him, her arm threaded through his, was a much younger woman, also smiling.

He gave the photo to River.

"That's the man who left the letter and the coin," he told his brother. "And our murder victim." He leaned toward his brother, studying the picture. "Fishbourne is wearing a wedding band. Is the woman his wife?"

"Dana Fishbourne passed away ten years ago," Addie said. "Her obituary mentioned a daughter, Ursula, who would be about the same age as the woman with Fishbourne last night. But there's no entry for Ursula Fishbourne with the Illinois DMV. Presumably she moved out of state. She's listed as Fishbourne's next of kin, and we're working to find her as well as the woman who was with Fishbourne before his murder. It's possible that woman and Ursula are one and the same—Ursula could be visiting."

She handed over a second photo.

"Here you see Fishbourne and the woman again, heading in the direction of the bookstore. The man behind them, the one in the tan trench coat, does he look familiar?"

Evan and River studied the new photo.

"It's hard to make out much of his face," Evan said. "But I don't believe he's someone I know."

"Agreed," River said.

She handed over a third photograph. "How about here?"

The third photograph showed an old man in a black hoodie and jeans. He appeared to be passing Fishbourne and the woman on their right.

"Isn't it the same guy?" River said, sounding puzzled. "Minus the trench coat and the glasses. He's wearing similar clothes to Hoodie Man."

"Could he and Hoodie Man be the same person?"

"The man last night . . . he didn't move like an old guy. My guess is no."

Addie looked disappointed as she collected the pictures. "We'll leave that alone for now. I've got one more picture to share, but first, has my team of experts made progress with the glyphs beyond wild-ass theories?"

"Define progress," River said.

"That good?" she said. "You must have something. An insight. A message of some kind."

Evan pulled out a sheet of paper from his messenger bag, unfolded it, and gave it to Addie.

She smoothed the paper out on the table.

Number	Glyph	Meaning	Location
N/A		Cat head	Victim's shoulder and TR's letter
001		Jumping man	TR's letter
004		Woman	TR's letter

005		Eye	TR's letter
011		Bull/bovine head	Victim's chest and TR's letter
020		Bee or wasp	Victim's chest and TR's letter
021		Fly	TR's letter
031/092		Trident?	Victim's forehead and TR's letter
038		Gate	TR's letter
042		Double-bladed axe	Chalked on side-walk near victim's body and TR's letter
043		Single-blade axe	TR's letter
044		Trowel	TR's letter
049		Arrow	TR's letter
051		Spearhead	TR's letter
054		Two-handled vase	TR's letter

057		Plow	TR's letter
070		Cross	TR's letter

Evan said, "The table shows the Cretan hieroglyphs found on the letter delivered by Fishbourne along with our best guesses for the glyphs on his body. The three tridents on Fishbourne's face don't match any known glyph, but they do resemble a couple of the Cretan hieroglyphs."

Addie narrowed her eyes in concentration. "Your table suggests that, even if we can't read this script, there is agreement as to what each glyph represents. Is that right?"

Evan nodded. "Among scholars, there is nearly universal agreement that, for example, glyph four is a woman, and glyph fifty-one is a spear-head. But for our purposes, since this is an undeciphered script written in an unknown language, we must accept that the killer might not be aware of how the scholarly community interprets the glyphs. Or agree with them if he does."

Addie's lips quirked in a half smile. "I understand our limitations, Evan. Give me those wild-ass theories you mentioned."

Evan squirmed. He wasn't fond of leaping into the void. What if he took Addie down the wrong path in this metaphorical maze, leading her to a dead end? Or, worse, took her in a direction that was far from the truth?

"As long as you realize all of this is highly tentative," he said. She nodded her understanding, and he plowed on. "The repeating glyphs on Fishbourne's forehead could signal—by their location—the idea of control over the victim."

"Explain."

"We think the glyphs represent the trident—the symbol for the Greek god of the sea, Poseidon, who started the chain of events that led to the birth of the Minotaur and the building of the maze. You could consider Poseidon the grandfather of the Minotaur since he created the white bull that sired Asterion."

"Asterion is the Minotaur," Addie confirmed.

"Yes. And we have two glyphs on Fishbourne's chest—possibly the glyph for a honeybee or a wasp and another one for a bull. I've no theories on those, yet. As for the cat, it doesn't appear in the actual script. It's found on decorative seals used for stamping impressions in wax, or worn as good-luck symbols to show a deity's protection. Which suggests that the killer's knowledge of the glyphs is wide ranging and that he had a reason to bring the cat into the mix. We also have the glyph that Hoodie Man—"

"Hoodie Man is the guy River followed?"

"Right. Hoodie Man chalked another glyph near the signs he wrote for the number six. That glyph was an axe, number forty-two."

"I remember," Addie said.

"Of course." He summed up what River and Diana had shared the night before about the labrys.

Addie tapped a rhythm on the table with her fingers. "You said this was *most* of what you have."

"I believe the mix of symbols and glyphs at the bottom of the letter might mean 'Solve the riddle before the sacrifice is made.'"

"The riddle is the game?"

"Presumably."

"And Fishbourne was the sacrifice?"

"I don't think so. The killer didn't give us time to solve any riddles before he murdered him. As River pointed out, Fishbourne's death was likely the opening move in his cruel game."

"Meaning there are more sacrifices to come? What if the killer has Fishbourne's companion? What if she's the sacrifice? Evan, I need to know what these glyphs mean. What I'm dealing with."

"No pressure."

"Oh, Professor," she said. "Lots of pressure."

The waitress appeared with their eggs and chili, and, for a moment, they focused on the food. Evan's tongue was burning pleasantly by the time Addie spoke again.

"How many Cretan hieroglyphs are there?"

"Counting syllabograms, logograms, klasmatograms, arithmograms, and stiktograms—" River began.

She glared at him. "You sound just like your brother."

"It's been a goal of mine."

"It wasn't a compliment." Addie pressed the heel of her hand to her forehead. "Sorry. It's been a long night. Please continue."

"There are a total of one hundred and forty-one glyphs," Evan interjected. "Cataloging them isn't important right now. Cretan Hieroglyphic is a logo-syllabic script—"

"Meaning some signs are words. And others are syllables," Addie said.

"Or morphemes," Evan clarified. "The smallest unit of language that cannot be further divided without losing its meaning. And some glyphs serve as both words and syllables."

"He's sexy when he talks that way, isn't he?" River said.

Unexpectedly, Addie blushed. She looked down, apparently perusing the glyphs for a minute before she looked up again.

Evan kicked River under the table.

Addie said, "Then if the killer's choice of glyphs is nothing more than his personal taste, there must be a reason why these specific images appeal to him. He's got a thing for weapons and plows and gates. Or"—she looked hopefully at Evan—"maybe he's using the glyphs as syllables to spell out his riddle."

"If so, it's a private language, his own personal music. Other than the *ma* sound for the cat—which we know due to the recurrence of that sign in the deciphered Linear B—no one knows what sounds are associated with these glyphs because we don't know what language they're written in. Presumably some long-lost Minoan language."

"Did you try using English?"

He looked at her with appreciation. "I did, since English is clearly a language the killer knows. But no matter what syllables I try, I only get nonsense." Evan tucked his hands beneath his chin. "I believe he's doing something else with these glyphs."

"But you don't know what."

"Not yet."

Addie pulled a fourth photograph from the file folder and passed it over the table.

"Last picture. A sergeant reviewing the videos found this guy."

"Good God," Evan said.

A man stared up at the camera. Or rather a monster. He had an immense bull's head with sharply curving horns, a broad bull's nose, and long, shaggy hair. The mask continued past the neck and over the man's chest in a thick pelt, disappearing beneath his clothes.

A chill touched Evan's neck—the photo was a strange juxtaposition between myth and modern man. As if a fable had risen from ancient times to walk the streets of Chicago.

He glanced at River, who appeared to share his discomfort.

"The video was captured at midnight," Addie said. "On State Street near Couch Place. Right around the time Fishbourne breathed his last."

"You think this is our killer?" Evan asked.

"Heck of a coincidence, otherwise."

"Maybe he was doing a reading somewhere else," Evan offered. "Like the woman playing Ariadne at the bookstore."

"I couldn't find any reference online for an event featuring the Minotaur."

"That is one hell of a costume," River said.

"Which brings us to the play at the Neverland Theater," Addie said. "A play set on Crete with a minotaur and a maze. The theater has a back door that opens onto Couch Place."

"You think there's a connection?" River asked.

"I know I want to see their costumes. And that's just for starters." She finished the last bite of her green chili and gulped water. "Tickets for the opening are sold out. But dress rehearsal is tonight. The website says to come early—there's some sort of interactive experience offered before the play, and they'll be rehearsing that as well. On other nights, this experience will be open only to people who upgrade their tickets for a hefty fee."

"An interactive experience with monsters and heroes?" Evan said. "Sounds faintly . . . ominous."

"We'll find out." She handed over three tickets. "I'll be off the clock, but the rehearsal will give us a chance to observe without alarming anyone. I want you guys there. And Diana, if she can make it. Dress code is business formal. Suits. Dresses. Everything pressed and neat. Which means"—she gave Evan a stern look—"no jeans. No hoodies. No tennis shoes."

"Have you watched the Oscars? Wearing trainers to formal events is a thing now."

"Not in my book."

Chapter 15

Evan

That evening, while River poured brandies, Evan unlocked the institute's front door for Diana. She arrived a few minutes later.

"Have you seen the reviews for the play?" she asked, breezing into the living room where Evan and River sat with their early evening glasses of cognac. The men set down their glasses and rose to greet her. Perro came running from the kitchen.

"I assume they're good if the play is hitting all the major US cities," Evan said.

"The reviews are ecstatic. The *New York Times* called it a 'tour de force.'" Diana scooped Perro into her arms. The corgi licked her face rapturously, and Diana gently turned his head away. "Not tonight, pal. I'm wearing makeup."

She eased Perro to the floor. The corgi trotted back and forth between Evan and Diana, giving his high-pitched happy-dog sound.

"Do you have one of those roller-tape thingies?" Diana asked, brushing at the golden fur now covering her black blouse.

Evan held up the gadget. "I had to use it earlier," he said. "Perro is a menace to good dress and proper etiquette."

She looked at Evan's suit. "I like the tennis shoes."

"Thank you."

She turned to River. "And your clothes are . . ."

"Rumpled. I know. My brother doesn't own an iron."

"Somehow it suits you."

"I don't clean up well, you mean. Don't worry. I have a blazer that will cover most of the creases."

She flushed. "No, it just shows that you have your mind on more important things."

His smile made her flush deepen. He poured a snifter of cognac and offered it to her. She accepted the glass and nodded her appreciation.

"The cast varies from city to city in an effort to promote local talent," she said. "But the principal roles are played by the same actors from New York. Musical accompaniment will be by members of the Chicago Symphony Orchestra, and a ballerina from New York City Ballet will dance the role of Ariadne just before intermission. Emma Gladstone Hargrave. I saw Emma in *Romeo and Juliet* last year when she danced for the Joffrey Ballet. She's impressive."

"You enjoy the ballet?" River asked.

She pirouetted. "I studied it from the time I was three until high school, when I decided my passion was soccer."

"Then we'll have to catch a performance," River said. "I haven't seen a show since the Royal Ballet in London a couple of years ago."

Her look was positively coquettish. "If you're serious, Joffrey is performing *Anna Karenina* later this summer."

"A Russian tragedy," River said. "What could be better?"

"A Russian comedy?" Evan suggested.

River laughed. "Now that's an oxymoron."

Diana took a sip of the cognac and briefly closed her eyes. "Lovely."

Evan wondered if she was referring to the cognac or River's love of ballet and Russian tragedy, or River himself. Again, he felt a protective urge, and again he pushed it down. River and Diana were adults. They'd figure it out. Maybe they'd have a fling and go their separate ways.

Or maybe something more long term would come of it.

He could only hope.

Diana raised her cognac. "Here's to catching a killer."

✣

The trio walked through the warm evening beneath a threatening sky, cutting through Couch Place to meet Addie in front of the Neverland Theater. With the clouds, dusk had descended. The air smelled of rain, and puddles still filled the city's potholes from the previous night's storm.

All traces of the murder that had occurred outside the theater's back door were gone. The police had had no choice but to process the scene quickly given the weather and the high rate of pedestrian traffic through the area—especially with the opening of the play.

The local papers, according to Diana, had not moved on. One typically sensationalist headline ran: A MONSTER ON THE STAGE AND IN THE ALLEY. Fortunately, the media hadn't uncovered the more lurid details. Nor did they know the identity of the victim, which CPD hadn't released while they tried to reach Ursula Fishbourne. Addie had informed Evan that they'd found Ursula's primary address in Houston, and they would work with Houston PD to locate her. Her Texas DMV record proved she was Samuel Fishbourne's daughter. The accompanying photograph resembled that of the woman who was with Fishbourne the night of his murder. But the photo was a few years old, and it wasn't confirmation. The woman herself remained unreachable.

"I'm deeply concerned," Addie had confided to Evan on the phone that afternoon. "That whole bit about sacrifice. We have an alert out for her with Chicago PD, too. Nothing, so far."

Tonight, Addie waited for them just inside the lobby doors. She'd put aside her usual business suit for flowing black pants and an emerald-green off-the-shoulder shirt. In the damp, her dark curls had escaped their coif to curl about her face, giving her a touch of unruliness despite the elegant blouse; the look suggested a barely restrained wildness that matched her restless energy and which Evan found irresistible.

While Diana and River went back outside the theater to admire a statue of a man wielding a sword, Evan approached Addie.

"It feels wrong," Addie said as he approached.

"It's perfect," he said, thinking of her blouse and her hair and the silky smoothness of her shoulders.

She blinked. "Perfect because the play is about Crete and a murderous monster?"

Evan did his own blinking. Of course she was talking about the same discomfort he'd shared with River earlier—the unease he felt in looking forward to a night's entertainment when, less than twenty-four hours ago, a man had been slain only yards away.

He recovered. "That's exactly what I meant."

Addie scanned the people walking past them. Men and women and a few children presented their tickets to tuxedoed ushers, who lifted velvet ropes and waved them into the main part of the lobby.

"I keep checking men's faces," Addie said. "Wondering if he's here. Wondering if he would bother with a dress rehearsal."

"If he plans to attend the play, which seems likely, I'd expect him to come tonight. He'll be flush off the murder and interested in any miscues or stumbled lines that would confirm for him the error-prone ways of humans. He might be looking for justification for his actions."

"He doesn't think of himself as human? Is this another wild theory?"

"It's the only kind I have. The Minotaur's mother was the daughter of Helios, the sun god. Thus, her son also carried the blood of the gods in his veins, making him a trinity of man, beast, and god. Which puts me in mind of the trinity of tridents on our victim's forehead. But I imagine our killer is most interested in his godlike attributes. There's a Greek term, *apotheosis*, which means to become a god."

"You think that's what he wants to do?"

"One murder at a time. If so, he picked the right mythos for it."

Addie was still scanning the crowd. "I see plenty of old men. But not the man from Sergeant Delarose's video. And I still can't imagine an older man having the strength to capture and kill even a soft-looking man like Fishbourne. Murder is hard work. I'm starting to think we might be dealing with a younger man who has disguised himself."

"Using masks? That's a scary thought. He could be anyone."

"As long as they share the same general height and build. Yes."

A shape-shifting killer. Evan knew from past events that tonight's attendees would consist of book and theater critics, bookstore owners, librarians, and scholars. And perhaps a few members of Chicago's well-to-do, whose donations helped make the play possible. But, like Addie, he didn't see the man from the video. Or any potential matches.

Warm air rushed in as the door opened for the hundredth time and River and Diana strolled in. They nodded at Evan and Addie and moved past them to present their tickets to the usher.

When Evan turned back to Addie, he was startled to see that, for a second, he had her full attention. A soft smile lifted her lips. "You clean up well," she said. "Even in sneakers."

✣

Inside the main lobby, visitors were directed toward a large wooden maze that filled one end of the foyer. The overhead lights above the maze were dimmed, and artificial torches flickered on the walls. A woman wearing the flounce-skirted dress of a Minoan priestess—although for modern propriety her breasts were covered—stood at the entrance, guarding a velvet rope across the doorway and waving people inside in ones and twos. Evan's group joined the line of people outside the entrance next to a sign that read:

WELCOME, FRIEND, AND BE NOT AFRAID!

THE MONSTER YOU ENCOUNTER IS YOUR OWN SHADOW SELF.

ENJOY TONIGHT'S JOURNEY OF SELF-REFLECTION.

"I'm not too fond of my shadow self," River said.

"He's a bad boy?" Diana asked.

"Let's just say there was a time when I wouldn't leave him alone with the cookie jar," Evan said.

"Now I'm a respectable archaeologist," River said. "Not a thief. But in my early twenties, I watched the Indiana Jones movies too many times. A life of adventure appealed more than the worlds of academia or dusty trenches. Plenty of people will pay millions for a golden idol smuggled out of a South American temple."

"To put in their private collection," Diana said.

He nodded. "Fortunately, I never succumbed to the temptation, and my frontal lobes caught up with the rest of my brain."

"You mean you've outgrown your shadow side?"

River gave her a lopsided smile. "Depends. Do you have any golden idols to sell?"

While his friends chatted, Evan studied the structure. On the outside, the maze's six-foot-high walls consisted of polished wood and mirrored tiles. The mirrors, Evan reasoned, were meant to emphasize the idea of self-reflection: among certain religious and new age groups, walking a labyrinth was a meditative process that encouraged the walker to explore his or her innermost self.

A prickle of unease cooled Evan's neck. He wasn't overly fond of mirrors. Especially of the head-to-toe variety. No matter how comfortable a physically limited person felt inside their own skin, no matter how much pride they might take in their difference, society was often less forgiving. The reminders could grow tiresome.

They shuffled forward. No one joined the line after them—their group would be the last to enter the maze. Periodically, from inside the wooden structure, came muted roars followed by screams, then shrieks of laughter. The two women ahead of them drew River and Diana into conversation.

Addie touched Evan's shoulder. "I read that there's a difference between a maze and a labyrinth."

Evan repeated what he'd told River: mazes offer choices, and labyrinths lead the walker along a single path.

"So the Minotaur's labyrinth led his victims around and around until they walked right into the lion's den?"

"That's one theory. But some stories say that his victims got lost and would wander around for days, which implies the famous labyrinth was actually a maze. And you have to wonder which would be more terrifying. A single path leading inevitably to doom—"

"Like birth to our inevitable death," Addie interjected.

"Cheery thought, but yes. Or a maze, which offers the hope of escape along with the fear of making a mistake and the crushing disappointment when—no matter what you do—you still end up in the monster's lair."

"Again, like life, with its good choices and bad."

"But some scholars refuse to distinguish between a labyrinth and a maze, although the words have different etymologies."

"Which I have a feeling you're about to explain to me."

"Only if you insist."

The line moved again.

"I insist," Addie said.

"Well, then." Evan drew a breath. "The word *labyrinth* is a late Middle English word that comes to us from the Latin *labyrinthos*, which itself comes from the Greek *laburinthos*. It is possibly from a pre-Greek language, which tradition connects to the Lydian word *labrys*, which means 'a double-edged axe.'"

"Like the glyph chalked on the sidewalk."

"Exactly like that. But not all scholars agree on the etymology. There's the pre-Greek word *laura*, which means 'a narrow passage or warren of passages.' Starting in the 1540s, the word came to mean 'a confusing state of affairs.'"

"Which is where my mind is right now," Addie said with a laugh.

The couple ahead of Diana and River disappeared into the maze. Diana turned back. She'd clearly been eavesdropping.

"But what of the etymology of the word *maze*?" Diana asked. "It's not Greek. Or Latin."

"It's possibly an Old English word, *mæs*, formed by combining *amasod*, 'amazed,' and the verb *amasian*, meaning 'to confound or confuse.'"

"Which means either word works," Addie said.

The line shuffled again, and now the Minoan priestess smiled at them. "I see you need no introduction to the mysteries of our maze. We allow six people in at a time." She nodded to Diana and River. "Enter and beware the monster."

Two minutes later, she unclipped the velvet rope and gestured Evan and Addie inside.

Inside, the labyrinth—for he suspected there would be few if any branching passages—was a thing of beauty. No cold underground cavern, this. It was a work of art. The walls were painted with frescoes crafted to resemble the inside of the palace of Knossos and other buildings from the ancient city. Evan identified for Addie the ones he recognized. Ceremonial scenes of priestesses accepting offerings, glimpses of nature replete with flowers, bluebirds, and monkeys, women drawing water, a sea battle, a fleet commander in an elaborate cloak. Warriors marching up a hill toward a walled city in what archaeologists believed might portray the Trojan War.

And the famous bull-leaping mural in brilliant blues and creams, yellows and ochers, in which Minoans—naked save for a loincloth—engaged in the dangerous game of hurdling over a charging bull. The bull's charge was so ferocious that all four of his legs were in midair, while the jumper at the front of the bull grasped the creature's horns in preparation for vaulting himself over the beast.

In a thoroughly modern twist, full-length mirrors were set between the frescoes to remind the maze walkers that they should be considering their inner selves, perhaps their shadow selves.

They turned a corner. Beside Evan, Addie sucked in her breath as a monster leapt in front of them.

Or rather a man. He wore a bull's-head mask and a loincloth over a tan leotard designed to simulate near-nudity. The man-beast crouched in front of them, his massive bull's head swiveling from Evan to Addie and back again. He tilted his head at Evan in a gesture that might have meant curiosity except Evan could see the man's eyes narrow behind the mask's eye slits in what looked like recognition.

For a breath, no one moved.

Then the creature rose to half his height and thrust his horns at Evan aggressively enough to make Addie cry out a warning and for Evan to backpedal until he hit a wall.

The Minotaur followed him, crouching inside Evan's personal space. The tip of one very sharp horn came within inches of skewering his right eye. Evan pulled his head back as far as he could and, feeling more threatened than entertained, tried to slip past him. But the beast clamped a hand on Evan's shoulder, straightened, then threw back his head and roared.

Chapter 16

Addie

The next sound out of the man-beast's mouth was a yelp.

The sound surprised Addie. She'd gripped the man's right wrist, but she'd barely squeezed.

The Minotaur yanked himself free of her and backed away from Evan, clutching his privates. "Son of a bitch," he choked out.

"Sorry," Evan said, not sounding at all sorry. "I'm rather fond of my eyes."

"You kicked me, you little freak."

"It was barely a love tap," Evan said.

"I could sue your ass."

"And I yours. Playacting is all fun and games until someone takes it in the family jewels."

Lights flickered above, warning the audience that the play was about to begin.

The Minotaur's snarl sounded frighteningly real. "I won't forget this, Professor." He spun on his bare feet and loped away, disappearing around a corner in the maze.

"You kicked him in the balls?" Addie asked.

"He grabbed me. You could say it was a knee-jerk reaction."

"Funny. He obviously recognized you. Any idea who he was?"

"Behind all the hair and those horns?"

"Just asking." She thought back to the video from last night. "This minotaur didn't have the same mask our potential killer wore in the POD video."

"That would have made the investigation way too easy."

"And what fun would that be?" She moved toward the exit, drawing Evan with her. "You head into the play. River and Diana are probably already in their seats. I'm going to get a name for our minotaur, and I'll see you inside."

"They'll stop you at the doors once the play has started."

She put on her cop face. "Watch them try."

✣

Rage boiled in Addie's blood. Her best friend—and someone had tried to hurt him. Nothing about that was okay.

Flitting at the back of her mind were the kinds of thoughts she'd been having more and more often lately, pretty much since Marcus Martin had asked for her hand in marriage. The thoughts went something like this: What if she lost Evan? What if he were no longer there with a shoulder to weep on, a joke to cheer her up, conversation to stimulate her? What if she could no longer tell him to trim his mop of hair or put on a suit? What if she had no reason to make tea in the British manner or pretend that she thought steak and kidney pie was an acceptable entrée?

None of it bore thinking.

Or perhaps it bore *more* thinking.

She was confused about all of it.

The woman behind the ticket counter took one look at Addie and got to her feet.

"Is something wrong?"

Addie held up her silver star. "I need to speak to whoever is in charge tonight."

"That would be our rehearsal director. But I'm afraid he's needed backstage."

"Get him." The woman opened her mouth as if she would protest, and Addie said, "Now."

"Yes, ma'am."

The woman made a phone call, and a few minutes later, a man in his thirties with a closely trimmed beard, stooped shoulders, and tired eyes strode into the lobby.

"I'm Tim Leck," he said. "One of the rehearsal directors. Is there a problem?"

"I'm Detective Addie Bisset with Chicago PD. Your performer in the maze tonight was dangerously aggressive toward a member of the public. I need his name."

Leck sighed. "You're talking about the Minotaur, I assume. That's Owen Teufel."

"You don't look surprised."

"He's a local kid, so I don't know him well. He's talented but a handful. Prickly."

"Prickly. Is playing the Minotaur in the maze his only role?"

"Not at all. He's what's known as the swing for several roles, including Theseus and the Minotaur. We like to use local actors as swings and standbys and understudies. It gives them a chance for the spotlight and looks good on their CV. And Owen is a fine actor, if a bit undisciplined. I'll speak to him."

Addie had already considered how she wanted to handle this. "I'd like to keep this between us for the moment. I'll be following up with Mr. Teufel on another matter."

"He's in trouble?"

"Thank you for your time, Mr. Leck."

She stepped away, then turned back. "One more thing, Mr. Leck."

"Yes?"

"Your costumes. Where do you get them?"

"They were designed by a company in New York. They travel with us."

"You don't rent anything locally, even for the standbys and understudies?"

"Not costumes, no."

She nodded her thanks then moved toward the doors where she could have privacy. She called the night sergeant.

"I need you to run a Chicago man for me. Owen Teufel. I'll wait."

"I can run him right now." A pause. "Only one Owen Teufel shows up. Age twenty-six. He's got two DUIs and one disorderly conduct. After the second DUI and the discovery of street drugs in his car, he did mandated time in rehab for alcohol and opiates."

"Any details on the disorderly conduct?"

"Public drunkenness and fighting. This was outside the Woodlawn Tap in Hyde Park. The bartender had cut him off, and Teufel took out his anger on a poor passerby. The passerby suffered a broken finger, and Teufel cooled his heels in a jail cell overnight before his parents paid bail. The victim didn't press charges."

Probably family money had helped smooth over the incident. A lot of UChicago students lived in Hyde Park. If Teufel was a student, that would explain how he knew Evan.

Addie thanked the sergeant and disconnected.

Anger-management issues, resentment, and easy access to a minotaur costume. And to Couch Place through the theater's back door. None of which made Owen Teufel a killer.

But it did make him their first person of interest.

Chapter 17

Evan

The performance, Evan and the others agreed, was magnificent.

The Greek myth offered in schoolrooms to children and teenagers was a sanitized version of the less savory and more bizarre aspects of the tales of Crete.

But the play held back little.

The action in *The King and the Minotaur* focused on a single night, hours before the Greek hero Theseus was to be sacrificed—along with thirteen other young tributes from Athens—to the cannibalistic desires of the monster. The action moved between each of the main characters: Ariadne, who had fallen in love with Theseus and longed to save him from her half brother; Queen Pasiphaë, whose son had become a monster; Theseus, heroic and brash; King Minos, whose hatred toward his queen's ill-begotten son ate at his soul; and the Minotaur, Asterion, alone and lonely in his underground labyrinth. A Greek chorus asked the audience to wonder if Asterion would have become a monster if his father hadn't hated him as a symbol of his wife's infidelity. Would Minos have hated the child, they asked, if he had looked more human?

The first act ended with a dance—Ariadne's elegant, leaping burst of grief and joy before she stole away to Theseus to give him a ball of red string that would lead him and the other intended sacrifices out of the labyrinth. And to gift him with a sword with which to murder her brother.

Impressed by the dance, Evan scanned the dancer's bio in the playbill in the faint light from the stage. Emma Gladstone Hargrave was a graduate of the School of American Ballet. Raised in Chicago, she had performed in multiple roles across the United States and now resided in New York City.

Hargrave. Why did that name seem familiar?

✣

In the lobby during intermission, Addie pulled Evan aside while River and Diana headed toward the bar.

"I had a background check run on the man who assaulted you," she said. "His name is Owen Teufel. Does that name mean anything to you?"

"It's not triggering anything, but I can check the records. He's a student?"

"Might be."

Evan scanned the crowd, wondering if the Minotaur would make another appearance. "Did you know that *teufel* is German for 'devil'?"

"Interesting and appropriate. But not immediately helpful."

"What did you learn when you ran him?"

"He's a local boy with two DUIs and an assault. He's also the standby for the New York actor playing the Minotaur, which suggests he's talented. But the rehearsal director says he's prickly and a handful."

"Why am I not shocked to hear that? Is he an older man, like the one in the videos?"

"Teufel's twenty-six, but that doesn't clear him. Not if we're talking disguises." She glanced toward the line at the bar. "You want to get a drink?"

"Go ahead. I'll join you in a minute."

She lowered her voice. "You seem pensive. You okay?"

"You mean aside from being nearly turned into shish kebab?" He gave her a smile. "Yes, I'm fine. Just introspective."

"Okay, my brooding friend. I'll give you a minute."

After Addie left, Evan found himself drawn to the monsoon lashing the street outside the doors. He crossed the lobby to watch as rain hammered the pavement. If the deluge continued, more basements and underpasses would flood. Power lines would fall. Cars would wash away.

He watched two men dart across the street as a car sped by, drenching them. One of the men spread his arms in a "What the hell" gesture.

What the hell, indeed. Evan sighed and resumed his gloomy study of the downpour.

Introspection isn't always wise, he reminded himself. He knew from experience that too much soul searching could lead a man down dark and thorny paths.

But the first act of the play had raised a question Evan had pondered more than once, given his own mother and father: how parents affected their children, and how their children, in turn, affected them. One's parents, through both genes and environment, helped create a human being. But who that child was—his or her intelligence, abilities, and disabilities—affected how his parents treated him, creating a sometimes vicious cycle of nurture responding to nature responding to nurture. In the worst cases, children became the battleground for their parents' moral failings.

He'd heard of parents who'd given up their dwarf babies for adoption, feeling unable to raise a child so different from themselves. Perhaps his own parents had wished to do so but had yielded to the conviction that a family takes care of its own. Then his father had fled physically while his mother retreated into bouts of self-absorption and depression. He'd studied pictures of his parents during their dating years and early marriage. They'd looked happy.

As a child, he'd thought his dwarfism was the cause of their unhappiness and the eventual breakdown of their marriage. As an adult, he no longer felt guilty. But he still wondered. In a family that prized aesthetics over diversity and individuality, having a dwarf child could shatter one's self-image.

A voice sounded behind him. "Dr. Evan Wilding!"

Evan turned. An older man of average height, with closely cropped gray hair, thin lips, and an imperial bearing, strode toward him. He pulled himself to a stop in front of Evan and held out his hand.

Bemused, Evan grasped the stranger's hand. As they shook, the man's name fell onto his tongue from some remote corner of his mind.

"Dr. Morgan Hargrave," he said. *Hargrave*, an old Anglo-Saxon name meaning "grove of the hares." *That's why the dancer's name was familiar.*

The man dipped his head in acknowledgment. "I'm pleased you remember me."

"Of course," Evan said politely. He took a few steps back when Morgan remained in his personal space. Having to constantly look up was hard on the neck and occasionally the spirit. He forced a smile. "I believe we've crossed paths at a few fundraisers?"

"Most recently, at the Minoan art opening at the Art Institute of Chicago. You gave a talk on the scripts of Crete. If you recall, you and I spoke afterward. I was there with my daughter, Emma Gladstone Hargrave."

"Tonight's talented Ariadne."

Hargrave's expression was smug. "She's amazing, isn't she?"

"She's a marvel."

Morgan Hargrave looked to be in his sixties. He was lean and fit, with narrow features and blue-gray eyes. He carried himself stiffly, like a soldier at roll call, and there was something pugilistic in his bearing; he appeared ready and even eager for a challenge. A hint of cruelty glinted in his expression. Or maybe, Evan chided himself, it was merely steely resolve.

"You might not know this," Morgan said, "but I'm a friend of your father's. Years ago, I funded one of his research projects, a search for a drug used by an indigenous tribe in Brazil. The drug was said to encourage empathy and compassion except—and here's where it got interesting—except in those for whom it created the opposite response. A subset of users became violent. And viciously cruel in their attacks. Your father called it the Jekyll and Hyde drug."

"I see," Evan said faintly. It sounded exactly like the kind of drug Oliver Wilding would go to the ends of the earth for. A chemical rationale for the mystery of good and evil. "And did he find what he was looking for?"

"Sadly, no. For all I know, he's still searching. We haven't spoken in years. Anyway." Morgan smiled. "I wanted to tell you how much I enjoyed your talk about Crete. You intrigued me. And now with Emma in this play, well, I've been following your work on the Phaistos Disc."

"I'm afraid my work has yielded few results."

"Nonsense! You know, I once heard a scholar, a professor of ancient history, I believe, say that the one thing a decipherer should never do is attempt the Phaistos. And yet, here you are."

"Here I am," Evan echoed. It appeared recent events were conspiring to remind him of both his hubris and his failures. "I'm familiar with the sentiment."

"Pshaw." Morgan flapped a dismissive hand. "Men like you and I spend our lives fighting in the arena. Our work demands it of us. I was pleased when your father took an interest in my work."

"Which is . . . I'm sorry, I—"

"No, no, even a brain like yours can't hold everything. I'm a social psychologist who studies moral psychology in children, particularly moral responsibility."

"Watching for budding Hitlers?" Evan said. "I'll have to look up your research. For now, it's been good to talk to you. I'm just going to—"

But Morgan interrupted. "I want you to meet my son."

This last was spoken as a man in his early twenties ambled up to join them. He wore Grecian garb: leather sandals, a short white tunic that fastened over one shoulder, leaving his chest bare, and a bright-blue cloak. A blue band held back his shoulder-length blond hair.

"This young man is my pride and joy," Morgan said. "My son, Peter. The hope of the Hargrave dynasty. He will pull us out of the doldrums of my own slow decline. Peter, this is Dr. Evan Wilding."

Peter Hargrave rolled his eyes at his dad, then shook Evan's hand. His grip was cool and firm. He had the chiseled good looks of a teen heartthrob.

"You'll have to forgive my dad, the dynasty builder. Sometimes he forgets all the good his own work has done."

"You're in the play?" Evan asked, even as he made a mental note to look up what, exactly, Dr. Morgan Hargrave's work covered. "I don't think I saw you onstage."

"I'm a standby for Theseus," Peter said.

"A standby? Not an understudy?"

"No, I'm—" Peter began.

"Standby is more prestigious," Morgan said, interrupting his son. He seemed blind to the anger that flashed across Peter's face. "A standby is someone who covers only principal roles. And where you might see an understudy on the stage as part of the crowd or in an ensemble role, a standby is never required to be on the stage, although he must be in the theater for all performances. He's only on the stage if he must step in for the role he was chosen for."

Pink crept into Peter's face. "Dad, I've already got the part. You don't need to keep selling me."

"Never hide under a lampshade, my boy." He clasped Peter's shoulder. "You know, when Peter was younger, I worried that my success would cast a shadow over his own ambitions. But my worry was unfounded. I should have known when Peter was accepted into Juilliard. Unlike some of the other local actors, Peter has *real* talent. And he has a backup plan, a degree in biochemistry."

Now Evan was interested. "Local actors like Owen Teufel? He's also a standby, isn't he?"

"For the Minotaur." Suddenly Peter grinned as if recalling a memory. "Owen's his own man. And better than he gets credit for."

Morgan sneered. "He's a savage, that boy. And I would know. I've spent my life separating those who contribute to society from those who would tear it down."

A series of expressions flitted across Peter's face—anger followed by what looked to Evan like sadness and then resignation. He struck Evan as someone braced against a constant headwind.

"I like Owen," Peter said. "We're friends."

"A shame," Morgan answered.

"So, father and son both do important work," Evan said weakly, and was relieved when River appeared by his side.

"Excuse me," River said. "Am I interrupting?"

"Not at all!" Morgan cried. "Another prominent guest. Dr. River Wilding, the archaeologist. You look just like your dad. Peter, we have a *real* hero as our guest tonight."

"Oh yes," River said in a clipped voice. "You should see what I can do with a trowel and a mound of dirt." He focused on Peter. "I flunked out of the third-grade school play. I don't know how you do it, standing up in front of hundreds of people. Thousands."

"And in a chiton, no less," Evan added, referring to Peter's short tunic.

Peter laughed. "I drew the line at shaving my legs. I told them—"

"But your exploits, Dr. Wilding!" Morgan continued forcefully, overriding Peter. "Or, if I may, River. I recall reading about the time in Afghanistan when you, armed only with—I believe—a World War One–era bayonet, hunted down a group of tomb robbers who injured one of your crew."

"What did you do with them?" Peter asked, his eyes wide.

"I merely handed them over to the local authorities."

Evan kept his grin to himself. As usual with River, there was much more to the story, part of which included scaling a cliff to reach the cave where the bandits were hiding. A story that ended in the capture of said bandits and a brief hospital stay for a wounded River.

River had Morgan Hargrave firmly fixed in his gaze. A crease marred the tanned expanse of his forehead. "Have we met?"

"Oh, surely not," Morgan said. "I would have remembered Oliver Wilding's son. But here is my card. Please give me a call while you're in town." He removed a slim gold case from the breast pocket of his suit jacket and handed both River and Evan a gold-embossed business card. "Although, as I mentioned, I know your father. Another adventurer. You must take after him."

"Not at all," River said firmly. He pulled on his spectacles and read aloud, "Dr. Morgan Hargrave, PhD, Harvard Distinguished Fellow, president of the Society for Philosophy and Psychology. Quite impressive."

Morgan smiled, although his gray eyes remained cool.

River slipped the card in a pocket and checked his watch. "It must be getting close to time to return to the auditorium. Evan, can I get you that whiskey I promised?"

Before Evan could respond, another young man approached their group.

Morgan's smile was fatherly. "And here's Bryant. Another person I'd like you to meet, Dr. Wilding. Or should I say, *Doctors* Wilding—plural? This is Bryant James. He's the husband of Jamal James."

"Jamal plays Theseus," Bryant said, offering his hand first to Evan, then to River.

Bryant was a rail-thin Black man with closely trimmed hair and a faint mustache. His expression was easygoing, his smile warm. He wore a stylish navy suit, a yellow-and-navy checkered top, and polished loafers. *Very* GQ, Evan thought. He appeared to be the opposite of the wild fierceness with which his husband played the role of the Minotaur.

As if reading Evan's mind, Bryant said, "I know, I know. I'm the mild-mannered high school chemistry teacher who couldn't possibly be with a man like Jamal. After seeing him on stage, people want to know what Jamal is like. The truth is, he's a pussycat."

"Jamal and I go way back," Morgan said, "to when he was just a boy. A friend of Peter's and"—there came the faintest hitch—"and their little group of friends. But don't let Bryant kid you. Jamal was always mischievous."

Bryant spread his hands in a "What can you say?" gesture. "Jamal's a practical joker. No question."

The lights flickered, indicating it was time for the play to resume.

"Wonderful to meet all of you," Evan said, echoed by River.

"Let's arrange a time to chat," Morgan said. "Give me a call. Both of you."

There was more shaking of hands, then Peter hurried across the lobby while Morgan and Bryant made their way toward the auditorium doors.

"For a moment, you looked as if you recognized Morgan Hargrave," Evan said to River when they were alone.

"For a moment, I thought I did." River tucked his spectacles away, and they moved toward the auditorium. "But I must be thinking of a painting of an emperor I saw somewhere. Bonaparte. Caesar. He's got that lordly air, doesn't he?"

"He certainly prefers to be the center of the conversation."

"Does he remind you of our father?"

Evan had been thinking the same thing. "Like two peas in a pod. Morgan seems to have the hubris to believe he can settle the issue of the origins of good and evil."

"And to think Dad merely wants to change how our brains work." River stopped outside the auditorium doors. "I got another text from Dad. He's coming to town in a couple of days to attend a conference and drum up support for his latest venture."

Evan's heart gave the faintest of lurches, an old familiar pain. "Are you going to meet with him?"

"Only if hell freezes over. Unless you want to go?"

"Maybe on the Twelfth of Never." Evan gestured toward the theater. "Go on in. I'll be right there."

After River disappeared inside, Evan hesitated, then scrolled through the contacts on his phone to find his father's number. More than once, he'd deleted Oliver Wilding's contact information from his phone. He always added it back in. His hatred of his father's abandonment seemed to run neck and neck with his desire to have a father.

Without understanding his own motivation—perhaps it was only to see if Oliver would extend the invitation to meet to his older son—he pushed the "Call" button. The phone rang once. Twice. Three times.

Evan was about to push "Stop" when someone picked up.

"Who's this?" his father asked. His voice was deep and throaty, an older version of River's and Evan's baritone. "It's the goddamn middle of the night here."

Clearly, his father did not have Evan's number in his list of contacts.

Evan hung up.

Chapter 18

Evan

After the play, Evan invited Diana and Addie to his house for some post-theater noshing.

While Addie helped Evan pull cheeses and meats from the refrigerator to make sandwiches, and while Perro ran about the kitchen in delight at the unexpected company, Diana challenged River to an axe-throwing contest.

"I have an axe in my car," she said, a playful glint in her eye. "What do you say to a little target practice?"

River looked at his watch. "Kind of late for a murderous play of blades, isn't it?"

"And dark," Evan added.

"And raining," Addie chimed in.

"There's plenty of light on the lawn in back." Diana kicked off her heels. "Or are you chicken?"

For just a moment, River's eyes carried a faraway look. He ran restless fingers through his hair and seemed to be searching for a memory.

"River?" Evan asked.

River shook himself and returned to the room. "All right," he said to Diana. "You're on."

"If you're really going to do this, there are some sections of plywood in the garage," Evan called after them. "Don't tear up the lawn or the trees. Remember, this place is a rental."

"Plywood won't work," Diana said. "It splinters."

River took her wrist and pulled her in the direction of the garage. "We'll find something," he said. "And don't worry, Evan. It will be just like when we were young."

Visions of broken windows, dented drywall, and a half-burned toolshed scrolled through Evan's mind.

"That's what I'm afraid of," he said.

Minutes later, River and Diana appeared in the backyard, carrying a broken-down pine picnic table between them. They propped it up against a tree, and Diana used a can of red spray paint to mark an *X* in the middle of the table.

"They can't do that!" Evan said.

But Addie laughed. "The table is falling apart. It probably hasn't seen the light of day in twenty years."

Evan moved toward the back door. Addie touched his arm. "Let them have their fun."

He came to a standstill. "But the table isn't mine."

"Take it out of the security deposit." She smiled, and suddenly the table didn't seem so important.

But he wasn't quite ready to give ground. "It could have sentimental value."

Addie's smile turned soft. "You're a good man, Evan. Now come on. Let's set out the food. I'm starving."

As usual, Evan found himself bewitched by her soft smile and husky voice. He let her steer him toward the island, and while she pulled a cutting board out of a lower cabinet, he used a step stool to reach a height that would put him eye to eye with Addie, and then began unwrapping the cheeses. She found the bread and deli meats, then he and Addie stood next to each other so that they had a view out the kitchen windows.

Perro ensconced himself at the kitchen's bay window, where a wide ledge and cushions offered comfortable viewing of the proceedings.

"Perro is a voyeur," Addie said.

"Best seat in the house. I should have brought Ginny in from the mews."

Outside, River marked off paces. Diana looked like she was checking his math. She was laughing. So was River. But there was a seriousness beneath River's humor as he eyed the table. A steadiness that people sometimes missed in the presence of his casual charisma.

It had always been thus. While River had never cared much about dares—letting the taunts of rougher boys pass over him—he'd also never been one to pass on what he considered a valid challenge. Those challenges came in the form of both mental and physical tests: navigating through boardrooms to raise money for a dig, facing the skeptics over a particular theory he had advanced, living in harsh conditions to reveal the past to the present.

It was all about testing himself, not performing for others.

"You and your brother are a lot alike," Addie said, startling him.

Evan became aware of her scent—perfume and rain and shampoo and whatever essence was uniquely hers. The scent washed over him like weather. Like a force of nature.

The stool he stood on made them of equal height. If he turned his head, his lips would be inches from hers.

He forced himself not to turn.

"What do you mean?" he asked. Outside, Diana was readying for the first throw.

"Sometimes your thoughts go winging off to places where I can't follow. It's as if you're not in the room at all. River is like that."

"You noticed, eh?"

Diana's blade flashed through the misty air, a whirl of bright steel turning end over end. The blade embedded itself with a loud thwack in the center of the large *X*. Diana's triumphant shout rang through the window glass.

Addie took a knife to a yellow block of cheddar. "Just a few minutes ago, he kind of checked out for a second. I can't count the number of times you've done that. Just gone on a mental vacation." She jostled him. "You two look alike as well. Dark and light, short and tall, it's true. But your features are similar."

His skin tingled where she'd touched him. "You mean that we're both incredibly handsome?"

She laid the cheese in a spiral on the wooden board. "I was thinking more that you'd be good as character actors."

"It's our father," Evan said. "His features are stamped on our faces."

"Sounds brutal when you put it that way."

"Our dad is a bit of a brute."

Addie touched his hand. "The way you and River are alike, though . . . it's lovely."

Suddenly self-conscious, Evan busied himself with the Stilton. He and River were nothing alike. Certainly not regarding love, which—with Addie standing so near him—was what he was thinking of. River had casual affairs. A quick in, quick out, in a manner of speaking. River's greatest passions were for his work and his freedom. In that order.

Evan's own relationships lasted for variable lengths of time, from a week to months. But they were never casual.

And lately, his love affairs had dwindled to essentially nothing. The last time there had been a woman in Evan's kitchen was almost four months earlier. Christina had left him because of his unspoken feelings for Addie.

"Penny for your thoughts," Addie said.

Now he did turn his head. His shoulder was pressed to hers. She didn't move away. He'd expected her to be watching River and Diana, but she was looking at him.

"Addie, I—" He stopped himself.

"I've been thinking about things," she said.

"What things?"

"That life is short. And that I've made a lot of mistakes."

"What kind of mistakes?" he asked.

"The kind I need to fix."

She set about rearranging the slices of cheddar.

His laugh was soft. "I get the feeling you aren't talking about the cheese."

Her hands stilled. She looked back at him, met his gaze.

He'd known her long enough that he could usually read her mind almost as well as his own. But tonight, confusing currents of contradictory emotion moved in the luminous depths of her eyes, leaving him at a loss.

"Evan, I—" She stopped. Started again. "I've been thinking about us."

His heart gave a single hard thump against his chest. Her eyes were—oh, cliché of all clichés—pools he could lose himself in.

"What have you been thinking?" His voice was little more than a whisper.

"That . . . I'm . . . that we . . ." Her voice trailed off, but still she didn't look away.

She'd never gazed at him this way before. Not, at least, outside of his dreams.

"That maybe you and I—" Again she stopped.

A strange panic rose in him. A fear that she would kiss him or tell him she loved him and then go back to Marcus Martin and that their friendship would be over and his heart would be broken. All because of a moment's mistake.

"This isn't what you want," he heard himself say.

She blinked. "It isn't? What isn't?"

"You're—" He struggled for words. "You're engaged."

She pulled away. Evan felt the coolness of the air swirl between them as she moved. A frown appeared in those luminous pools as she regarded him.

"Almost engaged," he said. "Isn't that right? You're going to marry Marcus. You told me you love him."

God, just give him a shovel so he could dig deeper. Or just shoot him now.

"Did I actually say that?" she asked.

He looked down, busied himself setting out crackers, no better than a lovelorn teenager.

Her phone rang where she'd set it on the counter. She grabbed it, spoke for a couple of minutes, then disconnected.

"It's Patrick," she said. "The judge approved the warrant for Fishbourne's home."

"You're not going in now?" Evan said.

She shook her head. "First thing in the morning. For tonight, we've got someone watching the place. But I'd better head home. We're going to get an early start."

She pulled her coat from where it hung over one of the chairs, slapped some turkey on a slice of bread, and smiled her apology at Evan.

"I didn't mean to make things awkward," she said.

"You didn't. It's me." He considered crossing the room to her. But from his place on the stool, they were nearly equals. It would kill him if she had to look down at him right now. "I was wrong. I—"

"It's okay." She stuffed a slice of cheese in her mouth and spoke around it. "I'll see you tomorrow?"

The moment was gone, if it had even truly been there.

"I'm at your disposal," he told her. "Let me know what you learn at Fishbourne's house."

She nodded. "I'll give you a call."

She breezed out of the kitchen. A moment later the front door opened and closed, leaving behind a wash of emptiness.

✣

After Addie left, Evan finished setting up the charcuterie board for his brother and Diana, then joined Perro on the window seat. The dog snuggled into him, resting his head on Evan's thigh. Golden fluffs of fur floated up, then settled on Evan's pants.

"I screwed up," he told Perro. "She was right there, and I pushed her away."

Perro's tail swept the cushion.

"It was for the better, right?"

But on this, Perro seemed to have no opinion.

Outside, laughter rose. Diana raised her hands in triumph while River conceded with a bow. From the black tick marks on the picnic table, the contest had been close. The center of the table had split beneath the blows of the axe.

He tapped on the window. When River and Diana turned, he gave them a thumbs-up. Diana curtsied, and she and River headed toward the door.

He dug deep and found a smile. If he never got more than this—his brother, his friends, his dog, his hawk, his work—he would count himself a lucky man. For the family we keep—whether it was one we were born into or one we created—provides a bulwark against all the darkness in the world.

CHAPTER 19

ADDIE

Addie stood in the backyard of Samuel Fishbourne's home and wished for a cigarette.

The day was close and muggy. The humidity had to be 90 percent. Storm clouds built in the distance, and a watery sun trickled through the leaves overhead to toss hazy patterns on the ground. Around her, old trees towered above a well-manicured lawn, and flower beds burst with midsummer blues and yellows.

She breathed in the warm rain-washed air.

She was purposely not thinking about Evan. Not thinking about the night before.

She was also trying not to focus overly hard on the still-missing Ursula Fishbourne. A detective didn't have the luxury of panic.

She and Patrick had completed their first walk-through of the home. The only bull symbols they'd found were a Chicago Bulls sweatshirt in Fishbourne's closet and a few pieces of the Bulls memorabilia in the basement—posters of Michael Jordan and Dennis Rodman, an autographed Spalding basketball, a red-and-black pennant. Addie spent a few minutes staring at the bull on the pennant. If there was a connection between this bull and the one inked on Fishbourne, the link was beyond her. At least for the moment.

They began their second tour through the house, moving slowly and taking a deeper look into the life of Samuel Fishbourne. They searched for threatening letters, illicit or illegal material, questionable finances. Any indication as to why a corporate attorney had been targeted for murder.

In the downstairs office they found two tickets for that night's performance of *The King and the Minotaur.* Next to the tickets was a flight itinerary for Ursula Fishbourne showing that six days ago she'd flown to Chicago from Houston's George Bush Intercontinental Airport and landed at Midway. She was scheduled to fly back to Texas in three days.

An empty suitcase lay open on a luggage rack in the second bedroom, and women's toiletries were scattered about the guest bath. They wouldn't know if these items belonged to Ursula until the lab had run tests.

But all of it gave Addie a bad feeling. Ursula had vanished.

Before leaving the bedroom, Addie had paused in front of the lone bookcase. The shelves were crowded with children's books and young-adult novels, as if the room had once belonged to a child and then a teen. On the bottom shelf, tucked next to a soccer trophy, were four high school yearbooks. She knelt and retrieved the last one, *Class of 2011*. Ursula Fishbourne's senior year.

She'd brought it with her, setting it on the dining room table where she wouldn't forget it.

Photos in the hallway included pictures of Samuel Fishbourne and the woman he'd been with the night of his murder. Laid out in chronological groupings, the photos began on the left with wedding photos of a young Samuel and his bride, followed by a family of three, with the baby growing into a child, then a teenager, and finally an adult. The bride, presumably Dana Fishbourne, disappeared from the photos when the child was in her early teens. A series of cats took her place.

Addie frowned at the cat-and-girl pictures.

Police could never assume anything when searching a home—the rule was to always question and verify. But she was certain that the now-grown-up baby—and Fishbourne's companion the night of his death—was his daughter, Ursula. The photos on the wall matched that of the young woman in the yearbook, the woman from the videos, and the Texas DMV photo. Houston PD was on their way to conduct a wellness check at Ursula's address. It was theoretically possible that Ursula had changed her itinerary and caught a red-eye flight back to the city, abandoning her personal items.

If Ursula wasn't back in Houston, they could hope she had parted company with her father after the show and was staying with an old Chicago friend. In the meantime, in addition to the wellness check, Houston PD had agreed to talk to neighbors, track down friends, and learn where Ursula worked. They'd create a profile of Ursula Ellen Fishbourne.

Perhaps that would give them a string to pull on. A way to find the missing woman.

Addie tapped her thighs with the palms of her hands. Through the open door behind her, she heard Patrick moving around the house. She thought again about a cigarette.

She didn't really want a smoke. It was a leftover habit from her rebellious teen years when one of the few ways to get back at her father and the nuns was to sneak a cigarette with her friends. But she still felt the longing now and again.

What she wanted wasn't nicotine, but answers.

To this case. To her life. To whether or not she should marry Marcus Martin.

Marcus was perfect. They were perfect together. He made her laugh. He appreciated her work catching bad guys. He claimed not to want to change a single thing about her.

And then there was Evan.

Her thoughts kept returning to him in ways that surprised her by moving into spaces beyond the comfortable and comforting friendship they shared. What on earth had she been thinking when she'd almost kissed him? Or whatever it was she'd been about to do—she was still confused about her own actions. One thing was certain: she didn't want to destroy what they had.

Focus, she told herself. *Focus.*

She'd come out here to think, and now she began a restless, winding circuit through the trees. Nothing in the house revealed why Samuel Fishbourne might have been targeted for such a bizarre and violent death. Or why, in the hours before his murder, he'd left a letter and a coin from Crete for Evan and River.

She knew the score: investigations like these took weeks, months, sometimes much longer. In the coming days they'd talk to neighbors, interview friends and coworkers, do a deep dive on Fishbourne's cases at the law firm where he worked, track down family members, find out if he attended church or belonged to the Rotary Club or had traveled recently. The usual plodding work that required persistence and patience.

But what if Ursula couldn't survive their patience?

She reached the back fence and stood on her toes to stare into the neighbor's heavily treed yard. A dog began to bark, and a moment later a golden retriever appeared, tail wagging.

"Some guard dog you are," she told it. The dog wagged its tail harder.

If Ursula was out there somewhere, the prisoner of a madman, then every hour counted.

Patrick's phone rang from somewhere inside the residence—he'd chosen a melancholy rendition of an Irish folk tune as his ringtone, and now the delicate melody called her back to the house. She turned and walked briskly back through the yard while overhead the leaves of oaks and elms and a few species she couldn't identify rustled in the merest whisper of a breeze, shedding last night's rain.

As she made her way, she spotted what had been invisible when she'd been walking in the other direction: someone had nailed a series of slats up the trunk of one of the oaks. The slats were just deep enough to allow someone to climb. She drew closer, rain-wet grass soaking the hem of her pants, and peered up.

High above her, mostly hidden by leafy branches, was a tree house. Her first thought was that it took a good father to build a tree house like that for his child.

Her second thought was that the tree house sat at a perfect height to give a voyeur a view into the upper two floors of the house.

She circled the tree, studying the ground for prints or cigarette butts or any indication that someone had been here recently.

Nothing.

She tugged on the rungs. They held. Glad she'd worn sneakers instead of her usual pumps, she stepped onto the first rung, then the second. As she climbed, more of the tree house came into view. It was larger than it had seemed from the ground. The boards that served as the floor of the tree house looked waterlogged; a few had rotted through. She tested the next rungs and kept climbing until she could poke her head through a square opening cut into the floor.

Silence greeted her. Shadowed by the leafy gloom, the tree house was lined with rough-hewn benches for sitting, and in the far corner stood a plywood four-by-four-foot hut, complete with a hinged door, peeling paint, and a glassed window in which hung a faded curtain.

Addie eyeballed the floorboards. Rot had spread outward from the center. A few rusted nails lay about. She should leave the place to the crime-scene techs. They could bring in a proper ladder and whatever else they needed to safely search the area. Plus, whatever she was looking for wouldn't be found here. No one had used the tree house in years.

The breeze pushed the leaves about, and a stray bit of sunshine struck the door to the little hut.

Someone had painted a symbol on the door. Once-red paint had faded to pink, but a sudden chill scurried down Addie's spine as she stared at the image.

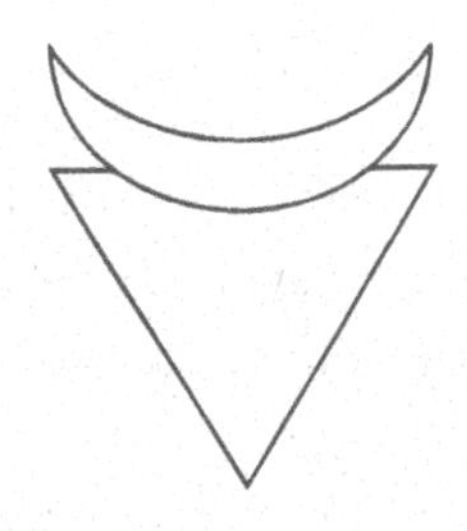

The shape looked similar to the Cretan sign that Evan had shown her—the one that resembled the head of a bull. The one drawn on Fishbourne's chest.

She took a photo with her phone, and texted it to Evan with a single word: Thoughts? She'd follow up with an explanation later. Then she pushed down on the boards near the opening, testing them. They appeared to hold firm, and she planted her palms and hoisted herself through the trapdoor. She perched on the edge, her legs dangling, and snapped more photos.

She eyeballed the floor. While the middle had rotted most of the way through, the boards were more solid along the edges where they had been nailed to the frame. She tucked away her phone and scooted on hands and knees along the outer edge, moving toward the hut.

The breeze came harder. The branches swayed, and the tree house suddenly felt like a ship at sea. She gripped the edge of one of the benches and waited until the wind died down. Then she moved forward.

At the hut, she took more pictures. Now she could see words above the symbol that had all but disappeared over time.

STOP AND FEAR: A MONSTER HUNTS HERE!

She pressed a hand to her chest, willing her suddenly slamming heart to calm. The words and the symbol were nothing more than kids playing. A macabre version of Keep Out!

She reached out and pushed down on the simple wooden latch. The door swung inward with a groan. Ancient cobwebs floated down, drifting through the musty air. She used the flashlight to check the floorboards, noted the shining spots on the floor where rainwater had seeped in, then rose to her feet and stepped inside. And found herself surrounded by faces.

For a moment, the staring eyes startled her. She let out a laugh when she recognized the images of silver-screen heartthrobs—Zac Efron, Robert Pattinson, Daniel Craig. Ursula Fishbourne had been a typical teenager, at least in her taste in actors.

She shone the light around the small space. An old plastic café table and a single chair. A ragged blanket tucked in a corner with a rotting pillow. Two moldering Nancy Drew books.

The wind gave a little kick, and the open door banged against the wall. The edges of the posters flapped. A once-glossy print of Pattinson as a vampire fluttered sideways. Beneath his image was the yellowed sketch of another man.

Addie held up the Pattinson poster and gazed at the new image, wondering why this drawing, which showed the face and neck of a thirtysomething male, had been hidden. And why it looked vaguely familiar. The man had a heavily crevassed face, a thick neck that suggested brute strength, and hooded lids over eyes as flat as a snake's. His thin lips held an arrogant sneer. Dark, neatly combed hair was shown parted down the middle. The collar of a T-shirt was just visible at the bottom of the sketch.

A tattoo marked the side of the man's neck. Addie lifted her phone with the flashlight app and leaned in to better see in the green gloom.

The symbol was the same as the one painted on the door. The triangle and crescent moon.

Goose bumps rose on her skin.

Carefully, she pried out the thumbtacks holding the sketch to the plywood wall, swearing softly when the rusting edge of one of the tacks tore her skin. She sucked at the thin welling of blood.

The drawing looked similar to a police artist's sketch. A straight-on mug shot created in dark pencil on thick paper and drawn by a skilled hand. She checked the back. The paper lacked a witness's signature that a true forensic sketch would carry—a signature that meant the witness agreed with the likeness.

She flipped the paper back to the front. The man glared out at her.

Her eyes caught on initials in the lower right-hand corner: TR.

TR—the same initials on the letter Fishbourne had left for Evan and River.

CHAPTER 20

EVAN

"Look at her!" River cried. "She's gorgeous!"

"She is," Evan agreed, shading his eyes. "But don't let that fool you. She's a terror."

The brothers stood in the forest reserve not far from Evan's home. Mist drifted along the edges of the meadow where shadows still clung. The leaves on the trees hung limp and sodden from the previous night's rain, their normal emerald glow dimmed to a mournful gray in the early morning light.

Far above their heads, darting in and out among the low-lying clouds, Evan's goshawk wheeled in graceful arcs. Ginny was hunting. But she also appeared to be soaring out of sheer love for the dance.

At the apex of one of her climbs, visible through a split in the clouds, she hovered. And then she dove. Down and down, plunging earthward and—an instant later—she extended her talons and struck the ground.

"She's got something," Evan said.

Evan noted River slowing his pace to match his own limited stride as they crossed the field to where Ginny crouched, mantled over her kill. She eyed them angrily, yellow eyes glaring, beak open in a pant. No matter how many times she and Evan went through this routine, Ginny never relinquished her kill except with barely restrained fury.

Evan raised his glove and slapped the leather with a tidbit meant to lure her back to him. Once, twice. A third time, and finally she heaved herself off the kill.

"Poor thing's still alive," River said.

"A hawk never concerns herself with what we consider the proper order of first killing and then eating."

Evan passed Ginny over to River, who was wearing one of Evan's gloves. Evan made sure River had the leather jesses wrapped between his fingers, then dropped to his knees next to the rabbit. Gently, he grasped the shivering animal and twisted its neck. River watched in silence as Evan field-dressed the rabbit, gave Ginny her reward of a morsel of flesh, then tucked the small corpse in his bag.

"Is that for you or for her?" River asked.

Evan looked up at his brother from where he still knelt on the ground, wiping the knife on the grass. "You remember Mother's rabbit cacciatore?"

"Of course. It was the only thing she cooked. And only because the cook wouldn't have anything to do with it."

"We'll have rabbit for dinner, tonight or tomorrow." Evan stood. "Now open your fist."

River did so, and Ginny flew to Evan's hand. He stroked her feathers. "There's my beautiful girl."

She watched him beadily for a moment, then set to cleaning her feathers.

✣

Back at the truck, Evan settled Ginny on her perch. The rabbit went into a cooler. Evan and River washed their hands with the bar of soap and jug of water Evan kept in the truck for just this purpose, then Evan unwrapped their egg-and-sausage breakfast sandwiches, which he had prepared early that morning. River poured tea from the thermos. They sat side by side on the lowered tailgate, River's booted feet kicking at the water-soaked grasses while they watched the rising sun struggle to break through the clouds.

Evan chewed and swallowed. "Not to beat a dead horse, but I still sensed last night that you found Morgan Hargrave familiar."

River set down his cup. "There is something about him, beyond his resemblance to Oliver. I thought we might have met when I was living here with Dad. Maybe they were talking shop, and I was hanging out on the stairs, eavesdropping. I did a lot of that when I was seven."

"Were you eavesdropping because you were curious or because you were bored?"

"Curious. I can't say I *liked* Dad, exactly. But I found him interesting. And people kept telling me how much I looked like him. I guess I was trying to decide if I wanted to *be* like him."

"I'm glad you chose otherwise," Evan said.

"Me, too, in the grand scheme."

Evan poked River the way he'd done when they were boys. Back before Oliver Wilding took his younger son to Chicago, leaving Evan friendless. "You should meet with him, River. See if there's anything there. Maybe he wants to be part of your life again."

"I don't want that. But I *am* curious." River kicked the grass. "You wouldn't mind?"

Evan poked him again. "You'd be taking one for the team."

"*I'd* mind," River said. "If it was you he called and you he wanted to meet."

Evan set down the remainder of his sandwich. "Sometimes, being a dwarf is a total bitch. Try reaching for your favorite coffee in the grocery store. Or stowing your luggage in the overhead bin. But in other ways it's also a gift. I learned long ago that either people judge me, or they don't. Those who do . . ." Evan shrugged. "I don't care about. It took years, but I've realized that their judgment of me is their problem, not mine. I wish Oliver wasn't one of the judgers. I've imagined over and over what it would be like to have a father who believed in me. Who supported me. But as they say, it is what it is. And I've accepted that, too."

River clapped him on the back. "You're a better man than I am."

"No. I've just had to make adjustments that you haven't had to make. And I'm not saying I'm a saint. I've had plenty of moments of miserable self-pity, just like anyone. But in truth, I'm okay with the fact I have no relationship with Oliver."

"You're okay that he's an asshat."

"Who else can I fault for my own asshattery? He taught me well."

"Always good to blame nurture over nature."

In the near distance, a dog set to barking. Evan looked out across the fields. It was rare for him to have company in the reserve this time of day. He spotted someone walking through the trees on the other side of the field. The man—if it was a man—was merely a silhouette in the mist, but something about his shape struck Evan as odd.

As if sensing Evan's perusal, the man stopped and turned in their direction. The form refused to resolve into the simple shape of a human. It was larger than a man, crowned by something Evan couldn't quite make out.

The dog kept barking, its voice going hoarse.

Not for the first time, Evan had the feeling that the merest wisp of a veil hung between his everyday life—the one where he sat in his truck eating an egg sandwich with his brother—and the mythos found in the subconscious of every human in every society.

A mythos that haunted dreams, that whispered near altars and in temples, that dwelt in graveyards and battlefields.

Myths that said the old gods weren't dead, merely abiding.

Evan knew that myth was—at its simplest—the sacred expressed through story, and as essential to the soul as breathing to the body. The ancients had created myths to provide a compass, a way of being in the world. Their primal stories served as a link between the everyday and the sacrosanct.

To ignore them, Evan knew, was perilous. Our ignorance robbed us of the divine—in ourselves, in the cosmos.

He jumped when River touched his arm.

"Is that your phone?" River asked, breaking his thoughts.

The figure vanished into the trees. The dog fell silent.

Into the sudden stillness, Evan's phone rang from the cab of the truck: "I Am Woman."

"It's Addie," he said.

CHAPTER 21

ADDIE

The thrill of the hunt ran through Addie like an electric current.

Standing in the tree house's plywood hut, she sensed images from the investigation coming into focus: shadowy forms like the first faint shapes developing on a photograph in a darkroom. She couldn't yet understand the connections, couldn't see what might link a young girl from ten years ago with a brutal killer.

But there was something here. Every molecule of her detective soul could feel it.

First there had been a girl—Ursula—with the typical interests of a child and then a teenager. Ponies and unicorns replaced by brooding movie stars.

And then something else had come in. An evil-looking man in a sketch, his picture hidden by the photograph of an actor playing a monster.

And a strange symbol: triangle and crescent moon.

The warning: **STOP AND FEAR: A MONSTER HUNTS HERE!**

What had happened in Ursula's life to shift her path from the usual teenage interests to something darker? Had it been only a brief curiosity, the way Addie herself had stumbled upon the Manson murders when she was sixteen and become, for a few months, utterly obsessed with the madness of such a terrible crime?

Or was it something that had stayed with Ursula, followed her into adulthood, linked itself—somehow—to her father's death and her disappearance?

Addie drew in a breath, released it, watched the cobwebs dance. Far away, thunder rumbled. She was jumping way too far ahead, reaching for connections that Patrick would tell her were leaps into the void.

Not solid detecting.

Still. A symbol that resembled a bull's head. A tattoo on the man in the sketch reappearing on a tree house door. The initials, TR.

Outside, the first drops of rain rustled through the leaves to fall as dark pennies on the tree-house floor. The door swayed, then banged against the wall. The moth-eaten curtain on the small window floated eerily.

Addie tucked the sketch inside her suit jacket to protect it from the rain, then retreated from the hut. She latched the door closed and edged her way back along the outside of the floor toward the trapdoor. The paper crinkled unpleasantly as she moved, and she had the weird feeling that the man in the sketch was staring straight into her soul.

She was almost to the trapdoor when something thumped on the floor behind her, then raced past. She let out a small cry as a squirrel barreled by and disappeared down the opening. The tree house felt suddenly ominous in the gathering gloom of the storm, and she retreated quickly down the slats, jumping the last few feet.

Patrick greeted her on the back porch and swept her into the house as the rain came down harder. He closed the door behind them. They stood in the dining room, a large space with a table for ten and an antique buffet. An abstract oil of the Chicago skyline hung over a mahogany sideboard. Brass candlesticks bolstered each end of the buffet.

Patrick leaned against the table and folded his arms. "Houston PD says there's no sign that Ursula has returned home. Her house is empty, and her car is still at the airport in long-term parking."

Addie thought of the tree house. "Something has happened to her."

"It's not looking good," Patrick agreed. "We'll keep the notice out, and we'll ask when we talk to the neighbors. Could be she parted company with her dad before he was murdered and went to stay with a friend."

"Ever the optimist."

"It helps in our line of work. Now you ready to get back to work, lass? Or did you find some answers out there in the trees?"

"Only more questions," she said, and showed him the photos on her phone of the door and its warning message.

"That looks a lot like one of the symbols on Fishbourne's chest," Patrick said, scrolling through the images. "Maybe Ursula was a fan of the Chicago Bulls, like her dad."

"I also found this."

She slid the drawing out from her jacket and set it on the dining room table. In the yellow glow from the chandelier, the drawing looked older and somehow more sinister. Moth droppings specked the paper. Crease lines showed where the drawing had once been folded.

Addie pointed to the lower right-hand corner.

"TR," Patrick said. His brow furrowed like a freshly plowed field.

"Right. The same initials on the letter Fishbourne left for Evan. Do you recognize the face? He looks familiar to me, but I can't place it."

"That's because when he was doing his nasty work here in the Midwest, you were off at your fancy eastern college."

Addie looked up, startled. "You know him?"

"Aye, lass, that's William Barlow. The Bogeyman."

She shook her head. "Never heard of him."

"He killed three people in Kansas, then made his way south and east through Missouri and up into Illinois, murdering as he went. They called him the Bogeyman because he was every kid's nightmare, and no one alive had caught a glimpse of him. Not until he returned to Illinois."

A memory tugged. Maybe her sister had sent her a news clipping. "Where is he now?"

"After he killed a kid in Springfield, his own father called in a tip, and detectives caught up to him. He was convicted on seventeen counts of murder and first-degree kidnapping, mainly kids, a few women. But detectives thought he was likely responsible for more. Plenty of kids disappeared between Garden City and Springfield, but Barlow never confessed, and the evidence never surfaced. His attorneys tried to use the insanity plea, and he sure seemed off with the pixies to me, that one. But it didn't work. After the attorneys finished their jurisdictional battle, he landed in the Pontiac Correctional Center, serving multiple life sentences."

"When was he active?"

Patrick scratched his chin. "I'm not sure. It was a few years before he was caught. He was arrested maybe ten years ago. In 2008, I think it was."

"Which would have made Ursula around age fourteen when he was arrested. A natural age for a kid to obsess over a child killer. Right along with vampires, werewolves, and the Thing Under the Bed." She shook herself. "Maybe I got ahead of myself thinking there was a connection between Ursula and the man in the sketch—something other than a youthful fascination with evil."

"If there is, I don't know what it would be. And that tattoo"—he pointed a finger at the ink on Barlow's neck—"that's pure fantasy. Barlow doesn't have a neck tattoo. At least, he didn't when he was arrested. It could be Ursula was studying Greek mythology in school and took a shining to the Minotaur."

"There are still the initials," Addie said. "TR."

"Not exactly uncommon. But I agree, it's odd. And there's another thing about Barlow." Patrick was still staring at the sketch. "His nickname is Bull Barlow. I don't know where the moniker came from. Could be because he's a big guy."

"Was the nickname mentioned in the press?"

"Must have been. That's how I heard about it."

"Then likely that's what inspired the artist to add the tattoo. Still, I'll follow up with the detectives who handled the case. Couldn't hurt to tie off that thread."

"I'm afraid that's going to be difficult, lass. The two primaries from Illinois are dead. I think a third guy also went to meet his maker. The others transferred and are probably retired. Not just our local boys, but the ones in Kansas and Missouri. As I recall, none of them were spring chickens."

The shadows in the room deepened as rain thrummed against the glass doors leading to the backyard.

"Doesn't that strike you as strange?" she said. "That the detectives associated with the case are dead or retired?"

Patrick scratched his stomach beneath the tie. "Nah. People get old. People die. The Illinois primaries died together in a crash during a high-speed chase six months after Barlow was convicted. Nothing suspicious. Just tragic as hell."

She nodded. But her mind was still reaching for connections.

"We've been wondering what compelled Fishbourne to deliver the letter and the coin to Evan's doorstep," she said. "What if Ursula had something to do with it?"

"Like maybe she asked him to play messenger?"

"Or the killer had snatched her, then threatened to kill her."

Patrick's hand moved from his stomach to his jaw. He stretched his neck and massaged beneath his chin. "Complicated. Risky."

"Which fits the profile of a man who dumps his victim in a public walkway in downtown Chicago."

"I'm not dismissing the idea," her partner said. "But I don't see the link between a killer who was snatching kids from rural areas ten years ago and a fourteen-year-old suburban girl. Other than morbid fascination, I mean."

"But the initials . . ."

"I know you hate coincidences, lass. But look in a phone book. It'll be crawling with TRs."

Addie rapped her knuckles on the table next to the sketch of Barlow. She and Patrick worked this way: playing devil's advocate to each other's theories. Sometimes they even convinced each other to shift their thinking.

But not always.

"Think I'll take a poke at the Barlow case, anyway," she said. "You never know what you're going to get when you kick over old logs."

"Vermin is what you get," Patrick said. "But knock yourself out, lass. We don't have much else to chew on right now. Just a couple hundred interviews to conduct, an autopsy to attend, Fishbourne's office to go over, camera footage to review."

"Good thing we're not busy," Addie said dryly. "The crime-scene techs are going to hate me. But I want them to search every crevice and behind every poster in that tree house. See if anything else pops up. If there's a link between Ursula and Bull Barlow, it might explain her father's death."

"How? Barlow's in prison."

"Maybe a copycat?"

"Barlow didn't cut his victims in half and make pretty drawings on their skin. He bit them a few times, then strangled them."

"There was a bite mark on Fishbourne."

Patrick followed her as she went to the back doors and stared out at the storm. His voice was gentle. "You sure this tree house is where you want to divert resources? The LT's not going to like it."

"You're the one who told me to follow my gut."

"Aye, lass." He sighed. "First time you ever listened to me."

CHAPTER 22

EVAN

Evan stared at the text Addie had sent him.

The photo showed an old wooden door on which someone had painted a warning above two symbols: a downward-pointing triangle topped by an up-tipped crescent moon.

STOP AND FEAR: A MONSTER HUNTS HERE!

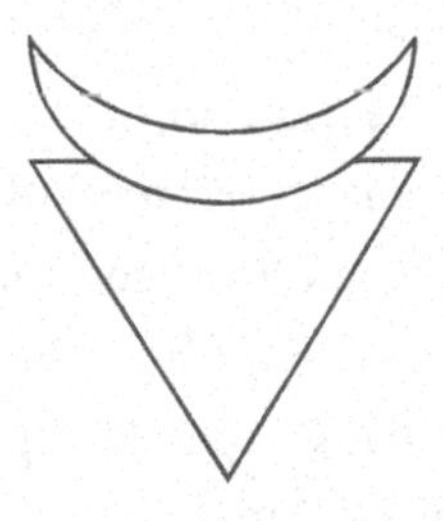

He turned his phone to show the photo to River.

"Where was it taken?" River asked.

"Addie doesn't say. But she and Patrick were going to Fishbourne's this morning."

"An odd warning. Like a child's version of *no trespassing*." River turned his brown ball cap backward and used his fingers to zoom in.

"The symbol could be a version of syllabogram number eleven, the head of a bull. Like one of the two glyphs drawn on Fishbourne's chest."

Evan nodded his agreement. "The artist used a triangle instead of a heptagon. And a crescent moon instead of the straight line we find in the actual glyph." He enlarged the image, turned it sideways, righted it again. "I'm pretty sure I've seen this specific iteration before."

"Where?"

Evan smoothed his beard. "I can't remember. Something someone sent me, maybe? It was a long time ago."

"So many symbols, so many years?"

"Are you suggesting that my mind is as overstuffed as a hoarder's house?"

"Your words, not mine."

Evan shot a text back to Addie.

Looks like a modification of Cretan glyph number eleven. Where is it from?

When a few minutes ticked by without a response, he hopped down from the tailgate. "Let's head home. I believe you said you need to check in with your site manager in Istanbul. And I want some peace and quiet to try and recall where I've seen that symbol before."

River folded up the paper plate from his breakfast and followed Evan out of the truck. "Time for a trip through your memory palace?"

"I was thinking of something far more mundane," Evan said. "Like old paper files and emails. But the memory palace isn't a bad idea."

A memory palace was a way to store memories within a familiar location. In Evan's case, he'd chosen an image of an English manor he'd visited as a child, populating the hallways and sunlit rooms in his mind with visual cues he used as markers for things he wanted to remember. The cues consisted of artwork that he mentally linked to poems, historical events, lines from classical literature, and statistics regarding semiotics.

"I live to serve," River said. "Before I call my site manager, why don't I look at your institute's financials, see what kind of mountain we need to climb in terms of funding?"

Evan cringed as he slammed the tailgate closed.

"It can't be that bad," River said.

"Perhaps you've heard of Mount Everest?"

✣

At the house, Evan released Ginny into her mews, settled River in the kitchen with a spreadsheet from the Institute of Middle Eastern Antiquities, then went into his library with Perro close on his heels.

The library was Evan's favorite room, although the gourmet kitchen came in a close second. A two-story space, the library was filled with floor-to-ceiling mahogany bookshelves, windows that overlooked the garden, lit display cabinets, generous wood trim, and a stone fireplace that looked medieval but could be turned on with the press of a button. A scattering of club chairs invited guests to visit, and a well-stocked bar encouraged them to linger.

Evan glanced longingly at the bar, reminded himself it wasn't yet noon, and settled himself in his favorite chair. Perro nestled in the chair next to him, head on Evan's thigh, and sighed contentedly as Evan scratched behind his ears.

Evan called Diana. She picked up immediately with, "Any news?"

"Not so far. Except Addie sent me a symbol painted on a door and asked my opinion."

"Context?"

"None. I assume Addie will fill us in. It's similar to the Cretan bull glyph, but I swear I've seen this particular iteration before. I wonder if you could go through my electronic files and emails and see if the pictogram or whatever it is shows up. I have a vague recollection of seeing it in an email, but I'll never find it. You, on the other hand, have an astounding grasp on technology that continues to elude me."

"Flattery will get you everywhere. Send the symbol over, and I'll see what I can find. You want me to start with your official UChicago email?"

"Yes. Thank you."

Diana disconnected. Evan closed his eyes and summoned his memory palace. He began by imagining himself approaching the house on the long gravel walk. It was a warm, sunny morning, the air filled with the scent of lilac and honeysuckle. A hummingbird whirred past. Larks sang in the trees. Overhead, clouds floated in the blue dome of the sky.

He sensed his heart rate slowing, his shoulders relaxing. He no longer felt the chair or Perro's warm weight.

He opened the front door and entered a large atrium. A hallway stretched into the unseeable distance. Rooms opened to either side. Evan mentally strolled to a room bearing a brass plaque that read **GREEK MYTHOLOGY**. Here, he'd stored his knowledge of the Greek gods and heroes and monsters—beings like Aphrodite and Perseus and the three-headed Cerberus, guardian of the underworld. Evan had populated the room with Greek artwork, including a marble statue of Theseus slaying the Minotaur, which stood just inside the imaginary door.

He paused in the doorway. It seemed likely that he would have placed the symbol of a bull in this room, along with his mental notes on it: whoever had sent it to him and when and why.

But nothing he saw sparked a memory; he had no hint where to look.

Plus, something felt off.

A shiver walked his back when the room in his mind dimmed as clouds covered the sun.

Always before, when Evan entered this imaginary estate of reminiscence, he had been alone. But now he sensed a shadowy presence, a vague not-quite-human form.

He forced his eyes open, was half-surprised to find himself in his library. Perro had fallen asleep. Clouds had closed in around the house, creating a bleak gray light, and soft rain caused the leaves in the garden to shiver-dance.

Evan pulled out his phone and looked again at the symbol Addie had texted to him. If it was meant to symbolize the Minotaur, then it represented shame, guilt, hubris. The Minotaur was the monster that dwelt in the labyrinth of our inner selves, skulking in the darkness, refusing to be dragged into the light. Had his thoughts of the Minotaur followed him into his memory palace?

For much of history, a labyrinth meant the unknowable, including whatever lay beyond death. It was a one-way path toward an inevitable end. But in the Middle Ages, the journey changed. It became one of enlightenment, a pilgrim's path that led to God.

He drew in a breath, closed his eyes. Found himself again standing in the doorway of the room of Greek mythology. He walked through the room while the gods and heroes stared back at him. But the symbol he sought wasn't here. Whatever the icon was, wherever he'd seen it, he apparently hadn't found it important enough to lock in his memory.

He walked up to Theseus and the man-bull. Theseus—the hero who slew many monsters, including the Minotaur. Who fled the island of Crete with the king's daughter, Ariadne, then abandoned her on another island.

After his father's death, Theseus became king of Athens. The word for king in Latin? *Rex*.

So, Theseus Rex. TR.

Just as in the play *Oedipus Rex.* In Greek, articles like "the" weren't used in the titles of plays.

Classical Latin didn't use articles at all.

At a sound, Evan opened his eyes. Perro lifted his head, ears cocked.

River appeared in the doorway, his face lit by his crooked grin.

"I might have it," he said.

Evan looked up. "A solution to the institute's financial woes?"

River waved a hand. "That's a piece of cake. I'm talking about the initials, TR."

"Theseus Rex," Evan said.

River laughed and leaned against the doorjamb. "Great minds think alike."

Sensing the archaeologist's jubilation, Perro hopped down from the chair and trotted over to see what the fun was about. River squatted to scratch under the corgi's chin.

Evan shook off his lingering unease from the presence he'd sensed in his memory palace and scooted out of his chair.

"Our killer thinks he's a hero," he said.

River gave Perro a final pat and rose. "Everyone is the hero of their own story, is that it?"

"Yes. But . . . also no."

River folded his arms. "You're not convinced."

"Once a killer decides to embrace his inner monster, in a manner of speaking, he tends to go all in. He doesn't switch back and forth between monster and monster-killer. We can consider Theseus Rex a possibility. It's interesting. And it links to the Minotaur myth. But we also need to keep digging."

River wandered into the room, picked up a book from Evan's stack on the table. "In that case, we need more to work with. One body, one set of half-erased glyphs—it's like deciding the function of a building at an archaeological site by digging a single test trench."

"You're thinking we need more victims?"

Frustration showed in River's eyes. "I'm thinking I shouldn't have let Hoodie Man get away."

"I'm quite glad you did. You're good, River. But this man is cruel and wildly unpredictable." Evan's phone buzzed: Diana. "Ah, maybe this is the cavalry."

River replaced the book on the stack.

"You're on speaker," Evan said when he picked up. "River is here."

"Good morning to you both," she said. "Evan, I found what you were looking for. Fourteen years ago, in 2004, a Detective Tom Walsh from Garden City, Kansas, sent you an email asking for your thoughts on a symbol, which he included."

"I wasn't even in Chicago then. Oh, was that when—?"

"It was when you'd agreed to teach here as a visiting professor. How quickly he forgets, eh, River? The symbol is an exact match for the text you forwarded from Addie. Downward triangle, upward tilted crescent."

A faint bell rang somewhere in Evan's mind. "You are amazing, Diana."

"That is true. And, anyway, it beats conjugating the verbs of a dead language."

"You don't mean that."

"That is also true. I've forwarded the original email to you, along with your response. I can't find any further communication between you and anyone in the Garden City police department."

After they hung up, Evan sent the emails she'd forwarded to a printer, then grabbed the printouts and laid them on the library table. River joined him.

> Dr. Wilding,
>
> My name is Tom Walsh. I'm a detective with the Garden City, Kansas, police department. We came

across this symbol (see below) during one of our investigations. Someone recommended you as an expert on signs and symbols, and I see that you've consulted with other police departments.

I would appreciate it if you would send me your thoughts on this symbol:

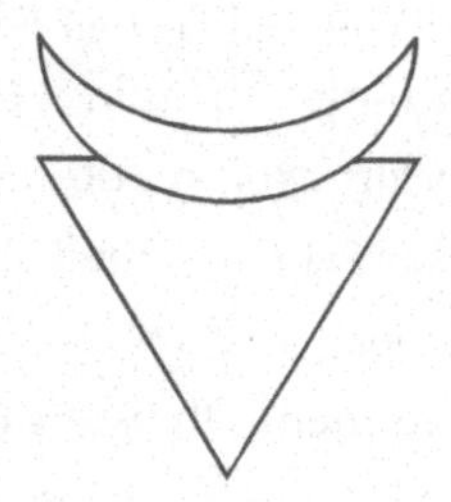

Sincerely,
Tom Walsh
Detective, Garden City Police Department

The second email was Evan's reply:

Detective Walsh,

The symbol you inquired about appears to represent a bull's head. The bull is a universal symbol of sacred power and masculinity. It is also used to represent fertility, earthiness, and the underworld. The horns stand for strength and aggressiveness—horned gods in various cultures were often warriors.

Biblically, the bull represents sacrifice.

In the Greek (and modern) zodiac, the bull appears at springtime, the season of rebirth.

Without the context in which you found this symbol, it isn't possible for me to offer further conjecture. Please let me know if I can offer any additional assistance.

Dr. Evan Wilding
PhD, SSA, IASS

River picked up the emails and reread them. "This was all you heard from the guy?"

"Apparently so. There's nothing more in my emails nor in my memory. When I didn't hear back from Detective Walsh, I must have expunged the entire thing from my mind."

"Saving valuable space?"

"There's a limit even to my brain's capacity."

"I never thought you'd admit it."

Evan's phone rang again. He answered with, "Addie. You're on speaker with me and River."

"And you're on speaker as well. Patrick's here. We're at Fishbourne's house. We've got a few things to cover, but let's start with the symbol I sent you. We found it painted on a tree house in Fishbourne's backyard."

"And you're wondering if a drawing from years ago might be linked to our killer?"

"I'd like your thoughts."

"Ordinarily, I'd say it seems unlikely." Evan clasped his hands in front of him. "It's a common symbol that Ursula or one of her friends might have seen in a comic book or on a television show. Or in a book of Greek myths."

"We found Chicago Bulls memorabilia in Fishbourne's basement rec room," Addie said.

"There you go," Evan said. "If the rec room was off limits to Ursula and her friends, she might have retaliated by using the same symbol to tell her dad to keep out of her tree house."

"You said *ordinarily* you wouldn't link the symbol in the tree house to the killer," Addie prodded.

"Right. There's more to the symbol." Evan paused while he gathered his thoughts.

Patrick's voice echoed through the connection. "No rush. It took God Himself six days."

"Sorry," Evan said. "When you sent the symbol from the tree house, I thought it looked familiar—beyond its similarity to a Cretan hieroglyph—and Diana did some digging to find out why. Fourteen years ago, a detective from Garden City, Kansas, sent me an email with the same image, wanting my thoughts on it. I sent him a few generalities on the symbol of a bull and asked for context. But I never heard back."

"What was the detective's name?" Patrick asked.

"Tom Walsh."

"Tom Walsh." Patrick's words came out in a sigh. "If it's the same Tom Walsh, I knew him years back. He started out in Chicago same as I did, and we shared a fondness for the Old Country. Last I heard he took early retirement."

"Garden City," Addie said. "Patrick, you said Barlow was active in Kansas."

"He was. I'll give Walsh a call."

Excitement ran hot and bright through Addie's voice. "Evan, inside the shack with the warning painted on the door, we found a sketch of a man Patrick has identified as a serial killer who targeted women and children—his name is William Barlow. Better known as

Bull Barlow. Barlow was arrested in Illinois in 2008 for kidnapping and murder in Kansas, Missouri, and Illinois. He's serving multiple life sentences."

In Evan's library, River imitated a basketball player dunking a ball.

"You're wondering if there could be a connection," Evan said.

"We're guessing that Ursula was fascinated by a serial killer doing his nasty work so close to Chicago. Which is mostly a big 'So what?' But here's the curious part. The artist placed his or her initials on the drawing: TR."

Evan decided not to bring up Theseus Rex. "Those are common initials," he said, ignoring the tingling in his gut.

Addie sighed. "You and Patrick. I need you to keep tugging on that thread. Find someone with the initials TR who knows you and River. Right now, Patrick and I are heading to the morgue. The ME is going to start Fishbourne's autopsy."

Evan's eyebrows lifted in surprise. "On a Saturday?"

"Since the crime happened in downtown Chicago to a law-abiding attorney, it's a high-profile case. But it's also because the ME has a crush on Patrick."

In the background, Patrick's voice rose in protest.

"Anyway," Addie said firmly, "tonight, after the play, I'm going to plant myself in the parking garage overlooking the alley in case Hoodie Man or the old man from the video footage decides to make an appearance. Seems like our best bet is to watch for them at the back door, where everyone gathers to get an autograph after the show."

"Because our killer will want to revisit the actual scene of his crime rather than hanging out in the lobby," Evan said.

"Right. Dinner at Petterino's first. I want to talk to the waitstaff. The three of you care to join me? I'd like River watching for Hoodie Man."

"Aye," Patrick said. "Just don't ask me to explain another missed dinner to the missus."

"Petterino's of the delectable Shrimp de Jonghe?" Evan said. "Nothing better."

"I'm in," River said.

"Good. But remember, Evan and River, you're there only to observe. No inserting yourself into the case by doing something to attract attention. If Hoodie Man shows up, and River IDs him as the same guy, I'll get patrol on him. No heroics from you two."

"Cross my heart," Evan said. "No heroes here."

River dribbled his imaginary basketball and remained silent.

CHAPTER 23

URSULA FISHBOURNE

The distant sound of metal clanging echoed through the space.

Ursula came awake with a cry. Awake in the way you might if you realized you'd overslept for an important meeting—suddenly and with panic. Except the panic she felt was like fangs in her stomach, tearing at her.

Of the sound, nothing remained. Perhaps it had been part of the nightmare.

I'm going to die here, she thought. *I'm going to die, and no one will ever know what happened to me.*

Had they found her father? Hot tears rose at her last memory of him, his eyes meeting hers as the animal dragged him away. Then, that awful sound of—

Stop. Don't give in. He is fine. He escaped. He is looking for me.

She pushed herself to her knees.

Keep moving.

It was mind-numbingly dark. Not a hint of ambient light. No clue to her surroundings beyond what she could touch—rocks and dirt. She was in a cave, and for all she knew, the hours—days?—she'd spent walking and crawling had taken her deeper into the earth and away from all hope of sunlight.

But she had to move. She had to. To stand still was to die.

She strained her ears. Was that the sound of someone breathing?

"Hello?"

Her voice echoed.

Hello . . . hello . . . ello.

The darkness swallowed her voice. The echo faded, and nothing more came back.

She'd heard that the human brain—deprived of all sensory input—created its own world. Smells, visual hallucinations. Sounds.

She sucked in air; the cold rushed down her throat and into her lungs.

Stay calm. Stay calm. Her father's voice rose in her mind, gently chiding her during one of their camping trips when she'd imagined a bear in the woods. *Panicking won't serve you,* he'd said. *At times like this, you must* think.

She ran a finger along the years-old tattoo on her forearm, traced the familiar outline of a cat's head. The tattoo had been a rite of passage. *Hieron poiesai,* he'd said. Ancient Greek words that meant "to make sacred." This was before they'd realized he was mad. Before he'd been sent away. Her first year in college she'd gone to have the tattoo lasered off. But the technician, a girl not much older than she, had told her the punctures were too deep, that the artist had used too much ink.

He would always be with her.

And now he'd come back. She was sure. How else to explain the attack? The stone labyrinth? The man-beast she'd glimpsed?

He was back, which meant all of them—every last one—were doomed.

Chapter 24

Addie

Late Saturday afternoon, Addie sat at her desk in the nearly empty bullpen. Phones rang, the television nattered, but most of the detectives working this shift were out chasing leads and catching crooks.

In front of her—on her desk and on the computer—was everything she'd pulled together on Barlow during the last hour. Newspaper clippings. Digitized police files. An e-book on child murderers.

None of it made for happy reading, starting with the fact that Barlow had killed himself in his cell a month ago.

William Barlow had been born in Pueblo, Colorado, in 1973, the son of a steelworker and a preschool teacher. He'd been a poor student who dropped out before completing high school. For years he'd drifted from job to job. He'd begun his murderous spree in 2002. Or, some detectives theorized, even earlier.

Journalists speculated that the Bogeyman might never have been caught if not for his own family. Barlow's father and younger brother had moved to Illinois in 1993 after his parents divorced. When William finally joined them, the younger Barlow was out of town, working construction in Florida. Barlow senior was semiretired, working as a woodcrafter and enjoying a few acres of farmland in northern Illinois. William said he needed a place to lie low for a time.

"My dad took 'im in, even with his lazy ways," Edgar Barlow was quoted as saying in one article. "That's the kind of man my dad was. But then he started getting suspicious. The late nights. Billy coming home with blood and dirt on 'im. The stink that was comin' from his room. Later, police said he'd probably kept his trophies there, skins he'd taken from the victim. But them skins was long gone by then."

Addie kept scrolling.

After Barlow's arrest, there had been speculation that he hadn't worked alone. Addie tried diving down that rabbit hole but found only aimless speculation. Barlow's attorneys had tried to get some mileage out of that theory so they could spread the guilt, but it had gone nowhere.

According to a feature piece, the Bogeyman's murderous exploits even drew the attention of a Chicago kids' mystery club who worked the Bogeyman case right along with police. Without, of course, police resources. They even sent the police a tip: "A guy in our club is pretty sure he saw the Bogeyman west of the city," said one member, a teenager with long blond pigtails. "William Barlow. And he wasn't alone." When this reporter asked who was with Barlow, the young lady replied, "Another man and a kid. Our club member told the police where he'd seen him, and Barlow was arrested three days later in that same area."

"The Bogeyman," said this same mature teen, "has made all of us interested in good and evil. We are determined to do good in the world." A giggle. "At least most of the time."

Addie picked up the phone, hoping to reach the reporter. The woman who answered said that Sheila Shaeffer had retired two years ago and died six months earlier. ALS. Lou Gehrig's disease.

Addie hung up thinking the case was like the curse of Tutankhamun. No one associated with it was left untouched.

She skipped ahead to what she could learn about Barlow's time in prison. According to the only journalist he'd agreed to speak with,

Barlow began studying mythology and working slowly toward a degree in the classics, despite his lack of any languages other than English.

There was no mention of a tattoo.

Addie skimmed through everything again, looking for a photo or a drawing that TR might have used as his model. But there was nothing.

So how had TR managed to draw such a skillful likeness?

Was he the kid who'd claimed to have seen Barlow?

CHAPTER 25

EVAN

When Evan and River walked into Petterino's, the first thing Evan noticed was the aroma of truffles. He took a deep breath. Perhaps he should reconsider the shrimp and order truffle risotto with an aged chardonnay.

The restaurant was in the middle of a lull. The theater crowd had cleared out, the after-show late-night diners were a couple of hours away, and only a few people waited near the front. A maître d' escorted Evan and River to the back of the restaurant, where Addie sat in a U-shaped booth.

She stood when they approached. Last night's fancy clothes were gone. Like Evan and River, she wore casual pants and sneakers. Tonight was about footwork.

"Greg will be your server tonight," the maître d' said before leaving them. "He'll be with you momentarily."

"Diana is on her way," Evan said as he worked himself into the booth next to Addie. River sat across from them. "After I filled her in on a possible link to a series of old murders and kidnappings, she figured four pairs of eyes were better than three. Especially when the additional eyes are hers."

"No hijinks or heroics," Addie reminded him. "Should our guy show up, patrol will be nearby."

"Cross my heart," Evan assured her. "Where's Patrick?"

"I'll explain in a moment."

A bowtie-and-vest-clad waiter appeared. Addie and River ordered light dishes, but Evan—after a brief debate—ordered the Shrimp de Jonghe and a glass of Montepulciano d'Abruzzo.

"It's not as if I'll be doing any running," he said to Addie's skeptical expression.

"Good thing." She sipped her water. Pointedly, Evan thought. She and River were ganging up on him.

"Maybe we should talk about the autopsy before the food arrives," she said.

"Always a wonderful aperitif," Evan agreed.

Addie glanced around the half-empty restaurant and leaned in. "The killing blow was done with a large, nonserrated blade. A machete. A sword. The ME says it's difficult with cutting wounds—as opposed to stabbing injuries—to determine the type of instrument or weapon used. More helpful is the bite mark, which has been confirmed by the ME. It will give us DNA."

They fell silent as the waiter arrived with Evan's wine.

"Go on," he said faintly after the waiter left. He found the crimson fluid suddenly unappealing.

"There's plenty of other information. The type of ink. The tape used on his eyes and mouth. Also the contents of his stomach, which confirm his dinner here and that the only alcohol he'd consumed was wine. His fists, which he clenched before he died, held nothing that would help identify his killer. It's all in the report, which I will forward to you. The other thing that stands out is that the killer thrust a red ball of yarn down the victim's throat before killing him. If Fishbourne hadn't been nearly cut in half, he would have suffocated."

"Ariadne's thread," River said.

Addie nodded. Just as they'd seen in the play last night. Ariadne betrayed her father and half brother by giving Theseus a weapon with which to kill the Minotaur and a ball of red yarn to lead him back into the world. Addie turned toward Evan. "The guy clearly has a thing for this myth. And given the savagery of the murder, it feels personal. The question is why?"

Evan pushed aside his momentary queasiness and took a healthy swallow of the Montepulciano. His gaze drifted up to the caricatures that covered the walls of the entire dining area: movie stars, comedians, politicians. The rich and the famous. People living the kind of life others longed for.

He set down his glass. "What drives an attachment to a mythos like this can indicate many things, but my guess is that our killer wants—needs—to be part of something larger than himself. If the role of hero is taken, he'll be the antihero."

"Then who is playing the hero?"

"Someone he both admires and loathes, would be my guess."

Addie made a note on her phone. "You said the Minotaur is part man, part beast, part god. Does our killer think of himself this way?"

Evan watched as the maître d' led an older couple to a table. The pair walked hand in hand, happy in each other's company.

He returned his gaze to Addie. "Someone who believes they are God is more a trope of fiction than an actual pathology. But consider someone who hides a massive inferiority complex behind an equally massive superiority complex. Leaning on the mythos of the Minotaur, believing yourself to be both more god and more beast than human opens a path to morally deviant behavior that is normalized under the rules of the mythos. A child like the Minotaur, who is descended from a god through his mother and made half beast through his father, that child could see himself as both superior and inferior."

Two waiters arrived with their food. Evan looked smugly at River's crab cakes and Addie's Caesar salad before tucking into his shrimp.

Addie took a few bites of lettuce and said, "Going back to these inferiority and superiority complexes. Do these complexes suggest issues with his parents? A father like King Minos who rejected and even imprisoned him? And a mother who was powerless to protect him?"

"It makes sense that the killer picked that myth because he sees a similarity between his life and that of Asterion's. But it might not be anything so outwardly dramatic. His father could have been strict, his mother detached. To a child already struggling, that could be enough."

The maître d' reappeared, this time with Diana in tow. He looked suitably awestruck by Diana's height and the copper flow of her hair.

River rose and motioned Diana into the booth. Their eyes met, and Evan saw that same look that had passed between them the first time they met. That certain *something*.

"No food, just a glass of your second-to-cheapest cab," Diana told the maître d' before sliding in next to River and flashing him a smile. "What have I missed?"

"We were playing armchair psychologists," Evan said while River helped Diana out of her coat. "And discussing the autopsy report."

"Oh, do tell!" Diana reached over and snatched Evan's salad fork and speared a shrimp off his plate.

Addie filled her in on the cause of death and the ball of yarn, then said, "A waiter from two nights ago confirmed that Fishbourne and Ursula were here and were, to all outward appearance, happy and relaxed. They mentioned they were going to the play at the bookstore. Fishbourne told the waiter that the beautiful woman dining with him was his daughter, who was visiting from out of town. And that he couldn't be more proud of her."

A waiter brought Diana's wine. She gave him a smile that made him blush before he hurried off.

Diana sipped her wine. "Then where is she?"

"We're looking for her, both here and in Houston. We've got someone watching her father's house. We have an alert out, the Chicago equivalent of 'Be on the lookout for.' Beyond that . . ."

"The killer took her somewhere."

Addie set down her fork. "That's our fear. Other than the videos from the PODs, the last confirmed sighting we have of her is at the bookstore, where we've established that she and her father attended the play. Per the store's receipt, Samuel Fishbourne bought Edith Hamilton's *Mythology*, a novel by Stephen King, and the current issue of *The Economist*. We're tracking down the attendees, hoping someone noticed something. There are no store cameras, and no one was allowed to record the performance."

Diana speared another shrimp off Evan's plate. "You said Bull Barlow was convicted on kidnapping charges as well as murder. Did anyone ever get away from him?"

"If so, they never came forward. He was caught when his own father turned him in. Barlow cooled his heels in prison for almost ten years before committing suicide. The chances of him having anything to do with Fishbourne's murder and Ursula's disappearance seem remote. Although I did learn that there was a group of kids trying to track Barlow back when he was known only as the Bogeyman. One of them phoned in a tip to the police that he'd seen Barlow with a kid and another man."

"Did the police figure out who they were?"

"The sighting was never confirmed. A teenager who might or might not have seen Barlow, who might or might not have been with two other people."

"The kids . . . you're thinking of Ursula and the tree house?"

"Absolutely. With the bull symbol and the words *stop and fear: a monster hunts here*."

"That sounds more like he's hunting them, not the other way around," Diana said.

"Kids scaring each other," Addie suggested.

"Or they figured it takes a monster to catch a monster." Evan pushed his half-eaten dinner across the table to Diana. She could carry the calories better than he could. "River and I have a theory that the initials, TR, could stand for *Theseus Rex*. After Theseus slew the Minotaur, he sailed back home to Athens, where he was crowned king after his father's death. *Rex* is Latin for 'king.'"

Addie's face fell. "So *TR* might not be a real name?"

"Impossible to know at this point," Evan said, with a glance at River, who'd been unexpectedly taciturn this evening. River nodded and Evan continued. "But I don't give much credence to the idea. It doesn't fit with what little we know about the killer, for him to consider himself a hero and a king. More likely, TR was someone Ursula knew as a teenager. A friend who shared in her interest in Barlow. Maybe even drove it. And now he's resurfaced."

"Whoever he is or was, he drew that sketch of Barlow from memory or imagination," Addie said. "Which means that if TR is our killer, his murder of Fishbourne could have been influenced by his teenage fascination with Barlow, even without any direct connection." She glanced at her watch. "Patrick is flying to Garden City tonight on the department's dime to see if Detective Walsh can shed any light. Walsh is in a nursing home. His ability to communicate is compromised by dementia, but the staff says he does okay when it's face-to-face. If we're lucky, he'll be able to tell us why he asked for Evan's help with that symbol. If we're really lucky, he'll give us more. A link between TR, Barlow, and maybe even Ursula. The lieutenant figured it was worth the cost of a ticket."

"And if he can't?"

"Then Patrick will talk to whoever was Walsh's partner back then, if he's still around. And go through his old cases."

When the waiter appeared, Addie handed over her credit card. After she'd signed for the meal over Evan's protests, she said, "Tonight's on me, not the department. Now let's get into position. And remember.

You guys aren't cops. You're civilians. This is strictly an eyes-on operation. The real cops will be nearby."

✣

Evan found that by balancing on a curved section of pipe—one designed for carrying electrical wires, he assumed—he could see over the cement wall of the aboveground parking garage to the alley below. The other three took up positions nearby while rain fell just outside. The garage was across from the theater, allowing a clear view of the stage door and up and down the alley.

Below them, an excited crowd milled in the alley near the backstage door of the Neverland Theater. Those gathered were mostly young; perhaps the theater's older patrons had decided to give the rainy, human-choked alley a pass. No older man with glasses and a wispy mustache. No tall white man in a black hoodie.

Evan watched the throng in astonishment. Who knew that theater actors were the new rock stars? He found it very satisfying.

"See anyone familiar?" Addie asked River.

River kept his eyes on the crowd. "Not so far."

Evan gave River a sideways glance. His brother had been quiet at the restaurant. Pensive. Evan wondered if he was thinking of the investigation or their father. Or if his silence was more about his obvious fascination with Diana. River's gaze had drifted to meet hers more than once during dinner.

Ten minutes ticked by. The rain slowed, then stopped. Umbrellas disappeared. A few more minutes, and the back door opened. A man wearing a jacket with the theater's logo and the word *Security* appeared and propped open the door. He waved the crowd back and set up stanchions and a velvet rope.

"Stay behind the velvet rope!" he shouted.

The crowd obediently stepped back. Four other men wearing *Security* jackets appeared, fanning out toward the east and west ends of the alley.

Moments later, the cast began to trickle out. First the original Broadway stars—the actor who played King Minos, and then the woman who'd acted opposite him as his wife, Pasiphaë, followed by Jamal James.

When Jamal James appeared—the local boy who'd made it big in New York—the crowd cheered. Jamal smiled and raised his hand. This was the young man who played Theseus and whom Morgan Hargrave claimed to have known since Jamal was young.

Behind Jamal came a man Evan didn't recognize. Then the man threw back his head and let out an immense roar that defied his narrow chest. As one, the crowd shrieked, and Evan realized he was looking at the actor—sans costume—who played the Minotaur. Hayden Lee Clark also raised his hand to the crowd. His smile was affable as he slung an arm around Jamal. Jamal mock-punched him. Hayden pretended to crash against the wall. When the actress playing Ariadne appeared, Hayden leaned over her with menace, and she swooned into Jamal's arms.

The crowd, as they say, went wild.

Behind the big names came the supporting cast: the understudies, the swings, and the standbys. There was Owen Teufel and Peter Hargrave. Between them stood the prima ballerina who played Ariadne in the dance portion of the play—Morgan's daughter, Emma Gladstone Hargrave. Emma was even more striking without her stage makeup and dressed casually in jeans, a low-necked turquoise blouse, and leather jacket. She wore her blond hair piled loosely atop her head.

As the fans moved in, waving programs to be signed, the actors spread out behind the velvet ropes, although Peter and Owen—perhaps because they weren't part of tonight's performance—stayed back, taking positions near the door. Most of the crowd were women who seemed focused on Jamal. Perhaps they didn't know or care that Jamal was gay. With his great height and strong features, he made an arresting figure.

One of the beautiful people, Evan thought. No wonder Bryant felt lucky.

Evan stuffed his hands in the pocket of his hoodie. Looking at the cheerful, jostling crowd, it was hard to believe that only two nights ago, this place had been deserted save for Fishbourne and his killer. And, perhaps, his daughter.

His mind went to the symbol scratched on the door of a child's tree house—the same triangle-and-crescent-moon sign sent to him by Detective Walsh. Why had TR drawn the image on the killer's neck? A tattoo that—according to Patrick—Bull Barlow didn't have.

Was the symbol simply a case of an independent creation of the same design, what archaeologists called *convergence*? After all, there were only so many ways to draw a representation of a bull. If TR knew of Bull Barlow's nickname, it could have inspired him to craft the design and include it on his drawing. And to paint it on the tree-house door.

Or had Ursula and TR stumbled upon the symbol because it *was* tied to Barlow? If so, what had they known that no one else had?

Addie glanced at her phone and stepped away with a "Be right back" gesture.

Beside Evan, River sucked in a breath. Diana moved closer to them.

"What?" she said softly.

"There." River nodded toward the alley's east end.

A solid-looking figure in a black Chicago Bulls hoodie and wearing a backpack was making his way through the crowd. He appeared to be on a beeline for Emma Hargrave, although it was hard to be sure with the way the crowd surged and shifted.

Evan glanced at Addie. She was still on the phone, a deep frown on her face.

The man reached Emma and held out his playbill. She signed it and thrust it back toward him, already reaching for the next admirer, the next program, her eyes and smile wide as she drank in the praise.

Then, abruptly, she paused and looked toward the man, her smile fading.

As Evan watched, the man reached across the rope, his hand groping for hers. She shrank back, visibly startled. Her expression turned angry, and her lips moved, but Evan couldn't hear what she said over the cheerful noise of the crowd.

"She's having a MeToo moment," Diana said.

Addie reappeared, her phone stashed. "What is it?"

"Someone has approached Emma," Evan said. He looked at River. "Is that him?"

River's gaze narrowed as he watched Emma and the man.

"No," he said, after several seconds.

"How can you be sure?"

"His hand," River said. "The man down there is Black. Hoodie Man is white. I saw his hand when he touched his chest."

Down below, the man glanced up as if sensing their scrutiny, revealing dark skin and a wild crown of locks.

"Definitely not him," River said.

The man turned back to Emma. She frowned. One of the security guards must have also noticed the man and Emma's reaction. He began plowing through the crowd toward them. When the man saw the guard, he backed away from Emma, turning and cutting his way east through the crowd.

"I'll be damned," River said. "That *is* him. He must be wearing a costume that covers his hands. His gait . . . it's him. Call patrol," he said to Addie. "Hoodie Man is here. He's about to exit the alley."

"He's moving east," Evan said. "Toward State Street."

Addie pulled out her phone again.

River hopped up on the cement barrier. "He's almost to the street. We'll lose him."

Evan watched as Hoodie Man left the alley and merged with the Saturday-night pedestrian traffic.

"Don't move. Patrol is three blocks away," Addie said.

River dropped lightly onto the arm of one of the streetlights that extended over the alley.

"River, don't," Evan said.

But River was already stepping along the metal arm toward the end of the lamp. Without hesitation, he threw himself across the alley, grasping the raised stairs of the theater's fire escape as he fell. Under his weight, the stairs sank obligingly to the ground. River hopped off.

"Go!" Diana cheered.

"Don't you dare. Stop!" Addie shouted.

River glanced up. "I'll just keep track of him until the cops catch up." He spun on his heel, jogging east.

"Dammit," Addie said. She still had the phone to her ear. "They got diverted to a disturbance two blocks south." She whirled on Evan. "Get him back here right now."

But Evan shook his head. "It would be like trying to stop a runaway train."

He stayed quiet as Diana edged past them and disappeared in the direction of the elevator.

"This isn't amateur hour," Addie fumed.

"The police don't know how to find the suspect," Evan pointed out. "River could be of help."

"Not if he gets himself killed," she said darkly.

CHAPTER 26

RIVER

River's memory of Chicago from his brief time in the city as a boy of seven wasn't much help as he followed Hoodie Man.

But cities were cities. Streets were streets. Alleys were alleys. And Chicago offered what many cities he'd been in didn't—pavement, street signs, and lighting. Far easier to follow a man through an American city than a Moroccan souk.

He turned on his phone's GPS tracker and stepped clear of Couch Place.

Hoodie Man had turned north. River followed. Pedestrian traffic in the theater district was heavy but grew lighter as the man headed in the direction of the Chicago River and its pedestrian walkways. River hung back so that his target was barely visible—easy enough, since although Hoodie Man moved fast, he was taller than most around him. The man glanced back twice but gave no indication he'd spotted River; his pace stayed steady.

How had River been wrong about the color of the man's skin? Had he been wearing white gloves that—in the dark and the fog—River had mistaken for flesh?

When Hoodie Man reached the bridge that spanned the Chicago River, he paused. Then he stepped to the right and disappeared.

River broke into a sprint. When he reached the bridge, he saw a set of stairs dropping from the street to the river. No wonder Hoodie Man had appeared to vanish.

He took a screenshot of his location and sent it to Evan. He glanced back the way he'd come, wondering if the cops were anywhere nearby. If so, they weren't approaching with lights and sirens.

Addie wants you back, Evan texted.

River stared at the message. He didn't want to get Evan in trouble with the police. But this was their chance to capture the man who'd taken an axe to another man and likely kidnapped that man's daughter.

Ursula Fishbourne's life could be hanging in the balance.

Eyes only, he texted back. Get cops here. South bank of river.

Without waiting for an answer, he stuffed his phone in a pocket and threw himself down the stairs after his quarry.

Hoodie Man was nowhere in sight when River reached the bottom of the stairway.

He raced to the water's edge and spotted his quarry jogging east. The man looked like any other recreational jogger enjoying the scenery on his evening run.

Which, River was sure, was exactly the point. If the police arrived, no one would have noticed a man jogging past.

River snugged down his ball cap and took up his own light run, going just fast enough to keep Hoodie Man in sight.

They reached a sparsely filled riverside brewhouse where a handful of patrons dined outdoors under umbrellas, determined to enjoy what was left of the evening before the next storm hit. Hoodie Man stopped at the entrance and glanced back. River was in clear view. He knew he'd been made.

The man tapped his chest three times, as he had done at the alley the night of Fishbourne's death, then grabbed a three-foot-tall planter the restaurant used to display its menu. He hurled the planter to the ground, blocking the path behind him.

"Hey!" shouted the startled hostess.

He broke into a sprint, his backpack jouncing.

So much for anonymous jogging.

River leapt over the metal planter and accelerated. The game was afoot, apparently. And at a dead run.

Hoodie Man reached the far side of the tables that lined both sides of the path. He glanced back, saw that River was gaining, and drove a shoulder into a waiter carrying a tray of drinks. The waiter crashed into a table full of diners, knocking table, chairs, and patrons to the ground. Glass and dishes shattered. A woman screamed.

"Asshole!" someone shouted.

"Call the cops!" River yelled as he zigzagged around the debris.

He grabbed an unopened bottle of wine from a serving tray and hurled it at Hoodie Man. It struck the man midback. For an instant he staggered, giving River a chance to narrow the gap.

Then he recovered and disappeared around a curve in the path.

River rounded the path after him and caught a glimpse of the man speeding through a darkness now lit only by glittering skyscrapers. The walkway stretched ahead of him, empty of pedestrians as the night grew late and rain began to fall.

Hoodie Man glanced back without slowing. Gave River a "Come and get me" gesture.

He was enjoying this.

And he was *fast.*

River kicked up his speed. His arms pumped. His breath bellowed in and out. It had been a year since he'd had to push himself this hard.

Another curve in the path. When River rounded the bend, Hoodie Man had again vanished. Shuttered businesses lined the right-hand side, offering alcoves where a killer could hide, waiting for his pursuer to go by. To his left, the river flowed darkly like oil. It stank of earth and algae.

River slowed as his sixth sense kicked in.

Hoodie Man was close.

He was wary of an ambush and of what Hoodie Man might be carrying in his backpack. River strained to hear the thump of retreating footsteps. No sounds came back other than the slosh of water and the distant rumble and horns of traffic.

He turned in place, studying the shadows. Rain trickled down the back of his collar. A private boat drifted by; voices floated across the water, beery and cheery, as the saying went.

River turned off his phone's password requirement in case he needed to access the phone fast, then sent another screenshot of his location to Evan. He edged forward.

And froze.

Something lay in the middle of the walkway.

A man's head.

River held very still. He stared at the object on the ground: the head of a Black man with a Medusa-like snarl of long locks. Blood glistened on the ragged edges of the man's neck and pooled on the pavement.

River backpedaled a few steps and glanced over his shoulder at the way he'd come, wondering how far behind the police were.

A sudden whiff of licorice and honey alerted him; he turned back as a man hurtled from a recess in the wall.

River crouched and curled his hands into fists, looking for the glint of a knife or the duller gleam of a gun. All he could make out was the man's vague form.

Then a sound.

River jerked away at the clean, heavy whisper of a blade slicing the air. He threw himself sideways, skidding on the wet pavement and going down on one knee.

The man followed, arms raised, everything but his eyes hidden behind a cloth mask.

Lights from the skyscrapers glittered on a blade.

"Wrong turn," the man said.

CHAPTER 27

EVAN

"He's on the Riverwalk, near the Chicago Brewhouse," Evan said, looking at his phone. "Going east."

He and Addie had moved from the parking garage to the now-deserted alley, taking refuge in the alley's only open docking bay. The air smelled of diesel and ozone. Lightning flickered distantly. Trash—empty beer cans and coffee cups, cigarette butts and food wrappers—lay flattened in the light rain. Nearby, a train rattled past on the "L."

Addie nodded at him and pressed her phone to her ear. He forwarded his brother's text to Diana, hoping he wasn't putting her in danger by doing so.

"Where are the police?" he said.

Addie held up an index finger: hold on.

He stared across the alley at the poster for *The King and the Minotaur*.

Why were the police so slow? Other than the fact that—according to Addie—they were also dealing with robberies, muggings, and traffic accidents. All of which took precedence over a possible sighting of a maybe killer.

He walked out onto the sidewalk along State Street.

The sidewalks and street glimmered in the misty rain. Cars and trucks whizzed by, but the pedestrian traffic had thinned. A homeless man stumbled by. Another man shouted from somewhere nearby.

There wasn't a cop or squad car in sight.

Evan pulled up a map of the Chicago River near where it ran beneath State Street. If Hoodie Man kept heading east, he'd eventually reach Lake Michigan. In between were a hundred places where he could divert away from the water and disappear.

Or lure River into a trap.

Addie appeared at his elbow.

"River and Hoodie Man made a ruckus at the Brewhouse," she said. "He's a problem, your brother."

Evan released his held breath.

"The police wouldn't have a hope of finding Hoodie Man without him," he said.

"I know. Which is why I don't know whether to send him flowers or arrest him." She checked the time on her phone. Scowled. "Where's Diana?"

"She hasn't reached out." More for him to worry about. "Addie, we can't just stay here while—while—God knows what is happening."

She bit her lip. Nodded. "You're right. Wait for me. I'll get my car."

Chapter 28

River

A long sword.

The hell?

River flung himself to the side as the sword's tip rang against the pavement hard enough to raise sparks. The blade missed River by inches.

River rolled onto his back. His struggle to escape put him within inches of the dead man's head. The contorted face leered at him through gaping eyes and an agonized mouth.

The sword sang on its downward arc. River caught a glimpse of the man's grip on the hilt—white skin, strong tendons. Light rippled along the blade's edge.

River raised his arms to knock the blade away.

The man twisted the blade sideways, slamming the flat of the weapon down on River's abdomen. Pain flared like a blowtorch through River's body. His breath left him with the suddenness of a slamming door.

He rolled again in anticipation of the next blow, sucking for air, scrambling to get his feet under him. Panting, he rose to a crouch, ready to dive low against his attacker. He would duck beneath the sword and bowl the man over.

He'd done it before.

Nothing stirred. Where the man had been, there was only the night.

River pressed his back against one of the shuttered shops. He unzipped his jacket and reached under his shirt, felt a sticky wetness.

"Shit," he whispered. He probed his flesh and found two parallel cuts where the edges of the blade had cut into his skin from the force of the blow.

How stupid he'd been not to anticipate that Hoodie Man could have stashed a weapon earlier. There were hundreds of places along the river to conceal things the size of a sword. He'd expected a knife, perhaps even a gun. But a man who killed another by cutting him nearly in two didn't do things in half measures.

The question that hung in the air was why hadn't Hoodie Man used his advantage to leave River's head on the sidewalk?

He pressed his shirt against the wounds until the bleeding slowed, then zipped his jacket to protect the injury and stepped back onto the pavement. He squatted next to the decapitated head.

To the west, lightning flashed. The wind kicked up, stirred the braided hair on the head. Rain fell.

Empty eyes stared blankly up at him. Not a human head. Just as they'd suspected, it was a mask. The latex was remarkably skin-like; the hair looked real. Even the fake blood seemed genuine.

Now they knew for certain: high-quality masks were how the killer was eluding them and the PODs.

He snapped a photo, sent it to Evan with a single word: mask.

He rose to his feet, ignoring the throbbing in his gut, and kept moving.

At the next bend, he once again slowed and rounded the curve cautiously. Straight ahead, an immense double-decker bridge spanned the water. The DuSable Bridge, according to a lighted sign.

He sent Evan another text.

Movement drew his eye. Halfway up the stairs, a figure stood with his back to River. When the figure turned around, a streetlamp revealed the face of an old man. In one hand, the man held a giant blade, the tip resting against the top stair. With his other hand, he tapped his chest three times.

River responded with his middle finger.

The man laughed, the sound of it echoing along the concrete.

"Your move," the man called. A young man's voice behind an old man's face. "What will it be, River Wilding?"

Lightning crackled. Clouds raced overhead.

The man turned and vanished into the night, the sword held aloft as if it weighed nothing.

His breath hissing between his teeth, River charged up the stairs after him.

✣

At the top of the stairs, the walls closed in, and River felt like he'd entered the belly of the beast.

Straight ahead, traffic whizzed through a tunnel. There was no sidewalk and no sign of Hoodie Man.

On his left, the path curved toward a pedestrian walkway that ran along a service road. The service road—part of the DuSable Bridge—lay beneath what River guessed was Michigan Avenue.

To River's right, homeless people slept beneath tarps and blankets, huddled as far from the traffic as possible.

River ran his gaze over the sleeping forms, looking for any sign that Hoodie Man might be hiding among them. There were ten, maybe twelve, people. Liquor bottles twinkled in the passing headlights, and the remains of a bucket fire smoldered. The area smelled of vomit and cigarette smoke and the fumes of cars.

But no one stirred. Nothing suggested a man's recent passage.

A cry echoed from beneath the bridge. River followed the sound, moving left onto the pedestrian path.

A dead gloom lay over the sidewalk and the steel structure supporting the bridge above. Occasional traffic rumbled by overhead, but down here, the only sound was the rising wail of the storm. Widely spaced LED lights cast an eerie glow as the beams reflected off steel and concrete.

Another shout, weaker this time.

River stepped onto the bridge. In the cold light, he spotted a homeless man who had set up camp behind the low cement barrier where the bridge's steel superstructure was anchored. He stared at River through one good eye.

The other eye was a bloody socket. Fresh blood sheeted down his left cheek.

A flash of lightning turned the world silver for an instant.

River blinked away the afterglow.

The homeless man had risen on shaky legs. "Why'd he hurt me?"

River held up his hands. "Stay there. I'll get help."

He pressed his back against the railing that separated the sidewalk from the river and its roughly fifteen-foot drop, standing as far away from the homeless man as possible. He didn't trust anyone.

He glanced up and down the pathway, then pulled out his phone. By now, the pain in his abdomen had turned into a white-hot fire that was eating him from the inside. His shirt was soaked with blood. Dizziness made his vision wobble.

With the grace of a leopard, the homeless man cleared the cement barrier and came at River.

In his gloved left hand, he swung a chain.

A thought flashed through River's head: *He's got an entire arsenal stashed.*

River ducked, dodging the chain as it whipped overhead. He scrambled sideways, looking for a weapon of his own. All he saw were plastic cups, crumpled take-out bags, cardboard drink trays. A discarded pacifier.

The man adjusted, following him, the chain snaking through the air. River darted behind a bridge girder. The girder vibrated as the chain slammed against it.

"You need to learn the rules of the game," the man said.

River tried to place the man's voice. Couldn't. "You're TR," he growled.

"Same."

There. Just on the other side of the road. A three-foot section of galvanized pipe next to the cement barrier.

Keep him talking.

"Theseus Rex?" River asked.

The chain struck the girder again. The man's laughter bounced among the steel supports. "Go on digging, pretty boy. You'll figure it out. Assuming you live long enough."

"Where's Ursula?"

The man and the chain fell silent.

River darted across the road, snatched up the pipe, spun around just in time to block the man's swing.

The chain struck the pipe and whipped around it, slicing away a piece of River's skin below his eye as it spun. River yanked the pipe toward him. The man gripped the chain and let River pull him close.

"Ursula is where she deserves to be," the man snarled. "Where they all deserve to be."

River pulled him closer.

"I'm Távros," the man said, and opened his mouth wide.

River shoved the pipe down, reared back, and headbutted the man, catching him in the ear as the man jerked away. The man roared in pain, spun River around, and rammed him. His greater weight broke River's grip on the pipe and sent him crashing into the street. The chain unspooled from the steel pipe, which clattered against the asphalt and rolled away.

River flipped onto his back, drew his bent knees to his face, arched his spine, and hurled himself to his feet. The man swung the chain and smiled.

A horn sounded, echoing in the tight space. Headlights flared.

River dove to the opposite side of the road, toward the railing. The car sped by with a long thrum of its horn.

"You dumb shit!" the driver yelled.

The car disappeared.

Távros had ditched the chain and picked up the sword. The blade rippled in the icy lights.

"That first time I hit you? That was a love tap." The man wove the blade back and forth. It hissed in the night like a snake. "I'd planned to kill you later. But now I'm angry."

Távros was built like a bull. Strong through the shoulders. Wide. Tall. He didn't fight like a street brawler. He'd trained somewhere. Trained well and often.

He cut the sword wide through the air; there came a whisper that could disembowel a man. Or separate a man's head from his shoulders.

River had won more than one battle through dogged determination—an ability to take a beatdown and keep standing. Three cheers for testosterone. But testosterone was a poor excuse for a fight, especially one you might well lose with, let's face it, fatal consequences.

Which left him with really only two choices: He could run. Or he could jump.

He planted his hands on top of the railing along the edge of the bridge.

The man raced toward him, the sword's fatal edge whistling.

River threw himself over the railing.

He dropped like a missile, arrowing cleanly into the river. Lukewarm water closed over him. He dove smoothly, then pivoted and pushed himself to the surface.

His head broke free. The water churned, and he swallowed a mouthful of what tasted like pond scum.

He spat.

All around lay inky darkness. Rain pelted the water, which rose and fell in the wind. Chicago's stunning skyline filled his vision.

Above him, the bridge was empty. Távros had vanished.

For a moment, dazed, River floated. River in a river. His parents had wanted all of them to have a *V* in their name. The patriarch, Oliver, and his wife, Olivia. Then Evan. And finally, River. The English aristocrat's version of everyone wearing blue jeans in the family photo. But why River? Why not Victor or Vince or Devin?

His feet were numb. The river was carrying him along. He shook himself and struck for the north shore, slicing through the water in an easy freestyle stroke. He reached the river's edge and swam along the cement embankment until he came to a pipe that extended over the water. He hauled himself out and lay gasping on the pavement while the blowtorch, momentarily stunned into quiet, resumed its merciless work on his stomach.

Footsteps. River pushed himself to his feet. He scrabbled in the near-dark for a weapon. His fist closed over a ballpoint pen. He raised his right arm.

Eyes or neck or throat. Or, with the right angle and enough momentum, a ballpoint pen could pierce a man's heart.

The beam from a flashlight ran over him, motes of light dancing in the rain.

Then Diana's voice, laced with worry and disbelief. "A pen?"

River glanced past her toward the stairs leading up to the service road and Michigan Avenue. Rain lashed the pavement, wind shook the handful of trees.

Nothing else moved.

He lowered his hand.

"I've always heard," he said, "the pen is mightier than the sword."

CHAPTER 29

EVAN

Standing in his gourmet kitchen, Evan yanked open the freezer door. River sat at the table behind him.

"You could have been *killed*," Evan said, eyeing a pack of frozen steaks.

"But I wasn't," River replied calmly.

Evan frowned into the freezer's depths.

Thus it had always been: Evan pointing out River's close calls, and River reminding him that close calls only counted in horseshoes and hand grenades.

"He could have *had* a hand grenade," Evan said. "He's a killer."

"But he didn't. And now we have a name. Távros."

"You couldn't bother getting a last name while you were trying to get yourself killed?"

"Other things seemed more important at the time."

Evan grunted, pushing aside a batch of frozen burritos.

After Diana had found River and phoned Evan, he'd alerted Addie. Nearly a dozen squad cars had descended on Michigan and on Upper Wacker. Addie steered River to one of the cars, sent someone off for an ice pack for his budding black eye, and peppered him with questions.

He'd huddled in his jacket and told them everything he remembered of what the man had said. He told them that the man—Távros—had a sword stashed, and a chain, and that he owned at least three masks, and no, he didn't recognize his voice. And no, he hadn't seen enough of the man other than when he was masked to offer a description. Addie had sent patrol and crime-scene techs back along the DuSable Bridge and the pathway on the south shore, hunting for River's assailant, collecting whatever evidence they could find.

They'd interviewed Diana as well, but by the time she'd reached River, his attacker appeared to be gone. She'd had little to add to his story.

After an hour, Evan had put up his hand and said enough. Addie relented after River promised to call if he remembered anything else. Evan and Diana had brought him home, propped him on a chair in the kitchen, and while Evan gave him the universal healing balm of black tea and milk, Diana went to the store for first-aid supplies and an antidiarrheal just in case. Drinking water from the Chicago River was never a good idea.

"Peas," Evan said, still riffling through the freezer's contents. "It's all I've got for the black eye. Diana will bring antiseptic for the cut on your cheek. Are you sure you're okay?"

"It's a flesh wound."

"That's what you said when someone opened your shoulder with a bayonet." Evan turned around, peas in hand, and said, "Oh, God."

River had removed his jacket and unbuttoned his shirt, exposing what Evan recognized as the imprint from the flat of a blade: two parallel cuts seeping blood with purplish bruising in between that revealed the sword's fuller—a groove in the metal used to lighten and strengthen the blade.

The imprint was as clear as a photo.

Evan tossed the peas onto the table. "God's wounds, River. You didn't say he *hit* you with the sword. Just that he had one."

"Help me with my shirt."

Evan helped River ease off the wet shirt. He dampened a clean dishrag and dabbed at the wound.

River winced. "He was well trained. It wasn't much of a fight."

"He tried to *vivisect* you. Why didn't you say anything about this to the police?"

"And get Addie in trouble because one of her civilian experts was in danger? And while I hate to say it, if Távros had wanted to cut me in two, I gave him ample opportunity. He wanted to hurt me, not kill me. At least during our first encounter. He got kind of pissed off after a while."

"Swive and sard, I'm not surprised."

"Medieval swearing, Evan?"

"Shut up. I could kill you myself." Evan heard the front door open and called to Diana. "Hurry, please!"

River stared glumly at his injury. "I fell for the innocent-bystander trick. I have *never* fallen for the innocent-bystander trick."

"It's because you're in Chicago. Cities make people soft."

"I'm now the poster child for soft."

"Remember that the next time you decide to go after a killer," Evan said. "You said he was trained?"

"Definitely trained."

Evan straightened. "I'll get you a shirt, and then we're going to the hospital."

"No hospitals. No doctors."

Diana walked into the kitchen carrying a plastic bag. She narrowed her eyes at the sight of River's abdomen.

"He could have internal injuries," Evan said. "But he refuses to go to the ER. That's because he's afraid of doctors."

"Doctors *are* scary," River protested. "Scalpels and needles."

"You talk him into it, Diana."

Diana washed her hands and knelt in front of River. She took the dishrag from Evan and finished cleaning away the blood. "The cuts are superficial."

"Told you," River said to Evan.

"Take a deep breath. Does that hurt?"

"No broken ribs," River said. "The only thing broken is my ego."

Diana glanced at Evan. "There's a risk of infection, but he doesn't need stitches. But you're right about internal injuries. He could have ruptured his liver or spleen." She turned back to River. "Either you go to the doctor, or you let me palpate your stomach."

Alarmed, Evan said, "You're not a doctor."

"I'm not. But I spent four winter breaks working search and rescue in the Colorado Rockies. I know how to check for internal injuries." She looked up into River's face. "It's going to hurt like a mother. Can you take it?"

"I've had shaving cuts that were worse."

"Tough guy. Evan, wash your hands, then bring that bag over." She looked at Evan and frowned. "And if you're going to be sick, go lie down. I don't need two patients."

"The hospital." Evan crossed his arms. "And a doctor. An actual doctor."

Diana ignored him, as she so often did. "Bring some whiskey, too."

"Single malt," River added. "Best you've got."

Seeing that it was two against one and knowing that River could go toe to hoof with the most recalcitrant mule, Evan threw up his hands. He hauled out a bottle of rotgut whiskey a friend had given him as a joke. "I'm not wasting my good stuff. You'll drink this for the pain, or you're off to the hospital."

River squinted at the label. "I drink that, I'll *need* to go to the hospital."

River gasped as Diana palpated the upper left quadrant of his abdomen.

"You're soft," she said. "That's good."

River frowned. "I am not soft." He gasped again as she shifted to his right side.

"Want to reconsider the hospital?" Evan asked.

River reached for the bottle.

✣

An hour later, a freshly showered and bandaged River lay snoring in the guest room. Perro snored on the floor next to the bed.

"I'll take first shift," Diana said. "Get some sleep. I'll wake you up in a couple of hours."

"You don't have to stay."

"You want me to leave?"

He shook his head.

"Well, then." She gave him a gentle push. "Go. Rest."

He took a last glance at River before Diana closed the door. He yawned and made his way down the hall toward his bedroom. Just as he finished brushing his teeth, his phone buzzed.

Addie.

She was at the front door.

✣

He turned on the bulb over the stove, keeping the lighting soft, and opened the refrigerator while Addie took a seat at the kitchen table. Evan had long ago realized that food fixed a lot of things. And those things it couldn't fix, it at least made more manageable.

He set out a plate of cold chicken and sliced peaches he'd marinated in bourbon. He placed dishes and napkins and cutlery on the table. He opened sparkling water.

"Coffee?" he asked.

"No." She gave a tired smile. "Thanks."

They sat next to each other at the table. Evan waited her out. He made small talk about Perro's upcoming vet check and Ginny's new proclivity for steak. He'd learned long ago that Addie would get to why she was here when she was ready.

She reached across him for the bowl of peaches, and Evan was aware of her warmth where their shoulders touched.

"Marcus called," she said.

"Ah."

Here it was. She'd come because Evan had a generous shoulder on which a friend could lean. He was glad for that.

But it wasn't always easy.

She picked up the bowl. "He wanted to know why I hadn't come over."

"You've been busy."

"That's what I told him. But it wasn't the only reason."

He waited. She stared at the peaches.

"About last night," she said. "I'm sorry."

"You're sorry for what? I'm still a bit confused as to what happened. Or didn't happen."

She sat back and scooped peaches onto her plate. "I think I *almost* kissed you."

"And I stopped you."

"I overstepped." Addie's gaze seemed glued to the damn peaches. "Which is why I'm apologizing."

Gently, Evan removed the bowl from her hand. He stood and carried it to the counter. He needed distance in order to give himself courage.

He cleared his throat. "In order for someone to overstep, there has to be a line. I don't remember establishing a line."

She kept her eyes down. "The line has always been there, Evan. From the beginning, almost from the moment we met, you've made it clear that we're friends and not more, and you don't want to mess that up. And now I'm supposed to marry Marcus. And you have a gaggle of girlfriends."

He busied himself putting plastic wrap over the fruit. "I never said that. And I do not have a gaggle of girlfriends."

She sniffed. "You could have a gaggle if you wanted. Half your grad students are in love with you."

"That's so not okay. And they're not. Or if they were, I wouldn't—I'd never—"

Addie plowed on. "It's the same with the faculty. They adore you."

"Adoration isn't love."

"Plus, you tell me all the time that friends shouldn't become lovers. You say things like—"

"*You* said friends shouldn't become lovers. I took my cue from you."

"I didn't." Addie lifted her gaze at last and scowled at him. "When did I say that?"

"When I met your oldest brother. You said John ruined the best friendship he ever had by marrying the woman. Their marriage lasted three months, and they haven't spoken since. And, lest you forget, there was that time we went to see *Romeo and Juliet*. You said Romeo should have stuck with his best friend, Mercutio, and left Juliet with the Capulets."

She burst out laughing, then quickly sobered. "Did I really say that?"

"You were mad at men, as I recall. Plus, you like your guys tall. Really tall."

"I can be shallow," she admitted. "But that tall thing was just a phase."

He was afraid to hear her. "Marcus Martin is tall, and you're practically engaged. And I, in case you haven't noticed, am not tall."

"That doesn't—"

"Matter? It doesn't matter?" He placed the peaches in the refrigerator and let the door slam. "Have you really thought about this, Addie? Dating a dwarf? There we'd be, walking down the street, content in our own little world. And then you'd notice people staring. Not because you're gorgeous, which you are. And not because you have spinach in your teeth, which you sometimes do. But because you're holding hands with me."

"Why do you focus on the one thing you can't change to the exclusion of everything else?" She drew a breath. "Maybe I'm not the only shallow one."

"Maybe I'm the only realist."

"Come sit down," she said softly.

"Why?"

"So that we can talk. Of course I've thought about this, Evan. I'm not willfully blind. But it doesn't matter. And that's my truth. And maybe I'm making a complete fool of myself. But I need to know your truth."

"My truth."

She gave a rueful smile. "I've heard it can set you free."

He took a chair, but he felt like he was standing on the edge of a cliff. He closed his eyes and made the leap.

"The truth is," he said, "when I met you, it was coup de foudre."

"It was what?"

Heat rose in Evan's face until he was sure he was the unappetizing color of beef. He willed his eyes open. "Coup de foudre. It's—it means . . ."

He stuttered to a stop and stared at Addie, who was staring back at him with an unreadable expression.

"I took French in high school," she said. "I know what it means. Love at first sight. Is that what you're trying to tell me?"

He looked down at his hands. His small hands. His short fingers. He was a man who'd wanted to play Liszt on the piano but could really only manage the controls on the stereo.

Oh, hell and damnation. What good was life if you didn't—at least once—reach for the brass ring?

What if, for once, it was your turn to catch it?

"Yes, Addie," he said. "'Twas always thus. Ever—"

She placed the tip of her right index finger against his lips, pausing his next words. Then she leaned in and kissed him.

Her lips were softer than he'd imagined, and her sweet scent was something the gods themselves would long for. He touched her hair, letting the curls twine themselves around his fingers, then dropped his hands to her shoulders. He pulled her closer. He tasted peaches on her lips and the smoky undercurrent of bourbon.

She pressed the palm of her hand against his chest and released a deep, trembling sigh.

"*That's* what I wanted," she whispered against his lips.

"And I. Ever since you spilled our drinks at that art show."

She laughed, her breath light on his skin.

It was a moment of pure, sweet joy.

Then came a sound at the entrance to the kitchen, and Evan and Addie sprang apart.

"Sorry," Diana said as she entered the room, eyes averted. "I came to get River some water."

Addie stood. "I need to go."

"Please don't let me interrupt," Diana said from the sink.

"No. It's late."

Evan walked Addie to the front. He was pretty sure his feet didn't touch the ground. He opened the door for her.

She grinned. "Still worried?" she asked.

"I confess to having visions of Marcus Martin paying me a house call."

"Sic Perro on him. He's terrified of dogs."

He took her hand. "Tell me this is real."

"It's real, Professor. We've spoken our truth."

"What took us so long?"

"Shared idiocy."

She kissed him once more, brushed her fingers through his tangle of curls, and walked away. He watched her until she got in her SUV, and then again until the car vanished around a bend in the long driveway.

The night felt suddenly empty.

✣

After Addie left, Evan knew he wouldn't sleep. He insisted that Diana go home and get some rest. He'd watch over River.

"Keep checking for fever," she told him. "But those old antibiotics you had will help with any infection and mitigate the effects of whatever sewer water he drank. If he complains of dizziness or takes a turn for the worse, get him to the doctor. No matter what he says."

He knew that in addition to River's injuries, she was thinking of CSO: the combined sewer overflow that happened in Chicago during the kind of monsoon they were experiencing. The thought of River—of *anyone*—taking a bath in that filth made Evan's skin crawl.

"Got it," he said.

"You sure you don't want me to stay?"

Evan wanted nothing more. But he said, "I promise I'll call you if he's having trouble. Get some sleep."

She eyed him frankly. "I'd tell you the same, but I won't waste my breath."

Evan watched her walk to her car, then closed and locked the front door and set the alarm.

He went back into the guest room. Neither Perro nor his brother had moved, although both—mercifully—had stopped snoring. Evan picked the most uncomfortable chair in the room so that he wouldn't fall asleep and settled in for the watch.

His thoughts, of course, went immediately to Addie. After all these years as friends, what had caused her to change her mind?

Our truth, she'd said.

His mind was a tumble of joy and terror. What might their future be? Did they have a future? Only if friends could become lovers without destroying their friendship. Only if being in love with Addie—a notorious serial dater—didn't turn into a train wreck and ruin their affection for each other.

River and Perro both stirred, Perro's tags jingling. Evan half rose from his chair. But the pair settled, and he resumed his seat. The clock on the desk ticked its relentless forward journey. Perhaps there was a place for him and Addie in the future. Perhaps not. He would do what he always did when events were out of his control: live fully in the moment and be grateful for what he had.

Calmer, he turned his mind to the task at hand.

He knew Addie would investigate the killer's use of masks—where the disguises might have been purchased and customized, any trace evidence or DNA from the mask that Távros had discarded. They were still waiting for DNA results from the bite mark. And God knew what else: possible witnesses; a conversation with last night's minotaur, Owen Teufel; further analysis of the POD videos; a search for any Chicago-based friends of Ursula's—friends she might be visiting.

Although, given what the killer had said to River, he doubted Ursula was laughing it up somewhere with her pals.

She was where they all deserved to be, the killer had told River. Did that mean she was dead? And what others was the killer referring to?

Solve the riddle before the sacrifice is made.

"What damn riddle?" he whispered.

As more information came in, Addie and Patrick would start to figure out the who.

Evan needed to focus on the why.

Távros. Not a real name, Evan suspected. Távros was the name of a suburb of Athens. And a hotel. It was also the Greek word for *bull.*

The name was part of whatever game the killer was playing.

Evan pulled up a map of Crete on his phone and zoomed in on castle ruins, monasteries, mountains, gorges, lakes, and beaches. Crete was the largest Greek island and the most populous. After its early Minoan history, the island had been alternately overrun and ruled by the Greeks, the Romans, the Byzantine Empire, the Arabs, the Venetians, and the Ottomans—all of whom had vented their empire-building tendencies on the local populace. Crete had suffered through two world wars and its own civil war before settling down to become a hugely popular tourist destination.

All of which Evan found personally fascinating. But none of which offered the faintest glimmer as to why the killer had become unhinged over Cretan Hieroglyphic and the Minotaur.

Which elements most intrigued him? The powerful flesh-eating monster? The man-beast who'd been betrayed by his father and sister? The symbolism of the labyrinth?

Or was it just a good kick-ass story he'd read in middle school?

Seemed like a good idea at the time, he could imagine the killer saying. *Vivisecting people. Biting their throats. Writing undecipherable symbols on them.*

All part of the fun, you know.

He pulled up the letter Fishbourne had left on his porch.

Evan, we have yet to meet. River, you won't remember me.

When had River met Távros? And had the man been using that name?

Evan opened multiple academic databases, looking for scholars with the initials TR that were linked to either Cretan history and archaeology or any of its scripts. He found exactly four, none with the first name Távros. The first researcher was deceased. The second was a woman, which didn't fit River's description of the killer or his voice. The third was—per the man's social media accounts—in his eighties and enjoying a vacation in Norway. And the fourth had been paralyzed from the waist down in a skiing accident three years earlier.

Across the room, River stirred and muttered.

Evan hopped off the chair and went to press his hand to River's forehead; his brother's skin was cool, his color good. As Evan leaned over, River murmured something incomprehensible before settling again.

Evan returned to the chair. He stared across the room at his brother and tried *not* to imagine a world without River in it.

A line of conversation drifted up from his past. Something his mother had said to his dad.

It's all you care about! she'd shouted as Oliver Wilding stood by the front door, suitcase in hand. *The next treasure. The next sacred drug. The next fleeting thing that will make you famous. You want to save humanity, but what about your own wife? What about your sons?*

River wasn't Oliver Wilding. Mainly because he wasn't a jerk. But the two certainly had a few things in common. Maybe that was why Oliver had kept the lines of communication open with his younger son. He sensed a comrade in arms.

Evan left the room long enough to make more tea.

When he came back, he checked on River—no change—then pulled up his university email account. Earlier that evening, the registrar had sent him the list Diana requested: the names of everyone who had preregistered for the talk he'd given a month ago on the Phaistos Disc. The registrar had also sent a scanned copy of those who'd signed in and paid at the door.

He recognized the names of several of his students, some of whom would be genuinely interested in the Phaistos Disc, others who would have been more interested in impressing Evan with their studiousness. Several faculty members had also attended.

There were plenty of names he didn't recognize—presumably classics or linguistics students and members of the public, and only one with the initials TR: Tijhomir Radoslaw, a professor of Slavic studies and an unlikely candidate for a sword-wielding killer.

He turned to the scanned sheet, which held twenty names.

Not even one TR.

But one name stood out. Morgan Hargrave had signed in with a flourish.

Evan chewed the inside of his cheek.

Morgan had mentioned his interest in the Phaistos Disc when they'd met at the theater. Did his interest stem from the fact that his son and daughter were in *The King and the Minotaur*? It wasn't as if the Phaistos Disc and its script had anything to do, per se, with the myth of the Minotaur. That is, outside of their birthplace on Crete. But Morgan struck Evan as the kind of man who'd enjoy dropping intellectual missiles into any conversation just to show he was the smartest man in the room. He could imagine Morgan saying, *Did you know that the Phaistos Disc is the world's earliest example of movable type?* while his son and daughter poured themselves more wine and thought, *Dad's shouting up our asses from atop his lectern again.*

But given that Morgan Hargrave had two links to the play—his children and his briefly mentioned relationship with Jamal James—Evan decided he'd do a little digging into the good scientist.

He fetched his laptop from the study and seated himself at the guest room's small desk. Perro woke and came over, ears perked. Evan found a toy for the corgi, and Perro settled on the floor nearby.

Evan opened a tab on his browser and typed, **Dr. Morgan P. Hargrave.**

Google returned a generous listing.

Morgan Hargrave was a social psychologist who had made a name for himself while still in his twenties through his carefully designed studies of good and evil in infants and children. Morgan had theorized that most children were born with a propensity to be good members of society, allowing, of course, for a few shades of gray. The rest would be social deviants.

Nurture could save some of the deviants. The rest were doomed by their genes.

And the sooner parents and educators knew about the doomed child, the more prepared they'd be for what was coming.

The idea that some children were born evil was an interesting, if deeply unpleasant, hypothesis. It was true that psychopaths had atypical brains—a larger-than-typical striatum, for example, and reduced gray matter in one area of the prefrontal cortex, among other differences.

But to suggest that any human was decisively evil before the world had time to act on him or her? Before he himself had a chance to act? That no matter what kind of parenting that child received, he or she was doomed to play the role of the devil?

What was next? Imprisoning those for whom childhood studies suggested a predisposition? Having them arrested, convicted, and sentenced by their brain scans and then sent off to the island of Dr. Moreau?

"It's chilling," Evan whispered to Perro.

Perro growled at his toy, which refused to relinquish its treat.

Morgan had conducted multiple studies with a large group of sixty children. Then a subset of more intensive research focused on a smaller group of children whom Morgan had followed from infancy to early adolescence.

Most of the children were designated "good" using the admittedly ingenious ways Morgan had devised to test even the very young for signs of compassion and altruism.

But two members of the group had shown signs in infancy of preferring bad actors. Both children went on to become troublemakers at home and at school.

Had the children known they'd been designated "bad"? Had their parents?

With all of Morgan's research, did he have any suggestions as to how to change the life course of such a child?

Evan scratched his beard and stared into the middle space.

More immediately relevant was how Morgan knew Jamal James. Were Jamal's friends—the ones Morgan had mentioned—other students in the study?

None of the children's names appeared, of course. Subjects weren't identified in studies of this type. Especially when the subjects were minors.

Evan returned his gaze to the screen and resumed reading.

Morgan was still very much a respected scientist. His most recent paper, "The Risks and Rewards of Empathic Thinking," had come out three months earlier. That paper listed his research lab as the Remington Foundation for Child Development. Evan googled it and found an address for a Remington Foundation in Arlington Heights. He went to the website and zeroed in on the logo for the foundation. The outline of a head in profile, with a unicursal maze where the brain would normally be.

What did the logo mean? The most obvious answer was that the human brain is a puzzle. But was Hargrave also using a metaphor to illustrate the results of his research: that, potentially, at the center of each human mind, there lurked a monster?

Evan pushed back his wayward curls, a distant part of his brain noting that he needed a haircut.

Perro squeak-growled his joy as his toy gave up its treasure.

What Evan truly needed were answers. He wished he could be as certain as Perro that the trail he was following led to a treasure.

He looked up Morgan's home in Daysville, a two-hour drive west from the heart of Chicago. An hour and a half drive from Morgan's home to his lab in Arlington Heights. The Hargrave residence was a mansion built in the Greek Revival style. Google Earth photos showed a large hedge maze occupying the space between the house and a river.

Another maze.

"No treat inside that puzzle," Evan murmured to Perro.

But the corgi had fallen asleep. Across the room, River began to snore again. Evan checked his brother's temperature, then went back to Morgan's earliest papers. The social scientist's fourth, fifth, and seventh papers listed a coauthor. Philomena Hargrave. Wife? Sister? Critical response to the articles suggested Philomena was the genius behind the studies, that her name should have been listed before Morgan's.

Philomena was a Greek name meaning "a loved one" or "a courageous lover."

Evan looked up the name and found a lengthy obituary.

> It is with great sadness that the family of Philomena Hargrave announces her passing. Mrs. Hargrave died at her home on July 13, 2010. Mrs. Hargrave was a brilliant social scientist who graduated with a PhD from Stanford University in 1988 and who worked alongside her husband, Morgan Hargrave, conducting child behavioral studies.

The next two paragraphs discussed Philomena's support of Doctors Without Borders and the work she had done to raise money for organizations that served the homeless.

> She is survived by her husband, Morgan, and their sons, Lowell and Peter Hargrave.

Evan reread that line. Lowell and Peter. No mention of Emma.

There followed a long paragraph about Philomena's hobbies—painting and embroidery—and her athletic awards in tennis and golf.

Philomena Hargrave had been a very busy woman.

> Numerous friends and colleagues came to St. Vincent de Paul to pay their respects to Mrs. Hargrave and her family. The eulogy was delivered by noted scientist and National Geographic Explorer, the Right Honourable Oliver J. Wilding.

Evan stared. Then glanced over at River, who snored peacefully on. He returned to the obituary.

The Right Honourable Oliver Wilding. British spelling and all.

Maybe it shouldn't have been a surprise. Morgan Hargrave had mentioned their friendship. But it still came as a gut punch that Oliver Wilding had time to deliver a eulogy when he didn't have time to visit his sons.

"Well, Dad," Evan said softly, "you never cease to amaze. Or disappoint."

CHAPTER 30

ADDIE

The alarm clock blasted Addie awake after only a few hours' sleep. Hours disturbed by nightmares in which she found Ursula Fishbourne tortured and dead, buried in a shallow grave.

Blearily, Addie planted her feet on the floor, pulled on leggings and a sweatshirt, then staggered into the kitchen. Bright sun slanted into her apartment. She glared at the light for a moment, then yanked down the shade.

She was still fuming over their failure to capture Hoodie Man. Or rather, Távros.

Távros not-his-real-name-world-class-horror.

She stabbed the "Start" button on her coffee maker, then dropped a bagel into the toaster and dug cream cheese out of the refrigerator. She checked her phone for messages, but nothing had come in while she'd been comatose.

She made herself slow her headlong dive into work and paused long enough to recall what had happened after the night went to hell.

Evan.

The thing she'd been afraid of for years—that romance would kill their friendship—hadn't felt that way at all. It had felt like she was exactly where she should have been all along.

She didn't know what she was going to tell Marcus. But the relief that she wasn't going to be Mrs. Marcus Martin felt as if she'd extracted a bad tooth. It left an ache, but the release was exquisite.

She guessed that pretty much said everything.

She reopened the blind, thinking that sunshine was a good sign. Maybe the monsoon had broken, just like her own idiocy. She hummed under her breath as she grabbed a mug out of the cupboard and returned to her coffee machine.

Which had done nothing in her absence. She pressed the "Start" button again, more gently. Nothing. Checked the plug. Made sure she'd filled the water reservoir.

Still nothing.

"I need coffee," she told it as if the desperation in her voice would persuade the machine to work. She wondered if smashing the thing against the counter would qualify her for anger-management classes. She was saved from having to learn the answer when Patrick phoned.

"I heard Evan's brother is a real chancer," Patrick said. "Got himself in a wee bit of trouble last night."

Word sure traveled fast. Especially for someone like Patrick, who was part of the good-old-boy network.

"He also got Hoodie Man to admit to being TR," she said. "Or Távros, as he apparently prefers. TR, the letter writer. And perhaps the same TR who drew Barlow."

"And he did it while managing to stay alive."

"I know, Patrick. It wasn't supposed to go down that way."

"For sure, lass, catching the killer is more important than the embolism the lieutenant's probably having as we speak."

"Thanks for that."

"We'll send flowers. And I have to give it to you, you were right to trust your gut on this whole 'TR' thing. Surprising, given how little you've got to work with. Your gut, I mean."

"As opposed to you."

"Ouch, Adrianne Marie. I'll have you know Mary's got me on a strict diet. But Rome wasn't built in a day."

Mary, Patrick's beloved wife, was straight from the green hills of County Cork.

"Or torn down in a day, either, presumably," Addie said.

"Keep digging."

Addie placed the toasted bagel on a plate and carried it to the table. She filled Patrick in on her version of the events of the previous night, leaving out only her private conversation with Evan.

She also shared what little she'd learned about William Barlow, including his death.

"I've been wondering how TR managed to draw such a good likeness of Barlow," she said. "I couldn't find any photo he might have used as a guide. Here's my current theory, which I admit is weak. Could the kid who reported seeing Barlow with another adult and a kid—could that have been TR? Which we now know would make him Távros."

"You think Távros knew where Barlow lived and was spying on him?"

"It would explain where he got that likeness. Maybe even go toward him growing up to be a killer himself. Have you heard the rumors that Barlow wasn't acting alone?"

"I thought it was an attorney ploy more than anything. But it makes for interesting speculation. If the kid was telling the truth, then it places Barlow with another adult and maybe one of his victims. Did the kid provide a description?"

"It wasn't in the article, and the journalist is no longer among the living."

"Things have to start breaking our way, Adrianne Marie."

"That they do, Patrick McBrady. Any progress in Garden City? Have you talked to Detective Tom Walsh yet? Was he able to shed any light on the bull symbol?"

"I just finished, if you could call it a talk. The good people of Sunset Village kicked me out and asked that I not return."

"What did you do wrong?"

"I so appreciate the leaps you take. It's not as if I stole someone's wheelchair and went joyriding. I showed Tom the symbol from the tree house, the one he sent to Evan, and he started a high-pitched cry that would give a banshee the shivers. When the staff couldn't get him to calm down, they bounced me out on my ear."

"You think he was reacting to the symbol?"

"I'm no mind reader, but I can put two and two together and not get five. He seemed fine just before I showed him the symbol. Not clear in the head, exactly. But he smiled and said something that sounded like hello, even if he didn't have a good goddamn who I was. Then I showed him our favorite sign, and the screaming started."

Addie was staring at a cow-shaped porcelain pitcher sitting on the table. She wasn't known for her housekeeping skills, but she was pretty sure the pitcher had been in the buffet her parents had given her, along with the rest of her mother's dishes.

A faint unease traveled along her skin, a prickle like an electrical current.

She reached out a finger and touched the porcelain cow. "What kind of years-old case would upset him that much?"

"I've been scratching my head," Patrick said. "Cops like Tom, the ones who've been around the block from age twenty until retirement, they've seen everything. They don't *get* spooked."

Addie grabbed hold of his words. *Cops don't get spooked.* She'd forgotten that she'd taken the pitcher out of the buffet, that was all. Maybe when one of her friends had dropped by a few days ago for coffee.

She carried the pitcher back to the buffet. "It could be that cops with dementia get spooked."

"Promise you'll shoot me before that happens."

"I'll probably shoot you long before then. You have a Plan B?"

"Tom's wife agreed to see me. I'm heading over there now. What have you got on your docket today?"

"I want to have a chat with Owen Teufel, the Minotaur who went after Evan in the theater maze. Then Emma Hargrave, see if she recognized Távros when he approached her last night. And I want to talk to Fishbourne's neighbors, see if any of them were living there when Ursula and her friends were using that tree house. Plus, I've got Ursula's yearbook."

"Don't forget to squeeze in Mass and a Sunday drive because you need your downtime. Isn't that what the sergeant is always telling us?"

"Not helpful, Paddy Wagon." Her unoriginal nickname for him, which usually made him smile.

"If the rest of the team's buried, let me call Bob Carlson, bring him up to speed, and get him to pitch in on the interviews with Fishbourne's neighbors. He's better than a father confessor."

"The lieutenant hasn't approved overtime," Addie reminded him.

"Bob will do it, anyway. He's been pining away on the weekends since his kids flew the nest and his wife decided she'd rather live with her sister. Now there's a blow to a man's ego. Have the techs gotten to the tree house yet?"

"Sergeant approved it after last night. It's on the schedule for tomorrow."

"Looks like you're juggling all the plates just fine. Don't forget I'm due in court tomorrow. The Eigsten case."

Addie had forgotten Patrick would be tied up the next day. She let loose with a mild stream of Irish profanity. Patrick laughed, promised to keep her updated, and disconnected.

Addie opened her laptop and found Ursula's senior yearbook online. She skimmed the names of the senior students, but didn't find a single TR. She searched Ursula's name and found a photo of the soccer team, Ursula wearing a goalie's jersey. Another photo showed Ursula as a member of the mock-trial group—an educational program that allowed students to role-play attorneys and witnesses under the guidance of actual attorneys. One of the attorneys was her father, Samuel Fishbourne.

None of the students had the initials TR.

Addie studied the picture. A group of ten kids dressed in suits or dresses, looking polished and studious. Ursula stood in the front. Another familiar face leapt out from the back row.

Jamal Jones.

Now that was interesting. She spent a few more minutes online, looking for connections between Ursula and Jamal. There wasn't much. A shared birth year and little else.

She closed the laptop and leaned back.

What did it mean, that Ursula and Jamal knew each other in high school? Probably nothing more than that Jamal might have reached out to his former classmate and mentioned he'd be performing in Chicago. Maybe that was what had made Ursula pick now to visit her father.

Their connection didn't suggest anything nefarious.

On the counter, the coffee machine released a thin stream of clear water.

A cloud drifted past the window.

By the time Addie went out to her car, the sky had turned dull, and the sun was a distant memory.

✣

She was halfway to Owen Teufel's apartment when a detective from the Near North station called.

"Got a call about a case of vandalism," the detective said. "Someone spray-painted a bunch of crap on a car sitting in a condo's parking lot. We ran the car. It's a rental, taken out by a New Yorker named Jamal James."

"The actor playing Theseus in the new play," Addie murmured. And Ursula's former mock-trial fellow.

"If you say so. No one answers at the condo James is renting. Half an hour ago, someone from the company that leased the condo let patrol in to do a wellness check."

"And?"

"And nothing. No one home. No sign of trouble. Looks like they had a party—beer bottles, dirty dishes."

Pretty much like a lot of twentysomething men's homes. Addie checked the time. "Maybe their car wouldn't start and they took an Uber. Or went with a friend. Is the vandalism threatening? Hate-crime stuff?"

"Nah. But I saw the report on your case. Looks like a couple of the images on the car match what you found on your victim."

Addie's breath came faster. If the vandalism on Jamal and Bryant's car was linked to the man calling himself Távros, then he'd had himself a busy night.

"I got more," the detective said. "Might not be anything. But the neighbor who phoned in the vandalism, she was outside the condo in the middle of the night, standing next to some trees so her dog could water them. Says she saw a man coming up the sidewalk. He scared her because he was a big dude. Tall, built like a weight lifter. Wearing a Chicago Bulls hoodie."

A description that would work for Távros. "Did she see his face?"

"Said from what she could see, he was an old white guy. But he didn't walk or talk like an old man."

Addie's pulse leapt. It had to be him. "Cameras?"

"Nah. But he stopped next to the entrance to the property and pulled out his phone. He was walking up and down the sidewalk, going in and out of earshot. But she heard part of the conversation. He used the name *Jamal*, which also got her attention. Made her wonder if he was talking to her new neighbor. She likes Jamal, this lady. Wishes he'd move back to Chicago permanently. She says, and I quote, 'He's a dish.' Anyway, the guy told Jamal they needed to meet. He said something about Jamal's car. Something like, 'They tagged your car.' Then he said they were all in danger. Our witness says she gave a little gasp. The man turned around and went silent, and she thought she was a goner. Couldn't tell if he saw her or not, her being in the shadows. But he started walking again, fast, and went out of hearing range."

What had River said? That Távros told him, *Ursula is where she deserves to be. Where they all deserve to be.*

"The witness is here if you want to talk to her," said the detective. "She also says Jamal isn't answering his cell phone."

"I'll head over now," Addie told the detective. "Text me the address."

When her phone chimed, she glanced at the screen; Jamal and Bryant lived in a condo near Boystown.

She hit the accelerator, cut north on Broadway. She called Johnny Sanchez on their team and asked him to pay a visit to Owen Teufel—ask a few questions, see if he had an alibi for the night of. Then she called Evan. And called him again when he didn't pick up. His voice sounded bleary when he finally answered.

"Hi," she said.

"Hi."

She felt suddenly shy; an awkward silence ensued.

We can't have ruined a perfectly wonderful friendship, she thought.

"Addie, you all right?" he said at the same time she asked, "Evan, you okay?"

They laughed, and the tension evaporated. Their friendship was still intact. The rest they could deal with later.

"How's River?" Addie asked.

"Tough as an elephant. Not quite as smart, given he voluntarily threw himself into the equivalent of a sewer. But he has an iron constitution, so I'm taking him out for breakfast burritos."

She hit her blinker and turned east on Newport Drive. The neighborhood was tree-lined and quiet.

"Then I hate to ask," she said. "But I need you to make a stop first."

"Something happen?" His voice was suddenly alert.

"Jamal and Bryant James have disappeared. Maybe. Their car was tagged with possible glyphs—I haven't seen them yet. And no one is answering their door. Bryant is the husband of Jamal, a.k.a.—"

"Theseus. I met Bryant at the dress rehearsal."

Addie pulled up to the curb near the front of the condo building. "A neighbor out with her dog in the middle of the night says she saw a big man in a hoodie, heard him on the phone telling someone named Jamal they were all in danger."

"Forget the burritos," Evan said. "We'll meet you there."

Chapter 31

Evan

Evan pulled his Jaguar to the curb near the address Addie had given him, and he and River got out.

The day was hot and muggy, the sky the soiled gray of dirty socks. Leaves hung limply as if the previous night's storm had beaten them into submission. Evan stripped off his hoodie and tossed it on the front seat. He smoothed down his rumpled tee and tucked it in his jeans. Ran a hand through his unruly hair.

River raised an eyebrow. "Never known you to care."

"It's a business call. I should look professional."

"In a T-shirt that reads, 'Half of everything a minotaur says is bull.' Where did you even get that?"

Across the street, a woman walking her fluffy bichon frise stopped and stared at Evan. He waved and she hurried on.

He turned back to River. "The shirt was a gift from a student. At the time I thought she was sending me a subtle message that half of everything I said in class was bull. But I reconsidered."

"First instincts are usually correct."

Evan lifted his chin and did a passable job of looking down his nose at a man nearly two feet taller than himself. "Perhaps. But at least in the proud and glorious halls of the University of Chicago, we offer only the finest bull."

Addie met them at the entrance to the half-full parking lot.

"Sorry to disrupt your breakfast plans," she said. Her eyes lingered for a moment on Evan—who returned the favor—before she glanced at River. "How are you feeling after last night?"

But River didn't answer. He was staring at the condo buildings—two structures rising twelve stories high on either side of the parking lot.

"River," Evan said.

"Great," River answered, still eyeballing the buildings.

"Okay." Addie took a few steps toward the far end of the lot, where two techs worked near a sedan. She stopped when River didn't move.

Evan could see she wanted to get straight to business. But he wasn't going to interrupt whatever River was doing.

She came back.

"Whoever tagged Jamal's rental car," she said, "used some of the same signs the two of you extrapolated from the marks on Fishbourne's skin. Which likely proves that your guesses were correct."

"That *should* feel like a win," Evan said.

"It *is* a win. Just not a home run."

Evan followed River's gaze. The parking lot had probably originally been intended to provide a grassy courtyard between the two buildings. But he suspected that for most leasers, the need for safe, accessible parking had won out over grass and flowers. The result was an area that carried the same labyrinthine feel that River had pointed out about Couch Place the night Fishbourne died.

"You're thinking of a maze," he said to River.

"A unicursal one," he answered. He pointed toward one of the condo windows. "Is that Jamal and Bryant's place?"

"The one with the 'I heart NY' sign?" Addie said. "Correct. How did you know?"

When River didn't answer, Evan jumped in for him.

"It's possible Jamal and Bryant are making a point of separating themselves from Chicago," he said. "Even while they're living here for the duration of the play. Maybe Jamal isn't fond of his hometown."

"Okay," Addie said. "That's potentially interesting? Now find me something that will be useful in court."

She started walking again, and they joined her.

"I interviewed the woman who overheard the phone conversation," she said. "She's agreed to sit down with a sketch artist. But it was the dead of night—two a.m.—and dark despite the lights from the building's lobby. Plus, I suspect the caller was wearing his old-man mask. What's more interesting is what she heard."

Evan skirted a pickup truck. "About Jamal and the others being in danger."

"Those are the words the man used, according to our witness." Addie opened the notes app on her phone and read, "'We need to talk. Like, tonight. He tagged your car, man.' The dude—her word—then said, 'We're all in danger. It's a warning.'" She lowered her phone. "The 'dude' walked away after that, and she wasn't inclined to follow him."

Evan stopped again, still taking in the scene. "You have a theory about what Jamal and Bryant's disappearance means?"

"Their *possible* disappearance. What I'm hoping is that Jamal and Bryant crashed with friends last night after the play. Or caught a ride this morning to their favorite Chicago breakfast joint. I'm hoping that Jamal has his phone on silent and doesn't hear his neighbor's calls."

"But you don't think so."

Addie looked down, kicked a round pebble back into place on the sidewalk's border. When she lifted her head, humidity had stuck a stray curl to her cheek. "Given the description of the man making the phone call, and what's been painted on their car, I'm worried it was a setup and the killer lured them somewhere."

"If so, then the question becomes—I mean, aside from *where* they are—the question becomes what do these four people have in common?"

"A few things, it turns out."

"Ah, our brilliant detective."

This time Addie didn't look at her notes. "Ursula and Jamal were born in Chicago in the same year. In 1994. Ursula's father, Samuel, helped coach a mock-trial high school team where the kids practiced prosecuting and defending a criminal. Both Ursula and Jamal were on that team. They *knew* each other way back when. At least as teenagers."

"How did you figure that out?"

"As you said, I'm a brilliant detective. I looked at Ursula's yearbook."

"Anyone named Távros in that book?"

"Not a one. And no TRs in her senior class. A few in the other classes. We'll talk to all those we can track down, along with everyone on the mock-trial team." She puffed out a breath as if realizing how big the investigation was getting.

For his part, Evan repressed a shudder. He would have loathed high school if he hadn't skipped it altogether. A lucky roll of the genetic dice—at least on the intellectual end—and it was straight to Oxford.

"Have we got a case of high school revenge?" he asked. "Maybe that's the reason for the 'I heart NY' sign. Leave Chicago in the rearview."

"High school can be miserable," Addie agreed.

"What about Bryant?"

"He's the outlier. His only connection, based on what I've learned so far, is that he married Jamal."

"Távros goes after pairs," Evan said. "Why? It's much harder for a single man to go against two."

River had been staring down the sidewalk, back the way they'd come. Now he turned around. "He likes the challenge. The harder the game, the bigger the thrill."

"I noticed you're walking funny," Addie said. "Hunched over."

River made a show of stretching his back. "Practicing my Quasimodo and hoping for an audition."

"Uh-huh." She clicked her tongue against her teeth. "Don't ask, don't tell?"

Seeking to distract her, Evan said, "How did the killer know which was Jamal's car?"

She let him turn the conversation. "I assume he followed them at some point."

"After one of the rehearsals, perhaps." Evan resumed walking. "Shall we continue?"

As they walked, the day grew heavier, the air as oppressive as a bigot's brain.

✣

Except for the techs, at first glance nothing looked out of the ordinary about Jamal and Bryant's rented Toyota Camry. It was parked between a Nissan SUV and a Mini Cooper, the undercarriage lightly splashed with mud from the storms. A rainbow pendant hung from the rearview mirror.

A closer look revealed a series of—no question—Cretan hieroglyphics painted on the driver's door.

"We've got the trident, the bull, and the bee or wasp," Evan said. "Just as with Fishbourne."

River squatted between the Camry and the Mini Cooper while the techs eyed him narrowly. "But instead of the cat's head, we have an eye."

Evan nodded. "Glyph number five. The killer repeated three of the signs and substituted the eye for the cat's head."

Addie motioned River away from the car. "What does that mean, the eye?"

"No one *knows*. Cretan Hieroglyphic is—"

"I know. Undeciphered. Give me something. Anything. A chink. A toehold."

Evan scratched the back of his neck where sweat beaded. He'd been giving the glyphs a lot of thought. "Our alleged killer, Távros, carries a narrative in his head. A story of how things should go. And he wants to keep tight control of it. The Minotaur signifies strength and power, power that he may believe to be supernatural."

"Meaning he thinks *he's* supernatural?"

"Maybe. That symbol"—Evan pointed toward the bull glyph—"is how he gathers and unleashes his power. And that one"—he aimed his finger at the trident—"is where he derives his power. He inherits his strength from his godly father and offers sacrifice to make sure the power keeps coming."

"And the bee? The eye? What about them?"

"No one—"

"Knows. Evan, I get it. But I don't think the killer just opened a book of Cretan Hieroglyphic and played spin the wheel. You just gave me possible interpretations of the bull and trident glyphs. What if—wait." She looked suddenly troubled.

"What?" Evan asked.

"At Fishbourne's house, there were pictures of a young Ursula with a cat. As Ursula grew older, new cats appeared. But there was almost always a cat."

"You're suggesting the killer knew she liked cats?"

Addie scratched her throat. "Maybe?"

"And Jamal likes, what, eyes?"

She rounded on him. "That is your job to figure out."

Fortunately, his mind was already off and running. "A personal symbol," he said.

She was listening.

He closed his eyes. "The bull for the killer, the trident for sacrifice, the wasp for . . . for something that links the victims together.

Something shared. Like a team logo, maybe. I'm hazy on that, and"—he opened his eyes and raised his palm like a traffic cop—"don't rush me. But if I'm right, then maybe the cat and the eye do, in fact, represent something personal to the victim. The killer seems to know Jamal, based on that phone call. Maybe he also knows Ursula."

"We're back to high school? A cat and an eye make for strange mascots."

"Not if you're forcing everyone into a specific mythos."

He looked to River to back him up, but his brother had returned halfway up the lot and was crouched next to the sidewalk. He looked back and waved a hand for Evan to join him.

"He's found something," Evan said to Addie.

She was nodding, thinking. "Tell him I'll be right there."

As Evan moved away, he heard one of the techs say, "We're done here," and Addie replying, "I want it towed to the garage. Fingerprints, trace, the works."

When Evan drew near, River said, "More numbers. This time instead of chalk, he used rocks and twigs."

Evan saw it immediately. Laid out on the sidewalk next to the grass were carefully arranged twigs and rocks. The twigs had been used to form three diamonds. These were followed by two round stones and another twig, this one angled. On each side were two more twigs in the shape of an X.

X ◊◊◊ O O / X

"Three thousand and twenty-one," Evan said.

"That's what I get."

"And the Xs—or Saint Andrew's crosses, if you will—signify the beginning and ending of the series."

"That's a bit of a leap," River said.

Addie walked up. "What's a leap?"

"They could serve as emphasis," River said. "The way they do on Cretan seal stones. Telling us which signs are important."

"Or they could be glyph number seventy," Evan pointed out.

"Mixing syllabograms and stiktograms." River rubbed his chin. "Unusual outside of an agricultural context. But we aren't even sure what glyph seventy is."

Addie held up a hand. "Stop nerding out and give me the layman's version."

"The killer left numbers again," River said. "This time using rocks and twigs. We're almost certainly looking at the number three thousand twenty-one."

Addie squinted down at the strange message. "And all those other multisyllabic things you were going on about?"

"A professional dispute," Evan said. "And probably meaningless in the context. Or at least unhelpful. The killer was either separating this string of glyphs from others that were ruined by the storm or pedestrians—"

"—the way you kicked that rock earlier," River said. "Which is what got me thinking."

"Or," Evan pressed on, "these are the only glyphs he left on the sidewalk, and the Xs serve to bracket his lone message."

Addie's expression went tight. "You're saying part of his message might be lost."

"Possibly," Evan conceded. "We're missing the axe that he left by the first set of numbers the night he killed Fishbourne. But I'm guessing no. This area is clear of other stones and debris. Someone could have come along and interrupted him before he added the axe."

Addie waved one of the techs over to take photos and measurements. While the woman worked, Addie drew Evan and River aside.

"First, we had the number six near the site of Fishbourne's body. And now three thousand twenty-one." She glared at Evan as if he was holding back on her. "What do they mean?"

"You're going to get tired of hearing this, but I don't have enough—"

"To go on," she said.

The heat pressed down like the lid of a waffle iron closing. Sweat prickled Evan's scalp and crawled down his back. Overhead, a flock of crows flew by in a flurried rush, and the smell of ozone wafted down as the air grew still.

"Sorry," Evan said.

Addie waved a hand and then pinched the skin between her eyes. "It's all well and good that the two of you can read Cretan numbers and somewhat interpret the glyphs. But twigs and rocks on a sidewalk? Chalk marks in the rain? I don't think *he* cares if we notice his signs or if we understand what they mean. These messages aren't for us."

"They could be messages to himself," Evan said. "A reminder of his purpose. Or they could be to Poseidon."

"The god of oceans."

"And the god who created the Minotaur."

Addie tugged on her earlobe. "Or, fresh take. Who was the Greek god of the underworld?"

"Hades."

"The messages are to him, more like." Addie looked back at the vandalized car, then crossed her index and middle fingers. "Because sure as hell, our killer is in tight with the devil."

CHAPTER 32

PATRICK

Alice Walsh met Patrick at the front door of her modest rancher. Utilitarian haircut, straight spine, lips narrowed to a 0.5 mm pencil line. And a softness around faded blue eyes that suggested she spent her free time raising puppies for orphans.

Patrick knew the look: you had to be tough to be a cop's wife. You also had to have compassion to ride through those times when a cop blew a gasket or went bottom-of-the-ocean quiet.

Patrick liked her immediately.

He showed her his star. "I'm Detective—"

"Patrick McBrady," she said. "Come in."

She gestured him to the living room. "I'll bring the coffee."

The coffee. Not *some* coffee. Because if there was a detective in the house, coffee was on the menu.

The room smelled of cigarettes and air freshener despite the open windows. Patrick had only a few moments to take in the simple but comfortable furnishings, the array of family photos and a bookcase with more golf trophies than books. Then Alice was back.

She set a tray with an urn and mugs on the suitably named coffee table and gestured for him to sit. He took a swivel chair across the table from her, noting as he did so the three-ring binder on the table.

"Cream and sugar?" she asked as she sat on the couch.

"Black. Thanks."

"Of course." The ghost of a smile. "I made the coffee strong the way Tom used to take it. I hope that works for you."

"Cop coffee. Exactly how I like it."

Patrick smiled his appreciation as she handed him a full mug.

She nodded toward his tattoo, which was easily visible with his short sleeves. "You're as Irish as they come."

Patrick glanced down at the line of poetry he'd had tattooed. W. B. Yeats. **FOR THE WORLD'S MORE FULL OF WEEPING THAN YOU CAN UNDERSTAND.** The line seemed especially appropriate here in the home of a woman whose husband had long since stopped being the man she married.

Alice poured a cup for herself. "Sunset Village called after you left there."

No small talk, then. Patrick loved small talk—it was a way to poke around the edges, to get a sense of a person. But he suspected Alice Walsh went from A to Z faster than most.

He said, "Tom and I both worked patrol in Chicago back in the '80s."

She regarded him over the rim of her mug. "I know. I talked to Tom's partner, Jim Murray."

"Ah." Patrick took a sip of the coffee; his tongue tingled. Strong, just as she'd said. Cop coffee.

Alice must have asked Murray to do a quick check on Patrick, make a phone call or two. Both Alice and Murray had worked fast: it had only been half an hour since he'd called Alice and asked if she would speak with him.

"Did I pass muster?"

Another flicker of a smile. "Flying colors. Now how can I help you?"

"Mrs. Walsh—"

"Alice. Please."

"Alice, I suspect you already know why I'm here."

"Because of Jake Kully."

Patrick blinked. A to Z, just like that. "Who?"

She leaned back. "Do you mind if I smoke?"

"As long as you don't offer one to me."

"Recovering?"

"Seven years."

She tapped out a cigarette and lit it from a book of matches on the table. She tucked her stockinged feet under her, blew smoke over her shoulder, then said, "There's only one thing you could have mentioned to Tom or shown him that would have upset him that much. And that has to do with Jake Kully. But let me backfill a bit, so you know what I'm talking about."

Patrick pulled out a pad of paper. "Mind if I take notes?"

"I'd be disappointed in you otherwise." Another pull on the cigarette. "Jake Kully happened in the winter of 2004. Fourteen years ago. Tom was working the body of a teenage girl who'd been dumped near Garden City Community College. Tom and Jim were juggling multiple cases—it was a bad year. In the middle of all these cases and this poor girl, a mom from a house near the tracks reported her teenage son missing. Both her son and the dead girl were fifteen. They'd disappeared within a week of each other. But outside of that, the kids had nothing in common. The girl was in the National Honor Society, a keyboardist in the school's jazz band, and a volunteer who worked at the homeless shelter with other members of her church. All those things that look good on a college application."

Patrick ignored the implied cynicism. "And Jake Kully?"

"He was a reprobate. A delinquent who smoked dope and probably did harder stuff, who couldn't be bothered to show up at school most of the time, who was suspected of petty theft, and whose best friend said Jake had sworn he was going to run away." Alice lit a second cigarette from the first. "Tom figured he probably *was* a runaway. And by then, Tom was working on linking the girl's death to all those others missing and dead in Kansas and Missouri. It didn't occur to him that Jake Kully might be one of them."

A calico cat sauntered into the room and hopped on the couch. Alice stubbed out her barely touched cigarette and stroked the cat, which began to purr.

"Tom thought the Bogeyman was behind the girl's death," Alice said. "You've heard of the Bogeyman? The real one, not the childhood nightmare."

"You mean William Barlow."

She looked mildly impressed. "I guess cases like that, everyone remembers."

Patrick nodded. "Pretty much."

"My husband believed—and I suspect still believes in some lost corner of his mind—that everyone matters." She gestured for Patrick's mug and leaned over the cat to refill it from the urn. "He managed to link the girl to Barlow. But he had nothing on Jake Kully. Just a kid who'd promised to run away. Tom certainly didn't think Jake's life was worth any less than that poor girl's. But . . ."

Her voice trailed off as she petted the cat.

"But Tom and his partner had other cases," Patrick guessed. "Cases with bodies. They got busy."

"I know you don't mean that as a criticism," she said. "Because you know that every cop has to decide which leads to pursue, which cases are more likely to break open. Everyone, even his mother, agreed that Jake was likely a runaway. Which, as his mother pointed out and Tom agreed, didn't mean the boy wasn't in trouble. But the mother's key indication that there was a problem was a symbol that had been scratched onto the family's front door. And that symbol had never been linked to any of the Bogeyman's other victims. It looked like a lot of nothing."

Patrick leaned forward in his chair, barely aware that he'd done so. The hair rose on his neck even before she flipped open the binder.

And there it was. The triangle and crescent Addie had found on the tree-house door. The one that Tom Walsh had sent to Evan and then never followed up on.

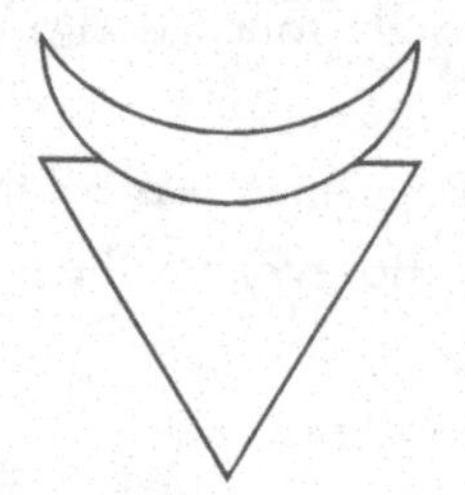

"You recognize it," Alice said. She'd had years of reading her husband, and Patrick suspected he and Tom were a lot alike.

He nodded. "It's come to light in a case my partner and I are working."

"Something to do with Barlow?"

Patrick sidestepped the question. "Barlow is deceased."

Her eyes narrowed as she scrutinized him. "And yet you're here."

"And yet I am."

"Okay." That flickering smile. "For sure, Tom didn't know what to make of the sign. A bull's head, presumably. But it didn't seem to have anything to do with his case. Barlow wasn't 'Bull' Barlow until after he went to prison. And like I said, as far as Tom knew, none of the other victims had been associated with this sign. Plus, Jake's body hadn't shown up anywhere. Tom sent the symbol off to an expert in codes and ciphers, but he didn't know what to do with the answer."

"He sent it to Dr. Wilding at the University of Chicago," Patrick said.

"Maybe. The name is probably in that notebook." She picked up the pack of cigarettes, flipped it around in her hands, then set it back down. "A couple of years later, Jake's body was discovered. By then, Barlow had already been found guilty on seventeen counts of murder and kidnapping and sentenced to serve multiple life sentences. Even before Jake's body surfaced, most everyone had moved on. Jake's father had never been part of the family picture, and his mother died of breast cancer before Jake was found. The body of a runaway was just another sad story. And that symbol was just some weird thing kids do. Jake Kully had never been at the top of anyone's list, and his corpse did nothing to change that."

"Except for Tom," Patrick guessed.

"Except for Tom. He never got over not moving fast enough on the kid. Not using every resource he could muster before the kid was a cadaver. He was sure Kully had been grabbed by Barlow."

The faintest of breezes entered the room. Patrick felt it cool the sweat on his scalp.

"What made him think that?"

"The condition of the remains. The kid's throat had been cut deep enough to sever the spinal cord. There were also cut marks on his collarbone and sternum, which is where Barlow branded his victims before taking their skin. You know about that, right?"

"I don't remember details."

"The Bogeyman—Barlow—cut away a large square of each victim's skin and took it with him. Presumably as a trophy. The skin came from near the breastbone, leaving cut marks on the bones."

The breeze died. The cat had fallen asleep. A clock ticked.

"Was there anything else about the body?" Patrick asked.

"There wasn't much to work with. The coroner for the county where Kully was found said she couldn't rule out the cut marks as animal damage. Which you and I both know is bullshit. But for sure, animals had worked those bones, and the coroner was the coroner. By then, Tom was starting to show signs of dementia. Memory problems. Trouble making plans. He'd get confused about what time it was, and twice he got lost on the drive home. He was diagnosed with early onset Alzheimer's. The department offered him retirement while he could still enjoy life, and since the doctors said stress would only make him worse, I pressured him to take it."

Alice's eyes shone, and Patrick looked away while she dabbed at them with her sleeve.

"More coffee?" she said a minute later, her voice husky.

"Always, thank you."

"Just like Tom. Telling him to take the offer was probably not the best advice I ever gave him. But he heard me out and retired. Took up golf because they said it would be good for him. But in his heart he was still a cop. And, at first, anyway, his mind was still on pretty solid ground. He spent those early months looking at other missing-persons cases that he figured Barlow could have been responsible for. He scrutinized databases looking at age and gender and geography, and all the things detectives use to link cases. He became obsessed with Barlow and with Jake Kully. Maybe because Tom had been exactly like Jake when he was young. Or close enough. Poor student, no dad, brushes with the law. It was while he was combing records that he learned about another kid who went missing. This one near Chicago."

All at once the hairs on Patrick's arms stood at attention. He held his breath as Alice flipped to a different section in the notebook. He scooted forward, his coffee forgotten.

A name leapt out at him. Immediately he thought of the description of Barlow in the article Addie had found: a kid who claimed he'd seen Barlow with another adult and a child.

"Colby Kaplan was only ten when he disappeared," Alice said. "In that regard, he didn't fit Barlow at all. Barlow liked them older."

"Then what got Tom's attention?" Patrick asked, although he suspected he already knew the answer. Colby Kaplan had disappeared from Ogle County, only fifteen miles from where one of Barlow's victims had been found.

"Geography," Alice said, confirming it. "But there was more. Tom called the detectives in CPD's Missing Persons. They didn't have much to offer except one thing—that the Kaplan kid's mother had mentioned a symbol scratched on her door. The same symbol you're looking at in that file. Tom called it a bull glyph."

Patrick told his racing thoughts to get out of the passing lane. He remembered his coffee and took a sip. "What happened when Tom brought up the symbol with CPD?"

"They figured it was a code shared by runaways. Like hobo code."

"They have good reason to think that?"

"Colby Kaplan talked about running away in his journal. And he'd drawn that exact symbol on the pages, which meant he might have drawn it on his own front porch."

"What else?"

"Like I said, Colby didn't fit Barlow's profile. Too young. And he was Black. Or biracial, anyway. All of Barlow's victims were white. And unlike Jake, Colby was never found."

The hairs settled on Patrick's arms. His shoulders dropped. If that were the case, if the symbol was a code for runaways, then Ursula and her friend TR were probably just kids who'd heard about the code on Myspace or whatever kids were using back then and briefly contemplated their own parent-free adventure. Nothing to do with Barlow other than TR's sketch. The drawing had remained, forgotten, in the tree house, papered over with Ursula's later interests.

"Did Tom believe Colby Kaplan was a runaway?"

"He figured that even if the kid had left home, it didn't mean he hadn't been picked up by Barlow. Same as Jake. At the trial, Barlow had bragged about branding his victims before he killed them—sometimes days before. 'Burned 'em like you'd burn a heifer,' he said."

Patrick looked up. "Tom thought this symbol was Barlow's brand? Not a sign for a runaway?"

"That was his working theory. But none of the skin cut from the victims was ever found. And Barlow never revealed what symbol he used when he branded those women and kids. That sign never showed up again, not in any of the cases Tom looked at."

Not until a tree house in a nice Chicago neighborhood.

William "Bull" Barlow. Had Barlow told another prisoner about his brand? Was that where his prison nickname came from? If so, how had TR learned about it?

"Does Tom still believe that symbol belongs to Barlow?" he said.

"I guess that scream you roused out of him this morning answers that."

"I didn't mean to upset him."

She nodded as if that were a given.

"Alzheimer's is cruel," she said. "With Tom, I sometimes think the disease ate away most of the good memories and left him the bad ones. Tom never stopped blaming himself for not looking harder for Jake Kully. He knew that Barlow sometimes held on to those kids and women before he murdered them. If he'd acted faster, there might have been time. When he heard about Colby, that made it even worse."

"But he did a lot of good, linking the girl's death to Barlow. Barlow served time for her murder—Tom has that in his pocket. Plus, he brought up the symbol with CPD."

"That's true." The puppies-and-orphan compassion in her eyes darkened to sorrow. "But almost as fast as you can snap your fingers, it didn't matter. By the time Tom learned about the Colby kid, it had become harder for him to connect the dots, to work things through. Jim Murray had a new partner and had to move on to other cases. CPD was busy, and I'm sure they could tell Tom was no longer fully capable. He was just a retired cop trying to run on one leg."

She stood. Interview over. Patrick closed the binder and stood as well. Her blue eyes were almost gray in the dim house.

"Take the binder," she said. "You might as well. It's got everything Tom managed to put together on the case before his mind sank in on itself. Maybe it will help you with whatever you're working on."

Gratefully, he picked up the notebook. She walked him to the door. He thanked her for agreeing to talk with him.

"I hope it was helpful," she said. But her eyes suggested she knew it was a long shot.

As Patrick walked down the driveway to his car, he wondered if his beloved Mary would ever look at another cop the way Alice had looked at him: appreciating that he still had what it took.

Knowing it couldn't last.

Chapter 33

Addie

Addie knocked on the back door to the Neverland Theater.

She'd called the theater as she was driving over; a man with a voice like a foghorn had directed her to wait by the alley entrance until someone could be there to let her in. Half an hour later, Addie huddled in her raincoat and scowled. She couldn't recall a summer so wet and gusty. Couch Place—Death Alley—had become a wind tunnel. Her ponytail was giving her whiplash.

Another year, maybe two, she'd chop her hair off. Get herself a more professional vibe. But she was as attached to her hair as Rapunzel. It was part of the femininity she'd clung to after her mother died, and she'd become the lone female in a home of four boys and a dad who'd cut her hair by placing a bowl upside down on her head and trimming around it. With her curls, she'd looked like Eraserhead from the David Lynch cult film.

Maybe she'd wait until she was forty. Forty was a good age to look respectable.

She had just raised her hand to knock again when the door swung inward.

Addie held up her star. "I spoke with someone on the phone."

"That was me," said a dour middle-aged man who waved her inside. He of the foghorn voice.

When she was inside, accompanied by a swirl of wind, he closed and locked the door behind her.

Addie loosened her ponytail, gathered her windblown hair, and pulled it back again.

"Is Emma Hargrave here?" she asked.

"They're all in the break room," he said. "Something we actually *have*, thanks to the theater's expansion."

"A break room is important," Addie said.

He flicked a gaze at her, checking for sarcasm, then sighed and glanced at his watch. "I'll take you there, but please be brief. There's an all-hands-on-stage meeting in seventeen minutes."

He turned on his heel and marched down the hallway.

"And Jamal James?" Addie asked, hurrying after him. "Is he in the break room?"

"He damn well better be. Or close by."

"I need to speak with him as well."

"Now you've got sixteen minutes."

"Actually," Addie said, "I've got as long as I need."

His disdain for the needs of the police fairly rang through his silence.

The break area was carved out of backstage space, put together with the kind of movable panels found in corporate offices. There was a folding table with chairs, a coffee machine on a smaller table with an extension cord that snaked under one of the walls, and a two-shelf bookcase heaped with what Addie guessed were scripts. The room was warm and echoey, the atmosphere drenched with the smell of fresh coffee, Danish rolls, and the coconut scent of a vape.

Four people were using the room. Two chatting next to the coffee machine. And Emma and Peter Hargrave, who sat shoulder to shoulder at the table, blond heads bowed as they read from the same book. She wore a cashmere wrap dress with tights. He, sweats and a long-sleeve tee.

Her hand rested on the book, holding it open.

His hand rested on hers.

They didn't look much like brother and sister unless you were taking a page from Zeus's marriage to his sister, Hera.

"The hell is everybody?" Addie's escort muttered. He cupped his hands and shouted, "Meeting in fifteen minutes on the stage! Everyone *will* be there."

Emma and Peter glanced up. Their gazes—his blue and hers gray—locked on Addie. Their respective hands retreated to their respective laps.

Addie's escort glared at one of the actors. "You. Go. Bang on doors. Make sure everybody knows." He gave Addie a flat stare, then snapped his fingers at the actor. "And get Jamal in here. Pronto."

The young man scurried out of the room, trailed by the other actor.

Addie's escort pointed to Emma as if there was some doubt regarding the identity of the lone female dancer in the room. Then he whirled out of the cubicle.

Addie's phone buzzed. A text from Evan.

Almost forgot. Ask Emma about her brother, Lowell.

Not Peter? she texted back.

Across the room, Peter stood and stretched. He was a looker, with a lazy smile he probably practiced in front of a mirror so he'd look as if he hadn't. He leaned down and whispered something to Emma, who laughed.

Evan had mentioned that Peter was firmly under his father's thumb. But there was no sign of that here. Peter's arrogance was locked and loaded.

Addie's phone buzzed again.

Name is Lowell, Evan answered. Mentioned in mother's obit. Also, ask re Morgan's studies: people genetically condemned to commit evil.

What??

Wild-ass speculation critical to all investigations.

Addie smiled, shook her head, and slid her phone inside her jacket.

Peter nodded at her in passing, then slipped out the doorway formed by two of the panels.

Addie approached Emma, who put aside her book. Her expression was nonchalant, bordering on blankness.

"I'm Detective Bisset," Addie said. "Do you have a few minutes to talk?"

"I have fifteen of them, according to Bert." Emma smiled, although only her lips moved; the rest of her pale face seemed carved out of alabaster. Her gray eyes held the middle distance as if seeing something veiled from the rest of the world.

"Bert is a taskmaster," Addie said.

Emma shrugged. "Our bunch needs one. Is this about the murder in the alley?"

Addie took the chair on the opposite side of the table. "You've only been in town a few days, is that correct?"

"Four. I flew into Chicago the night before dress rehearsal."

"A homecoming for you."

She tipped her head. "I grew up here and in Pittsburgh. Danced one year with the Joffrey Ballet. But New York is home now."

"Still, you must miss your family. Your parents and brothers."

"Brother," she corrected. "Just Peter. And my father. My mother is deceased."

The woman was poised. She didn't so much as blink at the suggestion of more than one sibling. What was Evan getting at with the second brother?

And what was Emma's relationship with Peter?

Addie opened her notes app. "I'm sorry about your mother. But I was under the impression you have a brother named Lowell."

The alabaster mask shifted ever so slightly. Was it annoyance? Or something else?

"Not Lowell," Emma said. "Peter. Peter Hargrave. You don't seem very well informed."

"It's just you, Peter, and your father."

Emma stared at her through heavy-lidded eyes. Apparently, Addie's comment was too obvious to require a response.

Addie said, "Let's talk about opening night."

"As you wish."

"After the play, you and the rest of the cast were in back, signing autographs."

"Not all of the cast," Emma corrected. "But a few of us."

"You drew quite a crowd."

"People love to touch the magic."

"The magic?"

Emma straightened, tucked one foot gracefully beneath her. "The human need for story. And not just any story, but the kind of tale that echoes back through the centuries. Back through millennia. All the way to when we didn't pretend to have the answer to everything. When the word *awful* meant 'full of awe.'"

The words spilled out as if something had come alive inside Emma.

"You believe passionately in what you do," Addie said.

"We all should, don't you agree?"

And as if a curtain had lifted, Emma was suddenly present. Sitting at the table, with one graceful arm stretched out, her body was lithe in the seat, humming with energy. She was Ariadne again, winding the ball of thread that would lead her brother's killer to freedom.

"I believe in storytelling more than anything," she said. "It's the best thing about humans. Our ability to weave a tale, to make the myths live again."

"Like the play you're performing in now."

"Like this play. And many others."

Evan had mentioned that often enough. How humans made stories out of everything—the position of the stars, the changing of the seasons. In Addie's world, stories were darker. The tales she heard were from men and women offering reasons for the atrocities they committed.

Addie found herself flat-footed in the face of Emma's ethereality. She had enjoyed the play. She appreciated the talent and dedication required to create something so beautiful. But her feet were too firmly grounded in this world for her to pierce the veil into another.

Maybe that was what her watercolors needed. A little veil piercing.

Addie put those thoughts aside. "There was one man in particular last night. An admirer, I presume. He said something that startled you."

A faint crease appeared on Emma's flawless forehead. She looked ready for a close-up in a script that said the actor should exhibit puzzlement.

"I don't remember anyone in particular," Emma said.

"He was a Black man. Tall. Had on a Chicago Bulls hoodie. You signed his playbill, but then he reached over the rope as if he meant to touch you, and you recoiled."

Emma sighed. "If you say so. There's one of those in every crowd. A man who oversteps, says something crude. Tries to touch me. After all these weeks on the road, I suppose I've just tuned it out."

"I would have expected the opposite reaction," Addie said. "Usually, a woman who attracts a lot of attention tries to memorize the faces of men who get too close so she can avoid them in the future. Or, if worse comes to worst, she can pick them out of a lineup."

"That isn't how it works for me. I don't like to dwell on the ugly."

"And yet, you're a beautiful woman. You must attract a lot of attention."

Emma didn't thank her or shrug off the compliment. Every morning, the truth would stare at her from the mirror—her flawless skin and classic features. The wide gray eyes and the blond waves that framed her face and rippled down her back.

"My looks haven't hurt my career," she said. "No shame in that. Even if I'd rather people paid more attention to my dancing than my face."

"Last night, you got angry. You said something to this man."

"You were watching me."

"I was watching everyone."

"Because you think someone associated with the play was involved in the murder."

"Do you?"

She wet her lips and lifted one impeccably plucked eyebrow. "Do you think I was approached by a killer?"

It's exciting to her, Addie realized. *A little dark magic for her offstage life.*

"We're looking at a number of things," Addie said shortly. "You get the magic, we get the cleanup."

Emma pulled back.

Addie's escort leaned into the room. "Seven minutes, Miss Emma."

"I'll be there, Bert."

He smiled as if she'd gifted him a winning lottery ticket.

"And Jamal?" Addie asked him.

"Probably filing his nails," Bert said. "I'll find him."

When Addie turned back, Emma was studying her as if Addie had turned into something unpleasant. A pile of dog crap, maybe.

"Why do you want to talk to Jamal?" Emma asked. "Because he's a tall Black man? I can assure you—"

"Because he's missing."

A beat. "And you suspect foul play?"

"If you know where he is or how to find him or his husband, it would be helpful."

"Bryant's gone, too?"

"And someone vandalized their car."

Emma's gaze went elsewhere. She plucked at the tie on her wrap dress. "I wouldn't worry. Jamal is notoriously unreliable. I'm sure he'll show up."

"You don't think he's in danger?"

"Why would he be?" She scooped up the waterfall of her hair and twisted it atop her head, securing it with a band from her wrist. "Unless he has some deep dark secret he's hiding. But even so, I wouldn't worry. Jamal knows how to take care of himself."

"Does Jamal have a deep dark secret?"

Emma smiled wickedly. "Doesn't everyone?"

"And you know that because the two of you are friends."

"Of course we're friends. Who doesn't love Jamal?"

Someone, apparently. "Did you know Jamal before the two of you were cast in this play?"

Emma tipped her head, amused. "This suddenly feels very personal, detective. Am I a suspect?"

Addie wanted to answer glibly: everyone's a suspect. But that wasn't the way to handle a woman like Emma.

"I'm establishing relationships."

"Because you think one of us is guilty of murder." She stood. Sudden anger lay on her like a shawl, elegant and assumed, another acting job. "You're looking in the wrong place, Detective. There isn't anyone in the cast or the crew who would do something so horrible."

"That isn't what your father would say. Your father would tell us that some people are born evil. That they can't help themselves."

"He's my adopted father. For the record. My father and Morgan were best friends. After my parents died when I was nine, Morgan took me in."

"Then you and Peter aren't . . . ?"

Emma laughed, the sound of ice crunching underfoot. "You thought there was something Oedipal going on between Peter and me.

But we're not related by blood. And, anyway, it's none of your business. However much you might be establishing *relationships*."

Addie said, "Let's go back to your father."

"Morgan Hargrave is brilliant. He knows that people who are born *evil*—they can't hear the music. They don't dance. They don't make art."

"Hitler painted."

"Oh, please," Emma snapped. "If you'll forgive me, I need to get to the meeting. Even the prima ballerina is not excused."

As Emma strode around the table, Addie said, "And Ursula Fishbourne? Do you know her?"

Emma hesitated, then continued walking. "No."

"And TR? Távros?"

Emma stopped. She waved a graceful hand in a gesture that suggested she was conducting an orchestra.

"If you're so curious about me, Detective, and about Jamal and Ursula, then do your homework. Do that *before* you barge into our lives with your ugly accusations, dragging in allegations like something the cat vomited up."

"I've hit a nerve."

"You hit nothing. No goals, no baskets, not a single touché."

Addie thought of the tree house and followed her instinct. "Are you sure that's what you want me to do, Emma? Look into your background and everyone else's?"

Emma tossed a look over her shoulder. "'Where ignorance is bliss, 'tis folly to be wise,'" she quoted.

"The poet Thomas Gray," Addie said, trusting her memory. "I know that Jamal and Ursula knew each other when they were teenagers. I'll ask again: Did you know them then?"

"No. And what is this interest in—who did you say she was—Ursula Fishlorn?"

CPD was still sitting on Samuel Fishbourne's name; they had yet to reach next of kin.

"Fishbourne. Are you safe, Emma? Has anyone threatened you?"

Emma turned away, lifted her shoulders. "Of course, no one has threatened me. What good is the ballet without its star?"

She stormed out of the room as only a prima ballerina could—with a toss of her head and a dignified step. Addie trailed after her to the stage and watched from the wings for a moment.

Emma went straight to Peter, took his hand, and whispered something in his ear.

Addie spotted Owen Teufel sitting on King Minos's throne, his knees drawn to his chest; she recognized him from the playbill. Johnny Sanchez had already spoken with him but still needed to check out the kid's alibi.

Jamal was absent. She heard Bert calling for him, but no one answered.

She watched the cast for a moment, turning Emma's words over in her mind. There had been something like a command in it.

Or a plea: *Do your homework.*

CHAPTER 34

EVAN

Back at Evan's home, River settled in the kitchen with his laptop to begin the search for potential donors for the institute and to research the coin Fishbourne had left on the institute's porch. Evan decided to take Perro for a walk around the neighborhood in the lull between storms. Maybe the fresh—if muggy—air would suggest new mental paths for him to pursue into the dark woods of the Minotaur's mind.

The Minotaur a.k.a. TR a.k.a. Távros.

Távros, a Greek name meaning "bull."

Their killer wasn't too subtle when it came to names.

The day was limpid and warm, the promise of cooler temperatures whispering behind the low cloud cover. Evan wasn't overly fond of walking about in public. People could be cruel. On the bright side, he reminded himself, people might sneer or laugh or take a video, but no one was likely to shoot him for the crime of being short.

After Perro had watered all the neighbors' bushes and Evan had stopped long enough to swap his cassoulet recipe for Mrs. Amrani's chicken-and-lemon tagine—Mrs. Amrani lived five doors down and was a splendid cook—Evan studied the lowering sky for a moment, then turned around.

He walked through the house, exited out the back, and strolled down to the small hedge maze. He took a seat on the bench placed within. Perro plopped nearby, clearly relishing the relative coolness under the hedges.

A murder investigation was—metaphorically speaking—a maze. A detective followed clues that sometimes led to dead ends, while others took unexpected turns. At no time during the early days did a sleuth have a clear sense of where he was headed. And once he had enough information to come up with a working hypothesis—the center of the maze—he still had to get back out with his theories backed by fact.

Evan didn't know where in the maze he was, but he was nowhere near the center. He needed more than half-formed theories. He scrolled through his phone, looking for information about the Hargrave family—especially Philomena and Lowell.

He found several laudatory pieces about the research Philomena had done with her husband. In the comments on one article about her tragic demise, he found a link to a true-crime blog. The link led him to a site rife with speculation that Philomena's death hadn't been accidental—that it was the result of foul play. But after a flurry of speculation, interest died. The last blog post on the site was years old.

The simple facts were that Philomena had suffered severe injuries as the result of her fall and died at the bottom of the staircase. An inquest determined that Philomena was home alone, her husband having taken their boys out for the afternoon. Alibis checked out.

Evan nodded to himself. There it was again, a mention of a second boy child.

But if Lowell Hargrave were still alive, he was a ghost as far as the internet was concerned. The only Lowells that Evan could find were decades too old to be Philomena and Morgan's son.

One more thing of interest did pop out in one of the articles about Mrs. Hargrave: Philomena was originally from Crete. That could certainly explain a child's interest in the myth of the Minotaur.

His phone buzzed. Addie.

"Talk to me about Lowell Hargrave," she said.

Evan tapped the icon for "Speaker." "Lowell's name appeared in the obituary for Philomena Hargrave, Morgan's wife. Philomena died in 1997. The obit said that she was survived by her husband and two sons, Lowell and Peter. No mention of Emma."

"Probably because Emma Gladstone Hargrave was adopted," Addie said. "Her father and Morgan were best friends, and Morgan stepped up after her parents died. Other than that tidbit, Emma mostly put me in mind of a clam. Oh, and she all but ordered me to do a background check on everyone in the cast."

"Why would she tell you to do that?"

A silence. Evan could picture Addie's scowl.

"I don't know," she said after a moment. "That's one of the many things about this case that just sits wrong. Maybe she wants me to learn something she isn't willing to state directly. Maybe she just thinks she's God's gift to the earth, and of course, I should know every detail. Only she didn't suggest I only investigate her background, but to look at everyone associated with the play."

A thought struck Evan: *Because you can't understand the truth behind the myth if you don't understand the players.*

"On a sidenote," Addie went on, "she and Peter have the hots for each other."

"Nothing illegal or immoral about that. Just unusual. What else have you learned?"

An exasperated sigh. "I've barely had a chance to start. Still, I'd bet my silver star Emma knows Ursula. And that she knew Jamal even before they were cast in *The King and the Minotaur*."

"But she didn't go to the same high school?"

"Nope."

"Meaning she met them somewhere else."

"My brilliant friend. I've got someone looking into a possible connection through the mock-trial group. Kids on those teams compete with other schools, so they could have crossed paths. Meanwhile, I'm actively looking for other ideas." A pause. "That's a hint."

"Church? Hobbies? Scouts? It's a mystery."

"Thanks for summing it up." Another pause. "Emma does seem inordinately fond of myths. Those are the best stories, according to her."

"They're certainly among the most powerful, as I'm sure our killer would agree. Maybe Emma is fashioning a myth for her own life."

"They call that branding. How did Philomena Hargrave die?"

Evan summed up what he'd just learned. "On a possibly interesting note, she was from Crete."

"A Cretan lady, a vanished son, and a tragic fall."

Evan waved off a swarm of gnats. "The stuff of myths. Emma won't have to dig far into her adopted family's past to create her—what did you call it?"

"Her brand. According to the myth, did the Minotaur—Asterion—did he love his mother?"

"An interesting train of thought, Detective. Are you suggesting our modern-day Minotaur is re-creating the ancient story?"

"It's possible, isn't it?" Addie pressed. "We talked about it at Petterino's. The potential parallels between the killer's life and the myth."

"It's not only possible, but likely. The question, as I said, is how closely the killer's life parallels that of the Minotaur."

"I'm guessing no Greek gods were involved," Addie said.

"I suspect not. Which isn't to say our killer doesn't believe in them. But back to your question about mother and son. While the Minotaur was born half human, half beast, he didn't develop a violent temper or a proclivity for human flesh until later. I imagine mother and Minotaur adored each other like any mother and child. Up until she let her husband imprison him in an underground labyrinth."

"If she loved him, why would she do that?"

Evan gave a half laugh. "It's hard to say no to a king."

"Especially a brutal one. Minos was brutal, wasn't he?"

"I'd put him on the top-ten list of brutal mythical leaders. Or top twenty, anyway. Are you thinking of looking into old domestic-violence cases?"

"Serial killers sometimes come from perfectly wonderful homes," Addie said. "But not usually. I'll get someone searching for cases of domestic assault or threats involving our principal players. But a few more details would be helpful."

Evan was quiet, thinking.

Addie said, "The bit about 'a few more details' was your cue, in case you missed it."

"I did try to learn more about Lowell," Evan said. "But outside of the obit and a crime blog that mentions two sons, I can't find anything else using my meager computer skills."

"As soon as we hang up, I'll start with the Cook County Clerk's office," Addie said. "See if I can scare up a birth certificate. I'll also see if I can track down a social security number for our ghostly boy."

They were both silent. Perro stood and barked his boredom. Evan rose and went back through the maze—Perro on his heels—to the lawn where River and Diana had played dueling axes. He dug the dog's tennis ball out of his pocket, unclipped Perro's leash, and hurled the ball as far as he could. Perro took off, a shot from a cannon.

After a moment, Addie said, "I should go."

"Will I see you later?"

"Cocktails at eight?" A smile in her voice.

"Music to my ears," Evan said. *And a song in my heart.*

✢

Back in the house, he gave Perro some fresh water and a treat, then went to his study. He laid out the printed copy of TR's letter to him and River, as well as the table he'd provided to Addie listing each of the glyphs used by Távros and their commonly accepted meanings. He added a note about the glyphs on Jamal's car and made a few other updates.

Number	Glyph	Meaning	Location
N/A		Cat head	Fishbourne's shoulder and TR's letter Not on Jamal's car. Personal symbol?
001		Jumping man	TR's letter
004		Woman	TR's letter
005		Eye	TR's letter and Jamal's car Not with Fishbourne. Personal symbol?
011		Bull head	Fishbourne's chest and TR's letter
020		Bee or wasp	TR's letter and Jamal's car

021		Fly	Fishbourne's chest and TR's letter
031/092		Trident	Fishbourne's forehead and TR's letter
038		Gate	TR's letter
042		Double-bladed axe	Chalked on sidewalk near Fishbourne's body and TR's letter
043		Single-blade axe	TR's letter
044		Trowel	TR's letter
049		Arrow	TR's letter
051		Spearhead	TR's letter
054		Two-handled vase	TR's letter
057		Plow	TR's letter
070		Cross	TR's letter

Dutifully, he studied the table.

He scratched his chin and tugged on his beard and stared at the glyphs some more.

They stared dumbly back.

His mind went to poor Wilfrid Voynich. Voynich was a Polish bookseller who'd spent his life trying to decipher a mysterious fifteenth-century book. The book, now known as the Voynich Manuscript, was written and illustrated in rare pigments, enclosed in an extraordinary cover, and filled with glorious drawings. It was also utterly unwilling to give up its secrets, likely because no key or biscript existed that would allow anyone to crack its code. Wilfrid Voynich died, heartbroken, having given only his name to the manuscript.

Perhaps the killer's message was of the same kind. Undecipherable, not because Evan didn't have the key, but because there was no key to be had outside the killer's mind.

Perro trotted into the room and came to stare at Evan, who dug out a puzzle toy strung on rope. He and Perro played tug-of-war for a few minutes before Evan relinquished the toy and Perro found a square of carpet to sprawl on, toy held in full triumph.

Evan returned to the glyphs. Again, he scratched his chin and tugged on his beard. Where could he find a path into the mind of the Minotaur?

After a moment, he smiled.

He opened his laptop, logged into his university email account, and went to a file labeled "Decipherments—False," then to a subfolder: "Decipherments—False—Cretan Scripts."

It was a long shot. But if the killer was fascinated by Cretan Hieroglyphic, and if he wanted to use them to send an actual message, maybe he was one of the hundreds who had submitted their decipherment theories to Evan.

He opened the electronic folder and began the tedious task of skimming through the emails with their various theories: Cretan hieroglyphs were the same as Egyptian hieroglyphs; Linear A was written in Hebrew;

aliens had brought Cretan Hieroglyphic to earth and buried the key to their decipherment on Atlantis before it sank into the waves.

There were other more studious attempts, and Evan had replied to those with an encouraging "Keep working." But not a single attempt had hit pay dirt.

Then he reached a letter that made him come to a full stop.

FROM: ahemming
TO: evanawilding.semantics@uchicago.edu
SUBJECT: An internal decipherment of CH

Dear Doctor Wilding:

I am writing—again—to inform you of my recent success in deciphering the ancient script known as Cretan Hieroglyphic. Despite the limited examples and an unknown language, I have solved the script! I have prepared a database of the inscriptions accompanied by a syllabic grid accounting for all characters. My work has been systematic and exhaustive, buoyed by the expectation that the rewards of deciphering this magnificent Bronze Age script will justify my efforts.

You have merely to reach out, Dr. Wilding, and confirm that you are interested in seeing my decipherment. (They tell me you're brilliant, but you've already passed up this opportunity once.) If we can connect, we will work together to finalize everything and present my success—our success—to the world.

Hygíaine!
Alex Hemming

A low tingling started near Evan's shoulder blades and moved down. TR had used the same sign-off, the ancient Greek word meaning "good health." Only here it was used, appropriately, in the singular form.

Beneath the typed signature were four Linear B glyphs.

𐀖𐀜𐀲𐀬

Evan sounded them out according to the phonetic values of the glyphs.

Mi no ta ru.

Minotaur.

Evan lowered his head to his hands. Had the answer to the killer's identity been hiding all this time in an old email folder?

Alex Hemming.

The email was dated three months ago. Evan had never responded, merely tucked it into an electronic folder. If Alex Hemming had ever presented his decipherment to the world, it had died a quiet death, like the supposed decipherments made by so many other would-be code breakers.

He raised his head and searched through his emails again, looking for Hemming's first correspondence. Nothing. Maybe he'd deleted it in one of the regular purges required by the university in the interest of saving server space. Or maybe Hemming had snail-mailed it, in which case the letter was likely filed in a cabinet in Evan's office.

He studied the email's return address, which came from a service provider he didn't recognize. The letter could be from anywhere. But surely a computer geek from CPD could trace the IP address.

Evan grabbed his phone and dialed Addie. When she didn't pick up, he returned the phone to his pocket and reread the letter.

He jumped out of his chair, went to stand at the windows.

Alex was a common, gender-neutral Greek name meaning "defender of humankind." *Hemming*, on the other hand, was a rare name derived from the Old Norse *hamr*, or *shape*. The name had an uncertain etymology but might have originally served as a nickname for men and women thought to be shape-shifters.

He was confident Távros was a pseudonym. Maybe Alex Hemming was also a pseudonym. An alias for a shape-changer.

A man of many names and many faces.

He tried Addie once more, then returned to the desk and hit "Reply," debating the wisest course of action. Engage and hopefully learn more? Or potentially scare Hemming away.

"Damned if you do," Evan said, "and damned if you don't."

"I assume you're talking about women," River said from the doorway.

Evan jumped at the sound of his voice. "I was just about to text you."

"It wouldn't have done any good. My phone is at the bottom of the Chicago River."

"Cuts down on nuisance calls," Evan said.

He regarded his brother, who leaned against the doorframe, arms folded, baseball cap snugged down, sunglasses tucked in the vee of his shirt. His comfortable physicality gave him a sense of confidence Evan could never, under any circumstances, possess.

Maybe in his next life.

"I'm heading out soon to meet Diana," River said. "She's agreed to keep me company at the Art Institute of Chicago. But I traced the coin. Or I should say, I *probably* traced the coin."

"Did you get us a name?"

"I think so."

River walked fully into the room. Perro woke from his nap and hurried over to greet his new friend, bumping River's leg.

River crouched to scrub behind Perro's ears. While Perro wriggled his joy, River looked around the room. "Ah," he said, "your *sanctum sanctorum.* It's even better than your office."

Knowing that River would share what he'd learned in his own sweet time, Evan followed his brother's gaze about the room. The bookcases and artifacts, the windows overlooking the garden with its small hedge maze, and—beyond—Ginny's mews. The sources of knowledge he'd collected and gathered into this one room made it feel like a fortress. Whatever a man needed to know, he could find many of the answers here. Through books. Through the internet. Through careful thought and hard work.

Eventually, answers gave themselves up, pearls in oysters.

As surely the Minotaur's identity would yield before their combined efforts.

Sanctum sanctorum, indeed. A secluded and mysterious place, a holy place.

"It is rather nice, isn't it?" Evan said.

"Dad would be envious if he could see it."

Evan abandoned his desk and went to stand in front of the Evan-size fireplace at the far end of the room. River trailed after him.

"Somehow," Evan said, staring into the empty depths of the fireplace, "I never thought of Oliver as much of a reader."

River came to stand next to him. Far enough away so that Evan wouldn't have to crank his neck to look at him. Close enough for his presence to be comforting.

"Not a wide reader, the way you are," River said. "But in his areas of passion, I get the sense he's damn knowledgeable. Mind-altering drugs from *A* to *Zed*. In a way, the two of you are after the same thing."

Now Evan turned. "I don't see that."

"Didn't ancient people write to capture the magic of humanity's shared experience? And also as a way to capture the gods? *Hieroglyph*, after all, means 'sacred carving or writing.'"

"That and it was an excellent method for tracking how many kilos of grain were supplied by the local serfs, and how many vessels of wine were required at the feast of the sacrifice."

River plucked a pottery votive of the goddess Hera off a nearby shelf. He ran a finger lightly down the figure, probably taking in Hera's braids and brooches, unconsciously searching for any chipping or wear. "Fifth century BCE?"

"Yes. Don't break it."

"In your work, you're looking for the essence of what it means to be human by studying the writing we leave behind. Dad is also looking for the soul of humanity. But he's doing it by peering into how our brains work."

"Hunting in jungles to find a drug-induced nirvana. It's a mad goal and a mad way to make a living. He's a dreamer."

River smiled. He carefully placed the votive back on its shelf. "So are you. Who else would tackle the Phaistos Disc?"

"That isn't a dream," Evan retorted. "It's a nightmare. And I'm coming to realize it. But Oliver is still traipsing around the world at—what is he now—sixty-two?"

"Sixty-three and happy as any man can be. Except for how he treated us."

Evan pivoted to take River's full measure. "You're saying he has regrets."

"So he says."

Evan bit off a laugh. "I hope you don't believe him."

"I'd like to."

"He made that bed," Evan said. "Now all of us have to lie in it."

River tipped his head and studied Evan for a moment.

"What?" Evan groused.

"He wants all of us to meet."

"No, he doesn't. He wants to see *you*. If I'm anything in this, it's as a mere afterthought."

One look at River's carefully blank expression and the truth hit Evan with the solid and unpleasant thunk of slop hitting the pail.

"Ah," Evan said, "I'm not Oliver's polite afterthought. I'm yours."

"You are never an afterthought."

Evan flashed back to their childhood when River had toddled everywhere after him, always wanting to know what Evan was thinking or doing. The perfectly formed little brother Evan had fully expected to hate. And whom he'd loved—and still loved—beyond all things.

River leaned against the mantel. In that moment, he looked very much like the country gentleman, if said gentleman liked to nip the master's brandy and bed the master's wife.

"What do you think, Evan? What should I—what should *we*—do?"

"You should meet him," Evan said firmly. "It will be good for you. Probably."

"To hold up a mirror to myself, you mean?"

"Not at all," Evan reassured him. "To satisfy your curiosity. And hear him out. Maybe he'll come up with some magic words that will wipe out years of pain."

River snorted, but Evan saw the faint hope in his brother's eyes. Ghosts that River wanted to either resurrect or lay to rest. Evan couldn't blame him.

"And if he does have some amazing explanation for his behavior all these years," Evan said, "you can share it with me."

"I'll share everything," River said. "You know that. But you should come."

"As if seeing his dwarf son will change his mind about me?"

"As if seeing Dr. Evan Wilding will make him realize what he's missed."

Now Evan snorted. And he knew his eyes held no ghosts of days past. "On my behalf, you can tell him he can bend over and kiss his—wait. I didn't tell you."

"Didn't tell me what?"

"Oliver gave the eulogy at the funeral for Morgan Hargrave's wife."

River shrugged. "That sounds exactly like Dad. A chance to humblebrag."

"Yes, but this could be our chance to get some dirt on the good doctor." Evan considered. Could the bastard who'd abandoned them be their best hope?

"What are you thinking?" River asked.

Evan swallowed that bitter pill. The case took precedence over personal feelings. "I'm going with you. We can ask Oliver about Morgan's vanished son, Lowell."

"He has a vanished son?"

"I'd tell you all about it if you weren't going on a date. But tell Oliver yes. Pick someplace neutral. Downtown is good. Near the lake, maybe. And not a place with food. Or drink. I want to keep this short."

River allowed a trace of a smile. "Any other demands?"

"The coin. I almost forgot. What did you learn?"

River pulled a folded piece of paper from his pants pocket and passed it over to Evan.

"I had to call in a favor from a disreputable dealer whose name shall remain out of this unless required by a court of law," River said. "Three months ago, he sold a one-stater coin with a description that matches ours to an American. A payment of $63,450 US was made in cash via a direct handover. Which means likely neither the buyer's name nor the purchase amount is valid. But that is as much as I'm going to get. The name the dealer provided was Alex Hemming."

"Alex Hemming? God's wounds." He stared at his brother.

"Have you heard his name before?"

Evan nodded. "Half an hour ago."

Evan returned to his desk and picked up his laptop, passing it to River, who perused the letter on the screen before handing it back.

"The Minotaur," River said. "This is three months old. Did you ever answer him?"

"Filed it in my computer's equivalent of the circular file."

"What does Addie say?"

"She's not picking up."

"Did you reply?" River asked.

"Not yet. I want to talk to Addie first."

"Afraid of chasing him away?"

"Or bringing him down on us."

River's smile was roguish. "Alex Hemming probably isn't his real name. Not if he used it with the coin dealer for a cash payment. But maybe he's created a false identity that can be traced. I'll stay and help."

"With what?" Evan waved a hand. "Addie and I will craft a response. The computer forensic people with Chicago PD can trace the address. Go enjoy yourself. I'll call if something comes up."

River shook his head.

"Look," Evan said, "if you really want to hang out here, maybe you can clean up after Perro in the backyard."

"Tempting," River said. "But no. Diana and I will mull things over while taking in Monet's lily ponds. Gazing at someone else's art is one of the best ways to clear the mind and let the subconscious have its say. In fact, why don't you come with us?"

"Thanks," Evan said, "but I'll stick to my *sanctum sanctorum*."

"As you wish. Diana and I will do a whirlwind tour of the museum and then come back here with dinner and hopefully our help."

"Addie and I were planning cocktails at eight," Evan said, not meeting River's eyes. "Mind if she joins us?"

"Cocktails? About time." River waggled his eyebrows, and Evan scooped up a magazine from a nearby table and threw it at him. River didn't even bother dodging.

"Just be careful," River said.

"*Sanctum sanctorum*, remember? You're the one who needs to be careful."

"Just ring me if you decide to go somewhere."

Just as River reached the door, Evan called him back.

"Don't break Diana's heart. She's on the rebound and fragile."

"If any hearts are to be broken," River said, "I suspect it will be my own." He turned away once more, and again Evan called him back.

"Do you ever think of settling down? Maybe here in Chicago?"

River's laugh was soft. "I love you, brother, but I'm not staying in Chicago longer than a month or two. After that, it's back to the trenches for me. The dirt. The bugs. The crappy food. Sunburns and snakebites. That's *my* life. And I love it." He narrowed his eyes. "Are you thinking of Mali? It wouldn't suit you."

"People change. Think about it. I head off to the wilds of Africa. You run a million-dollar institute in the Windy City."

"Us trading places is like that Mark Twain book . . . What was it?"

"*The Prince and the Pauper*," Evan said.

"Right! And how did that turn out?"

"I'm thinking about Diana."

River flushed. "Diana is lovely. She's wonderful. And she throws a mean axe. I'd be crazy not to be attracted to her. But if you're asking if we're going to fall in love and get married and raise two-point-three kids in some Chicago suburb, then no. Sorry, brother, but we're not." He wrapped his knuckles on the doorframe. "Swear you'll ring me if anything comes up. I'll see you in an hour or two."

After River left, Evan put aside the strange ache in his heart and tried Addie one more time. When she still didn't pick up, he sent a text: Can you do a background on Alex Hemming? Person of interest, calls himself Minotaur. Might be pseudonym. Could be same man as TR and Távros. Call me.

Evan returned to his stance by the windows. Perro came and sat next to him.

"In this myth," Evan said to the corgi, "I fear the monster is killing the heroes."

Perro wrinkled his furry brow.

Chapter 35

Patrick

Patrick carried Tom Walsh's binder into a diner he spotted on the Highway 83 business loop. The restaurant was recovering from what looked like one hell of a lunch rush. A harried-looking waitress with a messy ponytail and a weary smile cleared a table for him, handed him a menu, and promised to return shortly.

He'd come here after sitting in his car outside Alice Walsh's home, running the air conditioner and perusing the file Alice had given him. He called Garden City PD and spoke with a detective.

"Jake Kully was before my time," the detective had told him. "But I can ask around if you want to call back in five."

Patrick gave it ten, then called back.

"You want Donna Perry," the detective said. "She is—was—Jake's aunt on his mother's side. Closest relative now that Jake's mom has passed. Donna has lived in Garden City since the eighties, so she was here through all that mess."

Patrick thanked him, hung up, and dialed the phone number the detective had given him. A woman answered on the third ring. In the background, a dog howled. Patrick introduced himself, said he was running an investigation on a case in Chicago, and asked if she would be willing to meet him this afternoon.

"I can meet you in thirty," she said. "Then I have to go in for my shift."

Now Patrick called her once more and gave his location. She told him she lived five minutes away and hung up. When the waitress returned, he ordered iced tea and asked if they were still serving breakfast.

"Twenty-four-seven around here, honey," she told him.

"I'll have the biscuits and gravy, then." What the hell? What Mary didn't know wouldn't hurt her. He was only a few years out from retirement; there would be plenty of time to eat healthy then.

The sound of Tom Walsh's scream echoed in his mind. He called the waitress back, changed his order to a fake-egg omelet with mushrooms and spinach. "And toast with just a little butter."

She winked at him. "Whatever you want, sweetie."

Patrick mopped his face with his handkerchief. It was over a hundred degrees outside, and the diner's rattling AC couldn't keep up. Patrick was as fond of the heat as he was of the proctologist.

The door opened, and a woman came in. Midfifties, shoulder-length blond hair, nursing scrubs. Patrick stood.

"Ms. Perry?" he said.

She nodded—no smile—and came to the table. "Donna Perry. You're Detective McBrady?"

"Thanks for meeting me. Can I buy you lunch?"

"Just iced tea. I go on shift soon." She sat down across from Patrick. "Now, tell me why you're calling me about Jake after all these years."

Patrick handed her the symbol he'd removed from Walsh's binder. "You're probably familiar with this," he said.

She studied it. Handed it back. "I remember. The police said it was a kind of code for runaways."

"Is that what you and your sister thought?"

Donna crossed her arms. Patrick recognized the body language. Donna Perry was bracing herself for the unspoken accusations: Jake was a lousy kid. His mom was a lousy mother. Kids like Jake run away all the time. And so what?

"Does it matter what we thought?" Donna said. "The police had their minds made up."

"Meaning you don't think he ran away."

Donna uncrossed her arms and huffed out a breath. "He could have. His friend said he was talking about it."

"But you didn't buy it."

"Didn't matter whether I or my sister bought it. The police had all the power. And they bought it. And even if Jake *had* run away, wasn't it still the police's job to look for him? He was a *kid*."

Patrick knew he couldn't explain to this agonized woman why the police made the decision they had. Hell, he couldn't explain it to himself except to say that making tough calls was part of the job.

A waitress brought Patrick's omelet. She took Donna's order for iced tea and headed to another table.

Patrick tapped the paper he'd shown her. "Your sister found this symbol on her door, is that correct?"

Donna nodded. "Two days after Jake disappeared. Now you tell me: Why would a runaway come home just to leave a symbol that said he was a runaway?"

"Maybe to reassure his mom?"

"Reassure? *Reassure?*" Donna barked out a bitter laugh. "Carla had never seen that sign, didn't know what it meant, didn't know who left it or why. Now, why the *hell* are you bringing up all this painful stuff and asking me about that symbol?"

He weighed his options, how much to share. He said, "It's shown up in association with a case I'm working. If I knew what it meant, who might have left it, maybe it could prevent more deaths."

"Then I wish I could help you. But all I know about that sign is what I just told you."

"What about Jake's friends? Any still around that I could talk to?"

"Three of them are dead in the ground from opioid overdose. The fourth was smart enough to leave town. I have no idea where he went."

"You remember their names?"

"You can find three of their names in the cemetery, like I told you."

"I might want to talk to their families."

She softened. "No, I don't remember names. I do recall that the guy who left town, he was quite a bit older. My sister didn't much like him. But Jake said he was like a father to him. Taught him to hunt. Took him out for a good meal now and again. Debbie worried he was a pedophile. But Jake swore that wasn't so."

"Any way you could find his name?"

She lifted her tea and placed a napkin under it. "Maybe. I kept a journal back then. I might have written it down. But most of my stuff is in a storage unit. Buried under a bunch of other crap—mine and my ex's. It will take time. And timc is something I don't have a lot of."

"Any chance of a photo of the older friend?"

"Jake might have had one, but his stuff's long gone." She folded her arms again. "You really going to use that information? Because I have to tell you, I've got enough on my plate without going on a wild-goose chase because some cop has to fill out a report."

"I'd appreciate those names, Donna," Patrick said. "And whatever it is about my appearance that suggests otherwise, please try to see past that."

She caught herself in a smile. "You mean the buzz cut and the barrel chest and the look in your eyes that says you've heard it all and seen most of it and you're close to being done?"

Patrick blinked. He resettled himself in his chair, pushed aside his untouched omelet, and folded his meaty hands on the table. Close to being done? Was that what Alice Walsh had seen in him?

He put personal feelings aside. "Do you remember Detective Tom Walsh?"

She sipped her iced tea, replaced it carefully back on the same ring of moisture it had left on the napkin.

"Detective Walsh was decent. But he took early retirement."

Patrick speared a piece of the omelet but left it on the plate. "Because his mind was going. Dementia. But he never stopped thinking about Jake. Never stopped beating himself up for not finding your nephew."

"Good. I hope Jake haunts all those men who didn't do their jobs." She glanced at her watch. "I gotta go. I'll look tonight, see what I can find."

"Thank you."

Patrick gave her his business card, watched her leave. Then he opened the binder Alice Walsh had given him and flipped to a section Tom had labeled "Colby Kaplan." He read through it.

"Well, I'll be damned," he said.

A fly buzzed in the nearby window. Patrick picked up the phone and tapped a button for Addie. When she didn't answer, he tried her landline at the station, just for the hell of it.

She picked up.

"Something hinky is going on," he said.

"Says the master of overstatement," she said.

"Not this time." He filled her in on his conversations with Alice Walsh and Donna Perry. "I just finished looking through Tom Walsh's binder on the kids—Jake and Colby. Donna is going to look for the name of Jake's older friend. But you want to guess who Colby's bosom buddy was according to what his mom told CPD's Missing Persons?"

"Someone named Távros?"

"Close enough. Tav."

A silence. Then she said, "Maybe Barlow's rumored partner wasn't an adult. You think Tav was a teenage killer? And now he's all grown up?"

"Wouldn't be the first time."

"Teenage serial killers usually prey on younger children."

"Jake was fifteen. And according to Tom Walsh's wife, Tom is sure Barlow got him. But Colby was only ten when he disappeared near Oregon, Illinois."

"That's a couple of hours out from Chicago. You're giving me goose bumps."

"I'd have them myself if I weren't sitting here in a pool of my own sweat. Why don't you see what you can find out about young Colby on your end. In the meantime, where's your damn cell phone? And what are you doing in the office?"

"Sending out emails to the team. I've put Sanchez on the masks, trying to trace a source. The mask River found is at the lab. Rick and Frederica are tracking down members of the mock-trial team. Bob Carlson has found a neighbor who's lived next to the Fishbournes since Samuel and his wife moved in. A guy named Nick Macaluso. I'm talking to him right after I'm done here. And I'm looking for Lowell Hargrave, the alleged son of Morgan Hargrave."

"Who? Why?"

"Because Evan found a mention of a second son in the obituary of Morgan's wife, Philomena. I just talked to someone at the Cook County Clerk's office. Lowell Hargrave is real. He has a birth certificate that says he was born to Philomena and Morgan Hargrave in Chicago twelve months before Peter. And he has a social security number. But Emma denies he ever existed. Which I guess could be a weird form of dealing with grief. But I can't find anything else about him, and when I checked with the Illinois Department of Public Health, they didn't have a death certificate. I can contact American embassies to see what they know, but that's going to take time because I don't even know where to begin. And my phone is . . ."

He heard her rummaging around.

"I must have left my phone in the car. When are you coming back?"

"I'm catching a late flight. Who needs rest? I may just fall asleep in court tomorrow."

After they'd hung up, Patrick went to the men's room, taking the binder with him.

When he returned to his table, the omelet was cold, and the fly had gone belly up in his iced tea.

Chapter 36

Evan

Evan stared at the glyphs, hoping for something more to shake out. But arrows remained arrows, and plows were still plows. He decided to take a page from River's book and distract himself. Not with art, but with a Sunday drive.

He called the phone number on Morgan Hargrave's business card. No answer. He got the same lack of response at the Remington Foundation.

"I say we scope out the Hargrave mansion even if we can't go inside," he said to Perro. "We can take a stroll through the maze if it's not gated off. Let's go, boy."

✣

The city was a held breath, the eye of the hurricane waiting for the next round of storms, the reflooded basements and ruined cars, and plans thrashed by El Niño.

It was good to escape.

Once out of the city, Evan drove through farmland, and a countryside turned Irish green from all the rain. The sky was a dark gray, and he silenced the Bach fugues on the speaker long enough to dial in a weather station.

"Rain is in the forecast, folks. No big surprise there with our Midwest Monsoon. So enjoy the sunshine while you can. Stay tuned, and we'll keep you informed if anything really ugly starts coming our way."

So far, so good, then. Evan turned the radio to a classical music station. He glanced out at fields of corn and soybeans. Dirt paths led between emerald plots of vegetation. Farmhouses stood against the horizon.

He passed cows grazing in a pasture. Perro barked at them through the window, showing an optimism Evan hadn't known the corgi possessed.

"Maybe we can find some foul-tempered geese for you to herd," he said.

Every time his mind turned to the investigation and to the glyphs, Evan let the thoughts drift by without pursuing them. He knew from experience that anything of value that floated by would circle back. Letting thoughts come and go was the difference between thinking and ruminating. It was a way to quiet the monkey mind and let deeper thoughts surface.

Alex Hemming was a different matter. He had earned himself some hard focus.

Before he'd left the house, Evan had searched Hemming's name. He found a Swedish wedding photographer, a British gamer, and a US Marine stationed in Japan.

None likely to be Alex Hemming, would-be glyph breaker and buyer of coins.

A killer of men.

He tried again to call Addie's cell. Voice mail.

The haunting notes of the Fugue in G Minor filled the air. One of Evan's favorites. A fugue was the musical equivalent of a sonnet, subject to strict requirements and yet able to soar within those restraints. It consisted of a main melody—the theme—with simultaneous melodic lines played under and against it.

Point and counterpoint.

Like the murderer, Távros, who'd most definitely made a point. And the other melodies that swam around him: the Hargrave family; Jamal and Bryant; Samuel and Ursula; Alex Hemming; the play and the myth of the Minotaur. The problem for Evan was that he couldn't separate the principal theme from the supporting acts.

Nor could he think of a suitable counterpoint.

Was Távros also Alex Hemming? If so, then who, exactly, was the real Alex Hemming? Was he even real? Or was he another layer to the mystery they pursued?

He kept driving as the clouds raced by overhead, chased by a vast wind.

✣

After an hour, the car's GPS sent him south on Daysville Road along the Rock River. Two more turnoffs, a couple of long winding roads that brought him first close to the river, then farther away, then close again, and he spotted what had to be the Hargrave estate overlooking the river. The GPS had abandoned him a couple of turns back. But there wasn't much else around.

A call rang through the Bluetooth system, an unknown number.

"This is Dr. Wilding."

"Hi," Addie said.

"Hi," he said.

Her warmth embraced him. How could one syllable—a consonant connected to a single vowel—carry so much promise?

"What are you doing?" he asked. "Where are you calling from?"

"I've misplaced my phone. I'm using one of the department's burners. As to what I'm doing, I just finished delegating a boatload of work to the team on the Minotaur case. And I'm on my way to interview one of Fishbourne's neighbors. Also, you were right about Lowell Hargrave. He was born in Chicago twelve months before Peter."

"He's real."

"Very real. But maybe no longer alive. I'm still working it. What about you? What are you doing?"

"I'm out for a Sunday drive."

"But seriously."

"I am. River and Diana are taking in art and culture at the Art Institute, so I thought—"

She exploded. "You're supposed to be working on the glyphs. Evan, I need *something*. Ursula is missing, Jamal and Bryant have vanished off the face of the earth, and we have a sword-slinging murderer on the loose, a psychopath leaving cryptic messages around Chicago. And you're—"

"I have something for you."

"You're out for a flipping Sunday drive!" A pause. "Wait, what?"

"I have something for you. A name."

Addie's breathing came through the speaker. "For our killer? What name? Did you figure it out from the glyphs?"

"The name is a definite maybe, anyway. I went through some of the letters and emails I've received over the years—people who are sure they've cracked the code on one or another undeciphered script. Rongorongo, Cypro-Minoan, the Indus script, which some scholars argue isn't even linguistic, but instead is—"

"Evan!"

"Right. Sorry. One email stood out because the email's author said he'd deciphered Cretan Hieroglyphic. He didn't offer his solution, only suggested I email him back so that we can share the glory."

"You must get a million of those."

"Closer to a million and a half. But this particular decipherer signed off with the same Greek word TR used. And he identified himself as *Mi no ta ru*."

"*Mi no ta ru*?"

"The Minotaur. He used syllabograms from Linear B. It's not a perfect translation."

"And the name?"

"Alex Hemming. I sent you a text, but if you've lost your phone . . . Anyway, I suspect the name is a pseudonym." He explained the etymology behind the name.

"A shape-shifter?"

"If he's Távros, it seems appropriate, given the masks he wears. And there's more."

"Like in those commercials? If I order now?"

"Exactly like that. River managed to track down the sale of a coin that appears to be the same as the one that landed on the institute's front porch. It was purchased three months ago by a man in Chicago."

"Alex Hemming?"

"Ladies and gents, we have a winner."

"Evan, this is fantastic. Forward his email to my departmental email. I'll get someone on it immediately. Where are you doing your Sunday driving?"

"I'm about to knock on Morgan Hargrave's front door in Daysville. A friendly visit between two PhDs, so we can chat about work and the whole 'publish or perish' and whatnot. And I'll slip Lowell Hargrave into the conversation."

"Evan . . ."

"Evan what? He's probably not even here. No one answered the phone. Just call me curious. I want to see the place."

"Curious. We know where that got the cat."

"You're worried. That's charming."

"I'm not worried. Other than you might die of boredom with all that PhD talk, and I need you. Also, I'm never charming." A pause. "Am I?"

"You ooze charm. It seeps from your pores like the sweetest nectar. It rises from your hair in bounteous waves of delight."

"Are you done?"

"No. You—"

"You're done. Call me later. And don't do anything stupid in the meantime."

And just like that, she was gone.

Evan pulled the Jaguar into a paved curving driveway and parked near the front door of a white Greek Revival home loaded with columns and cornices, an immense pediment, a portico, and friezes. To Evan's admittedly limited knowledge of the classical style, Morgan hadn't missed a single architectural beat. Evan and Perro got out, climbed the front steps—ten of them so a man could get a little exercise when he went out to get the paper—and rang the bell. He listened for the sound of the buzzer echoing back to him, but there was only silence.

He stepped back, peering at the upper windows, looking for a light. What he saw instead were faint cracks running through the white-painted stucco, dirty windows, and shutters faded from the sun. A few tiles from the roof had landed in the garden.

"How very 'Fall of the House of Usher'–ish," he said to Perro, wondering if Morgan even lived here anymore. If anyone did.

He turned his back on the house and inspected the property. The mansion sat on a small rise so that the homeowner could be master of all he surveyed. Elegant landscaping near the house—hedges and flower beds, a groomed lawn—gave way after a few hundred yards to a wilderness of forest that surrounded the house on three sides like a fist curling around a child's playhouse.

Someone was at least tending the gardens, if not the manor.

Evan swatted at a buzzing fly, then he and Perro walked back down the stairs and toward the crest of the rise, looking for the hedge maze he'd spotted on Google Maps.

At the hill's edge, the land unfurled at their feet in a green carpet while above, the sky—now brighter—spread its immense dome: Wedgwood blue mottled with clotted cream.

The river laced its way through distant trees, a thread of glimmering blue and green.

At the bottom of the hill, a multicursal maze curved in on itself like a huddled child, a winding tangle of boxwood hedges. The maze's pattern was familiar—a version of the Hampton Court Maze, Britain's oldest surviving hedge maze—with a few deviations. From Evan's vantage point, it looked as if years had passed since anyone had taken a pair of pruning shears to the hedges. Weeds poked up through the gravel paths. Trees grew in the center of the maze, wild and ungainly. An empty stone fountain sat near the entrance.

The entire aspect was one of abandonment.

"Eerie," Evan said to Perro, who huddled against Evan's leg as if he agreed.

The maze was a puzzle that had been carved from the wilderness and then allowed to return back to nature. All such landscapes, Evan was sure, were haunted.

Stone steps led down the hill to the maze.

"Shall we?" he asked Perro.

As if sensing the need for an answer, the corgi barked.

"Then lay on, Macduff," Evan said. "And damned be him that first cries, 'Hold!'"

Down the stairs they went.

Chapter 37

Ursula Fishbourne

While she'd slept, he'd lit a candle and left it for her. In its soft light, she could make out a metal tub, partially filled with water. Also towels, a hairbrush, and a toothbrush. There was a white dress, long and flowing, trimmed with gold braid.

All of it laid out on a white blanket.

There was also cheese and bread and wine.

And a note.

She cupped her hands and drank from the tub. Then she snatched up the cheese and devoured it while she read and reread the note.

> My apologies that I could not be here to help you prepare, my dear Ursula. My work keeps me busy elsewhere. But please relax. Eat and drink. Bathe yourself. Great events will soon come to pass. You will see things denied most mortals. Experience things even the gods long for.
>
> Be of good cheer, and prepare to embark on your next journey.

She ate the bread. Drank half the wine. Then she pulled the dress over her torn suit for warmth and picked up the candle in its brass holder.

The flame's faint light revealed her prison as a hollowed space with walls of rock, an uneven floor of dirt and stones, and a backdrop of shadowy bends and openings. She stared at the shadows; any one of them might lead to escape.

Or plunge her deeper into the maze.

She folded the towel and set it at the center of one wall. That would serve as noon on an imaginary clock. Then, holding the candle high, she moved slowly in a clockwise direction.

The first shadow led to nothing but a rocky niche.

The same with the second and third.

Candlelight caught the fourth shadow, which seemed to recede away from her, sloping gently up and deepening into the heavier gloom of a narrow tunnel. She leaned down. The candle flickered as air brushed her cheek.

Her breath came in a sudden ragged gasp. Cold sweat prickled her back and between her breasts. She told herself to continue all the way around her imaginary clock. She should know every possible avenue that led to and from her prison.

But she didn't know how much time she had before *he* returned. And surely moving air meant that—not far away—there was an exit.

She set the candle carefully on a ledge. She grabbed the towel, took a final swig of the wine, then returned to the candle.

She picked it up and lowered herself to her knees. She set the candle on the ground and pushed it carefully ahead of her as she wiggled into the passage on her stomach. Stones ground into her elbows. The roof lowered until she could barely lift her head. But the breeze and the candle's faint light pulled her forward.

Sometime later—she had no sense of the passing of minutes and hours in this hellhole—the breeze grew stronger. She forced herself not to hurry. Not to let her haste tip the candle or cause her to strike her head against the rocks as the roof rose and fell.

"Almost there, Ursula," she told herself. "Easy does it."

The staccato boom of her heart was almost louder than her voice.

And then the tunnel ended in a wall of stone.

She stopped. Stared at the wall in shock. She looked left and right for a way around, searching for the source of the breeze. But there was no hidden passageway. No secret egress.

Slowly, she tipped her head up.

High above, at the apex of a skinny passage that would barely allow a rat to squeeze through, shone a small patch of blue. She blinked. Stared. Blinked. It was the sky. A cloud sailed past. The scent of grass wafted down. Warm air caressed her battered skin.

So close. She reached her hand up as if she could grab that piece of sky and hold it.

But it was as far away as the moon.

In a sudden fury, she knocked over the candle. The flame went out, leaving only the dim patch of sun.

She buried her face in the fold of her arms and wept as more clouds moved in and the light faded.

Chapter 38

Addie

Addie followed the address Detective Carlson had given her to the home of Nick Macaluso, the neighbor who claimed to have known Samuel and Ursula Fishbourne for years.

When a young man opened the front door, Addie held up her star. "Detective Bisset. I'm here to see Mr. Macaluso."

"That's me," the man said. He opened the door wider. "I'm Nick. Come in."

Addie lowered her star. Detective Carlson had mentioned a son, also Nick, who had answered Carlson's phone call.

"Is your father home?"

"He's here. But he's not feeling well and went to lie down. That's why I'm home—I flew in to look after him for a few days while his nurse is on vacation. I'm Nick Macaluso Junior. Hopefully I can answer your questions. The detective said you wanted to ask about Samuel and Ursula next door."

"You grew up here?"

"Until I left for college. I know the Fishbournes quite well. Want to talk on the back porch? It's cooler there. Air conditioner is on the fritz."

Addie stepped inside. Nick closed the door behind her, and shadows took over. She blinked, adjusting to the dim light, and followed the man through a maze of rooms and hallways. Putting aside Junior's intimidating size—he was well over six feet and built like a linebacker—maybe the young man would be a better source of information than his father. He looked close to Ursula's age.

"Here we go," Nick said, opening a door onto a covered back porch. "At least there's a bit of a breeze out here. Looks like more rain."

He gestured toward a wicker chair. Addie sat and pulled out a small spiral notebook she'd snagged from the office. She missed her phone with its notes app.

"Can I get you anything to drink?" Nick asked. He had shaggy dark hair, a beard, and one of those handlebar mustaches that seemed to be making a comeback. His nose looked like it had been broken long ago in a fight and never properly set.

"No. Thanks. What can you tell me about the Fishbournes?"

Nick scooted up a chair and sat, planting his elbows on his knees. "Can I ask you what this is about? Dad says he hasn't seen Samuel or Ursula around for a couple of days. Is everything okay?"

She gave him a polite smile. "I appreciate your willingness to answer questions, Mr. Macaluso."

He raised his eyebrows. "Oh, I get it. Not at liberty to say. I understand. But I do hope they're all right."

Addie uncapped her pen. "You've seen Ursula recently?"

"Sure. She came to spend a few days with her dad. Just like me. We were laughing over the coincidence."

"The two of you spoke?"

"Briefly. Hello in the driveway kind of thing."

"When was that?"

"Let's see, four days ago? Maybe five?"

"And how was Ursula?"

"Fine. Said she and Samuel were going to go see that new play in town. The one about the Minotaur. She suggested maybe the four of us get together for dinner one night."

"Did she mention visiting anyone else while she was in Chicago?"

Nick studied the porch's overhead rafters for a moment. "I don't think so."

"Tell me about when the two of you were children."

"Boy, that's a trip down memory lane. Dad and Samuel were friends from way back. I can't remember a time when they weren't our neighbors. That's how I got to know Ursula. She was a couple of years older than me, but we played together a lot when we were kids because of our parents. I was pretty lonely—no other kids in the neighborhood. And she was nice. But she also had her own group of friends, and I wasn't part of that."

"Friends from school?"

He shook his head. "Nah. I would have known those kids. Like I said, we were only a couple of years apart. I mean, there was one kid, Jamal, that Ursula and I went to high school with. But we weren't in elementary or middle school with him."

Addie kept her face expressionless. "Jamal James?"

"Maybe? I don't remember."

"So, a kid named Jamal. Any other names you remember?"

Nick's laugh could barely pass muster as such. "Oh yeah. The Hargrave brothers. And Emma Hargrave. Boy, do I remember them. Peter was mostly a prick, but he had his not-so-bad moments. Emma, now she was a stuck-up b-i-t-c-h. And Lowell? He was nuts."

Electricity stirred in Addie's gut. She wrote down *siblings*. Drew a square around it. "Tell me about them."

"Their dad was a friend of Samuel's, I think. Or maybe some kind of business partner. My dad could probably tell you more about that. But there were fourteen kids in their little clique, counting the Hargrave creeps, Jamal, and Ursula."

"Did you hang out with them?"

"Me?" Nick snorted. "I was beneath them. They were like the worst kind of school clique. Ursula wasn't even Ursula when she was around them. They used to play serial killer. I'm not kidding. Kind of like cowboys and Indians, but they'd pretend they were hunting serial killers. They'd be in, like, teams. Seven killers, seven—I don't know—detectives."

"And Lowell?"

"He was always a serial killer. Always. He was the team lead, from what I could tell. And Peter led the other team." Nick leaned back in his chair. He swatted at something on his arm, and a small bead of blood rose on his skin. "Not much love lost between those two. Sometimes Peter could be as mean as Lowell, but he was better at hiding it. Sneakier, you know? I think if you're going to be a bad dude, you might as well own it."

In her mind, Addie went back to her interview with Emma.

Brother, Emma had corrected her. *Just Peter.*

Was Lowell a banished black sheep, his name stricken from the family record?

"What was Peter and Lowell's relationship with Emma?"

"I was an outsider, remember?" He gave Addie a lopsided grin. "But I might have done some spying."

She nodded for him to continue.

"Even as a kid, I knew a love triangle when I saw one. Emma was always either with Peter or Lowell. Never by herself. Never tight with the other kids. Which I thought was a little creepy. I mean, I know they weren't, like, actually related. But seeing Emma hold hands with one of them or kiss one of them—it was still gross, you know?"

"How old were they at that time?"

Nick stared up, thinking. "By the time Emma came, I was probably eleven. Old enough to see she was a knockout. So, maybe thirteen?" He lowered his gaze. "I guess you'd call whatever those guys had going puppy love. It seemed to me that Emma liked Lowell better. Women love bad dudes, right?"

He smiled.

Addie refrained from comment.

From inside came a faint moan. Nick stood.

"That's Dad. Do you mind? I'll just go check on him."

"Of course."

Nick went into the house, letting the screen door bang behind him.

Addie stood and walked out onto the lawn. The Fishbournes lived right next door; she could see the tree house. No wonder Nick had been a spy. A lonely child living next door to a gaggle of kids. It must have been its own form of torture.

She glanced up at a sycamore tree. It was the kind of tree she would have spent most of her days in when she was a kid. Easy climbing. Wide branches that made for a good perch. Dense leaves in the summer if you didn't want to be seen. Addie would bet her phone—if she knew where it was—that you could look right inside Ursula's tree house from halfway up that tree.

The door banged, and Nick reappeared on the porch. Addie returned to her chair.

"Is your father okay?"

"He will be. He's got bad hips, but he's been putting off getting them replaced." Nick shook his head. "He thinks the cure is worse than the disease. I gave him some ibuprofen, but that will upset his stomach. He sends his apologies, says you can call later if you have more questions."

"Give him my regards." She picked up her pen and notepad. "So, Jamal and the Hargraves. Did you know the names of the other kids?"

He shook his head. "Sorry."

"Ever hear of someone named Alex Hemming?"

He looked away, scratched his ear. "I don't think so."

"What about Távros or TR?"

Nick dug a finger in an ear and rooted around. "Doesn't ring any bells."

"If anything comes to you, will you let me know?"

He turned back. His eyes met hers. "Sure."

Addie drew the bull symbol on her notebook—the triangle and crescent moon—then turned it around to show him.

"Have you seen this before?" she asked.

Nick's eyes went wide. "Sure, yeah. That was one of their signs."

Bingo, Addie thought.

"Signs? What do you mean?"

"They had this, like, code they used so they could leave messages for each other. I don't know how it worked. I mean, Ursula told me once that everyone had their own sign, and the teams did, too. I think they might have even given each other tattoos. Ursula said her sign was a cat head."

A coolness touched Addie's cheeks as if a breeze had blown in.

"You're talking about the serial-killer teams?" she said.

"Yeah, those. And also for, like, regular games. Kick the can and shi—stuff. I'd see those symbols around the neighborhood sometimes, carved on trees and fences. Their version of 'Kilroy was here.' That's what my dad used to say. Kilroy. You know how dads are."

Just as Evan had speculated. Personal signs and team logos.

Addie drew a couple of the glyphs from memory. Dang it that she didn't have her phone. She held up the page. "Signs like these?"

He leaned in. "Exactly like those. They used to be all over the tree house, but Samuel painted over them sometime after I left for college."

"He painted the entire tree house?" Addie was thinking of the symbol on the tree-house door.

"I assume so. I never actually looked." A winning smile. "I outgrew my spying days."

She pointed to the sycamore. "You climbed that tree?"

He nodded but didn't blush. "I would borrow my dad's binoculars. That's how I knew about the signs. And about Emma and her brothers."

"Let's go back to Lowell Hargrave," Addie said. "What else do you remember about him?"

"He killed Ursula's cat."

Addie looked up.

"Hung it from the tree house," Nick said in a matter-of-fact voice.

"Did that upset you?"

"Of course it upset me," Nick said, not sounding at all upset. "A cat, for Christ's sake. That would upset anyone, wouldn't it?"

The sudden disconnect between Nick's level voice and his unhappy expression was remarkable. The winning smile was gone. "Are you okay, Mr. Macaluso?"

He wiped his face on his sleeve.

"Just hot," he said.

"Did you tell an adult about what happened?"

He studied his feet. "I didn't want it getting back to Lowell in case he figured out who ratted on him. I was a big kid for my age. Tall. But not built like Lowell. Not back then. I was afraid of him."

"You were afraid he'd hurt you?"

"Lowell was a gallon of gasoline looking for a match. And it turned out I was right. He broke my arm. But it had nothing to do with the cat."

"Why did he hurt you?"

"Why the hell does a guy like Lowell do anything?" Again, that oddly mechanical voice. Maybe detachment was how Nick processed trauma. "Ursula's dad must have told her to invite me over. Maybe Samuel saw me watching them and could tell how lonely I was. Like an idiot, I accepted. This was around the time that Mrs. Fishbourne died, and I'd been seeing more of Ursula. She'd sit outside at night, and sometimes I'd go sit with her. We got closer, you know? The day that she invited me over was a day when all the kids were there. I thought I'd be part of the clique."

Addie took notes. "What happened?"

"Lowell sucked me right in. The thing about Lowell is . . . He was evil, right? I mean, anyone who'd hurt a cat like that, for kicks and grins, he's evil. Everyone agreed on that. But he was charismatic, too. Friendly seeming. Good looking. Smart. Made you want to be his best buddy. He invited me up to the tree house and apologized for the times he'd been mean to me. Told me he thought I should be a member of their club. Team Lowell, he said. Then he pushed me."

Addie looked up from her notepad. "He pushed you?"

Nick was sweating, his gaze bobbing around like a cork on a bloodshot sea.

"Out of the tree house," he said flatly. "He could have killed me."

"Mr. Macaluso, can I get you some water?"

"Yeah. No. I'll get it." He gave her a forced smile and stood. "I'll be right back."

Addie watched him go inside. She rose and went to the screen door and peered into the gloom of the house. The kitchen was empty. From somewhere in the house, she heard a door close.

The hair lifted on the back of her neck for reasons she couldn't articulate. Her gut was telling her something was off. It was probably the case getting to her. But still . . . Nick's stories about the cat and his own broken arm were weirdly out of sync with his robotic voice, even if unemotional speech was a coping strategy.

She eased down the door handle and slipped into the kitchen. The house was deathly quiet. She stood and listened for a moment, debating her approach. She decided to announce herself; the last thing she needed was to be shot as a suspected intruder.

"Mr. Macaluso?" she called. "Are you sure you're okay?"

She walked through the kitchen and into the hallway. On her right was a formal dining room. To her left, stairs went to an upper floor shrouded in gloom.

"Mr. Macaluso?"

A long, low moan.

Addie set her notepad down on the bottom stair and went up, staying close to the railing where the stairs would be less likely to creak. At the top, she found herself facing a series of closed doors.

Another moan. Louder. It came from the first door on the right.

She put her hand on the knob, turned it.

Inside, motionless on a bed, lay an older man she assumed to be Nick Macaluso Senior.

"Mr. Macaluso," she whispered. The air smelled of age and urine and a man's cologne that couldn't cover either one.

The man didn't move.

Addie sat on the edge of the bed and took Mr. Macaluso's pulse. It was strong. His eyes fluttered. He stirred, then began to peacefully saw logs.

A bottle of Motrin with a childproof cap sat on the nightstand next to a glass of water. She looked at the man's pants for any sign of wetness but now suspected the smell of urine was from an earlier accident.

She rose and returned to the door. With a last look at the sleeping man, she gently pulled the door closed and turned around.

Nick loomed behind her. In the gloom of the hall, she could see he was no longer sweating. He had his hands stuffed in his pants pockets.

He stared at her. "What are you doing?"

"Back up," she said.

"Are you spying on us?"

She pushed back the edge of her jacket to show him the butt of her gun. "Back up now."

He removed his hands from his pockets and raised them in an appeasing gesture.

"You invaded my home," he pointed out. "Why were you looking in on my dad?"

"I was worried about both of you. Keep backing up. Down the stairs, all the way to the kitchen."

He did as she said. At the bottom stair, she scooped up her notepad. As soon as they reached the kitchen, he collapsed into one of the chairs.

"What's going on, Mr. Macaluso?" Addie asked.

He grabbed a towel, pressed it to his face.

"I was having a panic attack," he said. "I get them sometimes. All that talk about Lowell and the kids."

"It brings up bad memories."

"I have . . . stuff I'm working through. And now you're asking me if I've seen Ursula and Samuel. What's happened to them?"

The sudden gust banged the screen door. Without taking her eyes off Nick, Addie crossed the room and latched it.

"Did Ursula say anything about Lowell Hargrave visiting?" she asked.

Nick lowered the towel. His eyes were wide. "Are they *dead*?"

"That's an interesting leap, Mr. Macaluso. Have you seen Lowell Hargrave around?"

"Lowell Hargrave." Nick chuckled. "Oh boy, are you guys ever barking up the wrong tree. You think Lowell Hargrave did something to Samuel and Ursula?"

"What do you think?"

Now he laughed. "Lowell Hargrave is dead. He's been dead for years."

He stood. Swayed.

"Please sit down, Mr. Macaluso, before you pass out."

He grabbed a kitchen chair and swung it into her.

Addie went down hard, crashing into the counter, bouncing off, falling to her knees. She grappled for her gun as Nick swung the chair again, slamming the side of her skull.

Pain brought flashing lights with it. The world shrank then expanded to a bleary whiteness. She reached again for her gun. As it cleared the holster, he uttered a guttural growl and kicked her. She toppled like a tree in a high wind. The gun skittered across the floor.

The sound of fleeing footsteps and the back door banging open echoed through her head.

"Stop!" she cried. She got to her hands and knees. A thread of blood fell from her mouth onto the floor. She stared at the coin of her own blood for a moment, watching it spread.

"Get up," she told herself. "Get up."

She used the abandoned chair to haul herself to her feet. She retrieved the gun, then drag-walked to the back door and out onto the porch. Nothing about her seemed to be working right.

From somewhere close by, Nick said, "You're losing the game."

Addie dialed 911. "Officer needs assistance." She rattled off the address. Then she half stumbled down the stairs, her gun up.

"Távros," she said, turning slowly in place while her brain tried to keep up. Part of her mind was telling her to get her back against something. To find a defensible spot.

She moved out into the yard.

He was so close. But where?

"Hands up!" Her voice sounded distant and tinny. "Don't make me shoot!"

He dropped on her from the sycamore tree, knocking her flat. He straddled her and pinned her arms.

"Moo," he said, and she understood that she wasn't the one who'd moved her porcelain cow from the buffet to the table. Távros had been in her home.

Nick Macaluso was Távros.

He struck her again, then stood and dragged her to her feet. A wave of darkness swamped her, tugging her down.

Thoughts batted at her as she sank toward oblivion.

How could I have been so stupid?

And, *Is Távros really Nick or just pretending to be?*

And, *If he is pretending, where is the* real *Nick Macaluso Junior?*

And, finally: *Evan.*

CHAPTER 39

EVAN

Evan and Perro plunged into the maze and into a fairy tale.

Mysteriously dying hedges rose high on either side of them, casting deep shadows, their patchy brown branches entangled with snarls of local flora. Wind coming off the river whipped the dead sticks together in a scratchy staccato. The former gravel path was a wilderness of weeds, in places giving way altogether to muddy earth.

A fairy tale, but one taken from a page in the Brothers Grimm. The kind where children got lost and were found by an evil witch who takes them home for dinner—hers.

"Worse than the house," Evan muttered, pushing onward.

He followed the rule of maze navigation by always going right. It wasn't the fastest way through a maze, but unless you ran into a closed area—an island—you would eventually find your way out.

He glanced back. The maze's entrance had long since vanished behind winding turns.

Part of him thought the wisest thing to do was to turn around, go back up the hill, climb into the Jaguar, and drive away without a backward glance. Something felt terribly wrong with this ruined maze, the crumbling house.

But he was a scholar—he prided himself as such. And he realized, as he took in the disarray, that he hadn't stopped to consider the other side of the Minotaur.

The Minotaur not as monster but as sacrifice.

Before the Greeks and then the Romans proved their superiority to Cretan culture by turning the man-bull into a flesh-eating beast, before the labyrinth was fashioned in the minds of men as a prison, the bull—sometimes shown as a god, sometimes a king—symbolized fertility and strength. Often depicted mating with a goddess or priestess, the bull provided the seed of life.

The maze path split. Evan stayed right, Perro nosing ahead of him.

And yet their killer was fully embracing his role as monster, not sacrifice. He served as the bringer of death, not life. How did he see himself?

Perro stopped. Barked.

Something rustled nearby. Something large.

Evan froze.

More rustling, a scrape, and then the hedge ahead of them exploded with a shower of leaves and broken branches. A creature leapt onto the path.

A buck with a rack that would make a hunter sell his soul.

The buck gazed at them in bewilderment. Its muscles twitched as it shook its great antlered head, then it turned and raced down the path in a whirl of thudding hooves. A moment later, there came more crashing sounds as the animal sought escape.

"Good luck to you," Evan said, pressing a hand to his chest to will his heart to slow.

When they rounded the next bend, the deer had vanished.

Evan guessed they were now near the center of the maze. An accomplishment, of sorts. Here, weed trees had sprouted among the planted evergreens. A former garden was so choked with bull thistles, bindweed, and dandelions that it was impossible to see what flowers had originally grown there. A stone wall had fallen to ruin.

He wondered if the garden had belonged to Philomena, and if Morgan had let it go to ruin in his grief.

Half-hidden among the weeds was a large slab of stone pressed into the earth. Evan paused next to it, hands on his thighs.

It looked like dark-green granite. Like a fallen gravestone, except it carried no words, only faint scratches that might have once meant something. The dirt around it was disturbed as if it had been recently moved. Some of the weeds were crushed.

Evan lowered himself to his knees. He tried pushing the stone, but it wouldn't budge. It would take someone with Diana's muscles—or at least a crowbar—to get any traction.

Perro laid back his ears and growled. Evan got to his feet. He had the distinct feeling of being watched. Perhaps the buck gazed at them from another row. Maybe rabbits hid in the hedges and crows in the pines.

And yet . . . this felt unfriendly. Evan crouched next to Perro and strained his ears. But he heard nothing save the breeze rattling the hedges and the trees.

He straightened. "Faster out than in," he told Perro.

Not long after, they reached the final turn. A distant rectangle of light revealed itself as the exit. As they drew near, a man stepped into the lighted square. He stood with his body in profile, ramrod straight with his right arm raised like a fencer about to go en garde. In his hand he held something Evan couldn't quite make out.

He jerked to a stop and gripped Perro's leash.

It wasn't a sword, which Evan half expected the man to have, but something rather different.

A gun.

Evan took a few steps back, wondering how well he and Perro could hide.

Then the man called to Evan in a voice he recognized.

"Dr. Wilding!"

Morgan Hargrave, patriarch, social scientist, and owner of this ruined maze and the decaying mansion.

"Are you going to shoot me?" Evan called back.

"Not today," Morgan said. He lowered the gun as Evan approached. "What are you doing out here?"

"I went for a drive to get out of the city and thought I'd pay you a visit. I rang the bell. Next time I'll pound on the windows."

Morgan didn't smile. "You were foolish to come alone to the maze."

For the first time, Evan could see that Morgan was nervous, and not because he was facing down a dwarf. The older man kept his finger near the trigger and looked around as Evan and Perro joined him and they headed toward the stone steps leading up the hill.

"You have a minotaur here?" Evan asked.

Morgan paused and looked down at him. The man's expression was grim. His gaze turned inward even as he continued his surveillance of the woods around them.

"It's—" He seemed on the verge of saying one thing before suddenly switching tacks. "A mountain lion," he said shortly.

"As real as a minotaur, then," Evan said. "I've heard we don't have mountain lions in Illinois."

"Tell that to the lion. We get one through here every few years. But I'd hate to have to shoot it, so let's get inside."

✣

Morgan Hargrave's home was what might generously be called shabby chic. Clean but worn, as if nothing had been done with the furniture or flooring in decades. As Morgan walked ahead of Evan, turning on lights, a warm glow filled the rooms. The scent of flowers wafted down the hallway—Hargrave must have a large bouquet somewhere.

"We'll sit in the library," Morgan said. "Just down here."

"It's a beautiful home," Evan said, seeing the potential.

"You're being kind. Since my wife died and the kids moved on, I've had trouble bothering myself with its upkeep. But Gretchen comes twice a week. You can thank her for the flowers and the lack of dust. And a gardener keeps up with the landscaping."

"He's not worried about the mountain lion?"

Morgan gave him a sharp look. "He carries a gun."

He stopped in front of a door and gestured Evan and Perro into a book-filled room with a fireplace, comfortable chairs, family photos arranged on the shelves, and a bar cart.

"Whiskey?" Morgan asked, waving Evan in the direction of a chair.

"One finger, thank you. I have to drive back to Chicago." Evan signaled for Perro to sit next to him. The corgi yawned and plopped down on the rug.

"Of course." Morgan poured two fingers into a crystal glass and passed it to Evan. He poured three generous fingers for himself and settled in a chair on the other side of a black-marble coffee table.

"I think you'll find it's an excellent scotch," he said.

Evan sampled it. Enjoyed the warmth on his tongue and in his belly; he reminded himself to take it slow. "It's exceptional."

Morgan accepted the compliment with a nod. He stretched out his legs. "So, what brings you here? Aside from a Sunday drive, of course."

"I hope you'll forgive me for bringing this up. But as I was looking into your research—"

"Thank you."

"Of course. You're doing fascinating work. And I'd love to come back to that. But on a more personal note, I saw the obituary for your wife. I'm so sorry."

Morgan's eyes widened, and his eyebrows rose in surprise. A flash of what Evan recognized as grief crumpled the man's face into a series of furrows. Morgan lowered his head and took a healthy swallow of scotch, and when he looked up again, his face was tight with rage.

"Cruel of you, isn't it?" he said. "To accept a man's hospitality and then bring up something so painful."

"I'm sorry," Evan said sincerely. "I didn't know her death would still . . ." His voice trailed off, lost in the sea of Morgan's grief and another emotion he couldn't identify. Regret?

"You didn't think bringing up my wife's death would still bother me?" He cleared his throat. "Philomena's death was a shock. You don't get over that."

It had been more than twenty years. That the man's grief was still so close to the surface surprised Evan. "Forgive me. I'm sorry that my own curiosity brings up such a painful topic. But you had mentioned my father the other day, and I couldn't help but notice that he gave a eulogy at the service."

Morgan stood and went to the bar cart. He picked up the bottle. "More?"

"No, thank you."

Morgan poured himself three more fingers and returned to his chair.

"I admire Oliver and consider him a friend. But I got the sense he was never much of a father."

Evan stayed silent.

"Ah, I see I've also touched a wound. Oliver was always married to his work. If he and Olivia hadn't gotten pregnant with you—but I can see by your face I've said too much."

Evan doubted Morgan's words were anything but calculated. A wound for a wound. Well, he might as well get what he could out of it.

"That's why they got married?" Evan said. "Because she was pregnant?"

"For a social scientist," Morgan said, "I can be a social idiot."

But his expression suggested smugness rather than repentance.

Evan went along. "No, it's all right. It clears up a question I've always had, which is why a man like Oliver would want a family."

"It's a difficult balance. I always knew that I wanted a family, and I love being a father. But Oliver—he had his eye on bigger prizes."

Evan opened his mouth to ask about Lowell, then stopped himself. What if something had happened to the boy? If Morgan was still grieving his wife, what would he feel about the loss of a child?

"That's part of what made my research so enjoyable," Morgan said. "The power to shape our children—first through their genes and then how they are raised. Even my decision to marry Philomena had an element of calculation. She had good genes. I, on the other hand, grew up in an orphanage, and my ancestry has only recently come to light. I've worked to defeat the defects that linger in my family's past, and my research has fed the decisions I make as a father."

"I wondered about your research in that regard," Evan said. "You talk about good and evil, and I can imagine how parents—upon learning their child is genetically predisposed to become a monster—might want to protect that child by whatever means possible."

Morgan glanced out the window. His expression was somber. "Or to hide him from the world."

"Like the Minotaur in its labyrinth?"

Morgan smiled. "You're thinking of the play, of course. Tell you what. Come by my lab. Tomorrow morning, if that's convenient. The address is on the business card I gave you. I'll share more of my research with you—give you an inside view."

"Thank you. I'd enjoy that." Before he could be what Brits called a melt—a coward—Evan said, "Tell me about Lowell."

Morgan startled, splashing his whiskey. He stared down at his damp shirtfront.

Evan rose and grabbed a dish towel from the cart and gave it to Morgan.

"You do seem determined to upend my evening," Morgan said, blotting at the whiskey. "Why are you asking about Lowell?"

Evan replaced the damp towel on the bar cart and resumed his seat. "I saw his name in Philomena's—in her obituary, and I was curious."

Morgan stood and went to the bookcases. He plucked a photo from a shelf and passed it to Evan.

"That's Lowell on the left. Peter on the right. They were sixteen and seventeen then."

The boys looked very much alike. Blond hair, the chiseled good looks Evan had noted in Peter when they met at the theater. Both boys tall and sturdily built, like rugby players. They stood with their arms slung over each other's shoulders, as any two brothers might. But there was a stiffness in their posture, a lack of warmth in their smiles. As if the photographer had told them how to pose.

"Lowell died four years ago," Morgan said, returning to his seat. "They ruled it a suicide, but I was never sure. Suicide isn't the Hargrave way."

"I'm so sorry." Evan set the photo on the coffee table. He was, indeed, sorry. He was also disappointed that one potential lead had just been closed off.

"No, it's all right. I never mind talking about Lowell. You just startled me. He was a handful as a child. Got in more trouble than I thought possible." Morgan swirled the remaining whiskey in his glass. "He was too smart for everyone else. Brilliant. And that's not just a doting father speaking. His IQ tests placed him at genius level. The apple doesn't fall far from the tree."

He glanced at Evan as if expecting a challenge. Evan nodded for him to continue.

"I tried the local schools, but they didn't know what to do with him. Then I tried homeschooling him. But I don't think he ever recovered from his mother's death. His senior year in high school, I finally sent him off to a boarding school in Switzerland. I thought a change of environment, a little firmness, would be good for him."

Evan waited. He was thinking of a boy with a strict father and an absent mother.

"He hated it. He ran away twice. The second time he went to Crete, and I thought that maybe that was exactly what he needed. To be with his mother's family, to have a slow, quiet life for a time while he met Philomena's relatives. You mentioned a labyrinth earlier, and Lowell was fascinated by the myths of Crete. Had been from the time he was very young. Maybe he remembered the stories his mother told him when he was a baby. He even made his own secret language using glyphs from the Cretan scripts." A soft chuckle. "He assigned a glyph to the kids he knew. He was domineering."

The implications of this sent a chill down Evan's spine. It took an act of sheer physical will for him not to sit up and dial Addie's phone.

Calmly, he said, "Did he share his secret language with you?"

"Let his old man in on his secrets?" Morgan chuckled again. "No."

"And the kids he assigned glyphs to. Seems like there wouldn't be a lot of children way out here. Who were they?"

Morgan's gaze turned shrewd. "Now that's an interesting question, Dr. Wilding. And not one I'm at liberty to discuss."

"But Jamal was one of these kids."

"You're clever, aren't you?" Morgan smiled the way a wolf might.

The room darkened, an early twilight brought on by the advancing storm. If it was an omen, Evan chose to ignore it.

"What about . . . ?" He dug out his phone and showed Morgan the triangle-and-moon figure from the tree-house door. "This symbol? Do you recall seeing this?"

Morgan leaned across the coffee table, then shook his head. "I either can't recall, or the answer is no. It's not a Cretan glyph, is it?"

"It's similar," Evan said. "Please go on."

The older man stretched his legs under the table. "Have you ever considered the Minotaur as a monster, yes, but also a sacrifice?"

Only about an hour ago. "What do you mean?"

Morgan looked into his now-empty glass. Lamplight made the crystal sparkle. "I pulled Lowell out of school and gave him my permission to stay on Crete. I thought I was helping him. I should have recognized the darkness in him for what it was."

Perro jumped to his feet and barked.

A figure appeared in the doorway. Evan hadn't heard anyone come in.

"Emma!" Morgan said, flushing as if he'd been caught in some wrongdoing.

Emma Hargrave. The aloof dancer who'd scolded Addie for not doing her homework. She rounded on Evan. "How dare you sit there, a guest in our home, and bring up Lowell? How dare you hurt my father this way?"

Perro bounced on his feet and kept barking. Emma looked like she wanted to kick him. Evan grabbed the dog's leash and firmly told him to sit and to be quiet. Perro obeyed with obvious reluctance.

Morgan pulled in his legs and stood. "It's all right, Emma. It's good to acknowledge the past." His words came out slurred as he peered past her toward the open doorway. "Are you here alone?"

"Who would be with me? Peter?" Emma looked at her father's empty glass and the open bottle and glared at Evan. "You're the one they call the Sparrow, aren't you? I saw that your name was linked to that dreadful murder in Couch Place."

Morgan frowned. "What murder?"

"Oh, God, Morgan, you really do need to get your head out of your ass now and then." She tossed her head, rippling the waves of her hair.

Was that a leaf caught in the long tresses?

"Emma!" Morgan said with quiet menace. "That is no way to speak to me or to our guest."

She shrugged. "Peter said to tell you he's staying in his apartment in the city tonight. There's a party or ten."

"Why are you here, then?"

"Why are you pretending that you care?"

The two glared at each other.

If this was a contest of wills, Emma lost. She spun on her heel and stormed from the room, regal even in her fury. Morgan followed her out. Evan clamped his fingers around Perro's muzzle to keep the dog from baying like a foghorn in her wake. From the front of the house came the sound of the dancer's steps as she fled to the home's upper floor, then Morgan's slower tread, returning.

Evan whipped out his phone, snapped a picture of the photo of Lowell and Peter just as Morgan reappeared.

"It's getting late," Evan said as if he'd been checking the time.

In the window, lightning fanned across the sky in a cascade of glittering white.

Morgan eyed the whiskey bottle. "Then you'd better head out, Dr. Wilding. Hell of a storm coming. The roads can get bad out here."

Evan followed Morgan to the front door. A few spats of rain struck the windows on either side.

"Just one more question, if I may," Evan said as Morgan opened the door.

"Please," Morgan said. "Ask away."

"Do you know the Fishbournes?" Evan asked. Behind him, lightning flared, irradiating the entryway. "Samuel and his daughter, Ursula?"

At first, Morgan's face registered only confusion. Then he turned pale. He gripped the doorknob until his knuckles stood out. Thunder rolled its way across the heavens. All that was needed to complete the Gothic scene was a madwoman hiding upstairs.

Maybe that was Emma.

"Was Fishbourne the poor man killed in the alley?"

"Why would you think that?"

"Because it's the Sparrow who's asking. I—I knew him years ago. Why?"

"Were Ursula and Lowell friends?"

"No, no. Never friends. Lowell didn't make friends."

"Enemies?"

Morgan recovered himself. "You'd best get back to Chicago before the storm breaks."

"Then thank you for the whiskey," Evan said. "And for your time."

"My pleasure," Morgan said.

In his eyes, something flickered and, for a moment, Evan thought he'd glimpsed an expression of a distant madness rolling in like the coming storm.

Then he shook his head. Likely just the eerie mix of dark and light in the entryway.

Once outside, Evan turned back and glanced in one of the windows.

Morgan was hurrying up the stairs after Emma.

Maybe she hadn't lost, after all.

Chapter 40

Addie

It was half past eight. Addie tossed the hospital gown on the bed and pulled on her pants and shirt. Her head and ribs hurt like a mother, but she felt clear again. The doc said she'd suffered a mild concussion and had substantial bruising.

"You're young and healthy," he'd said cheerfully. "Your scans are good. You'll heal quickly. Just don't drive, and make sure you have someone with you for the next twenty-four hours."

"What about the older man? Mr. Macaluso?"

"Sorry, I don't know. They must have taken him to a different ER."

It had been patrol who'd found her sitting propped against the sycamore tree, holding her head in her hands. They'd called an ambulance over her protests. She'd finally seen that if she wanted to win the war, she had to give up the battle. She agreed to go to the hospital after they'd taken her description of her attacker, issued an alert for an armed and dangerous suspect, and shut down the neighborhood while they searched for him. Which had yielded nothing. No surprise. Távros was no fool.

At least he hadn't taken her gun. She didn't have to add that humiliation to the fact she'd let him get away.

While she'd waited for the ambulance, patrol had verified that there was a real Nick Macaluso Junior, alive and well and living in Milwaukee. Nick told the officer who phoned that he'd head immediately for Chicago to see to his dad.

Addie had asked for and received his DMV photo. As she'd already suspected, the man who'd greeted her at the Macaluso home and assaulted her was not the real Nick Macaluso.

He was Távros. Which should have given them a description to go on. And indeed, she'd provided all the details of his appearance with the police alert. But she suspected the shaggy hair, the mustache and beard, the seemingly broken nose, had been part of a disguise. Távros hadn't even been trying to look like Nick Junior. He'd cared only to conceal his true face.

The question remained how he had known she was coming. She could only assume it had something to do with her missing phone.

Now Addie pushed back the curtain covering the cubicle in the ER and flagged a passing nurse.

"Doc says I'm ready to go. Do I need to sign anything?"

The nurse said, "One sec." When she returned, she brought a stack of papers, most involving instructions for recovering from a concussion, and a statement she had to sign that she would be under observation for the next twenty-four hours. Addie signed everything the nurse put in front of her and left the ER.

At the front desk, she asked if there was a phone she could use. Someplace private, she said. A nurse led her to a back office, apologized for the clutter, then left her alone.

She dialed Evan.

He answered with, "You okay?"

"I saw Távros tonight," she said.

She heard him draw in his breath. "Addie! God's bones, are you all right? What happened?"

She filled him in on her encounter with Távros, giving him a point-by-point review of their conversation and only minimizing the assault a little.

"Damn it to high hell, Addie. Where are you?"

"I just checked out of the ER. The doc says I'm fine. All I need is a little rest."

"I'm coming to get you. Which hospital?"

A knock and the door swung open.

"Sorry to interrupt," said the nurse who had brought Addie here. "But you've got a call at the front desk."

"I'll be right there. Evan, I have to go."

He said, "Which hospital?"

She dropped her voice. "Be patient, please. Let me see what they want, and I'll call you back."

She followed the nurse to the reception area, picked up the phone, and pressed a flashing button when the nurse pointed to it. She listened while dispatch told her of a body, another man ritualistically murdered. She leaned against the desk and stared unseeing at a medical poster on the wall. After a moment, she told dispatch to have whoever picked her up bring her a burner phone.

Then she hung up and called Evan, told him they might have another victim, then asked what he'd learned at Morgan Hargrave's home. He told her about Lowell Hargrave—four years dead, a suicide after being sent first to Switzerland and then Crete. He texted her a photograph of Lowell with Peter when the boys were teens.

She disconnected after promising to call back when she knew more, and studied the photograph. She'd been right about the disguise. Lowell was no one she recognized. She pondered Emma's staunch denial that she ever had a brother named Lowell.

Maybe Lowell was a bad seed. Still alive, but dead to his family.

She went out through the lobby doors to where a squad car was pulling up.

✣

An hour and a half later, Addie stood at the mouth of a paved side road that ran between two sprawling warehouse complexes. A drink manufacturer on the left. Paper goods on the right.

In the middle of the road was a circular maze made of white stones.

And in the middle of that lay the body of Bryant James.

A storm had blown through sometime between when Bryant had died and a security guard noticed the body and informed CPD.

Now the three-ring circus in blue had gone to work in the hazy night. Patrol officers walked up and down the roads looking for witnesses or anything the killer might have left. Techs worked the scene. The ME was already here. Addie had examined the body, spoken with the ME, then retreated to this spot to get a feel for the place.

She called Evan again and asked him to come to the scene, then stood with her hands thrust in her pockets, preparing to re-enter the fray.

On her way here, she'd texted one of the computer forensics guys and asked him to track Alex Hemming's IP address: the computer he'd used to send his email to Evan. He'd called back just as she'd exited her ride. As with the search for the living man, the search for his digital ghost was going nowhere fast. Addie didn't claim to be a tech guru, but she understood that Hemming had used something called VPN chaining to bounce his signal all over the world, making tracking difficult and filling the search with legal roadblocks. Worse, even if they managed to trace the address to a VPN company, those companies—unlike a normal internet-service provider—didn't usually keep logs. A subpoena would be worthless if there was no data.

"And if he connected to one VPN from another VPN," the computer guy told her, "we're looking at multiple companies we'll have to work our way through. If they even have anything to offer."

"Keep on it," she'd told him. "It's important."

Even if the tech couldn't track Hemming down in the next day or two, it would help when the case went to court. In the meantime, she'd told Evan to hold off on replying to Alex Hemming. She didn't want him to engage. Not yet, at least.

Her ribs ached. Her head pounded. Her lips felt bruised. She dry-swallowed two more Tylenol and made her way down the road, staying on the edge to avoid the stone maze. As she walked, she used her flashlight to search for security cameras or anything that might be out of place. But the warehouses on either side showed only blank faces behind chain-link fences. Employee and public entrances, along with loading docks, were elsewhere. This road was a convenient pass-through, Addie guessed, with only occasional vehicle or pedestrian traffic.

She noted a soggy cigarette butt and called a tech over. Due diligence.

Behind her, a car stopped. A door opened and closed, footsteps followed, and a moment later, Patrick stood beside her.

She decided to get it over with and looked at him straight on, knowing the police lights would reveal the bruising on her face.

"Mother, Mary of God. Addie, what happened?"

To her surprise, her tears flowed. Patrick walked her back up the road and around the corner of the paper-goods warehouse, away from curious eyes.

He handed her a handkerchief. "For moments such as this."

She accepted it. "These are tears of frustration."

"I recognize them. I've shed a few myself."

"I let Távros get the best of me, Patrick."

He drew in a breath, said, "And here you are, still alive, which is all that matters. It happens, lass. Távros is doing a damn fine job playing all of us. What you need to do now is get back into the ring. We're going to find this spawn of Satan. Don't you worry."

He waited while she sobbed her way to silence. Then he gave her a hug. She leaned in for a moment, allowing Patrick's strength to hold them both. Then she straightened and wiped her eyes.

"Now tell me," he said.

She filled him in on her encounter with Távros. How he'd pretended to be Nick Macaluso. The way he'd gone from normal to strange halfway through the conversation. "It was the murdered cat and the way that Lowell hurt him that triggered the change," she said.

She went on to tell Patrick how Távros had attacked her.

When she finished, he said, "Have you played with the idea that our missing Lowell Hargrave might be our potential teen serial killer and current murderer, Távros?"

"I have." She blew her nose into Patrick's handkerchief and had the courtesy not to give it back to him. "But Morgan says his son died four years ago on Crete."

"Families have been known to disinherit their kids."

"I had the same thought. I'll check with the embassy in Athens, see if I can confirm his death."

"This investigation gets weirder at every turn. Like one of Evan's mazes." Patrick zipped his jacket as if just now aware of the dampness in the air. Mist beaded on his face. "We can't even seem to answer a simple question: Is Lowell Hargrave dead or not?"

"We'll find out. In the meantime, we're also looking into someone named Alex Hemming. Hemming, whoever he is, sent an email to Evan three months ago claiming to have deciphered Cretan Hieroglyphic. He signed off with the same Greek word TR used in his letter. And he called himself the Minotaur. Also three months ago, a man identifying himself as Alex Hemming bought a maze coin like the one left on Evan's doorstep."

Patrick scratched his jaw. "I'm going to need a playbill just to keep track of one man. TR. Távros. Hemming. Are the computer forensics guys tracing the email?"

"Trying to. Hemming is good at hiding his trail."

"Why am I not surprised? We're running this case a day late and a dollar short."

She sighed, and he clasped her shoulder.

"Things'll shift," he said. "You ready to deal with the body around the corner?"

"It's Bryant James," she said. "Jamal is still missing."

"Same cause of death?"

"Looks like it. Along with the smell of licorice and honey, as with the first body. But we lucked out on one thing. When the ME turned him onto his back, the glyphs were there, undisturbed by the rain. Evan is on his way. From my newly acquired knowledge of Cretan Hieroglyphic, we have the trident, the bull, and the bee or wasp. No cat. Instead, we have an eye. Just as with Jamal's vehicle. Nearby, on the ground, Távros chalked what looks like the number one thousand and five, whatever the heck that means. Of course, after the rain, I can't be sure."

Patrick nodded that he'd heard. In the police lights, he didn't look like he'd just caught the redeye flight home and had to get up early for court. Indeed, he looked better than he had the night of Fishbourne's death. Maybe the trip to Garden City had done him good, gotten the investigative juices flowing again.

At least something was trending in the right direction.

Patrick said, "We've still got that possible link to Barlow. We'll look at his mail and phone records, see how much contact he had with the outside world. And check for any personal writing he might have left, like a journal or unsent letters. The prison will still have all of that. I've got court in the morning, but after I finish there, I can head down to Pontiac while you keep on top of things here."

The Pontiac Correctional Facility. She nodded. Prisoner mail was scrutinized, and any hard-core fan mail suggestive of a wannabe copycat killer would have been withheld from Barlow and kept in his file.

And while it was unlikely that Bull Barlow had written about Colby Kaplan—the vanished runaway with the weird glyph of a bull on his front door—or a potential partner, criminals had done stupider things. Barlow didn't have a lot to lose at this stage, and maybe he'd wanted to cleanse his soul before he died. Or bury his partner.

"You get a chance to look at Colby's file?" Patrick asked.

"What there is of it. His parents reported him missing when he didn't show for dinner. Said he'd gone out that afternoon with his dog. The family lived in Oregon, Illinois, just north of Daysville, and Colby liked to play along Rock River. He was a Boy Scout, knew his directions, knew how to swim. Knew how to build a fire and shelter in place if it came to it—the police report said the weather was nasty that afternoon, with a couple of tornado spouts, although nothing touched down. Hours later, the dog came home without Colby. They searched the river and surrounding area. Never found anything. Colby had taken his backpack with him, and he'd talked about running away in his journal. There were problems at home, the parents fighting."

"Was there anything about our glyph in the report?"

"The mother reported it. Detectives figured it was a sign for a runaway, just like you heard about that runaway in Garden City. That kid, Jake Kully."

"That didn't turn out well for Jake. You think the Bogeyman got Colby?"

"It would have been nice to ask Barlow directly. I've added Mrs. Kaplan to the list of people to talk to. On a side note, the area where Colby disappeared is near where the Hargraves live."

"Which makes Lowell even more of a suspect if he isn't six feet under. What about the other boy? Peter?"

"I ran him. Clean as a whistle. Same with Emma Hargrave."

"Those kind are the worst."

They walked back around the corner and along the road to the Minotaur's newest victim.

Police lights strobed against the warehouses and the chain-link fence. Portable lights shone their harsh glare on Bryant James.

"Same injuries," Patrick said. "Poor guy cut nearly in half. The bite to the throat. And, once again, his eyes and mouth were taped shut."

Another car pulled up. Another door opened and closed. Addie released her held breath. It was Evan. Maybe this second death would give him something to work with.

Something that would point to the Minotaur's identity.

Something that would tell them where Ursula Fishbourne and Jamal James might be.

And if they were still alive.

CHAPTER 41

EVAN

Evan bid Addie goodbye at 4:00 a.m. after contributing little to illuminate the scene of Bryant Jones's death except to clarify that the eye was Cretan hieroglyph number five, and that circular mazes created out of small stones, like the one surrounding Bryant, were commonplace around the world. They could be found in parks, churches, universities. But not, typically, in crime scenes.

Before she left, Addie asked Patrick if she and Evan could have a moment. Patrick moved off to chat with one of the techs while Addie sat in the passenger seat of Patrick's car. She left the door open and planted her feet on the asphalt.

"Patrick insists I go home with him," she told Evan. "Mary's already up, and nothing makes her happier than having someone to look after. She's throwing together some soup, she says. It will fix anything, she says."

"Even my disappointment?" He took her hand. "I suppose it would be foolish of me to offer to arm-wrestle Patrick."

She gave a soft smile. "He's a lot older. It wouldn't be fair."

"Then, by all means, let me at him."

This time she laughed.

"I'm sorry for what happened tonight," he said.

She blinked and looked down. "Thanks."

"Addie," he said.

She met his gaze. She must have seen something in his face, because she squeezed his fingers. "I'll be okay."

"Sure."

She brushed her thumb down his palm, tracing his lifeline. "We haven't had a moment alone since . . . Was it really only last night?"

"Feels like forever ago. But it just means we'll have lots to talk about when we can."

She nodded and released his hand. "As soon as we've found our killer."

He waited until she and Patrick had driven off before he got into his own car.

Távros had now injured two of the people most dear to him.

Lines had been drawn.

The gauntlet thrown.

They had to defeat Távros and win this appalling game.

He just needed to figure out how.

He had planned to return home to fly Ginny. But he had an 8:00 a.m. semantics class, and he was closer to the university than to home. When River called to check on him, he told him about his conversation with Morgan Hargrave. He didn't have the heart to talk about Bryant James. That would be an in-person conversation. He drove to the campus, availed himself of the tiny shower in his in-office bathroom, and crashed for a couple of hours.

When he awoke, he made tea and called the Remington Foundation, hoping to find another early riser. After someone picked up his call, he introduced himself and was transferred to Morgan's fellow researcher, a scientist named Dr. Grace Poole.

"I'm afraid Morgan was called out of town unexpectedly," Poole told him after he'd explained his reason for calling. "He's in Baltimore."

"I just spoke with him yesterday evening."

"I'm sure you did. These things happen. Morgan's research puts him in demand when there's a crisis. I'll be sure to have him call you when he returns."

"Perhaps you would be willing to give me a tour?"

She laughed. "I don't have time for nonsense of the show-and-tell sort. Who did you say you are again?"

Evan pushed a little pomposity into his tone. Sometimes arrogance worked wonders. "I'm Dr. Evan Wilding, professor of semiotics, linguistics, and paleography at the University of Chicago. I'm currently consulting on a case for which Dr. Hargrave's research could prove imminently valuable."

"Wilding." A pause. "You're the Sparrow."

How deflating that sounded. "Does that do anything to change your mind?"

"You're working on the man killed in Couch Place. I saw it in the news. Can you hold for a minute?"

Before Evan could answer, he found himself listening to a cover of Barry Manilow's "Mandy." When Poole returned, she spoke in a low tone.

"Meet me this afternoon at Buckingham Fountain in Grant Park. I'll find you. Two o'clock."

Evan was surprised. "But why? I mean, great, but is this—"

More loudly she said, "Thank you for calling."

She hung up.

✣

After two wide-awake nights, Evan slept-walked to class. Conducting a three-hundred-level course on Monday at 8:00 a.m. ought to be outlawed. Ten minutes in, it became clear that, like him, the kids were even more sleep deprived than usual. Probably half of them were thinking back on the weekend, not about Personal Identities as Social Semiotic Constructions. Despite the tongue-twisting title, his lecture on how we present ourselves in a way that draws meaning from our place in the world was usually a big hit, even on a Monday. But today, it failed to arouse interest in either himself or his students.

Presentation, he reminded himself. *Anything can be made boring if delivered that way.*

A student—one of the few alert ones—raised his hand.

"Yes, Mr. Phinjo? Please save us from this stultifying Monday morning."

"Um, yeah, sure."

"A promising beginning," Evan said.

"What I mean is, what you're talking about is how we brand ourselves across different mediums and modalities. Right?"

"That's partially correct. Which on a morning like this is a triumph. Are you working on your brand, Mr. Phinjo?"

A handful of students laughed.

Phinjo grinned. "You bet! I got a website, a blog, TikTok, YouTube. I'm on all of them, man. I'm like a meme."

"What about your BO?" said the kid next to him. "Is that part of your brand?"

The class laughed their approval, now fully awake.

Evan said, "Thank you, Mr. Phinjo, for doing what I could not, which is to wake the student body. I want all of you to work on your social semiotic constructions this week, focusing on multimodal processes and meaning-making through symbols. Class dismissed."

The students began packing up their laptops and textbooks. Not one person asked for clarification on the assignment. That, too, was a triumph.

Evan slid his lecture notes into a leather portfolio. He was thinking of Távros's chosen brand: that in looking at the trinity of man, god, and beast, Távros had selected the beast.

But perhaps that wasn't completely true. Maybe he considered himself a trinity. Alex Hemming, the man. Távros, the god. And Minotaur, the beast. Thus the three tridents on Fishbourne's forehead.

Maybe—somehow, someway—this could provide a chink in Távros's armor.

Rejuvenated, Evan told the post-lecture cluster of students that he would hold office hours the next day and hurried back to his office as quickly as his stature and dignity allowed. He heard voices as soon as he stepped out of the elevator: Diana's bright laugh and River's deeper one. A short silence followed by more laughter as he approached the door.

"I'm glad you're going to help him with the institute," Diana was saying. "He takes on too much."

"He does. We both do," River responded. "It's part of that mysterious directive that all sons feel from their fathers. Enough is never enough."

"Glad I missed out on that particular neurosis," Diana said.

Perro, perhaps sensing Evan's presence on the other side of the door, let out a cheerful bark. River must have brought the wee beast. Evan let himself into his office.

River and Diana sat together at the library table in the center of the room. They were wide awake and bursting with energy. Monet's water lilies must have done them good.

"Brother!" River stood. His posture still wasn't entirely straight, but he looked in good cheer. "After we talked earlier, I stopped this morning and picked up coffee for you. The kind that puts hair on your chest and leaves you awake for three days."

"Was it a romantic tryst?" Diana asked, looking hopeful.

Evan tossed his portfolio on his desk and bent to pet Perro. "They found Bryant."

Diana's sad sigh could be heard across the room. River resumed his seat.

He filled them in on the night with its brutal slaying, the additional glyph, and the white-stone maze. He suspected Távros had used the stones in place of the tiled maze on the alley wall at the site of Fishbourne's death. It was the presence of the maze, and not its particulars, that would matter to Távros.

By the time Evan had finished his coffee, he'd brought them up to date on everything he knew about the case so far.

"We've got a little bit of information ourselves," River said when Evan fell silent.

Diana nodded. "We headed off to see Monet's lilies, then realized that was so not okay with Ursula a prisoner. And now Bryant as well."

"We hope they're prisoners," Evan said.

"We hope," she agreed.

"So, instead," River said, "we availed ourselves of the computers in the Classics Department. They have subscriptions to everything we wanted. We spent the afternoon and evening online poring through back issues of newspapers from Crete and Athens."

"Which was exhausting," Diana added, "because neither my Greek nor River's is what it should be."

"We aren't awful," River said.

"We aren't," Diana agreed. "Passable undergraduate Greek. And there were some English-language papers. We found something."

River stood and shuffled through the papers on the table, then handed three sheets to Evan.

"They're printouts from the only Crete-specific news magazine," he said.

Evan thumbed through the papers. All of them were photos of a trident chalked onto stones.

"There were more than a hundred instances of someone chalking a trident on rocks and cliff faces around Crete," River said. "They occurred randomly throughout 2013 and stopped in 2014."

"Meaning," Diana said, "they appeared the year before Lowell's suicide, based on what Morgan Hargrave told you. Then stopped the year of his death. After that, the chalk marks the locals found were mostly of Cretan hieroglyph number eleven. The bull."

River set down more photos: chalked images of the glyph that had appeared at all the crime scenes.

Evan stared at the pictures.

"Which means," he said, "that 2014 is when Lowell became Távros. When he gave up on humanity's divine side and, through a symbolic death, man became monster."

In the silence, voices rose from outside on the quad. Closer by, feet trod on stairs and doors open and closed.

"That's good work," Evan said. "Thank you. I'll let Addie know."

He set down his empty coffee cup. Already the caffeine was buzzing in his system.

"Now we need to look further into the Alex Hemming angle." He crossed to the row of wooden filing cabinets in the back of the office and extracted several thick manila folders, which he brought back to the table. He opened the folders and set out the contents in several stacks, each consisting of stapled or paper-clipped letters.

"What are these?" Diana asked.

"Letters I've received from people wanting me to confirm that they've deciphered one of the great unsolvable scripts, up to and including the Codex Seraphinianus."

Diana's eyebrows shot up. "The Seraphinianus is an artificial script never meant to be anything but a pretense at writing. It *can't* be deciphered."

"That's never stopped anyone from trying," Evan said, organizing the stacks he'd placed on the table. "Few of us can resist the desire to solve the unknown. And to beat everyone else to the finish line. Now, we're looking for anything from Alex Hemming. Or any Távroses or

TRs. I've already got an email from Hemming. I want to know if he wrote me any actual letters."

River picked up a letter at random. "What is it these would-be decipherers want from you?"

"Usually, they hope I'll confirm their brilliance. Rarely do they ask for help. Not that I have any to offer other than to direct them to the basic steps of decipherment. I tell them to forget what they think they know. Forget what language they believe the script is written in. Set aside all their assumptions and focus on what the data alone tells them."

Diana nodded. "I assume you suggest they apply the Johari window."

"Right, since it essentially tells them that they need either a known language or a known script to solve the riddle. If neither the language nor the script is known, then decipherment is impossible."

"Like the Phaistos Disc," she said.

"You had to bring that up. I also wish to point out that what man has created, man can decipher. *Homo sum: humani nihil a me alienum puto.*"

"'I am a man,'" Diana translated. "'I consider nothing that is human alien to me.' Roughly speaking. Nice!"

"While you two were jawing," River said, "I found a letter from Alex Hemming dated two months ago."

Evan stopped sorting the letters. "Read it to us."

> Dear Doctor Wilding,
> I hate to open this letter by chastising an esteemed scholar such as yourself. Yet here I am, sitting on one of the greatest discoveries of the millennium, and I haven't heard from you. This is my third and final attempt.
>
> Imagine what a decipherment of Cretan Hieroglyphic and Linear A will offer the world! A

chance to understand Crete in all her glory. To realize that the Minoan culture was superior to anything that came after. The Greeks, the Romans, the Byzantines—they merely built on the glory of Minoan society.

You will note my return address. I hope—no, expect—to hear from you soon.

Hygíaine!

Alex Hemming

Evan took the letter from River's hand. "The handwriting appears to be the same as TR's in our first letter. Alex Hemming is TR. And TR is Távros. We've got him."

"Not quite." River's voice was dry. "There's no return address."

"On the envelope?"

"No envelope."

"You've looked all through the folder that came from?"

"I have."

"I will not shoot myself," Evan muttered. "Let's look through everything. If the email was his second attempt, and this letter is his third, then perhaps there's another letter from him somewhere here. I couldn't find anything else in my email."

They spent the next thirty minutes going through the letters piece by piece, looking for a loose envelope or another letter by Alex Hemming. Eventually, Evan returned to the file cabinet, stared inside, and made a small sound that was half groan, half triumph.

"Stuck to the bottom of the drawer along with assorted sticky notes and paper clips," he said. "The envelope."

"I'm going to shoot you myself," said Diana. "Where does he live?"

"Apparently, in a UPS box."

✣

Half an hour later, after speaking with Addie, Evan walked into the UPS store on Michigan Avenue. The middle-aged Asian woman behind the counter looked as if she thought the circus had come to town. She smiled.

"You selling tickets?"

"I'm afraid not," Evan said. "I'm trying to track down a friend, and I'm hoping you can help."

"Hmm." Her expression turned suspicious.

Evan showed her his university ID and then Alex Hemming's letter. "You can see he wrote this letter to me. And that he's hoping to hear back. Here's the envelope with his mailbox number and your UPS address. I did write him back immediately, but I've heard nothing. I'm hoping you can tell me if he still owns the box. I'd really like to find him."

She squinted at Evan, then his ID. A younger woman came out from a room in the back.

"What is it, Ma?"

"This man wants to know if a customer still has a mailbox with us."

The younger woman read the letter and checked Evan's ID. She shrugged. "Seems okay to me. You want me to look it up?"

The older woman nodded, keeping her eyes on Evan. Maybe she thought he'd try to steal the tape dispenser.

"Alex Hemming," the younger woman said. "He's still paying for the box. You want me to see if there's mail in there?"

"That would be wonderful. Thank you."

"Not a problem." She unlocked a cabinet and removed a key from a hook. She came out from behind the counter and opened one of the brass mailboxes. "There's nothing in here."

"I don't know what to think," Evan said. He pulled out his phone as if he'd just been struck by an idea. "Do you mind looking at this photograph? Maybe you can tell me if I'm looking for the right Alex Hemming."

Now the younger woman looked interested.

Her mother doubled down on suspicion. "We can't help you," she said.

"But it's—"

The woman frowned. "You know how many customers we get in here every day? A hundred. Two hundred. More. You think I'm going to remember anyone's face? Except maybe yours."

"And I yours," Evan said. He pulled up the picture he'd taken at Morgan's house of Lowell and Peter. "Here's the photo if you would just take a look."

The middle-aged woman snatched Evan's phone.

"Good-looking guys," she said. "But I don't know them."

"Let me see, Ma."

"We shouldn't—" her mother began.

"We should help. He's a professor at the university. They're good people."

"Thank you," Evan said.

The older woman folded her arms but made no more protest.

The younger woman took the phone and used her thumb and forefinger to enlarge the faces.

"I've seen the guy on the left," she said.

That would be Lowell Hargrave, according to his own father. Evan held himself very still.

"The guy on the left is Alex Hemming?" he asked.

The woman looked toward the ceiling, thinking. "He came in last month. I noticed him because, you know, major cutie. And built like the Terminator. He checked his box, and it was in the same area as Hemming's box, but I can't guarantee it was him."

The older woman nodded. "That's my daughter. She remembers everything. Names. Numbers. Faces."

"It's actually kind of a curse," the woman said, handing back Evan's phone. "But Ma's right. If I remember something, you can take it to the bank."

"And you're certain you saw this man just last month?"

"I'm positive. Three weeks ago, maybe. Definitely. It was the week before the Fourth."

"That's good, then," Evan said, allowing his actual relief to show. They had something. "Do you mind looking up his information? Maybe he left a street address where I can find him?"

But now, the older woman folded her arms. "Getting that information requires the police. The answer is no." She said this as much to her daughter as to Evan.

"I understand," Evan said. "Thank you so much for your help."

"Sure," said the younger woman.

Her mother said, "You gonna buy something?"

As Evan walked out of the store to where River and Diana waited with Perro, a glow of triumph buoyed his steps. If this woman's memory was as good as she claimed, then Lowell hadn't died four years ago on Crete. He was living here in Chicago under the name Alex Hemming. And someone had either given Morgan Hargrave false information, or Morgan had lied.

"We've got him," Evan told River and Diana and shared what he'd learned.

His friends cheered. Diana off-loaded bags from him and peered inside.

"What are you going to do with two hundred dry-erase markers?"

"And a heavy-duty stapler," Evan said. "They were on sale."

CHAPTER 42

ADDIE

Addie sat at her desk, wondering if it was wise to take the pain pills one of the detectives had given her. Her head pounded as if someone were inside it with a sadistic combination of a jackhammer, an anvil, and her father's voice shouting that she should go to Mass more often. The bruising along her ribs hurt like she was in a python's death grip.

Even her *feet* hurt, which made no sense at all.

She stared at the pills in her hand, then opened a drawer and dropped them inside. She used cold coffee to swallow a few Tylenol and considered the day's progress.

One: Owen Teufel, the actor who'd come after Evan in the maze, was on his way in, courtesy of patrol. Detective Sanchez had checked out Owen's alibi for the night of Fishbourne's death. It held. But Addie still wanted to talk to him. And she wanted to do it on her turf.

Two: The crime-scene techs had found nothing in Ursula's tree house that linked to their case. They'd tagged and bagged everything, but when Addie went through it, all she found was the usual teenage stuff—photos of Ursula's cat (presumably), the posters already noted, the Nancy Drew books, ditto.

And three: Colby's mother, Farah Kaplan, had listened to the officer on her doorstep, who explained that they wanted to ask a few questions regarding the glyph left on her home ten years ago. And no, sorry, they had nothing new on Colby's disappearance. Mrs. Kaplan had suggested exactly where the officer could go and what he could do once he got there, then slammed the door.

One step forward. Two steps back.

At least she'd confirmed that the real Mr. Macaluso Senior was all right. He'd been sedated by a man in nursing scrubs who told Nick Senior that he was replacing the usual home help for the day. The drugs had, presumably, been in the tea Távros prepared for him. After the sedatives cleared Nick Senior's system, the ER had released him, and CPD had sent an officer to keep an eye on him and the house.

Her phone rang. Patrick.

"I talked to a couple of people at Pontiac," he said.

The pain eased enough to give her breathing room. "What did you learn?"

"Two things. The first is that Peter Hargrave has been writing to Barlow, expressing admiration for his quote-unquote work. The good folks at Pontiac let Barlow see the letters, but they didn't let him keep them."

"You think it's really Peter who wrote him?"

"We'll ask the man himself. Letters were typed, not handwritten. No signature. Just a return address with Peter's name and his father's address. The other bit of news is that Barlow's last phone call was from his brother, Edgar Barlow. His last visitor, who came the day Barlow went to meet his maker, was also Edgar. In fact, the only person on Barlow's approved friends and family list was Edgar."

"You think there's a link between the brother's visit and Barlow's death?"

"I dunno. Nothing about this case has made sense in the normal use of that word. But the corrections officer on duty the night Barlow died said there was a marked change in Bull between the time his brother arrived and when he left. Bull was, and here I quote the officer, 'a total asshole before Edgar got here, just like always. And he was as quiet as I've ever seen 'im after the brother left.'"

Addie used a pencil to reach an itch on her leg so she wouldn't have to bend over. "Why would Edgar Barlow drive his brother to commit suicide? And how?"

"I'm not sure we can read anything into it. Barlow's only visitor, ever, was his brother. Same with the phone calls. Maybe Barlow was always sad after Eddie visited, watching his baby brother walk free. Maybe this time he just got more sad than usual."

At the sound of her name, Addie looked up. Patrol was escorting Owen Teufel to an interview room.

"They just brought in Owen," Addie told Patrick. "I'll make arrangements to talk to Peter."

"The way things are going, the judge will cut me loose by noon. So set up our chat with Peter for this afternoon. He feels like the bigger priority. In the morning, I'll head to Pontiac to go through Barlow's belongings."

"You got it."

✣

Addie strode into the interview room, forcing herself to walk upright so that Owen wouldn't notice that her entire body was ready to cut and run. Or, more likely, cut and take a nap. She would not start from a position of weakness.

As if he meant to taunt her, Owen Teufel sat in a comfortable sprawl on the small plastic chair, looking like he hadn't a care in the world. He was muscular, which fit River's description of Távros. But now that she was standing close to him again, she could see that he wasn't tall in the way River had described Hoodie Man; neither was he built like the false Nick Macaluso she'd encountered.

If she'd had any fading hope that Owen was Távros, it was now off the table. She didn't even need his alibi to prove it.

Owen sneered at her, doing his best to take up all the air in the room. Which was fine. Addie had just the needle to prick his ego balloon.

She dropped a folder on the table and sat down across from him. If Owen recognized her from rehearsal night, he gave no sign of it.

She'd originally planned to take the interview in one direction. But Patrick's news about Peter Hargrave had changed things even before she'd confirmed that Owen couldn't be Távros. Now she sat in silence, writing notes on a pad of paper, waiting for Owen to get impatient.

Kids like him always got impatient.

After ten minutes, he said, "You going to keep me here all day?"

She kept writing. Another five minutes ticked by while Owen adjusted himself in his seat.

"I've got rights," he said.

"Yeah?" She looked up. "What about them?"

"You can't bring me in and just make me sit here."

"I most certainly can. Or I can press charges. Would you rather go that route?"

"Charges for what? I haven't done anything."

"Other than assault a member of the public at the Neverland Theater?"

An angry flush darkened Owen's face. "The professor is a prick."

Addie went back to her notepad. When her burner phone buzzed with a text, she glanced at it. The text was from Evan.

Alex Hemming is Lowell Hargrave. He took out a UPS mailbox. Manager ID'd him in a photo. Also, Lowell likely left glyphs on Crete that reveal his desire to transform. Man to monster.

She texted back: Manager sure? Confirmed Lowell not dead.

Not unless he died in the last three weeks, Evan answered.

Addie sent a text to Sanchez on the team, asking him to request a subpoena for whatever information Alex Hemming had provided to reserve the UPS mailbox.

A sense of triumph swept through her as she tucked her burner phone away. One giant step for the investigation. Unless their newest suspect turned out to be well and truly dead.

She picked up her pen, jotted a note. "Why is Dr. Wilding a prick, as you so tactfully put it?"

"He flunked me out of a class I need to graduate."

"And that's his fault, not yours?"

"Did the prof bring charges?" Owen asked. "Is that why I'm here?"

"Is there another reason you should be here?"

"I've got rights," Owen said again, this time more quietly.

Addie set down her pen. In a situation like this, there was no law that said a cop couldn't lie. She recalled what she'd first learned about Owen Teufel the night at the theater and fabricated from there. She said, "That pre-med kid you hurt outside the Woodlawn Tap? His parents have changed their minds. They want to press charges."

Owen's eyes bulged. "No way. There's like, a statute of limitations, right? They can't just change their mind."

"You might want to become better acquainted with the law, Mr. Teufel. But if you're cooperative with me today, I'll see what I can do."

"That's blackmail."

"It's known as back-scratching. It's how the world works."

He sulked, screwing his lips up in a pout and staring over her head. After a minute, he said, "Cooperate how?"

"Where were you last Thursday night?"

"What?"

"The night of July twelfth. Where were you?"

"I was—I was—" He stopped. "I was with the theater troupe. Most of the out-of-towners got in that night. We met at a restaurant downtown. Is this about that murder in the alley?"

"And Peter Hargrave? What about him?"

"What about him? Peter was at the dinner, too."

"Why don't you tell me about Peter?"

"What about him?"

"You two close?"

"Not like gay close, if that's what you're getting at. But yeah, we're friends."

"Friends. He ever talk about his brother?"

A strange look came over Owen. As if pieces had just clicked together in his brain. He spread his hands on the table and looked down, studying them.

"Mr. Teufel?"

"Peter hated his brother," Owen said.

"Hated? Or hates?"

Owen looked up. Pulled his hands into fists. "If you're asking that question, then I guess the cat's out of the bag."

✣

Addie listened to Owen talk for thirty minutes. Then she cut him loose.

He might go to Peter, tell him the cops were nosing around about him and Lowell. But she thought it more likely Owen would want to bury the conversation he'd had with her in CPD's interview room.

No rat ever wanted to advertise the fact.

And once Owen decided to talk, he had plenty to share.

Peter and Lowell had loathed each other as soon as they were old enough to understand the concept. Based on what Peter told Owen, their hatred came down to their mutual desire to win their father's attention. Their dad ran tests on kids, looking for the good

Samaritans—that's what he called them—and the derelicts—also Mr. Morgan's word. The better behaved Peter was—the higher his grades, the more friends, the more sports trophies—the more dramatically Lowell acted out. It worked: both approaches got their father's notice.

Owen continued. Once, after getting shit-faced, Peter had confided his belief that three-year-old Lowell killed their mother. Morgan had taken Peter out for a stroll, and his mom and brother were home alone when Philomena took her fatal plunge down the stairs. This contradicted what the inquest had found: Morgan had claimed to be away with both boys. But if Philomena had stumbled over her young son, or fallen while carrying him, maybe lying about Lowell's whereabouts was the family's way of protecting him.

"Anything else?" Addie had asked.

Owen wouldn't meet her eyes. No doubt he hated her for making him betray his friend. He'd said, "A couple of times, Peter said it would be just like his brother to fake his suicide."

"Did he think that was possible?"

"Anything is possible."

"What do you think?"

"Me? I never met the guy. I think the whole thing is some seriously weird-ass shit. But Peter seemed like he thought it could be for real."

"Peter suggested his brother might be alive."

A shrug. "I guess."

Man to monster, Evan had texted.

After Owen was escorted out, Addie took the stairs down to the next floor, heading for the break room. The python around her ribs was taking a nap, thanks to the Tylenol. And the jackhammer in her head had muted to a dull pounding.

While walking, she wondered how best to approach Colby Kaplan's mother without getting another slammed door. She couldn't blame the woman. The police had done nothing for her ten years ago except to tell her that her son was a runaway and wasn't that too bad, so sad.

After a moment, she sent a text to Evan: Do me a favor? Talk to Colby Kaplan's mom? She won't talk to police. Ask re: Colby's friend Tav.

Evan answered immediately: I'm on it.

Back at her desk with a mug of coffee, she checked the time—it was eight hours later in Athens. Which meant the embassy was closed for the day. Sure enough, the phone rang through to voice mail. She left a message explaining who she was and that she wanted to verify the death of an American in Crete.

Next on her list was to track down Peter Hargrave so that she and Patrick could ask him why he'd been writing fan letters to Bull Barlow.

And if he thought his brother was alive.

And where he might be.

CHAPTER 43

EVAN

Evan parked the Jaguar on the street and walked up a path to a red-brick bungalow. The bungalow's front garden was filled with purple hyssops, white-and-pink arrowwoods, and cream-colored hydrangeas. Red geraniums filled a row of pots balanced on the railing of a small porch. Yellow curtains hung in the windows.

He climbed the stairs to the porch, where Farah Kaplan met him at the door. A short, slender woman with olive skin, thick black hair, and red eyeglasses, she took in Evan's height and smiled.

"Now I know why they call you Sparrow," she said. She pushed open the door. "Won't you come in?"

She led him through the house to a small backyard that she had turned into an oasis from the city and the heat. The space made Evan think of the courtyards he had visited on a trip through Italy. Flowers, shade trees, a red-slate patio. A fountain burbled on the other side of the patio, backed by miniature cypress trees. Evan smelled the sharp tang of lemons among the jasmine and hyacinths.

He drew in a deep breath. "This place is a marvel."

She gestured him toward one of the patio chairs. "My life has shrunk since my husband passed a few years ago. Colby's older brother works for an oil company in Paris. He calls often. He's a good son. But often, it is lonely. Gardening is how I occupy myself."

"I'm sorry for your many losses, Mrs. Kaplan," Evan said. "Especially your son. I'm told it's a pain that never goes away."

She collapsed in one of the other chairs. "And yet I have allowed you to reopen old wounds. I was rude to that police officer. But I am tired of hearing that they have nothing to offer. I don't know if it's because Colby's father was Black or because a runaway of any skin color doesn't get much attention. But they never really looked for him."

"You believe Colby ran away?"

"No." She shook her head firmly. "That was what the police said because of that symbol in his journal."

"The bull."

"Yes. But I never believed it. Colby struggled with knowing his dad and I were fighting. Booker traveled all the time, and I was tired of holding down a job and raising two boys on my own. But we were working it out. Colby knew that. And he adored his brother."

"I understand the symbol also appeared on your front door. Did you know what it meant?"

"Colby had told me about the sign. It was his and Tav's, a symbol for their secret club. If you can call two people a club. I think Tav left it on our door to let Colby know he was around. That he missed him."

"What did the police say about Tav?"

"They thought he was Colby's made-up friend."

"But you don't think so."

"I know he wasn't. I wish that boy would have knocked on my door instead of just scratching that symbol there."

"It must be incredibly painful not knowing what happened to your son."

"I have the hope, of course, that one day I'll look out the front window and see him coming up the walk, all grown up. He'd be twenty now. But mostly, it isn't like that."

She looked out to the garden where a hummingbird flitted around the hyssops. After a moment, she continued.

"Mostly, it's nightmares, imagining what might have happened to him. I see him getting hit by a car or a train. Drowning in the Rock River. There were tornadoes spotted that day. But mostly, I think about the Bogeyman. I imagine William Barlow grabbing him and hurting him and then I . . ."

She blinked back tears. The hummingbird buzzed away.

"I'm sorry to have brought this up," Evan said. It seemed to be his curse of late: wounding people already grievously injured. "I'm here because anything you remember might help us with another case. And perhaps lead to finding your son."

Her hands rose to her chest. "You mean his body."

Evan dipped his head. "I don't want to mislead you, Mrs. Kaplan. I have no news about your son. But it's possible that by solving our current case, it could help locate Colby's remains."

She folded her hands in her lap. "If I can't have Colby, then the most important thing now is that I have his body. I'm Persian. And according to my religion, according to what I believe is true, my son cannot find peace until his bones have been ritually washed and shrouded and properly buried to await judgment day. This is what is left for me. So"—she lifted her gaze—"tell me what I can do. Maybe we can help each other."

"What did Colby tell you about Tav? Anything about his age or what he did, or how they met? A surname?"

"He told me Tav's last name, but I don't . . . It will come to me." Her expression turned sadder. "Colby prattled on about Tav, and I didn't pay a lot of attention. I was working sixty-hour weeks as an administrator, and, as I mentioned, my husband traveled. I got Colby a dog and thought that made him safe. So, what do I remember about Tav?" She tilted her head back, staring at the sky as if the answer might be found there. "He was a few years older than Colby. A teenager. His father was strict. And I remember he liked spooky stories and old myths. He and Colby used to trade graphic novels."

"Did Colby offer a physical description of Tav?"

She brought her gaze back to his. "Not that I recall. It's not something a boy would mention. But he did say Tav had an older friend whom Colby didn't like. An adult. Colby said this man was always hungry."

"Hungry?"

"Yes. It was odd. I asked him if the man had enough to eat. I thought he might be homeless, and I didn't want Colby hanging out with Tav when this man was around. But Colby just shrugged. Sometimes I'd watch him pack snacks in the morning before he'd head out on one of his adventures. Crackers and those yogurt-in-a-tube things. Bologna sandwiches. Cookies. I would tease him. 'Your friend must be very hungry today,' I'd say, trying to get him to tell me if the man was going to be around. But he'd shake his head. 'He doesn't get hungry like that.'" Mrs. Kaplan closed her eyes for a moment. "I can't remember if I ever asked him what he meant."

"Where did Colby like to hike?"

"We lived in the town of Oregon then, a couple of hours west of Chicago. There were a lot of farms. Woodlands and bogs. Paradise for a kid, all that open space. I used to worry about snakes, but Colby said Rex was a good watchdog and wouldn't let him get hurt. I thought so, too."

"Did Rex disappear when Colby did?"

"Rex lived to the ripe old age of fourteen. He came home the day Colby disappeared. I found him lying on the porch, a puddle of misery. God, how I used to pray that Rex would develop a tongue for speech so he could tell me what happened."

Oregon, Illinois, was near Daysville, where the Hargraves lived. Perhaps the teen who mentioned seeing two men and a child walking in the fields had spotted them from the Hargrave home.

Had the Hargrave kids been members of the Chicago kids' mystery club that had reported the sighting? Did one of them know TR?

"Did Colby ever mention a house owned by Tav?" Evan asked. "Maybe going into that house?"

She shook her head. "I had a rule that he couldn't go into someone's home until I'd met their parents. Colby never told me where Tav lived. I'm not sure he knew."

"You said that Colby went out on adventures. Is that what Colby called it?"

"He wanted more than anything to be an explorer when he grew up. His thing was caves. He knew there was a network of caverns deep underground out there, and he and Tav were always hunting for entrances. He promised me if he found one, he'd mark it and tell someone about it. He promised not to go in alone. He promised he wouldn't even go in with just Tav."

"Did you tell the police about Colby's interest in caves?"

"Did I?" Her eyes flashed. "I begged them to send someone to search the caves. There was a spelunking club out there, although they didn't call themselves that. *Cavers* is the correct term now. Some of them agreed to search the caves they knew. They were mainly working north and east of our town, where Colby usually went. They didn't find anything. But they told me and Colby's dad—and the police—that there's a vast network of caves out there."

Evan nodded to himself. A cave. An underground labyrinth. Where else would a minotaur go?

He should have known.

Farah Kaplan straightened suddenly. "I remember now," she said. "Tav's last name was Rousse." She spelled it.

Tav Rousse. Sudden ice held Evan's spine in place.

Távros. The Greek bull. Távros with an older "hungry" friend.

Távros. All grown up, his friend—his mentor—dead in prison.

Távros, whoever he was, had learned his lessons well.

CHAPTER 44

ADDIE

"Please tell me you're kidding," Addie said into the phone.

"I'm sorry, Detective," said the officer on the other end of the call. "No one has seen Peter Hargrave since around two this morning when he left a downtown bar called the 2Twenty2 Tavern. He told his friends he was going to walk back to his place in the South Loop. We've checked Mr. Hargrave's apartment and the theater where he works. No sign of him. If there's anywhere else you want us to look, just say the word."

"I'll let you know," she said, and hung up. She dialed Sergeant Delarose and asked him to pull POD videos between the 2Twenty2 Tavern and Peter's apartment on Harrison Street. "Check Wabash, State Street, and Harrison," she said, looking at a map. "You'll find his photo in the DMV database. I'll also get a screenshot of him from the theater's website and send that to you."

"You got it," Delarose said.

She replaced the phone on its cradle and closed her eyes against the Monday chaos around her. Detectives coming and going, phones shrilling, the news on the television. The jackhammer had come back with a vengeance. She opened her eyes and dug the bottle of Tylenol out of her bag. She thought she'd read somewhere the stuff could give you an ulcer. But maybe that was ibuprofen.

She texted Sanchez: Any word on the subpoena for the Hemming UPS mailbox?

Nothing yet, Sanchez wrote back. I'll check with the judge.

Addie called Evan. He answered with, "How are you feeling?"

"The headache is better," she lied. "You get a chance to talk to Farah Kaplan?"

"She had a few things to add to our investigation. Per Colby, his friend Tav called himself Tav Rousse."

Addie wrote it down while Evan spelled it. "Sounds close to Távros."

"It's essentially the same thing," Evan said. "According to Mrs. Kaplan, the police thought Tav might not even exist."

"An imaginary friend?"

"Mrs. Kaplan wasn't having any of it. But it's possible. Colby also said that Tav had an adult male friend whom Colby didn't much like. No name. Just that the man was hungry. And not in the normal way."

"What does that mean?"

"Mrs. Kaplan didn't know. But it makes me wonder if it could have been Barlow."

Addie thought about it. "I don't know if this makes things any clearer, but the idea that Tav might not have existed does make me wonder if the male adult was also potentially a figment of Colby's imagination."

"You mean as with dissociative identity disorder? That Colby was mentally ill? Do you know how rare DID is, Addie?"

"I'm looking it up now. Fewer than two hundred thousand US cases per year."

"More than I would have guessed. But even if that were the case, who is our current Távros?"

Addie's thoughts were spinning in crazy directions. "What if Távros *is* Colby?"

"Addie, I don't think . . ." Evan's voice trailed off. "That would be pretty wild."

"I've seen wilder. Maybe the bull glyph really is the mark of a runaway."

"And Colby grew up to be a serial killer. It would be worth tracking down his medical records. On a slightly more cheerful note, Mrs. Kaplan also mentioned that her son loved caves. It's possible the kid went exploring and got lost."

"How is that more cheerful? That's a horrible way to die."

"Seems better than growing up a murderer. She said there used to be a caving club in Oregon, which isn't far from the Hargrave place and William Barlow's old home. I'm going to see if I can track down any of the members. We might be able to access maps."

"And possibly put Colby Kaplan's bones to rest."

"It would give his mother some comfort."

"Great information, Evan. It gives us some leads. In the meantime, Peter Hargrave is missing, and I need to talk to his father. You mentioned he's in Baltimore. Do you have a cell phone number for him?"

"Just landline and office."

Of course, it wouldn't be that easy. "I'll find it the hard way."

"Is Peter suspect or victim?" Evan asked.

"Until we find him, he's both. I should get going," Addie said. "Patrick and I are heading east to talk to William Barlow's brother, Edgar."

"Ask him about caves on his property," Evan said. "Just one more thing. Dr. Poole from the Remington Foundation has asked to meet with me this afternoon. I got the sense she didn't want to advertise that fact around her workplace."

"Any idea what she wants?"

"None."

"She could be valuable. All these tenuous connections. Peter and Ursula and Jamal are missing, Bryant and Samuel are dead. Lowell, a.k.a. Alex Hemming, is still an unknown. So far, the possible mock-trial link between the kids is coming up empty. What if the fourteen children—Ursula's friends—were part of Morgan's studies?"

"I'll learn what I can."

"Take River with you."

"Grace Poole is a scientist." Evan laughed. "If she comes after me, I'll beat her off with my briefcase."

CHAPTER 45

EVAN

Back at home, Evan looked up Illinois spelunking groups. None of them were based near Daysville, but it looked like most groups caved all around the state. He called the Chicago grotto club and told the man who answered that he was interested in exploring the caves in the northwestern part of the state.

"We cave in the south," said the man. "The area you're talking about has mostly sinkhole development and old limestone mines. There are rumors of bigger caves up there, but a lot of them would have entrances on private property, which means cavers are forced to find other access when that's even possible. You have experience?"

"I'm afraid not, although my brother does. Do you know of any caving groups in the Daysville area?"

"There's one guy in Oregon. Matt Sykes. Dude must be in his seventies. He used to cave up there, but I don't think he's been active for a long time."

"You have a phone number for him?"

"I don't. And I doubt the guy has a landline. He's more of an off-the-grid man. But I can ask around if you want. Some of the older members might have it."

"Thank you. Consider it urgent. What about maps? Are there any available for that area?"

"Maybe Sykes has something. But cave maps aren't like surface maps. They're tricky to read. And tricky to make. It's hard to swear to their accuracy. Especially on the longer, more complex caverns."

"I understand." Evan thanked the man and hung up. He looked online for Matt Sykes in Oregon, Illinois, but found nothing.

Next, he pulled up a map of caves produced by the Illinois State Geological Survey. Most of Illinois's caves were in the south and southwest. But there was also a cluster in the northeast.

Restless, his gut churning, he went into the kitchen where River was making a snack. Perro watched nearby, scouting the floor for any stray bits.

"I was just about to come find you," River said. "We're all set up with Dad. We're going to meet near the Bean in Millennium Park. The location takes care of all your requirements. Downtown near the lake. Outdoors. No food or drink."

Evan found himself surprised—and a little annoyed—with River's obvious enthusiasm. He tried to match it with his own. "What time?"

"One thirty. We need to head out. Dad is fitting us in between meetings."

Of course he is, Evan thought. He shook his head.

"I'm meeting Morgan Hargrave's research partner at two o'clock," he said. "But it's less than a mile away. Why don't I drop you off near the Bean, meet with Dr. Poole, then come back? Shouldn't be more than fifteen minutes. It will give you and Oliver some time together before I barge in."

River offered Evan half his turkey sandwich. "You think Poole might have light to shed on the case?"

Evan filled River in on his conversations with Addie and Mrs. Kaplan and some of the theories he and Addie had tossed back and forth, especially about Lowell and the caverns.

"Meeting Poole might be a chance to get the names of the other kids who were involved in Morgan's experiments," he said. "Find out if there's a link between those kids now and the Minotaur. Poole was willing to talk only after she realized I'm consulting on the case. Which means there's a connection."

"I'll go with you."

"You can't. This is your window with Oliver."

"I'm still on the fence, anyway. The last time I met Dad, it didn't go well." He set his sandwich on the counter and poured a glass of water. "I've been thinking of Dad hotshotting it around the world while we waited at home. He believed his work as a scientist was more important than his identity as a dad."

"No argument there."

"But what I'm wondering is, are you and I all that different? You and Diana and me—we've all given up any idea of having a family. Spouses and kids, I mean. And we've done it for our work. We've just been smart enough to make that decision before we had children."

Speak for yourself, brother, Evan thought. *I haven't given up, romantic fool that I am.*

"Because our work is important, right?" River went on. "Lifting the veil that covers the past. It matters."

"Do family and work have to be mutually exclusive?"

"Maybe not. But we spend a lot of time in the kind of places where you can't raise a family. It's essential to be in the field. To be willing to drop everything and travel at a moment's notice when something new appears that might be relevant. Staying in one place is a sort of surrender."

"I hadn't thought of it that way." Evan's voice came out stiff.

River flushed. "You know I didn't mean it that way. But you've been in Chicago for only a few years, and you're talking about Mali. Because a scholar, a researcher, must be willing to go where the job requires.

You're restless, Evan. I don't think you like being tied to the university or the institute any more than I would."

"Now you sound like Oliver. Mom always said that for him, it was a form of surrender to have a permanent address."

River's eyes sparked. He waved a hand around the kitchen. "Why are you tying yourself to this? This house, this city, a place behind the lectern? You could go anywhere, be anyone you wanted."

"No," Evan said carefully. "I can't. I don't have the options you do."

"That's bullshit!"

Perro barked. Evan just managed to avoid flinching. This was the closest he and River had come to a fight in years.

"You can't let your height get in your way," River said. "Every time we've been in the field together, you've held your own and then some. No one but you considers your height a problem. Including Addie, I'm guessing."

Evan shook his head. "I've done okay being out in the field because *you've* been there."

"Bullshit," River said again, but more quietly.

"I'm not leaning on my disability. But you have to understand there are limitations. The grocery store is a problem when everything I want is on a shelf that's just beyond my reach. Same with the hardware store or the bookstore or even the damn doctor's office when I'm struggling to reach the sign-in sheet."

"But you—"

"Hold on. That's the easy stuff. Refitting a car, refitting the furniture. Renovating the kitchen and bathroom. That's nothing. And so what if I can't leap on a horse or ride a camel or travel incognito? The hard thing isn't how I move through the world, but how the world reacts to me moving through it. In the eyes of a lot of people, I'm a freak. They point at me, whisper about me, even laugh at me. They take goddamn videos so they can post them on social and talk about how they met up with a circus geek. So maybe I'm okay with having found a place where, for the most part, I fit in. Sure, some of my students titter the first time I walk into the classroom. Or try desperately not to. But I fit in here, River. It's the first place that's worked for me."

"Then why Mali?"

"I don't know. I don't know." It was true that while he felt accepted at UChicago, and while he loved the work and his students, he also sometimes felt stymied. But maybe everyone felt that way now and again. It might be that a little discontent was good if it made you push yourself without running away.

"Are you happy here, Evan?" River asked.

"I am," he said firmly. "But that doesn't mean I don't want a sabbatical now and then."

River raised his hands. "Okay. We'll circle back to this conversation. In the meantime, we'll go with your plan. Drop me off near the Bean, meet with Poole, then join Dad and me."

"I knew you'd see things my way."

River sighed. "I always do."

CHAPTER 46

EVAN

At a few minutes before two, Evan found a bench near the Buckingham Fountain and sat down to wait. He told himself to bring Perro the next time he came. The corgi would love all the action.

The day was a mix of sun and clouds. Wind whipped in from the lake. Mothers pushed strollers, and children played around the fountain. Pigeons congregated. Tourists in shorts and T-shirts took photos.

Promptly at two o'clock, as the fountain was starting its hourly display of grandiosity, a woman in a pink pantsuit appeared on the far side of the fountain, heading across the brick plaza from the direction of downtown. Late middle age, stylish haircut that the breeze toyed with, maroon leather briefcase, and designer sunglasses. She saw Evan, pivoted slightly, and came to sit beside him.

"Dr. Wilding, I presume." She held the briefcase in her lap.

"Dr. Poole."

She didn't offer a hand but instead stared forward. As if she and the short person just happened to pick the same bench.

Evan refrained from looking at her. "Why am I here?" he asked.

"Because I'm scared for my daughter," Poole said simply. "Because I worry that Morgan has completely lost his marbles, and the house of cards is tumbling down around us."

Evan struggled to follow. "Perhaps you could back up a bit."

She breathed in, breathed out, and gripped the handle of her briefcase. "Perhaps you could, too. The man in the alley? It was Samuel Fishbourne, right?"

The police had released Fishbourne's name that morning. "Did you know him?"

"He and his daughter both. Ursula was one of ours."

"Meaning?"

"Meaning I'm going to share information with you that I shouldn't. I have signed papers swearing I wouldn't. But I have Anna to think of. She's safe for the moment on a mission with her church in Ghana. But she'll be home in a couple of weeks. That's why this information needs to come out. I'm going to give you what I think you need, and in return, I ask that you not share my name with the police. I'd rather not be divulged as a source. That's why I came to you instead of the cops."

Evan debated, and finally said, "A detective already knows I'm meeting with you."

"Then tell him or her that we met, and I changed my mind. But then, like an idiot, I walked off without my briefcase. A terrible oversight on my part. And you, naturally, looked through the contents."

"Her, not him," Evan said. "I can work with that. But if the case goes to court, we'll almost certainly have to ask you to step forward."

"I can't be a confidential source?"

"I don't think so. But I can't say definitively. I'm not an attorney."

Another deep breath, which sounded shaky. "Okay." Here, she risked a sideways glance at him. "I can live with that. But you must swear that the children from our studies, those who aren't already missing or dead, their names must remain out of the media. And this includes my daughter."

"Anna took part in the studies?"

"I enrolled her myself."

"Are she and the others in danger?"

"I believe so. That's why I'm here. I expect you to share their names with the police. But they and their families don't need the world to know that they were part of the so-called good and evil studies. If these children, all of whom are adults now, want to come forward later, that's their choice. But they don't deserve the attention that this will bring."

"I can't make that promise, Dr. Poole. If the murders are linked to Morgan's studies, journalists will start sniffing around."

"Then let them. Just don't hand them everything on a silver platter."

"I promise to do my best."

She lifted her chin. "Then I guess that will have to do. Now listen carefully. I'm going to talk quickly. Then I'm going to get up and walk away, leaving my briefcase here. It contains the names of the participants in the latest study, which began twenty-four years ago and continues, in a much-reduced form, to today."

"I am rapt," Evan said honestly.

"Good. Morgan and his wife, Philomena, began their work together with the best of intentions. They were young, brilliant, in love. Philomena became pregnant with their first child, a boy named Lowell, while they were honeymooning on Crete. She gave birth to their second child, Peter, only twelve months after Lowell was born."

Evan nodded. So far, only the honeymoon was news.

"But Philomena had a love of the bottle. When Lowell was three and Peter two, she fell down the stairs and struck her head. She died instantly."

"I heard there might be more to the story."

Poole moved her hands on the briefcase. "Lowell was home at the time, if that's what you're referring to. And maybe Philomena tripped over him or slipped while she was carrying him. There was even talk that Morgan had—" She stopped herself.

"Morgan had what?"

"That Morgan and Peter were home as well. That Peter was napping, and Morgan was puttering around the garden. It doesn't matter. What does matter is that it was her drinking that killed her, not her son. He can't be blamed."

"Of course."

"Philomena's death broke Morgan. And the fact that Lowell was there made it worse. First, Morgan was afraid it would scar the child for life. Then he became afraid of the child."

"But why—"

"Because Lowell was a frightening child. He'd only ever been loving toward Philomena. After her death, he became reclusive. In small ways, he tortured Peter, the cat, other children. By the time he was six, he had failed all our tests that would have proven him to be a good child, a normal child, happily in the middle of the bell curve."

"And Morgan blamed him for Philomena's death?"

"Morgan became obsessed with the idea that Lowell was responsible. I was a witness to all this. I helped run the studies. Lowell was a naturally difficult child who became more difficult after he lost his mother. But he wasn't a monster. It was Morgan who became the monster. He let his own son think he'd killed his mother."

"I'm guessing you tried to reason with him."

"For all the good that did. You must understand that a lot of money was coming into the Remington Foundation during those years. Politicians from both parties decried the rising crime rate, and they invested state and federal dollars in anything that promised a way to identify criminals and offer intervention before they acted. Morgan was entranced with his new fame and the money. In his own way, he thought that pigeonholing Lowell would help him heal his son." She lowered her head. "Then again, I sometimes wondered if Morgan's real goal was to see if he could *create* a psychopath, just to prove it could be done. Let's hear it for nurture, right? But to even attempt something like that would require a level of depravity I don't believe Morgan is capable of."

Evan let that sink in.

"What was Morgan's relationship with Peter?" he asked.

A neon-yellow rubber ball flew their way. Poole flinched as Evan deflected it. A little girl came running to grab it and stared at Evan.

"Are you from Oz?" she asked, wide eyed. "Do you know the wizard?"

Evan placed a finger to his lips and leaned forward. "I *am* the Wizard of Oz. The real one. But don't tell anyone."

The wide eyes opened farther. "I won't. I swear. Have a good day, Mr. Wizard."

Poole waited until the girl was out of earshot. "Peter was Daddy's pet. I don't mean that to sound as harsh as it must. But for every awful thing Lowell did, Peter did two good things. Morgan pushed Peter hard, and Peter went right along with it. He became the apple of his father's eye. Things went on this way for years. Then something happened."

Evan waited. Poole crossed her legs, shifting the briefcase.

"The problem is, I don't know what. I just know that one morning, Morgan came in as shell-shocked as if he'd been through the Blitz. Two days later, Lowell was shipped off to a boarding school in Switzerland. Several years after that, we got word that Lowell had fallen from a cliff while hiking in Crete. It would have seemed like an accident except he left a note."

"Do you know what the note said?"

She gave a slight shake of her head. "I believe it was something to the effect that Lowell's death was Morgan's fault. Morgan himself made a brief comment that Lowell blamed him. But I wasn't privy, and whatever it was, it sent Morgan further around the bend. His work became everything. He was obsessed with finding the source of evil in humans. He pushed the kids in the study. Pushed the data to show things it really didn't. His donors ate it up; Morgan's research appeared to give them hard facts they could use for their crime bills. But it was too much for the families. Most of the parents pulled their kids. We went from our original fourteen to nine to five. Now, Peter remains the only subject, and that's a farce. Morgan stopped publishing the results of these studies, although he shared the research with other private donors: wealthy families with troubled—or potentially troubled—children. Now he's trying to recruit more kids for a new study. I imagine that's one reason he's in Baltimore."

Evan had a sudden realization. "The kids were assigned nonsequential, random numbers."

"Of course. In keeping with policy."

Evan recalled the number Távros had chalked on the sidewalk after Samuel Fishbourne's murder. "Ursula was number six."

"Zero zero six, to be exact." She recrossed her legs. "How did you know?"

Távros was writing down the children's randomly assigned numbers—the number given to each child to keep their names out of the paperwork.

"It doesn't matter," he said. "Why fourteen children?"

"It was a convenient number to work with. Seven girls and seven boys. It was a large enough pool to give us good data without it becoming unwieldy, especially as the kids turned into teenagers." She raised her hands, pushed back her hair against the warm draft. "We ran subsets of the tests on larger groups to get a good statistical analysis. But the core fourteen were the Foundation's focus. *Morgan's* focus. In the early days, if a child was removed from the study—the family moved or the child became ill—we found replacements. We'd learned that early childhood indicators toward prosocial or antisocial activity didn't deviate. Whatever tendencies a child showed at six months, he also showed at six years. We'd simply run a battery of tests on the new child and then popped him or her into the study like a widget."

Evan was thinking of the fourteen Athenian tributes sent to Crete every nine years to be sacrificed to the Minotaur as revenge for the death of King Minos's firstborn son in Greece.

"You said something bad happened one night. When was that?"

"The summer of 2008. But truly, I don't know what happened. That's a question for Morgan."

"Have you heard of Colby Kaplan?"

"No."

"Alex Hemming?"

"No. Why?"

"What about Tav Rousse or Távros?"

"I know that *távros* is Greek for 'bull.' I remember that from my undergraduate days. Why are you asking me about these names?"

"Just wondered if you'd come across them."

"I haven't. And I've shared as much as I can. Now I'm going to leave you with a list of names so that you can make sure these people are safe." For the first time, she turned to face him. She removed her sunglasses, revealing tired brown eyes. "I'm not here to bring down Morgan. He's done nothing illegal. But it's hard to trust a man who will do anything for his family. Or *to* his family."

She lowered the briefcase to the ground and used her foot to slide it under the bench. She started to rise, then eased back down.

"There is one more thing," she said. "It might interest you to know that your brother was in one of Morgan's early studies. Your father was a family friend, and he agreed to let River participate. River was seven at the time. The study didn't amount to much. A few experiments, which River—if he remembers them at all—would recall as play dates. Watch a film. Play with these toys. Answer the pretty lady's questions. Get a cookie."

Evan gaped.

Grace Poole stood and strode back across the plaza in the direction she'd come from. She didn't look back. Evan stared after her, considering the implications of what she'd just said.

Was this why they'd received a minotaur coin? Did TR know River from the childhood studies, and did that make River a target? Yet Távros hadn't killed him when he had the chance. Perhaps because killing River then didn't fit the ritual.

Evan retrieved the briefcase from under the bench. He looked down when his phone vibrated. A text from River's new burner phone.

Dad a no-show. I'll be at the curb when u r done.

On my way, he texted back. Sorry about Oliver.

Evan picked up the briefcase and walked in the same direction as Poole, heading toward his car. A second text stopped him.

Just heard. Dad knifed in parking garage nearby and now at Northwestern Memorial hospital. Dad gave EMTs my number before he fainted. On my way. C u there.

Evan turned around to face Lake Michigan and let the wind off the water toss the spray from the fountain against his suddenly cold skin.

Oliver knifed.

Not a mugging, he suspected. Something worse.

He phoned River, but the call went to voice mail. Maybe River was talking to medical personnel. He hit "Reply."

You were part of the studies. That's the reason for the coin. Maybe this is how TR knows you. Minotaur after Oliver. And you.

Chapter 47

The Minotaur

He was *compelled.*

Compel meant "to drive together," "to irresistibly urge," "to push to a single place." The force could be applied physically. Or by moral imperative.

He found it an interesting word, *compel.* From the Old French *compeller*, which itself derived from the Latin *compellere.*

All creatures were compelled, weren't they? By biology. By need. By nature and nurture.

No harm in doing what you were compelled to do.

After all, when had choice ever been involved in anything he'd done? What choice had he ever had? He'd been marked from birth. And what his genes hadn't done, his father had finished, compelling him to find himself in new and different ways. He'd banished himself from home, exiled himself to the land of his forefathers. But when he'd learned of the traveling production, *The King and the Minotaur*, he'd recognized the play for what it was: a sign from the gods telling him to return home. Compelling him to finish what he and they had begun years ago.

Now, it was Ursula's turn to be compelled. She and the others. In the early days, they had scorned him, mocked him, tried to drive him away.

But look at Ursula now. Crawling like an animal. Compelled to seek the sun. Making a mockery of his offerings.

And with each dragging pace, she went deeper into the earth.

CHAPTER 48

ADDIE

Addie drove.

The rutted dirt road that led to Eddie Barlow's house took her and Patrick a mile through the woods before dead-ending in a flattened area of dirt and gravel. A ramshackle house sat on the far side of the open space. It drooped listlessly in the heat and humidity, cowering beneath the immense sky. Nearby, a pickup truck was parked in the shade, its original blue paint barely visible beneath the rust. The vehicle looked as if it would have trouble traveling fifty feet, much less back to civilization.

Addie emerged from the air-conditioned car, her ribs protesting. Immediately, her skin turned tacky in the heat. Her hair clung heavily to her scalp as if an animal nested on her head.

On the other side of the car, Patrick groaned. "It's hotter than Hades out here. How about I stay with the car? Keep the engine running in case we need to make a fast getaway?"

Addie rolled her eyes at him. "Man up, partner."

"This would be better with a side of ocean and a beer."

His joke fell flat, swallowed by the oppressive air.

All around, the land sprawled, a riotous spread of green. Birds called, and insects hummed, but beneath that, an unforgiving silence filled the hollow spaces between the animal calls. A forest of oaks and hickory trees rose all around, putting Addie in mind of border guards. *Here and no farther,* the trees seemed to say. Visible through the tall trunks, rocky outcrops pointed ragged fingers toward the heavens.

The area smelled of mud and damp, underlain by a throat-tickling sickly sweet odor.

"Something is dead," Patrick said.

"He's a hunter." Addie pointed toward a pile of deer antlers. A weather vane creaked on the roof of the single-story house. "You ready?"

"I forgot my stock of moonshine and a possum bag."

As they neared the house, a flock of crows burst from the trees to the north. Addie jumped. The birds were after a hawk that had ventured into their territory. Half of the crows dive-bombed the predator from above while the other half came at her from underneath. Whatever the hawk had been after, she gave up and fled the area, fading to a black speck against the sky as she wheeled north.

The crows circled victoriously.

"This place gives me the willies," Patrick said.

Addie's eyes stayed on the crows. "I've only now realized how close Edgar Barlow's place is to where Colby Kaplan used to go hiking. And to the Hargrave place. Less than an hour's walk."

"Which makes it even more likely that Colby was snatched by Bull Barlow or his understudy."

There was no sound or movement from the house. Addie led the way up the sagging, unpainted wooden stairs, Patrick close behind. Curtains hung over the open windows at the front of the house, limp save for the occasional waft of air.

She stopped at the door. On either side, old metal tables held wooden boards on which the skins of rabbits and other small animals had been tacked. Flies landed and rose and landed.

Addie wrinkled her nose. "At least now we know what's dead."

"You thought I was kidding about the possum bag," Patrick said.

Addie drew a shallow breath and knocked on the wooden doorframe where it held a tattered screen.

Silence. Patrick shifted his feet, and the boards creaked. Addie knocked again.

"Leave and come back?" she said. "Or wait?"

Patrick moved to the side window, shading his eyes to peer through the thin curtain. "Looks like someone's down on the kitchen floor. Not moving. Try the door."

Addie pulled her gun, opened the screen door, and turned the knob. It gave easily, and the door swung inward. She took one side, Patrick the other. She went in first, gun up, Patrick right behind her.

"Police! Hello!"

Nothing stirred. Addie stepped from the tiny entryway into the kitchen and leaned around the table. She took in the form lying on the floor—old clothes, boots, a hat, and straw—and her breath came out in a rush.

"He's making a scarecrow," she said.

Patrick came to stand beside her. "My mistake." He scratched the back of his head. "But now that we're inside, we'd better make sure no one in here needs our help."

"You *knew* it wasn't a person. You're skirting the line, Paddy Wagon."

He shrugged. "I'm not going to feel bad taking a quick walk-through of the place a serial killer once used as his base of operations. Especially when we've got another killer."

Addie frowned.

"This one's on me," Patrick said. "If we see anything suspicious, we'll back right out, drive away, and return with a warrant."

✣

The place was small, maybe a thousand square feet, and for the moment, it was devoid of human life. There were two bedrooms—both of which looked used based on the tangled bedding and a scattering of men's clothes—a living room barely big enough to turn around in, and a bathroom. In the kitchen, the table was set for two.

The walls were empty of art. A bookshelf held a few car manuals and an illustrated guide to hunting. A fishing rod stood in one corner of the living room. A few photos were thumbtacked to the wall.

Edgar Barlow appeared to live a simple life.

Addie and Patrick studied the photos. One photo was clearly older: a man, a woman, and two young boys stood in front of the family car. The Barlows, presumably, in happier days.

In the other photos, a man recognizable as William "Bull" Barlow stood with a second man close to the same age. Their resemblance was striking. The brothers posed with deer they'd shot, fish they'd caught, and once with an older man who looked like both of his sons.

"William looks a wee bit daft, doesn't he?" Patrick said. "Edgar looks more like the brains in the family."

Addie agreed. In all the photos, Edgar appeared cunning. As if he knew something no one else did. William mostly looked blank, although in one photo his scowl suggested a model for TR's sketch: she recognized the glare.

"Those rumors about Bull having a partner," She said. "You think it's possible it was Edgar?"

"Those rumors were mostly dismissed," Patrick reminded her.

"What happened to Barlow Senior?"

"Gone the way of the angels, like his son. Heart attack, if my memory is what it should be. It wasn't long after he turned in William to the police."

Addie returned to the kitchen, wondering who Edgar's houseguest was. She glanced through a window at the back porch where Edgar had placed more hides.

Very small hides. She stepped out onto the porch for a closer look, then gave a small cry.

"Patrick!" she called.

He pushed open the back door and came to stand next to her.

"Look at these," she said softly.

Next to the stretched and pegged hides of small animals were two boards that held three-by-three-inch squares of what looked like human skin. On each skin, someone had tattooed the bull glyph they'd first found on Fishbourne's body.

"Mother Mary—" Patrick began.

A creak on the far end of the porch warned them just before a man appeared. He stopped and stared, surprised to see them. He must have come from the woods to the north of the house and missed their car.

"Who are you?" he growled.

He was compactly built, under six feet, probably in his early fifties. He was the same man who appeared in the photos with Bull. Edgar Barlow.

Addie could only see one of his hands. The other was hidden by the corner of the house. The man himself stood in shadow.

The whisper of Patrick's gun leaving its holster reached her ears. She shifted to her left so that Patrick would have a clear shot if he needed it.

She kept her voice casual. "We're with Chicago PD. Are you Edgar Barlow?"

"What if I am?"

"We'd like to ask you a few questions about your brother."

"He'd dead," Edgar said. "Not much more to say about 'im."

"We heard about his death. We're sorry for your loss. Would you mind coming all the way around the corner, Mr. Barlow, where I can see your hands?"

He took a single shuffling step forward. Suspicion lay heavy in his eyes. She could now see his other hand. He held a hammer.

"We just want to talk, Mr. Barlow," Addie said. "How about you put down that hammer and we chat for a few minutes?"

The suspicion in Edgar's eyes deepened. He held on to the hammer.

"It won't take long," she said.

Addie felt as though she were coaxing one of his small animals into a trap. Drawing him close enough so that Patrick could slap on cuffs.

Because finding those branded squares of skin had changed everything.

A shaft of sunlight spilled through the cracked boards of the roof that hung over the porch. It illuminated Edgar, and the tattoo on the side of his neck came into view.

The bull glyph. Just as in the drawing of William Barlow in the tree house.

Addie acted on instinct. "Where's Távros, Mr. Barlow? Is he here with you?"

Barlow threw the hammer. Addie ducked. Patrick shouted. Edgar spun on his heel, leapt off the porch, and took off running.

"Damn it," Patrick said. "He winged me."

Addie turned. No visible blood. "You okay?"

"I'm fine, no thanks to that low-life bastard."

"Call the sheriff," she said.

She sprinted after Edgar, ignoring the protests of her bruised body. She jumped off the porch and caught a glimpse of Edgar—black shirt, camouflage pants—darting into the woods. Behind her came Patrick's voice on the phone talking to the Ogle County Sheriff's Office.

She dashed across the open space. As soon as she moved into the forest, the world darkened. Sunlight came in patches, alternately dazzling and then gone. She spotted Edgar far ahead, racing along a deeply rutted trail.

"Stop!" she shouted.

Barlow put on a burst of speed. Addie tried to do the same, but the python around her ribs squeezed. Every breath pulled the python tighter.

Barlow darted left off the path and deeper into the woods. By the time Addie reached the place where he'd doglegged off the trail, he'd disappeared. She listened for his footsteps, but the only sound was the angry chattering of a jay. She wiped sweat out of her eyes.

He could be anywhere. Watching. Deliberating. Perhaps, like Távros in Chicago, he had a weapon stashed. Perhaps he was even now circling around to approach her from behind.

Addie sidled off the trail and into the woods, placing her feet carefully to avoid tipping off Edgar. The jay followed her, scolding, flying away only after she remained motionless for a few minutes. She strained to hear other sounds. Something rustled in the undergrowth. A crow cawed in the distance. Her own heart thrummed in her ears as loud as the ocean.

Finally, her heart slowed. The python eased.

Up ahead, the foliage thinned, and sunlight shone down in full glory. She approached cautiously, moving from tree to tree and periodically glancing back the way she'd come. When she reached the edge of the clearing, she stopped with her back pressed against the wide trunk of an oak.

A single insect buzzed by her ear, then it was as if the world had fallen silent.

Someone had built a circular maze out of stones—fifty or more, each boulder roughly two feet in circumference. Now she understood the ruts in the trail. Whoever built the maze had used a small tractor.

On the far side of the glade, a rocky ledge rose fifteen feet high. Deeply etched on the rock was a circular maze. And in the center, someone had used chisel and hammer to carve an image of the man bull.

The Minotaur.

At a sound behind her, she whirled.

It was Patrick, approaching her with gun drawn, his breath coming hard. She pressed a finger to her lips as he drew near.

Her eyes returned to the maze on the ground.

Something lay at the center.

She pointed toward the figure, then gestured for Patrick to cover her. When he nodded, she stepped guardedly into the maze. Her foot wobbled on a loose fragment of stone, sending it skittering into one of the boulders, and she ducked, waiting for Edgar to come rushing out of the forest. She glanced back at Patrick. He shook his head, indicating he'd seen nothing, and she pressed on. She ignored the designated path and moved in a low crouch between the stones, heading toward the heart of the maze. Periodically, she stopped to listen.

Nothing except a rising breeze filled with a welcome coolness that touched her cheeks. Clouds gathered overhead.

She neared the center of the maze and sank to her haunches. She peered around one of the stones.

A figure lay huddled on the ground. Someone had pounded a metal stake into the earth and attached a chain and a pair of manacles. The manacles gripped the person's wrists.

The figure lay on its side, curled in a fetal position, half-covered by a tarp. She couldn't tell if it was a man or a woman.

Or if they were still alive.

She took a step forward, flinched when the figure moved. Now she could see it was a man. Badly beaten in the face, a scab of blood near one ear, another across his forehead that still seeped blood.

"Help me," said Peter Hargrave.

CHAPTER 49

EVAN

Evan found River sitting in the emergency room lobby, twirling the Indiana Jones hat Oliver had given him so long ago. He stood as Evan approached.

"They're taking him into surgery," River told him. "We can wait upstairs."

Evan took in River's strained expression, the slump in his shoulders. "What happened?"

River waited to respond until they'd made their way across the lobby and through a set of doors.

"He was attacked after he got out of his car. A man was waiting for him in the parking garage."

They stopped at a desk with a security guard and signed in. The guard pointed them down the hall toward a row of elevators.

River continued. "The man approached Dad as if he recognized him, called him Dr. Oliver Wilding. Dad, of course, stopped to talk. I don't know what the man said to him—witnesses heard the first part but not anything after."

"Wait," Evan said. "How do you know all this?"

"Witnesses told the EMTs, and they told me. Lucky for Dad, he's been through his share of rodeos. Witnesses said he shouted and jerked back, which means he must have seen the knife. If he hadn't, he'd be dead."

"The shout must have scared off his attacker," Evan said. "How serious is it?"

They stepped into the elevator, and River punched a button.

"The ER doc says it's not life threatening as long as he doesn't get an infection. The knife sliced through the abdominal wall and nicked his liver. He'll be laid up for a time."

"Slow him down a bit, anyway," Evan said. "Maybe this will be our chance to get to know him. Unfortunately."

They both tried to laugh.

The elevator opened onto another waiting room. The air smelled of coffee and antiseptic. Lights flooded the space, making everything overly bright.

A family of three huddled in one corner, and a man paced back and forth in front of the windows. River almost ran to an empty receptionist's desk and rang a bell. When a nurse appeared, she nodded, had him sign something, checked her watch, and went back through the door she'd come through.

"He'll be out of surgery in forty minutes or so," River told Evan when he caught up.

Evan bought two water bottles from the vending machine, then he and River found seats near the center of the room. River set his hat on a side table and rubbed his face as if trying to wipe away worry.

"That text you sent," he said. "What were you talking about?"

"Grace Poole told me you were in one of Morgan's early studies."

Evan shared his conversation with Dr. Poole. He hadn't had a chance to look inside her briefcase, which was locked in the trunk of his car.

"I don't remember any of that," River said.

"It probably wasn't memorable enough to stick. As Poole mentioned, you would have thought you were going on playdates."

River uncapped the water and took a long swallow. "I wonder how my tests came out?"

"Psychopath," Evan said with a straight face. "Through and through."

A smile found River. "Then you'd better play nice with me." His expression shifted. "You think it was the killer who came after Dad?"

"Hard not to think so," Evan said. "He killed Samuel and Bryant."

"But how did he know where to find Dad?"

"It wouldn't be rocket science. If he learned that Oliver was at the conference, he could have followed him from the hotel. But there's also your phone."

River shook his head. "You mean the one at the bottom of the Chicago River?"

"What if it's not? What if Távros slipped it out of your pocket while the two of you were doing the tango? If Dad forgot you were using a burner and texted you on your old number first—"

"Távros would have gotten the message."

"On the other hand, surely your phone is password protected."

River looked for a moment like he wanted to shoot himself. "I turned off the password requirement before I went after Távros. I didn't want to fool with it while I was sending you screenshots of my location."

"That was either very clever or really stupid."

River's smile was twisted. "I believe the phrase you want is 'too clever by half.'"

"That will work."

The elevator doors opened, and Diana strode into the room. She saw them and made a beeline. The man pacing by the windows stopped long enough to admire her as she sailed past.

She hugged Evan, then took a seat next to River. She took his hand in hers. "Thanks for letting me know," she said to him. "I'm so sorry about your dad. What's the word?"

While River gave her an update, Evan felt a surge of pleasure: River had cared enough about Diana to call her.

"Have you guys heard the news?" Diana asked, scattering Evan's thoughts. "There's a manhunt going down in Ogle County. They're looking for Edgar Barlow."

Evan and River exchanged glances.

"Addie and Patrick went out there this afternoon," Evan said. "I'd better give her a call."

The pacing man had disappeared into the bathroom. Evan took up a spot by the windows and called Addie. She picked up right away.

"I just got off the phone with the embassy in Athens," she said. "Some functionary burning the midnight oil. Apparently, they did create a Consular Report of the Death of an American Abroad for the death of Lowell Hargrave. Drafted it after they received notice of his passing from the authorities on Crete. But get this, they never found a body. The reason they agreed to issue the report is that after six months, Lowell Hargrave hadn't reappeared."

"Fascinating," Evan said.

"Exactly what I thought. I'll fill you in on the details later. Meanwhile, in other news, Edgar is a killer, just like his brother. But he's not Távros. Still, I'll bet dinner at the best restaurant in Chicago that they know each other."

Evan listened while she recounted the events of the afternoon, concluding with finding Peter Hargrave in the forest and with the manhunt now going down.

"I guess that clears Peter as a suspect," Evan said.

"Actually, no. Maybe he and Edgar had a falling-out, and Edgar got the best of him. He hasn't said much. He was in and out of consciousness while we got him back to Edgar's place. The EMTs have stabilized him, and he's agreed to talk before they transport him to Rochelle Community Hospital. The kid is scared to death."

"Minotaurs have that effect on people."

"Sheriff's deputies have gone to keep an eye on the Hargrave place, in case Edgar shows up, hoping Peter escaped on his own and ran home. Or in case Lowell makes an appearance. Maybe we can put a nail in that coffin."

"In a manner of speaking."

Her laugh was dry. "Evan, you mentioned caves. We've got most of Ogle County's Sheriff's Office here, and they're bringing in dogs. But so far, we can't find a trace of Edgar Barlow."

"There are rumors of caves in the area, and if there's anything a minotaur loves, it's a cave. There's a spelunker named Matt Sykes in Oregon. He's in his seventies now and no longer active, but he could help you find cave entrances. And maybe he's got maps."

"That's good. I'll reach out."

"Also, if you think Edgar Barlow has gone underground, River can lead a search team. He has hundreds of hours of caving experience. And he can read the maps. Without him or someone like him, any deputies who manage to find the caves run the risk of getting lost."

"You want to put River in a cave with Edgar Barlow and maybe Távros?"

"Not for all the lost documents in the world. But I'm not my brother's keeper."

"River isn't a law enforcement officer."

But he heard the desire in her voice, a need to do whatever could be done.

"He's an expert," Evan assured her. "Have the sheriff deputize him for this specific mission."

She sighed. "I didn't take much convincing, did I? I'll talk to Patrick and the sheriff. And if you don't mind, ask River. Time might be running out for Jamal and Ursula. Especially since Edgar knows we're on his trail. If the sheriff agrees and River is willing to help, I'll send a squad car for him."

Evan started to say that, of course, River would help. But he held off. Maybe River would want to stay at the hospital with their father.

"I'll talk to him," he said.

A doctor appeared from behind the surgery doors. "River Wilding?" he called.

"I've got to go," Evan said without telling Addie about Oliver. Cops were already working the scene of the attack, and she had enough on her plate. "Let me know what you learn from Peter."

After they'd hung up, Evan joined River and Diana near the receptionist's station.

"Your father came through just fine," the surgeon said. "I don't see any damage to the liver other than what we picked up on imaging. There is blood in the abdominal cavity, but not as much as we sometimes see with injuries like this, and I was able to repair the damaged blood vessels. He's lucky. A few inches deeper, we'd be looking at injury to the intestines, possibly the stomach, with an accompanying risk of peritonitis or abscess. For now, we'll keep monitoring him for infection or other complications."

Wary relief flooded River's face. "When will we know he's out of danger?"

"Typically, any issues appear within a few days. Occasionally, problems can appear months later. He'll need to be monitored regularly."

"What's next?" Diana asked.

"He's being moved to post-op, where he'll remain for an hour or two. After that, we'll get him into a private room. You can see him then, although he'll likely be sleeping. In the meantime, you're welcome to wait here. Or we can call you at home when he's awake. Just let reception know what you want to do."

They thanked the surgeon, and he left.

"Dad is one lucky son of a bitch," River said.

"Or maybe just too stubborn to die," Evan suggested.

River squeezed Evan's shoulder, hugged Diana, then went to stand by the windows. A minute later, he prowled past the elevators as if considering flight, then stopped in front of the vending machine for a time. He walked past their chairs, took a slug of water, then returned to the windows.

Diana, too, was watching him.

"He needs you," she said to Evan.

Evan nodded. River did need him, but not in the way Diana imagined. What River needed was a distraction, and work would serve. Even if Evan hated what he was about to ask.

He steeled himself and went to his brother.

"If you want to put that energy to good use while we're waiting on Oliver," he said, "I know just the thing."

Chapter 50

River

A CPD squad car picked up River at the hospital's front entrance. He directed the officer to make a quick stop at a hardware store and a longer one at a sporting-goods outlet. When he had what he needed, River returned to the squad car, and they sped west, lights flashing.

He stared out at the passing city and thought of Oliver and all the times his dad hadn't been there for him. Birthdays and holidays. Graduations and awards. It should have made him feel better. Instead, all he could think was that Oliver lay in a hospital bed with an IV and a heart monitor and all the other devices meant to save a life he'd come close to losing.

And if he died, his youngest son wouldn't be by his side.

The city slipped behind them, its skyline gray and hulking. The countryside opened, and late-afternoon sun slanted through the windshield while a light rain spattered the windows. The cop turned off the air-conditioning.

After Evan told him about Morgan Hargrave's studies, River had begun pulling up hazy recollections of time spent with other children. A tall shining building. Brightly lit corridors. A memory of wanting to hold Oliver's hand but not wanting to ask. They'd put a device on his head—a cap with wire leads, which he now realized must have been an EEG. Then he'd watched movies of puppets helping other puppets. Or sometimes not helping them. After each film, he was taken into a room with other children. He had no memory of what games they might have played.

Had he helped the other children? Fought with them? Where did he fall on Morgan Hargrave's spectrum of good and evil?

His thoughts turned to Diana, and his shoulders relaxed. He felt a smile touch his face.

"We're forty minutes out," the officer said. "Driving right into another damn storm. The rain going to be a problem in the caves?"

"It might."

River put aside all philosophical thoughts and his unexpected longing for Diana. He opened the bags holding his purchases and began ripping off tags.

Chapter 51

Addie

Peter sat huddled in a blanket at Edgar Barlow's kitchen table. A mug of tea cooled in front of him. Someone had brought him a pizza, which sat untouched. He had bandages on the fingers of his left hand and on his ear, and an adhesive butterfly on his left cheek.

The EMTs had checked him over. Bruises, abrasions, a nasty sunburn on his legs, and a nastier cut near his ear. And a serious case of shock. As soon as Addie gave them the go-ahead, they'd take Peter to the hospital. In the meantime, they said, he was stable.

But even with sheriff's deputies all around and Addie in the kitchen with him, he was still shaking.

"You're safe, Peter," Addie reassured him. "There's no way Edgar or anyone else is getting to you here."

He made no response. He wore scrubs from the EMTs, which were too short and too tight for his frame—he'd been naked when Addie found him. He looked like an overgrown child save for the vacant look in his eyes.

"Do you want to call your dad?" Addie asked.

Something surfaced in Peter's eyes. He looked at Addie as if seeing her for the first time. He reached out suddenly and grabbed her arm.

"Where is my dad?"

Addie resisted pulling away. She saw that the nails on his unbandaged fingers were broken and dirty. "He's in Baltimore. You can use my phone."

Peter relaxed, released his grip on her.

"Are you worried about him?" she asked.

He said nothing. The vacant look reappeared.

"Peter, I know this is hard, but I need you to tell us what you can about what happened. Who chained you in that maze?"

A noise burbled between his lips. It sounded like sobs, but his eyes were dry.

"Who was it?" she asked.

He blinked. "Eddie. It was always Eddie."

"Eddie. You mean Edgar Barlow?"

Peter nodded. "He was the one who told Billy what to do."

"You're talking about William Barlow?"

Another nod.

"Did Billy always do whatever Eddie told him?"

"Seemed like it," Peter said.

Addie was thinking of a man suddenly subdued by a visit from his brother. A man who had killed himself right after that visit. Maybe Eddie had been worried that, with Lowell back on the scene, the truth would come out about who had really been in charge when people died.

Addie leaned forward, made sure she had Peter's attention. "Peter, what did Eddie tell his brother to do?"

The shaking grew worse. Maybe it was a top-notch act from a talented actor. Peter might be guilty of terrible crimes. After all, the young man had written fan mail to Barlow.

But right now, Peter didn't look as if he could swat a fly without vomiting.

"Can you tell me what Eddie told Billy to do?"

"To hurt them."

"Who did he want Billy to hurt?"

But Peter pulled on the blanket and looked down.

"How do you know this, Peter? How do you know Eddie was the one who told Billy what to do?"

Peter's voice came out with the thinness of thread. "Lowell knew them. He was friends with them. Eddie was the smart one. He wanted me to be his friend, too."

"Were you? Were you Eddie's friend?"

Peter wiped his nose with the back of his hand, then winced when his fingers caught the butterfly bandage. "Sometimes."

"And you, you must have liked Billy. You wrote to him in prison."

Peter's eyes grew large in his battered face. "I did not. I didn't. It was Lowell."

"You think Lowell wrote to Billy?"

Silence.

She decided to test his reaction. She said, "But Lowell died, didn't he?"

Now the tears came. One, then another, then more. She found a clean tissue in her bag and offered it to him. He ignored it.

She held her breath. Released it. She changed tactics. "Did Lowell hang out with Billy and Eddie?"

The sobbing turned to a sort of chortling. "You mean, were they drinking buddies? Fishing buddies?"

"Did Lowell help Billy and Eddie hurt people?"

Peter closed in on himself so quickly it was like watching a box fold itself shut.

Addie sat back and tried to regroup.

The US embassy staffer in Athens had said the police statement attached to the consular report indicated that a body had been spotted at the base of a cliff by a fisherman. But when the fisherman returned with the police, the body was gone. Police found Lowell's backpack with his ID near where the fisherman reported the body. And a suicide note.

They presumed Lowell's body had been swept out to sea.

But what if there was another explanation?

"Peter." Addie risked putting a hand on his shoulder. He didn't flinch. "Is Lowell alive?"

Peter lifted his head. "Dad told us he died. Four years ago."

"What do you think, Peter? Do you think Lowell is alive? How else could he have written those letters?"

Silence.

"Did Lowell ever call himself Távros?"

Peter squeezed his eyes shut. After a moment, he nodded.

A deputy came into the kitchen. "Detective Bisset? The caver guys are here. Both of them. A local guy and someone named River."

"Thank you, Deputy."

Peter opened his eyes and watched the man leave. Then he leaned in toward Addie and spoke in a whisper.

"You know what fucking kills me? No matter what Lowell does, Dad always cleans up the mess. No matter what."

Chapter 52

Ursula Fishbourne

She didn't know what time it was that he came for her. There was no morning, noon, or night here. There was only darkness, lit now and again with flame.

He was dressed as a monster. The Minotaur. The flesh-eating beast of Cretan myth.

She thought of the sound she'd heard as he tore her father from her, and she crumpled to the ground.

He grabbed her by the wrists and hauled her to her feet.

She said his name, and he laughed.

"No longer," he said. "I am Távros. The Minotaur. Slayer of men. Soon, very soon, I will send you to meet the gods."

The chill that ran along her spine spread to encompass her entire body. Flesh and muscle and bones and organs. She couldn't move. She couldn't speak. She could only weep.

He threw her over his shoulder and moved toward the dancing flames.

Chapter 53

Evan

Evan jerked awake trailing nightmares.

For a moment, he took in his surroundings without processing them. He didn't know where he was or how he had come to be here. His first thought was that he was in an overlit antechamber to the underworld.

Then it came back: his meeting with Grace Poole, River's frantic text, their dad's surgery.

The fact of Lowell's death and that a body had never been recovered.

The killer had come after Oliver. And now Evan had sent River straight into the monster's lair.

He sat up. His phone showed it was late evening—he'd been asleep only an hour—but it was impossible to tell in the brightly lit waiting room; the large windows reflected rather than revealed. Beside him, Diana dozed: head back, legs sprawled, still somehow graceful. The pacer and the family of three had left.

Evan stood and worked out the kinks in his neck.

A woman—nurse or technician—appeared at the receptionist's desk. She called out, "River or Evan Wilding?"

Diana didn't stir.

When Evan reached the desk, the woman gave him a reassuring smile. “Your father is doing just fine. He’s been moved to a private room. Would you like to see him?”

About as much as I’d like to be bitten on the nether regions by a scorpion.

He smiled back. “Yes. Thank you.”

✣

For a moment, standing in the doorway, Evan didn’t recognize his father.

The last time he’d seen Oliver Wilding, the renowned pharmacologist had been a decade younger and in the prime of health. Now gray had taken over his shoulder-length hair, and his large-boned frame was thinner than Evan recalled. Oliver had ditched the beard somewhere along the way, revealing a face carved by time and sun. Pale now, but still handsome.

“Hey, Dad,” Evan said from the doorway.

Oliver opened his eyes. “Bastard,” he growled.

Definitely him.

Evan edged into the room. Being around his father always made him think of walking on marbles. One wrong step and down you went.

“Can I get you anything?” Evan asked.

“Where’s River?”

“Out trying to catch the man who hurt you.”

Oliver closed one eye. Squinted. “Seriously,” he growled.

“As a heart attack. Seems you came to a killer’s attention because of Morgan Hargrave.”

“Who?”

“Your old friend, the social psychologist. You enrolled River in his studies.”

Oliver lifted his head from the pillow. "The good and evil guy? God, it's been years."

"Scale is tipping more toward evil at the moment, but yes. Do you remember him?"

"Get me some water."

Evan retrieved a glass of water and positioned a straw so that Oliver could drink. Oliver took a few sips and lowered his head back to the pillow.

"I remember Morgan," he said. "And his sons. Lowell and that pansy, Peter. Lowell sure as hell didn't fall far from the family tree."

"What do you mean?"

"Pair of psychopaths, he and his dad." Oliver pierced him with a glare. "The hell would either of them have to do with the bastard who stabbed me?"

"Tell me what you mean by calling them psychopaths."

Oliver's glare deepened to a scowl. "Doesn't my height-challenged, allegedly brilliant son know what a psychopath is? Lots of successful men are psychopaths. Brilliance in your work requires a rather cruel dedication, don't you think?"

"I know that's how you've lived your life."

Oliver blinked. "Touché."

Was Evan imagining it, or did Oliver's expression now hold a hint of respect?

Evan said, "Someone is murdering former members of Morgan's study group. And people close to them."

"Are you still serious as a heart attack?"

Evan nodded, and Oliver forced himself to a sitting position. He pressed his hands to his stomach, in obvious pain, but his scowl turned ferocious. "And you let River go out to find him?"

Evan swallowed his guilt. "I believe that's the first time you've given me credit for anything. As if I could tell River what to do. Now tell me what you know so that River has an idea what he's dealing with."

Oliver's harsh gaze remained on Evan for another moment. Then he settled back against the pillows. "Morgan's a psychopath when it comes to his work. The man laid everything at the altar of his studies. Including that beautiful wife of his. Philomena. He ignored her. Maybe worse." Oliver looked up at the ceiling tiles. "Maybe much worse."

"Meaning what?" Evan asked. "Meaning Morgan might have had something to do with his wife's death?"

"Read whatever you like into it. I'm well into the realm of speculation. It was Lowell who was the violent one, not Morgan. Lowell started showing the classic signs when he was six. Ten years later or so, Morgan finally sent him to a facility in Switzerland."

"I heard it was boarding school."

"Is that what Morgan told you?" Oliver laughed softly. Spittle glistened on his lips. "Boarding school my ass. It's a treatment center for the untreatable."

"Violent psychopaths."

"Maybe you're not a complete idiot. Once Morgan realized Lowell was psychopathic, he knew it was a terminal diagnosis. But he thought the violence could be managed. He tried redirecting the boy's attention by stuffing him full of the things the kid loved. Classes on mythology. Lessons in Greek and Latin. A trip to Crete to meet his mother's family and see the palace at Knossos. There was nothing he didn't do for Lowell. He was going to change his son and thus change the course of psychology."

Evan thought of the hedges in front of the Hargrave estate. "He built Lowell a maze."

Olive shook his shaggy head. "The hedge maze? That was Philomena's. What I do know is that something happened. Ten years ago, there was an incident."

Colby, Evan thought. "What happened?"

"I'm just speculating, so don't go trotting off to tell the world. A boy disappeared. The police called him a runaway, and who was I to suggest otherwise? But around the same time, Morgan mentioned to me that Lowell had become unmanageable. And he was tired of cleaning up his son's . . . messes. You connect the dots."

"You didn't go to the police?"

"With what? I was making guesses from four thousand miles away. I let them do their job."

Evan forced himself to set aside his disgust with his father. "So, Morgan sent Lowell to Switzerland."

"The foolishly optimistic work in every field, and the doctors at the facility said they could help Lowell."

"Did they?"

"How the hell would I know? Last I heard, the boy had run away from the center. He ended up killing himself on Crete. Now what has any of this got to do with me getting gutted like a fish in a parking garage?"

Oliver's face had gone paler. His heart rate had shot up. Evan was sure a nurse would appear any moment to tell him to leave his father in peace.

"I don't know yet," he said.

"Of course not. Your work is all speculation. Nothing concrete." His eyes drifted closed. "I wanted my firstborn son to be just like me. Or better than me. You threw off my plans."

"Children tend to do that."

"I know. God, do I know. And I was a bastard about it, Evan. But there was my work to consider."

Evan thought he must have misheard his father. Oliver didn't make mistakes. He made course corrections.

But instead of leaning in, Evan pushed the comment away with a joke.

"They say recognition is the first step," he said.

Oliver barked a laugh, then yelped in pain. "Damn it. I thought they gave me something. Our current pain meds are worthless. Addictive. Brain killing. There are better substances out there."

"And you'll be the one to find them."

"Damn straight," Oliver said.

When Oliver's breathing had evened out, Evan left without saying goodbye.

✣

Back in the lobby, Diana still slept. One of the staff had made coffee, and gratefully he poured a cup. He carried it to the window and stared out at the night.

Lowell a confirmed psychopath.

An *incident* that had happened ten years ago, the same time that Colby Kaplan had disappeared.

Morgan's indulgence of his son's interest in Greek mythology and Crete. Oliver had said the hedge maze was built for Philomena. And what Minotaur would be satisfied with an aboveground maze made of greenery?

And then there was Philomena. Had Morgan been afraid her death would scar Lowell, as Grace Poole had suggested? Or had something else happened? Was Morgan right in what he'd told Poole? That he believed his son had been involved in Philomena's death?

Evan poured himself a second cup of lukewarm coffee, drank it in quick gulps, tossed the cup in the trash, and went downstairs and outside.

Wind buffeted him as he crossed Superior Street to the parking garage. Thinking of Oliver's attacker, he quickly retrieved Poole's briefcase from the Jaguar's trunk and hurried back through the ER and onto the elevator.

In his mind, he kept seeing the mix of glyphs Távros had written at the bottom of his letter: *Solve the riddle before the sacrifice is made.*

He'd thought the riddles lay in the Cretan hieroglyphs Távros had placed in the letter and on his victims. But he was now confident that

Távros hadn't buried a deeper riddle in his glyphs because nothing Evan had tried coaxed any meaning out of them. Távros had used them as symbols of tribalism: team icons, individual signs. There was probably a reason why a particular glyph had been assigned to a specific child, but Evan doubted that was relevant to identifying and finding Távros.

The real riddle was Távros's true identity.

And at the moment, Lowell Hargrave—despite the report from the consular in Athens—was his top suspect.

Evan emerged from the elevator. Diana had kicked off her shoes and curled into a ball, her face buried in a pillow. A young couple now sat in the corner previously used by the family. Evan poured himself more coffee and resumed his seat.

Addie had sent him a text with a list.

Hemming's ID used for UPS is fake

Convo w PH:

L called himself Távros

L hung out as teen with B brothers

Conclusion: With lack of body, likely L alive and our Minotaur

Figuring she didn't have time for a phone call, Evan typed back his own message.

Agree w your conclusion re: L

False "death" symbolic: shed old self and became Minotaur thru rebirth.

Per M Hargrave's research partner, something bad happened mid-July 2008, right before L sent to boarding school/treatment center. L "dies" around same date six years later.

Suspect MH covering for his son. MH in danger if not in Baltimore.

Addie responded with: Treatment center?

Evan: Likely not a boarding school L attended. Rather, a facility for treating psychopathy.

Addie: Got it. Deputies delayed but on way to MH's. I will warn them MH at risk, L might be there.

Evan set his phone on the table and brought his hands to rest on his stomach. He stared unseeing at the ceiling.

Solve the riddle before the sacrifice is made.

They had, quite possibly, solved the riddle. Now what? How could they prevent the sacrifices—presumably of Ursula and Jamal?

Did the riddle suggest that Távros would lay down his sword if his identity was revealed? Did he seek acknowledgment more than whatever revenge or punishment drove him?

If so, what kind of acknowledgment? And how would they reach him?

He picked up Grace Poole's briefcase and opened it.

Inside were two slim sheets of paper stapled together. Fourteen names, two of which he knew: Ursula Fishbourne and Jamal James. Both missing. The Minotaur had murdered Ursula's father and Jamal's husband. He'd possibly taken his own brother. Was his goal to collect the fourteen tributes that—according to the myth—had been sacrificed to the Minotaur every nine years? Did he plan to eventually murder seven people while imprisoning seven more for later sacrifice? He shuddered. It was said that the Minotaur took his time with the sacrifices rather than devouring them all at once.

A third name, Anna Poole, confirmed what Poole had told him and why she'd shared this information. She would do anything to keep her daughter safe.

A final piece of paper lay inside Poole's briefcase: a photocopy of part of a painting Evan recognized as Michelangelo's *Last Judgment* from the Sistine Chapel. In the lower right-hand corner of Michelangelo's famous piece, he had portrayed King Minos at the entrance to hell, entwined by a serpent that had sunk its fangs into the man's genitals. According to myth, after Minos's brutal slaying—death by boiling water—he became one of three Judges of the Dead in the Greek underworld.

Beneath the copy, Poole had written a note: *Lowell mailed this painting to me seven or eight years ago after he left for boarding school. I didn't understand what it meant, but I held on to it. Maybe you can figure it out.*

Below that, she'd written a phone number with the words *If you want to discuss.*

He picked up his phone again and dialed. Grace Poole answered.

"Do you really think Morgan is in Baltimore?" he asked.

"I thought you would be calling about the painting," she said.

"Please think, Dr. Poole. Morgan's trip was sudden. Was it unusual in any way?"

"A little. He normally has our receptionist arrange his travel through a service. This time he just sent us a text, notifying us of his departure. But if the trip was as urgent as he implied, there wouldn't have been time to use a travel service. He flew out last night."

"And he texted you from his phone?"

"Of course. What did you think about the painting?"

"I think Lowell believes his father can't rightfully judge the dead until he is among them."

"What does that mean? Judge which dead?"

"The only dead man who can still care what his father thinks."

Evan hung up.

He wondered if Morgan had fled before Lowell decided it was time for the king to pay the ultimate price.

Flight seemed unlikely, given Morgan's ego—he wouldn't believe himself to be in danger. He'd always controlled Lowell in the past. He'd feel certain he could control him still. And someone else could have sent that text from Morgan's phone.

His mind wandered back to the flat, heavy stone he'd found in the hedge maze. The one lying in recently disturbed earth amid flattened weeds.

If Oliver was right, and Morgan had worked to distract Lowell from his violent tendencies, then maybe there was more to the family's hedge maze than met the casual eye.

He stared out at the night. What better way to keep a child from becoming a monster than to let him pretend to be one?

He sent a final message to Addie: Lowell will be in or near the maze at the Hargrave place. I suspect the maze leads to an underground chamber bc I believe Morgan let L play Minotaur. If so, I know where the entrance is. Tell the deputies it is in the hedge maze. At the center under a flat stone. I'm on my way.

He put his phone away without waiting for an answer. He didn't want Addie to try and stop him. He checked in with the nurse on Oliver's status—vitals good, sleeping soundly—and scribbled a note for Diana, which he propped on the table next to her sleeping form. Then he picked up Poole's briefcase, headed for the elevator, and pressed the button.

The doors opened. As he stepped inside, Diana came running and slid in next to him. She had his note clutched in her hand.

"I'm going with you," she said.

"Did you bring your axe?"

"It's in my trunk."

"I'd prefer it in your hand." He allowed a small smile and pushed the button for the ground floor. "We just need to make a quick stop at my office."

✣

Darkness had fallen by the time they reached the Hargrave estate. Evan pulled in behind two sheriff's cars parked in the driveway. He checked his phone—Addie had texted that the deputies were expecting him. She'd also sent a text telling him he should stay in his car with the door locked. *For your sake, she'd added. And mine.*

He killed the engine, pocketed his phone and keys, and they stepped out into the suffocating air.

Outdoor lights illuminated the front of the house and the drive. Inside, the house was dark. No one answered the bell.

"Maybe Morgan took the deputies down to the maze," Evan said. "If I'm right, you must go through the maze to get to the labyrinth—that is, you have to travel through the hedge maze to reach the entrance to the underground labyrinth."

"How do we find this entrance?"

"I believe it's concealed under a stone in the center of the maze where there used to be a garden."

"How do you even know there's a labyrinth?"

"I don't. It's all guesswork right now."

She cast him a look. "Guesswork, huh? Okay, Professor."

They walked to the crest of the hill. The maze lay below them, a coiled, brooding serpent in the darkness.

"There!" Diana pointed.

A light, unmoving, its glow seeping through the dying hedges.

Diana insisted on going down the stairs first. She had her axe gripped in her right hand and her hair in a braid. Even in her thoroughly modern rain jacket and trainers, she looked like a goddess. She ran down with the grace of a leopard while Evan followed with the gait of a short-legged munchkin cat.

She waited for him at the bottom.

"From here on, I lead," he told her. "If for some reason we get separated, always turn to the right."

"It's better if I go first."

"Look at it this way. If we're attacked from the rear, he'll have to go through you to get to me. And if he attacks from the front, I won't even have to duck for you to sink your axe into him."

Diana couldn't argue with his logic.

Evan used his phone as a flashlight and plunged between the hedges.

The maze was a nightmare in the dark. Gusts flowing in from the east shook the dying hedges so that they resembled monsters with squat bodies and long claws. Unexpected roots and stones lay in wait to trip the unwary. Clouds scuttled overhead, chased by the same wind, hiding then revealing a sea of stars.

After several turns, the light they'd spotted from above glowed more brightly. Diana gripped his shoulder. When he turned, she nodded toward the light, used her fingers to pantomime a slow walk, then pressed a finger to her lips.

He nodded. Quiet and measured.

When they reached the last bend before the light, Diana again set her hand on his shoulder. She gestured for them to crouch as they turned the corner.

Evan wanted to point out that if Diana crouched, it made them the same height. Which meant crouching on his part was unnecessary.

But he followed orders.

They turned the bend.

A heavy-duty flashlight lay on the ground. Its wide beam revealed two men dressed in the olive-and-tan uniforms of the Ogle County Sheriff's Office. The men lay on their backs in the gravel and weeds.

They'd both been shot dead.

CHAPTER 54

ADDIE

Matt Sykes, the caver from Oregon, had no difficulty leading River, five deputies, and Addie to the nearest cave entrance. It lay concealed below the rocky ledge where someone had carved the Minotaur and a maze.

Sykes aimed his flashlight at the rock. "I remember seeing that years ago before getting spooked by Edgar Barlow about being on his property. Some landowners are cool about it, but I didn't get a good feel from Barlow or his dad."

"Did you know the other brother?" Addie asked. "William?"

"The killer, right? No, ma'am. Lucky for me, I didn't run into him. But I was part of the team that searched for that kid who got lost. Colby Kaplan. We never found hide nor hair of him."

Hide nor hair. Addie tilted her head back and studied the heavens and the first spangling of stars.

River used the top of one of the maze stones to lay out Sykes's maps.

"Those maps will guide you through the caves," Sykes told him. "But I couldn't map the area under the Barlows' property since I didn't have access. I compared topo maps with my underground ones, and I figure I got within a quarter mile of this entrance while I was caving. I could have pushed closer, I guess, but it felt better to avoid the Barlow property altogether."

Addie lowered her gaze and stared at Sykes's map. It looked like the Etch A Sketch doodles from her childhood.

Sykes pointed to one of the squiggles. "There's a large cavern here, complete with some gorgeous decorations—flowstones, stalactites, stalagmites, columns, the works. Real unusual for this part of the state. But I haven't been there in fifteen years or more. If your fella is making a home away from home down there, that's likely to be the place. I just don't know if you can get there from here."

River nodded. "Guess we'll find out."

Addie said, "Did you ever see anything strange down there, Mr. Sykes? Carvings? Any remains?"

"I've seen the bones of little critters down there. Animals looking for shelter and getting more than they bargained for and—" He seemed to realize what Addie was asking. "Human remains? No, ma'am. Like I said, I was part of the team looking for Colby. But we were working north of here, where they thought the kid went hiking. There could be miles of tunnels we never got to."

"Miles of tunnels?" she echoed faintly. Her ribs gave a sympathetic twinge.

Pain aside, she wasn't sure if she was claustrophobic. She'd never tested herself. Not since her brothers locked her in a neighbor's toolshed so she wouldn't follow them and then forgot about her.

She shone her light. The cave itself began as little more than a slit in the ground, mostly concealed by large slab-shaped rocks.

"He used smaller rocks to hide the passageway, pulling the stones after he was inside," River said, pointing to scrape marks in the dirt. "If he'd covered the opening from the outside, he would have used the larger stones."

"Meaning Edgar is in there," Addie said.

"That's how I read it."

It was nearly full-on dark now. Which Addie supposed hardly mattered if you were going into a cave. But somehow, it made the prospect of crawling underground with a killer even less appealing. Especially when, for all they knew, there were *two* killers down there. Edgar and Lowell, working in tandem. Just as they'd done in the past.

Patrick had tried to talk her out of going.

"What do you plan to do, lass? Slap handcuffs on our killers and frog-march them out?"

"What do you suggest? I tase and drag them out?"

He'd looked at his feet. "Just gives me the heebie-jeebies, you down there. Not fifteen minutes ago, I heard from Donna in Garden City. She found the name of her nephew's older friend. Jake Kully's pal was—"

"Let me guess. Eddie."

But the sheriff had agreed she should come. She knew Távros better than any of them.

"And she's the smallest of the lot," he said. "In case they reach a narrow passage."

Addie hardly cared for the sound of that. But River shook his head. "We know Távros is a big man. If he's down there, then the passages must be good-sized."

Now Addie looked over her crew. Three deputies had volunteered to go in with her and River. They would use handheld radios inside the cave for line-of-sight communication, and whistles as backup. Two more deputies would follow them, staging themselves at various stopping points. These deputies would monitor the single-wire telephone that Sykes had brought for them.

"Built by an amateur," Sykes said. "But it's rugged and easy to use. We can reach each other in case you have a problem or we need to alert you to possible flooding."

The hair rose on Addie's neck. Was it too late to change her mind?

But River just nodded. "Thanks," he told Sykes. "This is good to have."

River handed out whistles, gloves, knee-and-elbow pads, helmets, headlamps, granola bars, water bottles, and small backpacks.

"I'll leave chalk marks every time the tunnel splits," he told the deputies and Addie. "If we get separated, you can crawl backward and check your location against the marks."

Worse and worser, Addie thought. She popped three Tylenol in her mouth and took a sip of water.

"Right now, everyone find a tree and take a leak," River said. "Rule of caving is that everything you take in must come out. But I didn't bring bottles."

Addie sighed. *And worstest.*

When they'd returned from the woods, River said, "Everyone ready?"

Nods and affirmatives. Most of the deputies looked more excited than nervous.

A bunch of grown-up Boy Scouts. Just like her brothers.

✣

Addie learned quickly that caving involved a lot of crawling, slithering, and the occasional hunched-over crab walk through narrow passages. Rarely was there room to stand. Her bruised ribs hated every inch of it. The air, per what Sykes had told them, was a constant fifty-eight degrees Fahrenheit, but moving kept them warm. Addie was second in line, which meant breathing in the dust stirred up by River. But she was afraid to allow more of a gap between them.

She couldn't imagine the terror of getting lost down here. Or being held prisoner.

They proceeded this way for an indeterminate number of minutes—it was impossible to gauge the passage of time in a cave—periodically stopping to drink water and catch their collective breaths. At each branch,

River marked their direction. Twice they went down dead ends and had to backtrack. River would erase his original chalk mark and draw another.

After what Addie guessed was more than an hour, they eased down a narrow ledge and into a space where the cave opened enough for them to stand together. Addie only sipped at her water, afraid she'd need to pee again, and took a few bites of the granola bar. Her ribs throbbed.

River laid one of Sykes's maps on the floor. He spoke in a low voice. "I figure we're only fifteen minutes or so from the large cavern that Sykes mentioned. I'll keep guiding, but if Edgar is there, how you guys want to handle it is up to you."

They'd discussed this up top. As an unarmed civilian, River would find somewhere to pull out of the way and let Addie and the deputies continue. They'd move forward with tasers drawn. Guns were for emergency use only: a ricochet against rock could be as deadly to them as to Edgar.

A short time later—or maybe it was a long time, Addie couldn't tell—River came to a stop. They were all crawling on their stomachs; the tunnel here was just wide enough to allow a single person to wiggle through.

River managed to turn enough to signal to Addie that he would pull over at the first opportunity. It was time to let her and the deputies pull ahead.

She gave a thumbs-up.

They kept going. After another span of time, River's light went out, which was the signal they were almost to the cavern.

Addie turned off her own headlamp. Behind her, the deputies did the same. She strained to see a glow of light from up ahead that might signal Edgar Barlow had holed up here.

But the darkness was entire. Addie couldn't see her hand in front of her face—she'd always thought that was a cliché, but this cave proved it to be true.

She pulled her headlamp strap from around her helmet, tucked the light inside her jacket, and flipped it back on. She couldn't move forward without the light—she'd risk knocking herself silly on a low-hanging rock, even with the helmet. But through the material of her coat, the light gave only a soft glow.

River had vanished. Had he found a slot to tuck himself into? She struggled to hear anything.

She edged forward on her forearms.

She felt the cavern before she saw it. Air touched her cheeks, and the sound of her own breathing echoed back.

Once again, she turned off the headlamp. Again, the darkness was complete.

Had Edgar heard them coming and prepared an ambush?

When a man's voice cried out, Addie at first thought it was her imagination. The voice was weak and thin, sounding both close and faraway.

"I'm here," said the man. "Help me!"

Addie's heart thrummed against the tunnel floor as she edged forward, her face almost pressed to the floor.

The man was begging them to hurry. Addie could hear nothing else.

Where was River?

There came a sudden scuffle up ahead. A man yelled, something thudded like a body hitting the floor, followed quickly by more thuds, and then a light flared back into the tunnel, nearly blinding Addie.

"Edgar Barlow is now unconscious and trussed," River said. "The coast, at least for the moment, is clear."

Addie flipped on her headlamp, strapped it once more around her helmet, and crawled forward. As promised, the tunnel ended at a vast cavern. All she had to do was maneuver headfirst down a seven-foot drop. River reached under her arms, pulled her free, and set her gently upright. When he grimaced as if with pain, she pretended not to see.

Whatever injury he'd sustained in his own encounter with Távros, he'd chosen not to share.

Edgar lay on the cave floor, wrists and ankles tied. He looked dead except for the faint movement of his chest.

"Decked him with my backpack," River said, holding his hand to his stomach. "He stuck his head into the tunnel, maybe looking to see if he'd imagined hearing us or if we were really coming. As soon as he pulled back enough for me to get a swing, I did. The chance was too good to pass up."

"I'm not complaining," Addie said. She retrieved handcuffs from her backpack, rolled Edgar onto his back, and cuffed him.

Was it really going to be this easy?

The deputies crawled and slithered their way down the ledge and into the cavern. Addie shone her light around the echoing space, looking for the man who'd cried for help.

"Here!" a man shouted. The voice came from behind a place where the wall sloped down into the cavern, creating a high barrier that almost merged into the far wall of the cavern.

River touched her arm. "Could be a trap."

Addie nodded. She pulled out her taser and gestured to the deputies. As they drew near, the stench of pus and blood and vomit filled the unmoving air. One of the deputies gagged. Addie scooped up a rock and tossed it past the opening.

No reaction.

She moved to the wall and gripped her electroshock gun. There wasn't room to allow more than one person passage.

She drew in a breath and extended her headlamp around the corner, hoping Távros wasn't waiting with his sword to separate her hand from her wrist.

Still no reaction.

She said a silent prayer and peeked around the rock.

A man lay on the ground. His right wrist was chained to a pipe hammered into the rock; the length was so short that the man would be unable to stand.

Addie holstered her taser and approached. The stench was both heartbreaking and unbearable.

The man lifted his head. Frightened brown eyes stared into hers.

"Jamal James?" she asked. She knew the answer. But there was so little left of the glorious Jamal who'd portrayed Theseus onstage that she almost couldn't be sure.

He wet his cracked lips. "I'm Jamal. Please get me out of here before he comes back."

She knelt beside him and looked at the chain. There was no way to free him without bolt cutters.

"Edgar Barlow is handcuffed and unconscious," she said.

"Not him," Jamal whispered. "He's just the evil sidekick."

"Who then?"

Jamal blinked back tears. "The Minotaur."

"You saw him?"

"Half man, half bull." A scraping laugh. "Oh yeah."

Addie ignored the way the hair rose on her arms, and icy fingers gripped her neck. Monsters generated a primal, superstitious fear. Even when the monsters were human.

"He's coming back."

She laid a reassuring hand on Jamal's shoulder and looked him in the eye. "I understand. But I'm here with three deputies, and there are more deputies farther back in the cave. I promise we won't let anything happen to you. We're going to get you out of here."

Jamal didn't look reassured. "Better hurry. He said tonight was the night of sacrifice." He touched her hand. "What time is it?"

"It's early," she lied. "Where are you hurt?"

She asked because only a wound could explain the blood caked on Jamal's skin. And the smell.

"My back," Jamal whispered. "They branded me and took my skin."

She was calm now. In cop mode. Unsurprised by anything he could tell her. "You're going to be okay," she said.

She called to the deputies.

"Get a stretcher," she said. "And tell someone to come with bolt cutters." She turned back to Jamal and took his pulse. Too fast, but steady. She offered him her water bottle and a granola bar. "Not much longer now."

"Is Bryant okay?" Jamal asked.

Addie's heart clenched, but she made her voice brisk. "Don't worry about anyone else right now. Focus on getting your strength back. I'm going to talk to the deputies for a minute, then we're going to get you out of here."

She backed away and returned to the main cavern. One of the deputies was calling for supplies using the single-wire telephone Sykes had constructed.

"We need to move fast," she told the other deputies and River. "Jamal says the man working with Barlow is coming back tonight."

"It's already 'tonight,'" someone remarked.

"That's why we need to move fast."

She let her gaze take in the stark beauty of the cave while, in her mind, she traveled north to where Evan had gone to meet the deputies at Morgan Hargrave's home.

She walked over to the deputy who'd just gotten off the phone. "Any word from up top on your compadres who went to the Hargrave place?"

He stood and pulled on his backpack.

"Just got word," he said. "They haven't checked in."

CHAPTER 55

EVAN

Evan gaped at the bodies.

"Who shot—?" he began.

But Diana grabbed his arm and hurried him forward, past the dead men and toward the maze's center. He knew what she was thinking: the deputies' flashlight made them sitting ducks.

The thought made him shudder. What if the monster was still in the maze? What if the hedge maze *was* the lair of the Minotaur, and he was wrong about a cave?

And since when did the Minotaur use a gun?

He turned off the flashlight app on his phone. They'd have to make do with the light of the silvery moon, such as it was.

He waited while Diana, shielding her phone inside her jacket, called the sheriff's office to report two officers down, an armed killer on the loose. Then they resumed their half run along the path.

When they reached the center with its overgrown garden and forlorn trees, they paused. They listened for footsteps or voices, then Evan risked using the flashlight app again. He ran the beam around the space. The wind and the light made the trees jitter like berserkers. The tumbled stone wall grinned at him with broken teeth.

He turned off the light.

"You ready?" Diana whispered.

"Guns are scarier than blades," Evan whispered back. "That whole distance thing. He *murdered* two sheriff's deputies."

"We aren't going to die," Diana said.

"We're *all* going to die. I'd rather it not be tonight."

"Think about Ursula and Jamal. They could be sacrificed at any moment."

Reluctantly, Evan nodded. "Right. Okay."

"Where's the entrance?"

"There's a flat rock, like a gravestone." He pointed. "It's somewhere near the wall."

Again, Evan risked the light as they made their way through the weeds. The green granite of the stone caught and held the beam.

Evan saw immediately that the stone had been moved. Where it had lain gaped a deep, dark hole.

Most certainly a cave. With a minotaur.

"We should call the sheriff again," Evan said.

Diana ignored him and used her phone to shine a beam into the void.

"There are stairs," she said.

Evan peered into the opening. She was right, as she usually was. Stone steps like those that led from the house to the hedge maze now spiraled deep into the earth, a mirror image of the stairway in a medieval tower.

"I can't believe the amount of work this took," he whispered.

"Like Minos with his maze."

"Which was built by the famous engineer, Daedalus. Who also built wings for himself and his son so that they could escape the maze."

"But Icarus flew too close to the sun."

"And when the wax melted, he fell to his death."

Another myth with a message, Evan thought.

Had Morgan built a labyrinth for his sons as a macabre playground? A dark mirror to the once-beautiful hedge maze and the garden Evan suspected had belonged to Philomena?

"I'll go first," Diana said.

"Not this time."

"What are you going to do, bite them?"

He gave her an injured expression. "I have a gun."

She raised her eyebrows. "That's why we went by your office. Excellent thinking, Professor."

"And you'll agree that a gun beats an axe, at least under these circumstances. You're rear guard."

"If you get hurt, I'm going to kill you."

"Likewise," he said, and took the first stair.

✣

A faint light shone at the bottom of the shaft. Evan and Diana pocketed their phones and descended into the gloom.

Even in the dim light, Evan could see that the staircase was a work of art. The carefully carved stone of the steps. A burnished-metal handrail. Brilliantly hued murals that echoed those in the palace of Knossos on Crete.

Only the drifts of dirt that had crept in around the gravestone indicated they were anywhere but in a palace.

Evan continued down, the air growing cooler, his thoughts returning relentlessly to the bodies of the deputies. The small, brutal holes at the base of their skulls.

What had made Lowell use a modern weapon? The myth of the Minotaur demanded a sword, an axe, a club.

Not a gun.

He recalled Morgan Hargrave standing at the entrance to the hedge maze, his pistol raised and pointed at Evan.

You have a minotaur here? Evan had asked him, joking.

Morgan had seemed about to say one thing and then abruptly shifted. *It's . . . a mountain lion. We get one through here every few years,* he'd said.

Grace Poole had told him: *It was Morgan who became the monster.*

Before he had time to decide what this meant, Evan heard voices. He felt a moment's panic that someone was approaching the stairs. But then he realized the voices came from whatever lay beyond.

He turned to make sure Diana was still behind him—the woman moved like a ghost—then peered around the corner.

Before him stretched a long tunnel, naturally formed, and almost tall enough for even Diana to stand in. The light was brighter here, coming from the far end of the tunnel, its glow revealing multiple cavernous side branches.

The voices rose. Evan heard Morgan's deep baritone. And another man's even deeper pitch, his tone angry, insistent.

Evan couldn't catch their words, but it was clear the men were arguing.

He thought of the adventure movies he'd watched. He thought of the times with River when their plans had gone astray, and they'd made it out alive, anyway. He thought of River's steadfast belief in him.

Time to storm the castle.

He spoke quietly to Diana. "Here's the plan. We clear each side passage in case Lowell has allies. It would be a shame to get shot due to inattention. Since I have the gun, I'll go first. As soon as I clear a passage, I'll give you a thumbs-up and move to the next one."

She looked as if she wanted to argue.

"No arguing," he said. "For once, please do as I say. If I get shot or disemboweled or decapitated, I order you, as your boss, to run like hell away from here."

"That's a terrible plan."

"Do you have a better one?"

He was half hoping she did, but she frowned and shook her head.

"Then steady as she goes," he whispered to himself, and moved into the tunnel.

✣

It took them only minutes to clear the passageway. Each side tunnel wound into the darkness in a way that suggested a vast, branching network of caves. A maze created by nature and likely used by Lowell.

All appeared empty.

The voices of Morgan and the other man—it had to be Lowell—stayed in front of them, calmer now, a low rumble.

Just before the tunnel widened, he stopped and looked over his shoulder.

Diana had disappeared.

His bowels clenched. She wouldn't leave him voluntarily. Unless she'd come up with a better plan.

A cool and efficient part of his brain made a mental note to speak with her about good communication.

He took a few steps back and found her waiting for him in the side tunnel they'd just cleared. He stepped in beside her.

"What are you doing?" he whispered.

"I tapped you, and you just kept going. This passage circles back to the main cavern. You can see the light. Shall we divide and conquer?"

It was a good plan, or at least as good as they could do in the moment. He nodded. She squeezed his shoulder and moved away, heading down the tunnel, and he returned to the main passageway.

There, with nothing to do but proceed, he stepped into the cavern.

He stared in wonder at the startlingly beautiful space that materialized before him. Glittering selenite crystals. Immense columns sheathed in flowstone. Icicle-shaped stalactites that pointed down at the melting candles of stalagmites.

Into this space, someone had brought in a wooden plank table and chairs. A sofa. Artificial plants and thick rugs, and even a few paintings that leaned against the cavern walls. Battery-powered lanterns glowed from points around the room, periodically interrupted by the flickering flames of actual torches.

A labyrinth created by a king for his damaged son.

On the floor lay a woman Evan recognized as Ursula. Her hands and wrists were bound, her eyes closed. But she looked unhurt and alive, and Evan held on to that.

On a chair nearby, someone had tossed a discarded costume: the horns and shaggy features of the Minotaur.

There was no sign of Jamal.

It took only a few seconds for him to process his surroundings. All of it was peripheral to the center action: in the middle of the room stood Morgan and a much younger man—a big, handsome, and somehow unexpectedly *present* man who stood with his hands behind his back, his posture at ease.

"Gentlemen!" Evan called, grateful that his voice wasn't as small as his stature. "I'm here to tell you I solved the riddle."

The men turned from each other and stared at him in astonishment. He held his gun in clear view.

Morgan raised his eyebrows. "Do you plan to shoot us with your little gun?"

"The hand holding it isn't overlarge," Evan replied. "But the gun, I assure you, is exactly as big as it needs to be." He nodded at the younger man. "Lowell Hargrave, I presume. Or should I call you Alex Hemming? Or Távros? Or, simply, the Minotaur?"

The man tipped his head. "Lowell will do for the moment. It isn't yet time for the monster to reemerge."

"And what of Alex Hemming, the man? The decipherer?"

Lowell turned his face to the shadows. "Alex is no more. And his decipherment—failed as I now know it to be—died with him."

"You signed your letters TR. Not Alex Hemming. That suggests that you were already on your way."

Another tip of the head. "It was always a back-and-forth. The eternal question of which aspect of myself would claim victory."

Movement on Evan's left told him that Diana had reached the main cavern. She remained back, out of Morgan's and Lowell's sight.

He swaggered forward a few steps as if he had an army at his back. Diana was nearly that.

"And if I'd answered your letters?" he asked Lowell. "If I'd checked your decipherment, would that have changed your course?"

"I thought it might," Lowell said. "The decipherment was important. Important enough to distract me from urges I didn't want to follow. But it turned out false. And when I realized how wrong I'd been, I could no longer contain the Minotaur."

"You can't know if you're wrong," Evan said as a weight threatened to crush him. What if he had answered Lowell in his guise as Alex Hemming?

But Lowell said, "Whatever else I might be, Dr. Wilding, I'm not a fool. My decipherment was based on the false premise of a larger link between Crete and Egypt."

"Did you come to Chicago hoping to finish that work?"

Lowell pivoted to face Evan full-on. "I did. I came here six months ago, moved in with my old friend Eddie Barlow."

"Did you know he was here?" Evan asked Morgan.

Morgan nodded.

"You knew he was alive. You paid for the papers he would need to start over as Alex Hemming. Passport, probably a birth certificate. You had the money to buy the best. But you were still afraid of him. That's why you greeted me in the hedge maze with a gun."

"Lowell can be—" Morgan shot a look at his son. "Erratic."

"So, what happens now?" Evan said to both men. "With the riddle of Távros's identity solved, what comes next?"

Morgan leaned against the table and folded his arms, a man at a rather dull cocktail party. "You were foolish to come here," he said. "Even more foolish to expose my son."

"Possibly. But I believe Lowell made a deal with my brother and me. That if we figured out who he is, the game was over. Now you give me Ursula and Jamal, and I leave."

Lowell smiled.

He didn't look much like a killer. They already knew he was a big man—tall and broad. But his face held a sweetness that belied his actions. If someone who knew nothing about him were to see his photo, they'd mark him down as a student of literature or philosophy. The kind of man who means well but who never wows the world. Who floats through life and is content to do so.

Don't let him fool you, Evan warned himself. *Don't be sucked in. He managed to fool Ursula and her father, Jamal and his husband. And look what it cost them.*

Lowell's smile broadened. Even his grin was endearing. "But I didn't tell you the ending to the riddle," he said.

He brought his hands out from behind his back. He held a knife.

For a moment, Evan worried he'd miscalculated. Even if he shot Lowell—something he was loath to do—the young man might still manage to murder his father, if that was his goal.

Evan decided on diversion. He sighed dramatically. "I believe the finale is where you tell your father all the things he's done wrong. A reckoning of sorts. Up to and including killing those deputies."

"I did no such thing," Morgan said. His tone suggested Evan had accused him of running a stop sign.

Evan tilted his head as if taking Morgan's measure. "How much of what you've done has caused you regret, Dr. Hargrave? Tell me, have you found the root of evil? Did you even need to look past your mirror?"

Morgan merely sighed.

But Evan had been thinking about what Poole had told him. *It was Morgan who became the monster.* And about Colby Kaplan. He'd been pondering Morgan's need for control, which had been evident from their first meeting. He decided to play his hand and find out if it held nothing more than a 2-7 offsuit at a poker table—the worst possible hand. Or if he'd come up aces on the flop.

"Your son, using the name Tav, befriended Colby Kaplan. But Tav had been watching the Barlow brothers. He knew they were doing terrible things, and he was curious. He wanted to know what it was like to have control over another person. He decided to bring his friend here."

"I see."

"It was Lowell's first real dance with the dark side. But he wasn't a killer. Not yet. He'd been torturing his brother and the cat, but only in small ways, or so I was told. Kidnapping was the most audacious thing he'd done. I'm not sure he was ready for more. Were you, Lowell?"

"I wasn't—"

"Don't answer that," his father snapped.

"You weren't what?" Evan pressed. "Ready to commit murder? Especially the murder of a child, a boy, a *friend* who looked up to you?"

"It wasn't—"

Morgan roared. "Stop, Lowell. Not one more word."

Lowell growled.

"Why so worried, Morgan?" Evan asked. "What's one more death to what Távros has already done? Or is it that Lowell didn't kill Colby? Perhaps you were the one to pull the trigger, just as you would have shot a lion that threatened you. You couldn't let Colby go. Killing him was the only way to protect your son. And your reputation. A Hargrave can be eccentric. Even aggressive. But kidnapping is rather beyond the pale. They put teenagers in jail for that."

"Kill him," Morgan said to Lowell.

Off to Evan's left, Diana shifted. But Lowell merely twirled the knife in his hand.

Evan let out his held breath and pressed on. "Fortunately for the Hargraves, the news of Colby's disappearance died quickly. But you couldn't risk Lowell giving in again to his impulses. You sent him to Switzerland with the hope that the doctors at the treatment facility were right. That a violent psychopath can be made less so. That while they couldn't cure him, they might manage to put a brake on his less desirable proclivities. And although I can't know, they might even have been successful. Until the opening of *The King and the Minotaur*."

Morgan looked amused. "No one would minimize your ability to fantasize, Dr. Wilding." He reached a hand toward his jacket.

"I wouldn't," Evan said. "I'll shoot you with the same good cheer I'd shoot a rattler that showed up in my kitchen."

Morgan lowered his hand. Fury glowered in his eyes like banked coals, but he remained silent. Evan had won that hand. He continued.

"Do you want to know the worst thing your father did, Lowell?"

Except for that single growl, Lowell had listened to his father's and Evan's exchange with an expression that suggested he found it highly entertaining. Now he nodded.

"By all means," said the Minotaur.

"The worst thing he did was to make you, his eldest son, into a monster. You were his creation, whom he loved and loathed equally. The problem is, he couldn't be sure what parts of you were due to his own ancestry—and your mother's—and what behaviors came about because of the environment you grew up in. He'd done his best to plan and control your world. To divert you from your violent tendencies. But you know what they say. If you want to hear God laugh, tell Him your plans."

"Lowell had the best possible upbringing," Morgan interjected.

He'd pricked the man's ego.

"But he didn't, did he?" Evan said. "You'd altered things early on. You let your son think he was responsible for his mother's death."

The smile slid from Lowell's face.

"When I brought up Philomena's death to your father, I tried to understand his grief," Evan said. "He was, of course, saddened. But his pain went beyond what I would expect after more than twenty years. And there was something else in his reaction. A second emotion I couldn't put my finger on."

"And now you think you have," Morgan said. "This has gone far enough. Lowell, do what you do best, and take care of our little problem."

Evan slid his finger onto the trigger. But Lowell tossed his father a glance that made Morgan go still.

Evan willed his voice to hold steady. "I learned today that the inquest into Philomena's death was incorrect. Your mother wasn't home alone, Lowell. You were there. And the same source also brought up the rumor that everyone was home the day Philomena fell to her death. Not just you, Lowell, but also your father and Peter."

"Is that true?" Lowell asked Morgan. "You always said I was the only one home with her."

Morgan curled his lip. "He's making this up. How could he possibly know who was there?"

Evan said, "Good guesswork rests on a foundation of fact. Bring enough facts to bear, and others reveal themselves." He watched Lowell. "Your father knew how malleable people's memories can be, especially a child's. You can tell them things happened that never did, and they'll believe you. It's called memory implantation."

Lowell's mild expression had vanished. His face was blank now, as if he were searching his past.

"You and Mama fought," he said. "I remember that."

"Sometimes," Morgan said. "But not that day. I wasn't there."

"No, no, I remember. You fought, and I was there, and I fell, too. Just a few steps. That's how I got the scar on my knee. The one you said I got from tripping outside, near Mama's fountain."

"You can't possibly remember these things," Morgan said.

On the floor, Ursula moaned.

"You lied to the police about Philomena's death," Evan said to Morgan. "But maybe you didn't do it to protect Lowell. Maybe you did it to protect yourself. And Lowell, like Asterion, wasn't a monster until you made him one."

"Why would I murder the woman I loved?"

"You alone know the answer to that," Evan said. "Perhaps you were angry about her drinking and meant to alarm her, not hurt her. Perhaps you were jealous of her professional success. Maybe she had seen the man beneath the erudite surface and threatened to leave."

Lowell abandoned his place near his father and narrowed the gap between himself and Evan.

Evan stiffened. He didn't underestimate Lowell's skill at close quarters. He needed to keep his distance. He sidled left, closer to where Diana was hidden. He'd lost sight of her, but he knew she stood at the ready for whatever might come.

"You chose the myth you did, Lowell, because somewhere inside you knew that your father was to blame for your mother's death. You also know that what we find at the center of the maze is enlightenment. Whether that illumination reveals a hero or a monster is up to us. You made your first choice, which was to become the Minotaur. Now you can make a different one."

Lowell shook his head. "And how do you picture that?"

"I'm not going to lie and say you get to waltz out of here. Instead, you confess to the police what you've done. Show them how badly you need help. There isn't a therapist on the planet who wouldn't agree that you need a lengthy stay in a place where you can be both monitored and cared for."

Lowell's laugh was rich and warm, in keeping with his deep voice. "A fairy-tale ending. But none of the characters in the myth of the Minotaur enjoyed a happy ending. The Minotaur, of course, was slain by Theseus. Minos was boiled alive. Ariadne was abandoned by the hero for whom she'd betrayed her father and brother. Theseus himself died when he was betrayed and thrown from a cliff."

"Is that why you chose the supposed death you did? The slaying of the hero so the beast could take his place?"

Lowell dipped his head in acknowledgment.

"But those stories are only myth," Evan said. "And we—for good or for ill—live in a world where the gods have been forgotten, the heroes are broken, and where beasts generally get shot." He waved his gun without shifting his aim. "I suggest you embrace your human side."

Morgan pushed himself upright. "I've heard enough."

"So have I," Lowell agreed.

Lowell spun with the grace of a dancer, leaned in, and thrust. The blade pierced Morgan's throat, the pommel protruding like the period at the end of a fatal sentence. Morgan made a gurgling sound and brought his hands up to grasp the knife's handle.

"Don't!" Evan cried.

Morgan yanked the knife free. Uncorked, his blood poured over his hands in a waterfall. His knees buckled. His gaze went to his son, but the blade had taken his ability to speak.

Evan sighted the gun on Lowell. The younger man yanked his knife from his father's hand and turned it toward his own throat, arms extended—apparently, Lowell had chosen for himself the rarest form of suicide used by people and one guaranteed to succeed.

"Here's a riddle for you," he said. "If Theseus and the Minotaur are two sides of the same man, is it homicide or suicide when the hero slays the monster?"

Evan fired. The bullet pierced Lowell's left forearm and then the right. Lowell screamed in pain and struggled to bring the knife to his neck.

Diana flew out of the shadows. He pivoted the knife toward her with his crippled arms, and she stopped.

She and Lowell stared at each other. He must have thought that Hera had come to see him to the grave.

"Don't," she said.

Again, Lowell turned the knife. He thrust the blade into the tender notch between his clavicles. He gave a soft sigh as his knees gave out.

Diana caught him and lowered him to the ground. She used Lowell's own shirt to try to staunch the blood. But such damage couldn't be repaired.

It took only a few moments for him to die.

When Evan turned to Morgan, he saw that the older man had slumped to the floor, his eyes open wide, seeing nothing.

From far away came the wail of sirens. The cavalry as sheriff, riding in to save the living and clean up the dead. Evan went to Ursula and took her gently into his arms. Her eyes fluttered open.

Evan glanced to the far end of the cavern, where a tunnel disappeared into the dark. It surely led into deeper caverns. He wondered if the caves reached all the way to the Barlows' property. If he could walk through them and find Addie at the other end.

He looked down at Ursula and then past her to the Hargrave men.

"The most difficult riddles of all," he said, "are the secrets we hide from ourselves."

CHAPTER 56

EVAN

Two Weeks Later

Petterino's bustled with diners as River held open the door for Evan, Diana, and Addie. Walking in, Evan inhaled the scents of truffles and garlic and marinara sauce. A maître d' in bow tie and vest led their group to the same table they'd sat at the last time they were here. Several days and a lifetime ago.

"Bring us a bottle of your best red," Addie told him.

"Of course, madam."

They were here to celebrate the judge's ruling in favor of Evan's Institute of Middle Eastern Antiquities, a ruling that had been handed down that morning. Evan was now the proud curator of the Theodore Watts collection. The part of the collection, at least, that he wouldn't repatriate to the countries of origin.

They were also here to celebrate the successful conclusion of the investigative part of the case the media called the Minotaur Murders.

As they took their places around the table, Evan relished the laughter of his friends, the cheeriness of the restaurant, the sunlight falling through the windows. He thought of all they had to be grateful for.

Ursula had been bruised and dehydrated and traumatized when EMTs took her to the hospital. She'd broken down after hearing of her father's death. But friends and family had come to support her, and while she had a lot to work through, she had survived the Minotaur and his maze. She and Jamal had met and shared their stories and promised to help each other.

It was a start.

Cavers, led by Matthew Sykes, had found remains believed to be those of Colby Kaplan in a rocky niche halfway between the Barlow property and the Hargrave estate. The remains would be returned to his mother as soon as they were positively identified by the coroner. There was already talk of naming the caves the Colby Kaplan Caverns and opening them to the public; a memorial to the adventurous Boy Scout would be erected near one of the entrances.

The Ogle County Sheriff's Office had brought multiple charges against Edgar Barlow, including sharing joint responsibility for the murders William Barlow had perpetrated in Kansas and Illinois. Other charges were forthcoming.

Two days after Lowell's and Morgan's deaths, DNA from the mask discarded by Távros and the bite marks on Samuel Fishbourne and Bryant James had been confirmed as a match to DNA from Lowell Hargrave. The artist who had made the custom masks confirmed that a man calling himself Alex Hemming had ordered them.

The inquest into Philomena's death was being reopened, although Evan couldn't imagine who they would find to interview. Grace Poole, perhaps. Friends of the family. Maybe employees at the Remington Foundation.

Speaking of which, an investigation would soon begin into the foundation. After learning of the crimes committed by Morgan Hargrave, Grace Poole had agreed to cooperate.

Addie settled next to Evan at the table and took his hand.

He squeezed her fingers.

He'd spent a lot of time thinking about why Lowell had chosen to go after Ursula and Jamal. He thought it likely that if he hadn't been stopped, Lowell would have murdered other kids who'd been in his father's study. He'd simply started with the easiest: those in Chicago, where he had a place to go to ground. He'd punished them by taking them prisoner and leaving behind the corpse of someone they loved. No doubt, Lowell was following the dictates of the myth: seven men and seven women slated to die. Fourteen sacrifices to the Minotaur. Peter, who had also been part of his father's studies, had finally admitted it was his own brother who chained him in the maze he'd created on the Barlow land, perhaps as an eventual sacrifice. Eddie had been glad to help.

Evan also thought that the Chicago kids' mystery club—the kids who had tried to solve the Bogeyman case—were made up of members of the study. It would have been natural for them to hang out together while Morgan took notes. Sometimes at Ursula's tree house playing serial killer. Sometimes at the Hargrave home where, perhaps, one of them had glimpsed a real killer.

Evan was less certain if Morgan had really been trying to turn his son's propensity for trouble into psychopathy. With the investigation into Remington, he'd likely learn more. Not that he was eager to dive in. It was bad enough for a father to push a child too hard. Unimaginable for him to push a child into madness.

Who would ever be able to fully parse the man who had been Lowell Hargrave? How much of his personality was steered by genetics—Morgan had implied an unsavory ancestry—and how much by the tests his father ran, the rivalry with his brother, the likely fact that he'd seen his father murder his mother, then been persuaded that he'd only dreamed it? He would have spent his life not knowing who to trust. Certainly not himself, with his faulty memory. And not the family who was supposed to love him.

Lowell had recognized in the ancient myths a pattern of truths as old as mankind. The heroes, the villains. The gods and the monsters.

The archetypes of our psyches. As Lowell's identity fractured, he had latched on to these myths to provide guidance the way a drowning man grasps at a bit of flotsam. The myth of King Minos had given him his choice of a hero and a monster. When the hero—Alex Hemming—failed, what was left was Távros, the Minotaur.

A waiter arrived with the wine. He uncorked it and poured a tasting for Addie.

"Excellent," she said.

The waiter nodded with satisfaction, poured more wine, and took their orders.

Evan asked for the Shrimp de Jonghe. He'd promised his fretting brother he would stick to a high-protein, low-carb, heavy-on-the-vegetables diet. And he would. After tonight.

River raised his glass. "To the investigators. To Addie and Patrick. To Diana. And, of course, to my big brother."

"And to River, the fighter of swordsmen," Diana said.

They clinked glasses.

"And to Oliver Wilding," River said, "who is confined to a hospital bed and must, for a few more days, pay attention to his sons out of sheer boredom."

Another clinking of glasses.

Evan cleared his throat. "Speaking of family, what are your immediate plans, River?"

"Are you suggesting you no longer need me now that you've gotten your hands on the Watts collection?"

"It's nothing like that," Evan protested.

"Are you tired of the fact that I leave wet towels lying around and muddy shoes in the vestibule?"

Evan considered. "Not to mention cracker crumbs in the library and dirty scotch glasses stacked everywhere. You're turning my house into a twenty-first-century archaeological dig."

"I'll try to be better. Because I'm going to hang around for a few more weeks until I'm sure you aren't going to drive your own institute into the ground. Then Diana and I are going to hike the Carpathian Mountains in Romania."

Evan didn't bother hiding his smile. A week in the mountains, and River would come to realize how dull life could be without Diana.

The waiter appeared with their food. Before he left, Addie requested another bottle of wine and also asked him to leave the dessert menu.

River speared a tomato from his plate. "What about Timbuktu, brother?"

Nothing like being put on the spot. "It's all settled."

River froze with the fork halfway to his mouth. "What's all settled?"

Addie frowned. "Yes, what's all settled?"

He avoided her eyes. "I was considering a sabbatical among the libraries of Timbuktu. But I've worked it out. The university is donating a scanner, although I'm not quite sure how we're going to get it there. Somehow, we will. And once it's in place, the librarians of Timbuktu will send me copies of their most urgent manuscripts." He met Addie's gaze. "I can do all of it from the comfort of my office. Traveling to Mali is an adventure for another day."

"Glad to hear it," Addie said, still sounding peeved.

He tried to smooth it over. "This was before you and I—before we—you know—"

"Before we kissed?"

Evan was sure he was as scarlet as the tomato River was now contentedly chewing.

"Speaking of romance," Diana said, coming to the rescue, "what do you guys think about Emma Hargrave? Was she in love with both brothers?"

"In my humble opinion—" Evan said.

"The only kind you ever have," Diana cut in.

"Thank you. In my humble opinion, Emma cares only about herself. She loved neither Lowell nor Peter but played them against each other. An Ariadne who would not choose between Asterion and Theseus."

The talk turned to other things. Evan pushed aside his shrimp—it was important to leave room for dessert—and let the others' talk wash over him. He was, indeed, a lucky man. None luckier. His chosen family was sitting together at dinner, talking, laughing, sharing stories. Life's ambrosia.

When at last dinner and dessert were done, when the bottles were empty and the after-dinner brandies consumed, they paid their tab and left a generous tip. River and Diana caught an Uber while Addie and Evan went for a post-dinner walk. The monsoon had finally stopped, and the evening was that rare kind of July night where the temperature was perfect, the humidity low, and the downtown crowds reasonable. They headed in the direction of the setting sun, the light casting its golden glow over the world.

She slipped her hand in his. "First time we've walked hand in hand."

He smiled. "I'm thinking there are going to be a lot of firsts."

"Oh, do tell. Like what?"

"Me bringing you coffee in bed at five a.m. before we take Ginny out for her morning flight."

"Funny. I was picturing you bringing breakfast to me in bed at nine a.m. before getting back into bed with me."

"Your view does have a certain charm," Evan said. "I'll take it under advisement."

"Now you're being reasonable." She stopped at an intersection, waiting for the light to change. She looked down at their clasped hands, then back up to him. "What happens next?"

"What do you mean?"

"I mean, what are we? Are we a thing? A couple? Whatever it is people say now?"

He smiled. "We are what we've always been. Best friends. And now partners. In whatever form you want that to be."

"Even if it's a church? A wedding dress, and you in a tux and polished shoes, the whole shebang? Even if it's that?"

He swallowed the sudden lump in his throat. "Even so, my love."

"My love," she echoed softly.

"'Twas always thus."

Addie laced her fingers between his. "Ditto."

The light turned.

Her steps matched his as together they crossed the street.

The Minotaur

From the personal papers of the Minotaur Killer, July 2018
Cited in *Criminal Behavioral Analysis of the "Minotaur Murders" for the Chicago Police Department, August 2018*
Dr. Evan Wilding

- How is it that I once believed I could choose my future?
- How could I have been so guileless, so gullible, so damnably naive when I knew that the myth that came before me and then embraced me and that will remain after I am gone—that this myth is not mere story? It is my destiny. And the story never changes. Only the players.
- Our fate is carved into the stones of life's labyrinth—it directs us to our future, without us ever being aware that we are only hands unspooling fortune's thread.
- In the papers, on the news, in the words of both amateur and professional profilers, they say I'm a psychopath. How else to explain what I have done?
- But I answer back: Do psychopaths feel regret? Sorrow? Pity? I'm told not. So maybe I'm not a psychopath. Maybe I'm just an ordinary man who went badly wrong.
- Can I be blamed for what my father did?
- Can I be blamed for the path the fates chose for me?

GLOSSARY

Arithmogram – In Cretan Hieroglyphic, a symbol representing a whole number.

Cretan Hieroglyphic – An undeciphered script used during the Bronze Age from around 2100 to 1700 BCE. Cretan Hieroglyphic is the earliest writing system of Europe.

Hieroglyph – A hieroglyph is a stylized picture used in writing to represent a sound, syllable, or word.

Klasmatograms – In Cretan Hieroglyphic, symbols that sometimes follow numerical signs and may be intended to indicate fractions.

Labyrinth – A mazelike structure consisting of a single path that winds its way through a series of twists and turns, eventually leading to a central point or goal. Labyrinths have been used for thousands of years for a variety of purposes, including as spiritual or religious symbols, as well as for entertainment or exercise. They are found in many cultures around the world and are often associated with mythological or symbolic meanings.

Linear A – An undeciphered writing system used by the Minoan civilization of Crete.

Linear B – A syllabic writing system that was used by the Mycenaean civilization in ancient Greece. Linear B was discovered on clay tablets during excavations at the palace of Knossos in Crete in the early twentieth century, and it was successfully deciphered by the British architect and amateur linguist Michael Ventris in 1952.

Logogram – A written symbol that represents a word or phrase.

Maze (Multicursal) – A type of maze with multiple paths or branches that lead to dead ends or to the final destination. Multicursal mazes offer multiple paths and options for the solver to choose from.

Maze (Unicursal) – A type of maze with a single nonbranching path from the entrance to the exit.

Minoans – An ancient civilization that flourished on the island of Crete from approximately 3000 to 1400 BCE. The Minoans were highly sophisticated, with elegant architecture, art, and technology. The decline of the Minoan civilization is believed to have been caused by a combination of factors, including natural disasters, invasion, and internal conflicts. The Mycenaean civilization, which arose on the Greek mainland, ultimately took over Crete and adopted many aspects of Minoan culture.

Morpheme – The smallest unit of meaning in a language. It is the part of a word that carries a semantic (meaningful) or grammatical function. Morphemes can be individual words, such as *dog* or *run*, or parts of words, such as the *-ing* in *running* or the *-ed* in *walked.*

Pictogram – A symbol or picture that represents a word or idea.

Rebus – A puzzle or word game in which pictures or symbols are used to represent words or parts of words.

Stiktograms – In Cretan Hieroglyphic, symbols that serve as punctuation, often used to mark the beginning of an inscription.

Syllabograms – Symbols or characters that represent syllables in a writing system. Syllabograms are used in contrast to alphabetic writing systems, in which individual characters represent individual sounds.

Acknowledgments

I continue to be grateful to the people who have gone with me on this journey, from my first novel to this one.

Deep gratitude to my beta readers, who enter and exit at various stages of the book's development. To Michael Bateman, who encouraged me and edited pages from the book's inception. Thank you, Mike, for your friendship and our weekly talks. To Michael Shepherd and Robert Spiller—longtime critique partners and dear friends who have made every book better in multiple ways. To Cathy Noakes, whose brilliance I have leaned on since middle school. A shout-out to my sister-friend Deborah Coonts, who powered through the novel in a couple of days and didn't hesitate to point out problems I should have seen but didn't. And thank you to Angela Crowder, editor extraordinaire, for her work on this book. Angela, you raised the game to a new level.

I am so appreciative of my kind and tireless editor, Liz Pearsons, who has always had my back and encouraged me to find my passion in the stories I tell. Thanks for everything you do, Liz: the gentle suggestions, the great conversations, and for shepherding my books on their journey. Thanks as well to Sarah Shaw, my author liaison, and to the rest of the incredible people at Thomas & Mercer.

To Charlotte Herscher: brilliant editor and wonderful human. You bring terrific insight to my stories while making me feel great about all of it.

To my wonderful agent, Christina Hogrebe; and to my assistant, the marvelous Christine Conlee.

I'm always indebted to subject-matter experts. Thank you, Mary France, ancient Greek and Latin lecturer in the Languages and Culture Department at the University of Colorado Springs. Mary offered translations I found both enlightening and entertaining. I am grateful for your patience and willingness to help. I look forward to studying ancient Greek with you!

To mythologist Francesca Ferrentelli, PhD, for our delightful correspondence. Thank you for letting me know that there are people called "mythologists" and for pointing me in the directions I needed to go for further information.

For answering my questions about caves in northwestern Illinois, I am grateful to the following individuals: Dr. Donald Luman, principal geologist, Illinois State Geological Survey, Prairie Research Institute, and University of Illinois at Urbana-Champaign; retired biologist Steve Taylor; and members of the Illinois Speleological Society. Thanks to their input, I decided to play with geology and transport the kind of cave more typically found in Southern Illinois to Ogle County.

And to Mary Tostanoski for her artful renderings of Cretan hieroglyphic and other scripts throughout this book.

In addition to the people I get to chat with, there is an endless list of fascinating books and articles on some of the subjects covered in this novel. To name just a few: *Walking a Sacred Path: Rediscovering the Labyrinth as a Spiritual Practice* by Lauren Artress; *The Greatest Invention: A History of the World in Nine Mysterious Scripts* by Silvia Ferrara; "The Making of a Script: Cretan Hieroglyphic and the Quest for Its Origins" by Silvia Ferrara, Barbara Montecchi, and Miguel Valério; *Minotaur: Sir Arthur Evans and the Archaeology of the Minoan Myth* by J. A. MacGillivray; and *Minoan Crete: An Introduction* by L. Vance Watrous.

To my readers who support my work. To my friends who keep me sane and grounded, including Lori Dominquez, Patricia Coleman, Maria Faulconer, Virginia Sweeney, and my friends and beta readers listed above.

Last but not least, to Steve and Amanda. And to Kyle. Love you always.

ABOUT THE AUTHOR

Photo © Trystan Photography

Barbara Nickless is the *Wall Street Journal* and Amazon Charts bestselling author of *At First Light* and *Dark of Night* in the Dr. Evan Wilding series as well as the Sydney Rose Parnell series, which includes *Blood on the Tracks*, a *Suspense Magazine* Best of 2016 selection and winner of the Colorado Book Award and the Daphne du Maurier Award for Excellence; *Dead Stop*, winner of the Colorado Book Award and nominee for the Daphne du Maurier Award for Excellence; *Ambush*; and *Gone to Darkness*. Her essays and short stories have appeared in *Writer's Digest* and on Criminal Element, among other markets. She lives in Colorado, where she loves to cave, snowshoe, hike, and drink single malt Scotch—usually not at the same time. Connect with her at www.barbaranickless.com.